The Nine Moons of Adjemir

by

Tyler Dhensaw

authorHOUSE

1663 Liberty Drive, Suite 200
Bloomington, Indiana 47403
(800) 839-8640
www.authorhouse.com

This book is a work of fiction. Places, events, and situations in this story are purely fictional and any resemblance to actual persons, living or dead, is coincidental.

*© 2004 Tyler Dhensaw
All Rights Reserved.*

No part of this book may be reproduced, stored in a retrieval system, or transmitted by any means without the written permission of the author.

First published by AuthorHouse 08/27/04

*ISBN: 1-4184-4840-0 (sc)
ISBN: 1-4184-4839-7 (dj)*

Library of Congress Control Number: 2004094126

*Printed in the United States of America
Bloomington, Indiana*

This book is printed on acid-free paper.

The Renegade Town of Darmonarrow

It has been a long time since this land has seen peace, Elves Humans Dwarfs and Krugs have been at war for almost sixty years. And through all this turmoil in the land of Adjemir, the powerful renegade town of Darmonarrow has survived.

The town of Darmonarrow is located in Human territory very close to the Elf/Human border. It is referred to as a renegade town because it is made up nearly completely from outlaws, thieves and people who just want to get away from the rest of the world. But here they have to live in peace. In Darmonarrow, because Ram the leader of Darmomarrow is a very strict and powerful Sorcerer. Ram would never allow any fighting inside the town by the people who live there, nor would he allow for any person who lives in Darmonarrow to break any of the town laws.

Darmonarrow is very hard to attack because of its location. It's on the top of a steep hill surrounded by rugged terrain, making it tough to ride fighting animals against, or to march a large number of soldiers onto.

Darmonarrow is on a small plateau, so there isn't much room to walk or move around outside the walls making it impossible for troops to circle. It has only one well in the middle of the city. Food is imported from other cities near Darmonarrow, sometimes in exchange for weapons.

All inhabitants live in the same type of house, in Darmonarrow, which is a small one-story gray brick house with a thatched roof, except for the leader's house. Ram's house, which is considerably larger than the other houses in Darmonarrow, stands alone almost in the exact center of the town.

There is only one gate leading into the Town of Darmonarrow, which is the only opening in the twelve-foot, well built high rock wall surrounding the town. There are at least always two guards in plain sight guarding the gate and a hidden archer in the nearest tower, with a small opening in which the archer can shoot arrows through.

The archer in this tower is always ready and always has an arrow notched in his bow. He would shoot anyone who didn't belong to Darmonarrow, or who looked even slightly dangerous. There are also guards patrolling the walls, and there are four guard towers surrounding the town which also have a number of guards in them. All guards, no matter what their rank is, are trained to alert the town if danger is approaching. This is done by giving three sharp short whistles, in a secret way, by using both thumbs.

The reason why there is a required secret whistle, to warn of an attack against Darmonarrow, is so that there would never be any false alarms. The earlier leaders of Darmonarrow, had wanted a special warning system, so that no young prankster could create any confusion, or scare the residents of the town.

The town makes most of it's income by exporting the best made weapons, in all of the land of Adjemir, selling to the Elves, Humans, Dwarfs and occasionally the to the Krugs.

The town gets it's main income from these four combating races.

Weapon's purchases were always made outside of the walls, in a small trading Gazebo, which was located a short distance down the road from Darmonarrow.

Ram was very strict about this rule, because he did not want any large group of any of the combating forces inside the walls at any given time.

Ram knew how difficult it could be to defend Darmonarrow from an attack from outside the walls, and he also knew that if there was ever any infiltrator inside the walls during an attack from the outside, then Darmonarrow would be very difficult to defend.

Due to the fact that Darmonarrow is located on the Humans land called Chesfeld the Humans have tried many times to defeat Darmonarrow, without much success.

Ram, a very powerful sorcerer, is the leader of Darmonarrow and young Bobbiur is a senior Captain. Bobbiur has been very close to

Ram for a very long time and although Ram doesn't show it, he thinks of Bobbiur, as more of a son, than that of a Captain.

The Young Captain Bobbiur

Ram, the sorcerer had been sent on a mission, by the Elders of Darmonarrow, when he was still young man himself and this was before he became the leader of Darmonarrow. The assignment was to track down and destroy a very large meandering band of Krugs, who had been attacking small defenseless Human Villages which were situated close to the town of Darmonarrow.

Ram knew that he and his soldiers from Darmonarrow were closing in on renegade Krugs, when he came upon a burnt out Human Village. All the inhabitants had been murdered.

Or so he had thought.

Just as Ram and his men had decided on the direction which the Krugs had departed, when they left the village, Ram heard what he thought was a very faint babies cry. The sound had been coming from a small shed, which was situated in a narrow dusty alley at the edge of this town. Ram had signaled to his men to surround the shed and that they should be at the ready. Ram did not feel that there had been any present danger, but he was always careful in these types of situations. Ram, even at this young age had some magic powers, so he was able to personally surround himself with a protection shield, before he had walked slowly up to the shed with his sword drawn.

Ram had slowly pushed open the shed door with his foot but he never saw anything at first. Then as his eyes adjusted to the darkness of the shed, he saw some old cloth sacks in the farthest corner of this small building. He had reached out with the point of his sword and very gently removed the sacks, one at a time. There he was, a baby which Ram would later name, Bobbiur. It was as Ram was picking up this baby from the shed floor that Ram had remembered when he had been a child himself. A young Elfin boy who had been a friend of Ram's, had been called Bobbiur. Ram had never forgotten his childhood friend. Ram's friend Bobbiur, had been killed by an incoming arrow, during a Human attack on Darmonarrow.

Ram and his childhood friend Bobbiur, had been practicing with wooden swords in the center of Darmonarrow at the time of the Human attack. Ram had been standing very close beside his friend Bobbiur when it happened. An errant arrow which had been shot over the wall by a Human attacker, had hit his friend Bobbiur right in his heart. Ram's young friend Bobbiur had died almost instantly. When Ram's young friend Bobbiur had been injured, Ram had run over to the dying Elf boy and cradled him in his arms. Bobbiur, while dying had stared straight into Ram's eyes. Ram did not know it at the time, but the way Bobbiur was staring into Ram's eyes as he died, had a very strong effect on him. Ram at this tender age cried, but it was also to be the very last time he would ever show this type of emotion.

As Ram had reached into the shed on this day and picked up this baby boy, he had instantly thought of his childhood friend Bobbiur. He didn't know why he thought of his childhood friend Bobbiur, but he just did. Later Ram thought it must be a message from the Gods, or just an omen, but Ram had never forgotten this moment. Ram was certain that the babies parents were amongst the dead in the Village. It also appeared to Ram the child's parents had hidden the baby in this shed, when they had returned and helped the other villager's to defend against the raiding Krugs.

Ram had sheathed his sword and then he had picked up the baby, which he held very close to himself as he turned to his men. Although Ram only had a small band of men with him on this day, nobody even tried to argue with him when he handed the baby to one of his men with the fastest horse, ordering him to return to Darmonarrow as quickly as he could. Without even considering what the Elder's of Darmonarrow might say, he told the rider to take the baby straight to his friends house. His friend was an Elf, by the name of Arthorn. Ram knew this young baby boy would be well cared for by Arthorn and his wife.

Even Ram was not sure why he felt close to this Human boy child, but as he had picked up the baby boy, he had felt something which had brought an instant smile to his face. This feeling had made him feel good inside.

As the rider started to ride back to Darmonarrow with the baby, Ram turned to his men. There was such a strong, determined, fierce look in his eyes, which had sent cold chills up the backs of some of his men. The look of fierceness on Ram's face was so strong, that it had caused some of the men to involuntarily take a step backwards. Nobody in their right mind would even want to, in the slightest, argue with Ram when he was like this. There was such a vicious look of deep hatred and a need to get the job done. Ram's eyes did not even look Human when he was like this. The men knew when they caught up with this band of Krugs, these Krugs were going to get a severe thrashing.

His men knew what kind of a fierce fighter Ram was and they also knew that when they saw this look in his eyes that there would be no turning back. Some of the men who were with Ram on this date, after the incident at the village, noticed a greater confidence coming from Ram. This show of confidence that Ram had found on this day, in this village, would stay with him the rest of his life and would serve him well in the future.

It was like the men had thought. When Ram and these men caught up to the band of Krugs, they were greatly outnumbered, but Ram did not even hesitate in the slightest. The men noticed that Ram didn't even stop to set up a protection shield for his safety, or his men's safety, but he rode swiftly and straight into the center of the Krugs. The battle itself was brutal. The Krugs didn't stand a chance and literally in minutes there was nothing but dead Krugs all over the place. Ram had fought without reserve and he had acted possessed. His men had never seen him like this before and although they respected his judgement, it was somewhat unnerving to see anybody fight this fiercely, or this viciously.

While Ram was fighting, his men saw his eyes and Ram's eyes said it all. They were almost like the eyes of a demon. The eyes of Ram, during the battle, did not seem Human.

Even his own men were nervous of him at this time. It was a strange look and they did not want to see this look again. None of the warriors who were with Ram during this battle, on this day ever mentioned this look to Ram, nor did Ram ever speak of this day again.

New Recruits For Darmonarrow

Recently two new recruits have joined the ranks of Darmonarrow. Hagjel and Salbuk are their names and they are wanted for assassinating a Human emperor's nephew. The Emperor's nephew had been a very cruel Human. Although both Hagjel and Salbuk are new to Darmonarrow, Ram trusts both of them very much.

Before any new recruits are added to the ranks of Darmonarrow, they must be interviewed by Ram himself. It is during this interview, when Ram, unknown to the any new recruits would search their minds to make sure that they are honest and would remain loyal to Ram and the citizens of Darmonarrow. Ram was more than satisfied when he interviewed Hagjel and Salbuk, regarding the loyalty which he felt was present in the minds of these two individuals.

The one called Hagjel, was a good looking and very friendly Elf. Hagjel was not like other Elves, and from most of his behavior, he acted more like an Adjemirian Human. Hagjel liked to party whenever he got the chance. In fact some of his closest friends thought, Hagjel acted more like a Human, than the Elf he was.

Why Hagjel acted more Human than Elfen, was probably because when he was growing up, his father's best friend was a Human and both families spent a lot of time together. The Human behavior must have rubbed off on Hagjel. The one who they called Salbuk, was a Human with some magic powers. They had been friends for quite some time and had seen quite a few battles together. Most people, who had seen these two together, thought that Salbuk was more like a big brother to Hagjel, that is how close their relationship was.

Ram had found both Salbuk and Hagjel quite interesting.

The Four Combating Races of Adjemir

Adjemirian Elves are just like Elves from other lands. They are tall slender Human type creatures, who have pointed ears, narrow eyes, pointed noses, with thin eyebrows.

The Elves weapons of choice are the bow and the spear. Some Elves are born with very strong magic powers, but for some unknown reason, most Elves don't have any magical powers at all. The Elves hate Krugs and dislike Dwarves. When Elves catch some Humans, they like to enslave them and use them for all the hard labor, because Elves themselves really aren't very strong. The Elves live for about two hundred, to three hundred years. The Elves live in great cities to the West of Darmonarrow, in the land called Volkjynn.

The Human race of Adjemir, are shorter than Elves but are much stronger. Their weapons of choice are the bow and the sword. The Humans have some people with very strong magic powers, which they are also born with, just like the Elves.

The Humans hate most Elves, all Krugs and are neutral about most Dwarves. The life span for a Human is sixty to eighty years and the Humans live in a land called Chesfeld. Chesfeld is located in the Eastern part of the land called Adjemir. Out of the four races the Humans control the largest amount of land in Adjemir.

The Adjemirian Dwarves are short stout creatures and are very strong in the upper body. The Dwarves have short stubby, but very powerful legs and all male Dwarves have long beards.

The Dwarves have round ears that stick out from their heads, and they can hear really well. Their weapons of choice are the 'war hammer' and the 'war axe.' They have no magic to speak of. The Dwarves are natural born craftsmen and they are able to build very strong weapons, but their weapons are not as good as the weapons which are made in Darmonarrow. Dwarfs are very experienced at building underground tunnels.

The Dwarfs hate Krugs more than any other race. They live in the Southern part Adjemir. Adjemirians call the Dwarves land, Axpen.

The Dwarves have tunnels all throughout the Humans and the Elves territories. Dwarves like to steal food, weapons, and treasures.

The life span of a Dwarf is about two hundred years.

The Krugs of Adjemir are tall, gray skinned, hairy creatures. They hate all living things and all living things hate them. Krugs never smile.

Krugs have a very flat nose and very small ears. They have no skill in making anything, so all of their weapons are stolen, or are traded for.

Krugs can be very mean. They have a low intelligence and most Krugs aren't very skilled in battle. The only thing that allows them to win battles, is their numbers. They like to overwhelm armies with their larger numbers.

There is a large Krug population. Krugs have no magic at all. Some Krugs have been educated by Elves who have been trying to civilize them, but they always remain evil at heart.

Some Krugs like to camp near Human, Elfin and Dwarfen towns so they can steal things when they get the chance. Krugs have their own land in the North East corner of Adjemir, which is called Krugland, bordering the Human and Elfin territories.

Stolen Weapons

Ram sat quietly at a large desk effortlessly calculating his funds after the latest weapons' trade. The only sounds in the room were the scratching of his quill and the whirling of the magically guided feather fan above his head.

It was fairly warm for September. There was a quiet knock on the door and without stopping his calculations he waved his hand and the door magically swung silently open. A tall broad-shouldered young man with a medium build stood at the doorway, he was wearing a black cloak over a suit of dull grey steel chain mail. He stood tall and straight, his face was dark with his eyes sunken back into his thick brows. He had shoulder length chestnut hair and a short beard growing on his chin.

He was, a good looking, but serious type young man.

"Enter" Said Ram quietly.

"Milord." The man said standing directly in front of Ram.

"What is it, Bobbiur can't you see I'm busy!" Ram had replied abruptly, still calculating his figures.

Looking down, Bobbiur quickly said. "Yes sir. But I thought you should hear this."

"Well spit it out Bobbiur!" Ram had said this in a slightly raised voice.

"Well sir." Stated Bobbiur. "It's about the last weapon shipment we had sent out to the town of Garriton."

At this, Ram put down his quill and looked slowly up at Bobbiur.

"Well what about the last shipment we sent to the town of Garriton?" Ram asked. Lowering his voice and looking up from the papers on his desk.

"Sir, it was ambushed by a band of Krugs from Krugland." Bobbiur quickly added. "The Dark Storm Clan, I believe."

This statement got the complete attention of Ram as he quickly looked up at Bobbiur, with a questioning look, on his face. "And how might I ask, do you know this Bobbiur?"

"There was one survivor sir." Replied Bobbiur.

"Bring him to me right now, Bobbiur." Demanded Ram.

" I can't sir." Stated Bobbiur.

"And why----". Ram was interrupted in mid sentence

"Because." Bobbiur mentioned, as a matter of fact, while nodding his head.

"He's dead sir. He died of his wounds shortly after returning."

Bobbiur continued, speaking in an urgent tone. "His mount brought him back to Darmonarrow, and I was only able to speak to him for a few moments."

Interrupted Bobbiur.

"Well about this Krug problem....." Ram was rubbing his chin as he spoke. Bobbiur could see that Ram's mind was working at a very high speed.

After thinking for a moment, Ram spoke softly, but in a determined fashion to Bobbiur. "You and that strange new Elf-Archer, Hagjel and his little Human 'mage' friend Salbuk, will get our weapons back. We can't have Krugs, running around stealing our best weapons, now can we?" Ram suggested.

Then Ram, looking down added with a wave of his hand. "You will find them both at the Forge."

Both Ram and Bobbiur had worried looks on their faces because they knew that it could be very dangerous if these, top of the line weapons fell into the wrong hands.

These swords were so well built that they can cut right through armor and could even slice through other weapons such as, spears and swords.

The spears could go right through even the heaviest armor and were nearly impossible to brake.

The bows and arrows, which were built in Darmonarrow, were the straightest and fastest in all of Adjemir.

The Nine Moons of Adjemir

The daggers were so well crafted and sharp, that they could also go right through some of the best built war armor.

The other problem which was recognized by both Ram and Bobbiur, was in regards to the knowledge that if an arms shipment could be attacked this easily, it might start a trend. Both Ram and Bobbiur recognized that there must be something done quickly and with a very strong fashion against this raiding Krug band.

"Yes sir." Said Bobbiur, as he had turned and quickly hurried out the door and down the street.

Ram smiled to himself, as Bobbiur left the door.

Ram knew Bobbiur had no magic powers, but Bobbiur has been a good assistant and that someday he would be a good person to lead Darmonarrow. Ram in his own mind knew, he was starting to get old and someday he would have to step down. Ram could not think of a better individual to lead Darmonarrow than young Bobbiur.

Bobbiur had come up through the ranks and had always been very loyal, to Darmonarrow. Ram has seen Bobbiur in battle and his leadership abilities had always been evident. Bobbiur had never sent any of his men into a battle, or into any dangerous situations, unless he was willing to do the job himself. Ram had also noticed that Bobbiur, inside Darmonarrow had always treated the citizens the same and it didn't matter if the individual was Human, Dwarf, Elfin, or even Krug. Ram knew that this type of leadership quality was hard to find.

As Bobbiur left Ram's house, he noticed, the streets were nearly empty, as the Human Empire had been attacking Darmonarrow quite frequently. But on his way, a little further on, to his surprise he did see quite a few Dwarves, Humans and Elves and even a few Krugs. Bobbiur was thinking to himself, as he walked along, that it was really quite strange to see Krugs here, due to the fact that they hate all races.

Bobbiur surprised himself, as he spoke out loud to himself. "A very strange sight, to see all four races living together like this. A very strange sight indeed."

After a short while Bobbiur could here the banging and clanging of the Forge, his destination, in the distance.

The noise grew louder and soon he could see the Forge as he turned the final corner.

He walked up to the Forge where all the new recruits were trained in making swords, war axes, war hammers, bows and arrows, spears, and armor.

Sure enough, there they were.

A tall slender Elf with long blond hair, a bow over his shoulder and wearing some well built, expensive looking, green leather armor. The Elf stood beside a slightly shorter Human with a short beard, long black hair, wearing black robes.

The Human was watching Bobbiur, very closely as he approached and Bobbiur noticed that this Human's eyes, seemed intensely observant. Bobbiur, who was more observant than most citizens of Darmonarrow, noticed that both these individuals, were watching him very closely. Bobbiur also observed as he approached Hagjel and Salbuk, that both these new recruits had friendly smiles on their faces.

Bobbiur walked up to the Human, called Salbuk, who was closest to him and said. "Hello my name is Bobbiur and master Ram has a mission for you and your Elf friend Hagjel."

Bobbiur then turned slightly and nodded towards Hagjel.

"Hello." Said the Human called Salbuk, or at least Bobbiur thought he did.

"Wow, what was that, your lips didn't even move." Bobbiur exclaimed as he turned back to Salbuk.

"He's a mind mage. He's uses his mind and he just talked to you in your head."

The Elf named Hagjel pointed out, smiling, while almost laughing.

"Oh well, stay out of my head and speak normally to me." Bobbiur demanded sternly of Salbuk.

"He can't!" Said the Elf, who was now grinning ear to ear. "He took a Krug arrow in the throat in his last battle and he lost the ability to speak."

Then Hagjel said. "See the scar." At this Salbuk raised his chin and pointed at a large scar on his throat.

"He's lucky to be alive." Hagjel still smiling, tilted his head and with a slight chuckle, raised his eyebrows while observing Bobbiur's reaction.

"My name is Hagjel." Hagjel put out his hand to hand shake in the formal Adjemirian fashion. The Adjemirian formal handshake, is done by firmly gripping each other's elbow.

The Nine Moons of Adjemir

"And this is Salbuk." He said pointing towards the Human. Bobbiur then shook hands with Salbuk in the same fashion and was thinking to himself.

"These two warriors seem quite likeable."

Bobbiur could still not argue with Ram's decision to choose these to strangers to help him get the weapons shipment back, but he wished the new recruit Salbuk could speak. He also noticed that the Elf called Hagjel had a very large 'pot belly,' and this was probably from drinking too much ale over the years. Also, Bobbiur could not help but notice that Hagjel had a very large tote bag over his shoulder. This tote bag was larger than any other tote bags which most peoples of Adjemir normally carried.

Bobbiur had made a mental note to ask Hagjel why he would bother to carry such a large tote bag, but he put the thought aside, because he would be very busy getting things ready for the trip.

He would have to ask later.

Both Hagjel and Salbuk had noticed that Bobbiur had shown considerable interest in the tote bag carried by Hagjel, plus Salbuk had caught Bobbiur's thoughts. They looked at each other with a knowing grin on their faces.

"Okay." Said Bobbiur stepping back and taking a deep breath, before adding.

"Anyway, Ram has decided that you will accompany me on this mission and we leave in one hour. So pack your things."

Bobbiur went on to say.

"The last arms shipment which was headed to Garriton, has been ambushed by Krugs and all of the escort has been killed. We shouldn't be gone long, maybe a day or two is all."

Bobbiur, with a feeling of pride had said this while nodding, smiling and glancing over his shoulder at the workers in the Forge.

The Horses of Darmonarrow

Bobbiur was thinking that the three of them should be ready to leave in about an hour. Bobbiur had told Salbuk and Hagjel to meet him at the stables, where he would be waiting with his favorite Spaggidon already saddled.

Darmonarrow Spaggidons were always his choice of mount because they could travel for a long distance without needing to rest and the Spaggidons did not need a lot of food. Therefore they could forage while traveling.

The Darmonarrow Spaggidons were larger than other horses from Adjemir. Nearly thirty percent larger than the size of other, ordinary horses from Adjemir and considerably more intelligent. They could travel very quietly and could also carry a heavy load if required. These Spaggidon, from Darmonarrow, were not fighting animals, but they were very obedient.

Bobbiur took it upon himself to choose two Spaggidons. One for each Hagjel and Salbuk and also a spare Spaggidon to help carry some supplies if required, or to send messages back to Darmonarrow if needed.

Bobbiur did not know that in the past, Ram had taken all of the ordinary horses from the stables of Darmonarrow, trained them and then changed them with his magic. Spaggidons were much stronger, much faster and much more loyal than any other horses in all of Adjemir. These mounts would always return to the town of Darmonarrow, regardless of being captured by other peoples away from Darmonarrow. They would always try to return, because the homing instincts placed in them by Ram's magic was very strong.

If the Spaggidons were away from Darmonarrow for more than ten days, then the magic which had been placed in them by Ram, would diminish completely and they would simply turn back into ordinary horses.

If these Spaggidons were captured by any peoples other than citizens of Darmonarrow, they would also be impossible to ride.

Yes, these were the best mounts in all of Adjemir, but these magically changed horses were only reliable and loyal, for the citizens of Darmonarrow. The horses of Darmonarrow after Ram had altered their appearance, became know as Spaggidons. From that time forward they were not called horses any longer.

Leaving Darmonarrow

Soon after Hagjel and Salbuk arrived and started to load their gear onto the Spaggidons, Hagjel whispered to Salbuk, in front of Bobbiur.

"Should we tell our new friend Bobbiur, why I carry such a big tote bag?"

Salbuk sent a message to both Hagjel and Bobbiur. "Better now than later."

Both of the new recruits were smiling.

This last statement had gotten Bobbiur's interest so completely, he turned to ask innocently of Hagjel, why he had been carrying such a large tote bag. Hagjel, now knew he had Bobbiur's complete interest. He flipped up the lid of his tote bag.

Bobbiur still had a friendly, boyish, relaxed grin on his face, when suddenly a fully grown GymmKat slowly raised it's head up out of the tote bag which hung on Hagjel's side. This GymmKat, was staring Bobbiur, full in the face.

Bobbiur was caught completely by surprise. Bobbiur gave a surprised yelp as he jumped back. He had instantly lost the boyish smile. He covered his face and as much of his body as he could, by reflex he was guarding against a possible sting from the GymmKat.

Clearly the trick being played on Bobbiur, by Hagjel and Salbuk had worked out perfectly. They were both laughing so hard that Hagjel almost fell over.

GymmKats, who are actually quite rare, have a sting which was about one hundred and fifty time greater than a wasp sting. GymmKats were by far and away the most feared animals in all of Adjemir. At least a person could defend against Dragons and such, but the sting from a GymmKat could all but paralyze a person, or animal who was stung by one of these small creatures.

GymmKats were actually quite a beautiful animal. About the size of an ordinary house cat, with pointed ears, a long curly ringed tail and a short stubby face. The tail could be used for hanging from trees and for fluffing up to keep warm at night.

This GymmKat was a very dark brown with golden stripes flashing along it's sides. But not all GymmKats were the same color and this animal was no exception.

The most interesting thing about a GymmKat, are the eyes. The eyes of a GymmKat are big rounded and always very beautiful. But that is where the beauty, of the beast, comes to a grinding halt.

The eyes are where the GymmKat, launches it's powerful sting. The GymmKat can send an energy sting up to about thirty feet. The sting it has been said, moves faster than the fastest arrow. The sting from one of these animals is so strong and painful, that people who have had this sting, on occasion, have committed suicide by jumping off of cliffs, just to end the pain.

The pain can last for over an hour and the sting will also leave the victim very weak for days.

Yes, the GymmKat is very beautiful, but they are also very powerful and dangerous.

Bobbiur, in his panic had taken about fifteen quick steps backwards in total. When he felt he was at a safe distance, it finally dawned on him that Salbuk and Hagjel were actually playing a game on him.

They were still laughing when he started to get mad. "What the hell are you two doing?"

"We are supposed to be on a very serious mission and you two want to play games." Then changing the subject, Bobbiur in a raised voice yelled. "I'm not sure why Ram said I should take you two with me but I'm starting to think it's all been a big mistake."

Bobbiur was just shaking his head, as he raised his voice and was getting madder by the second.

Hagjel walked up to Bobbiur and without explaining, said. "Meet Jakka."

Salbuk sent a mind message, to Bobbiur. "You should not be mad because..."

Salbuk seemed very relaxed and he still had a big grin on his young face, as he finished his mind message. "Hagjel does this to everybody."

Salbuk's next mind message was almost like an apology. "Don't worry Bobbiur, after a couple of days you will actually find yourself liking Jakka."

Then Hagjel said while nodding his head and still grinning. "And besides you will find that Jakka is a great assistance in a fight. Consider what your reaction was and then think of how it takes the ability away from the enemy during a fight, when they suddenly see Jakka, staring them straight in the face."

Bobbiur was considering this information about Hagjel's pet GymmKat, Jakka and quietly musing about the surprise it must be for an enemy when this GymmKat, would show himself in the middle of a fight. Bobbiur was thinking that this could be a good asset and an advantage in a fight. Salbuk was able to catch Bobbiur's thought and he just smiled and nodded to Hagjel.

Hagjel nodded back that he understood, then he also put a thought in his mind that. "Bobbiur is not such a stick in the mud, as we first thought."

Salbuk sent a message back to Hagjel. "I agree."

Then Salbuk sent another mind message to Hagjel, which was actually quite amusing.

"Hagjel, this Bobbiur seems kind of young and a little green behind the ears, but I think we can train him. What do you think?"

Both Hagjel and Salbuk were almost laughing again when Hagjel put the thought in his mind for Salbuk. "Sure I think he's trainable."

Bobbiur thought that something was up when he asked of Hagjel. "What's so funny?"

Hagjel just rolled his eyes, looked at the sky, while shaking his head and said innocently. "Oh nothing. Nothing at all."

Hagjel turned back to his Spaggidon.

Once all the supplies were loaded onto the Spaggidons, Bobbiur, Hagjel and Salbuk rode out of the renegade town of Darmonarrow and down the narrow winding road, past the Weapons Trading Gazebo, eastward towards the old town of Garriton. Garriton was about five hours away and it was on this road where the weapons shipment had been traveling, when it was ambushed by the dark Storm Clan from Krugland.

Bobbiur was very curious because he had never heard that any person, regardless of whether or not they were Elf, Human, Krug or Dwarf, had ever become a friend of a fully grown GymmKat. He had to ask Hagjel how he had befriended Jakka, the now fully grown GymmKat.

Bobbiur knew he had to get this question out of his mind so he rode his Spaggidon up to the side of Hagjel. He asked the Elf. "How did you ever became friends with a GymmKat?"

Hagjel, after hearing the question from Bobbiur, glancing side-ways at Salbuk, stared momentarily at the sky and then turned his tilted head towards Bobbiur, with a slight boyish smile on his face. Started to speak about Jakka.

Salbuk who had heard this story many times, never tired of hearing it, so he rode his Spaggidon nearer to where Bobbiur and Hagjel were riding.

Hagjel, took a deep breath and started telling Bobbiur how he had become a friend of Jakka. He started by saying. "I had been to a pub in a village called KyLee, not to far from the Village of WynnFred and it was late at night when I was walking back to my camp. I heard a noise coming from a ditch beside the road."

Hagjel went on. "It sounded just like a baby kitten, crying for help. In the dark and with as much ale as I had drank that night, I probably thought it was a baby kitten."

Hagjel was shaking his head, shrugging his shoulders and looking off into the distance, as he went on. "I really can't remember."

"But I had picked up, what I thought at the time, was a baby kitten."

Hagjel continued on telling the story, with a distant look in his eyes as he was rethinking everything. "The mother must have been killed, or Jakka had somehow became separated."

Hagjel paused and looked down fondly at Jakka, who was now fully awake and looking up at Hagjel.

"But this little guy trusted me." Hagjel, patting Jakka on the head had a fond look on his face, while glancing ahead down the road and remembering how he had come upon Jakka that night. Hagjel took another deep breath as he continued.

"Anyways I had some small fruits in my tote bag, which I fed to this baby GymmKat and I guess we became instant friends. At this time and as dark as it was, I still did not know that this was a baby GymmKat. The next morning in my tent when I woke up, this baby GymmKat was sitting on my chest, and staring me right in the face. I never moved, because I was afraid, and I stared at Jakka for a long time. I was afraid to move." Shaking his head in a mild disbelief Hagjel continued. "I wasn't sure if a baby GymmKat could sting."

"When I was able to feel comfortable with this little guy sitting on my chest, I picked him up." Hagjel thought for a few moments, then continued. "Jakka must have thought that I was his mother, or something like that, because he just snuggled up and went into my tote bag looking for something to eat." Hagjel laughed before he went on. "I had some problems explaining to my friends in the camp, that this GymmKat was not dangerous and after awhile, they grew to accept Jakka."

Hagjel was shaking his head as if he still did not completely understand what had happened when he first found Jakka. Then, still smiling, he continued on. "For me Jakka has been a really good friend."

Then Hagjel went on to explain, just what kind of friend Jakka was and how reliable Jakka could be. Hagjel speaking quietly and with the same friendly look on his face kept talking. "One time I was traveling alone, going from the city of Domerge to the village of WynnFred, looking for a friend of mine, when I was surprised by about ten young Krug scavengers."

Hagjel added. "I was all alone so these young Krugs must have thought I was easy to rob."

Hagjel, smiling, looked down and patted Jakka's head as he continued with this amusing part of the story. "They had caught me completely by surprise so I never even had time to get my bow off of my shoulder."

"Basically I had been surrounded by a bunch of young rascals."

Still smiling, Hagjel went on. "They were really confident. Ten to one odds, was a pretty good feeling for them, I guess."

Hagjel looked at the sky, trying to remember all of the details and Salbuk noticed that Bobbiur was listening intently. Hagjel looked off into the distance, while patting his tote bag where Jakka was curled up and was now sleeping. "Just when I thought I was about to get robbed or even killed by these Krug rascals, Jakka must have sensed the danger to us."

"Jakka was almost fully grown by this time and his sting was just as powerful as a fully grown GymmKat."

Hagjel went on in a matter of fact fashion, with a smile on his face. It was becoming clear to Bobbiur that Hagjel had told this story many times. Hagjel spoke further. "I had been so concerned about the danger from the Krugs that I had somehow forgotten about Jakka in my tote bag."

"The Krugs must have thought I had a lot of money, or gold on me because of the size of the tote bag."

The smile on Hagjel's face grew even bigger when he told the rest of his story. As he continued to look off into the distance, Hagjel came to the most interesting part of his story.

Hagjel said. "I remembered Jakka was in my tote bag when I heard his attack sounds."

"Bobbiur just in case you have never heard it, it sounds something like this."

Then Hagjel imitated the sound of a GymmKat as best he could. "Ka,Ka,Ka,Ka, HaWussss." Nodding Hagjel said. "Made in a very rapid fashion."

Hagjel glanced off towards Salbuk, with a knowing smile on his face and then he continued.

"The faster the sounds are made means the closer to attacking, the GymmKat is. When I heard Jakka's attack sound coming from the bag. So did the Krugs."

"But apparently none of them knew what this sound was."

Hagjel had a very amused look on his face as he continued. "As I had said early I don't think any of these Krugs had heard this sound before."

"I quickly got the idea and flipped open the tote bag. Then Jakka suddenly stretched up out of the bag and went into his battle stance."

Hagjel made a guttural sounding laugh which came all the way from his belly, as he continued to tell his story.

"The rest of the battle was amazing."

Hagjel was continuing with an even bigger smile on his face. "Jakka continued to make his attack sound and these young Krugs were actually frozen in place. None of them even dared to move."

"These Krugs didn't seem to know what the GymmKat sound was but they sure knew what a GymmKat was when they saw one face to face."

Glancing downwards to the tote bag Hagjel spoke with friendship for Jakka. "Jakka sent his eye stinger at the closest Krug and at this close range Jakka made a direct hit. This was happening so fast that the other Krugs were also caught completely by surprise."

Hagjel made some movements, as if he had a bow in his hands, as he showed how he reacted to the Krugs. "I had my bow out and got off four shots before those Krugs could recover from the surprise of seeing Jakka ."

Salbuk's sides were shaking, because he was laughing so hard at this part of the story. "Those four Krugs died within minutes. The rest of the Krugs turned and fled. I was going to kill the Krug on the ground, which Jakka had stung just to put him out of his misery, but I decide against it."

Hagjel looked off into the distance and his smile grew larger.

"I thought it would be better to let him return to his people and tell his story to them. Glancing at Bobbiur Hagjel said. "I thought it might send a message to other Krugs that they should stop raiding travelers on the roads of Adjemir."

Hagjel was just finishing up his story but decided to say just one more thing.

Hagjel concluded. "If you have never seen a sting from a grown GymmKat then you will be surprised by just how strong Jakka can sting an enemy."

Salbuk, who was doing most of the watching for possible ambushes, knew that the story was almost over. He quickly sent a message to both Hagjel and Bobbiur, that they should give all their attention to watching for the Krugs. Bobbiur nodded to both Salbuk and Hagjel that he understood and agreed.

It was no coincidence that Ram had chosen these three warriors for this mission. He trusted them very much and had complete confidence in their abilities.

He had picked Salbuk because of his mind abilities. If he could he would have sent just Salbuk alone, but his powers although very strong were limited against a large force. It must have been a large force which could intercept an arms shipment.

Ram sent Bobbiur for his exceptional sword skills, his quick mind and his ability to lead. Plus Bobbiur needed more training. Ram was comfortable that Salbuk and Hagjel would add to Bobbiur's further training. Ram had smiled to himself when he had made this decision.

He also decided on Hagjel for his skill with the bow. Hagjel could shoot arrows faster and more accurate than anyone else in Darmonarrow and maybe in all of Adjemir for that matter. He could give cover-fire to Bobbiur and Salbuk. Because Hagjel had worked as a tracker before coming to Darmonarrow, his tracking skills would come in handy while looking for the Krugs.

Ram had chosen wisely. He felt very comfortable with his choice of only sending a small group. Basically he did not want to send a larger group because it might weaken the garrison at Darmonarrow.

After the group had left Darmonarrow and even though they were moving slowly because they had to watch out for possible ambushes, it wasn't more than two hours before they found signs of the ambush of the weapons shipment. Black Krug blood and red Human blood painted the ground. The remnants of a wagon, was charred and still smoldering in the middle of the road.

Hagjel said "What a mess."

They all looked around at the bodies on the ground and glanced into the surrounding woods worrying about possibly being ambushed themselves. There was no time to bury the dead from the arms shipment, as the tracks from the Krugs might get old and they might become difficult to follow. Also Bobbiur was not sure how good of a tracker Hagjel actually was, so he decided to press on.

Bobbiur instructed Hagjel and Salbuk to remove any supplies which they had loaded onto the spare Spaggidon and he wrote a message onto a piece of paper, which he put into the side pocket of the pack saddle.

Jakka had poked his head out of the tote back and Hagjel had fondly stoked Jakka's head and given him some nuts and small fruits to nibble on. Even though Bobbiur was very intense regarding the task at hand, he could not help but notice that Hagjel and Jakka had a very deep friendship. There was an uncanny communication between the two of them and although Bobbiur had seen Salbuk watching and knowing that Salbuk was reading his thoughts on this matter, it did not seem so bad any more. Bobbiur was starting to like these characters more all the time.

The Nine Moons of Adjemir

The message which was being sent back to Darmonarrow with the spare Spaggidon, was addressed to Ram. It stated that Darmonarrow should send out a burial party to look after the mess, which was left at the ambush sight.

Spaggidons were very reliable and loyal mounts about returning to their home when not being ridden or being used as a pack animal, so Bobbiur felt more than satisfied that the message would be received by Ram.

Hagjel, being a scout and archer for the Elf armies in the past, was also supposed to be an excellent tracker. He easily picked up on some Krug tracks leading into the bush.

The group did not talk much because they did not want to make any sounds. So they, by way of old habits, started to use hand signals amongst themselves, but Salbuk, did not need any signals because of his ability to send and to receive mind messages. Salbuk just smiled to himself when he saw Hagjel and Bobbiur giving signals to each other.

They followed the tracks which were easy to follow, because the tracks were less than a few hours old.

Bobbiur knew that they might be catching up to the Krugs so he wanted Hagjel in the front and Salbuk in the rear of the group, guarding their backs. Bobbiur had decided that he should be behind Hagjel, so he could cover for him. Because Hagjel would be concentrating on the ground, looking for signs, he would need somebody to look out for his back. Hagjel's total attention would be concentrated on the ground when tracking the Dark Storm Clan.

After a short while Bobbiur looked up and noticed that it was starting to get dark, so instead of continuing and maybe getting into a night battle, or an ambush by the Krugs, he decided that they should set up camp. He motioned to the others and they nodded that they understood what was happening. Bobbiur had simply made a tent shape with his hands and put his hands against his cheek to signify a sleeping position. Then Bobbiur picked a location on a small hill which was just in front of them and which was close to a stream. Bobbiur pointed to the others.

When they had ridden up the small hill they all dismounted. Bobbiur and Salbuk set up the tent while Hagjel stood guard.

They all ate some food while the Spaggidons ate some grass growing nearby, beside the little stream. They were all very tired but before they went to sleep Salbuk put up a mind barrier, a shield of protection, around their camp to protect them while they slept. Although none of them wanted it the Spaggidons, mostly because of their size, which made them noisy sleepers, were tethered close to the tent.

The Spaggidons, were tethered close to the tent, because they had a very good sense of hearing, and if any Krugs or other enemy tried to sneak up on them while they slept, the Spaggidons would hear them before anybody else would. The Spaggidons were also trained to make enough noise, to wake them up it there were intruders.

The next morning the group woke early, filled their canteens and had something to eat. It was still a little bit dark when they packed up and set out again. Bobbiur was quite amazed how Hagjel could follow tracks with such a small amount of light and he was forced to admit, that Hagjel was very good at tracking. Bobbiur smiled to himself because Ram had chosen wisely.

It wasn't long before Hagjel could smell the smoke from the Krug camp. Hagjel turned and pointed to his nose and both Bobbiur and Salbuk motioned that they had also smelled the same thing.

As it turned out, most of the Krugs were still sleeping but some were moving around doing their morning errands. The men looked at each other and without saying anything they backed up a little ways and tied the Saggidons to some trees.

Then they began sneaking up closer to the Krug camp. When they got close to the Krug camp, Bobbiur signaled to Hagjel that he should go first and Salbuk sent a mind message to both Hagjel and Bobbiur, that he understood and was in agreement.

Hagjel found a good spot and from a kneeling position, picked a target. He fired an arrow into the camp and it hit it's mark dead center in the throat. Krug dropped silently to the ground in a puddle of black blood. He fired two more arrows in a rapid fashion hitting two more Krugs, before the war horn was blown and all the Krugs scurried out of their tents looking for the enemy. Bobbiur figured that there were about thirty Krugs in total, in the camp.

Salbuk made two telekinetic swords, with his mind, which he sent into the camp and these swords started hacking up the Krugs. Hagjel kept firing arrows into the camp and had to switch spots a couple of times, so the Krugs didn't catch onto his location.

As for Bobbiur, a very skilled swords-man, he waited until the 'telekinetic swords' spell wore off and then ran into the camp and began fighting any Krug that he could find. He was not worried that Hagjel was continuing to fire arrows at the Krugs, because by now he knew that Hagjel was such a good shot that he would not be hit by a stray arrow from Hagjel's bow.

Just then Salbuk saw a Krug advancing on Bobbiur's flank which apparently Bobbiur was not aware of. Thinking quickly, Salbuk sent a message into the Krugs mind, which caused him to stab himself with the same dagger he was going to use against Bobbiur. Bobbiur saw the Krug was under one of Salbuk's spells and Bobbiur nodded his thanks to Salbuk by raising his sword up to his face. Bobbiur lightly touched his sword handle to his helmet and then with a smile, nodded his head. Salbuk smiling gave a short bow in return.

Eventually the remaining Krugs retreated into the forest followed by a barrage of arrows, complements of Hagjel.

The only injury acquired by the three was a small slash on Bobbiur's arm made by a Krug's spear. The injury was easily repaired by Salbuk with his magic powers.

While searching through the Krug camp they realized there were no weapons to be found. Bobbiur was puzzled, as was Hagjel and Salbuk.

Then Hagjel said with a bit of a surprise in his voice. "Jakka slept through the whole fight. And this surprises me."

Hagjel then said. "He has never slept through a battle before."

Then shaking his head Hagjel added. "He enjoys a good fight. He must be really tired."

Bobbiur looked somewhat puzzled and Salbuk said in a mind message. "Maybe he has a cold or something, or maybe he just felt that his services were not needed."

Then changing the subject Salbuk said in a mind message. "It's a good thing this the battle ended when it did because I was starting to get very tired and I would not be able to cast many more magic spells. I barely had enough strength left to heal Bobbiur's arm. I'll need to rest for a little while, so I can regain my strength."

Just then they saw a figure in the forest walking quickly toward them. All three got ready for another battle. As the figure got nearer they saw what looked like an old Human with a beard down to his knees. He wore really old blue robes and a green pointed hat with a worn out rim.

"Hello" The old man yelled as he neared them. "Congratulations on the victory. Jolly good. Jolly good."

The old man was yammering, and grinning ear to ear. His head was bobbing up and down, like a leaf in a strong wind.

"Who are you?" Bobbiur asked loudly while all three were still ready to fight, because they did not know who this funny little old man was.

"They call me Zorp" He replied.

"But you can call me. 'The King of Adjemir'."

This funny little man, with a twinkle in his eye was laughing to himself as he approached.

"No! They can't." Bellowed a voice from beneath them. The sound was coming from the ground.

"Oh shut up you flee bitten, scaly-worm."

Zorp yelled, shaking his fist at the ground.

"What was that?" Bobbiur demanded as he stepped back. All three were looking at the ground around their feet with their weapons at the ready.

"Oh that." Zorp, nodding his head said calmly. "That was just my Dragon."

Then looking towards the group Zorp said. "You can call her Dorothy. If you want?"

Zorp suggested with the wide grin remaining on his face. His head was tilted slightly to the left and there was a friendly twinkle in his eyes.

"No they can't." Bellowed the voice from the ground.

"My name is Dymma and don't you believe everything this old man tells you. He's such a boring old liar."

"Fine but you don't let me have any fun." Zorp whined glancing towards the ground.

"Anyway I know where your missing weapons are." Zorp said suddenly looking at Bobbiur. "Have you ever heard of Smarge of the 'Dark Storm Clan'? He's an educated Krug."

Zorp went on without waiting for a response. "One of the smartest and strongest. He has been trained by the most evil and skilled, Elf swords-man in all of Adjemir."

Then Zorp continued on while waving his arm in a circular motion with the same twinkle in his eye. "This Smarge is the leader of these Krugs."

Said Zorp while shaking his head and waving his arm at a pile of dead Krugs. "They call themselves a clan." He nodded towards the Krugs again.

"But it's more like they are, just a gang."

"Oh. And where might we find him?" Hagjel had asked with a quizzical look on his face.

"He just found you." Said Zorp looking up and pointing towards the sky.

They all looked up to see a magnificent green Dragon with a mighty Krug, bigger than they had ever seen before, on the Dragon's enormous back, sailing down toward them. The Krug on the back of the Dragon looked like he meant business. He had a miserable, vicious and mean look on his face, as he surveyed his dead warriors on the ground. This Krug was dressed in a shinny yellow suit of armor. Which was probably made from bronze, or a type of copper. Smarge's war helmet was made with some strong looking bluish metal. It had a complete face guard, with small eyes holes and no ear holes. A blue feather plume was attached at the back of the helmet, which was flapping in the wind behind him as he flew closer.

"Dragon!" Zorp had loudly screamed for Dymma.

"I'm on it." The deep sounding voice from the ground roared.

The place where they were all standing started to rumble and shake. With a great explosion of crackling sounds, a swirling golden mist began quickly rising out of the ground. Then a huge body exploded into being, right before their very eyes with such force, that it knocked Salbuk and Bobbiur to the ground. Right before them stood a very large and fully mobile, beautiful golden colored and magnificent looking Dragon. This very large Dragon, quickly jumped upwards from the ground and started flapping its enormous wings, just in front of where Salbuk and Bobbiur, were still sitting after they had been knocked down. The Dragon, while hovering just above them smiling, turned its mighty head and said apologetically.

"Sorry I knocked you down. But as you can see, I was in quite a hurry."

Bobbiur was thinking, to himself that he had never heard a Dragon speak before, or even smile for that matter.

Salbuk sent a message to both Hagjel and Bobbiur. "A talking Dragon is completely unheard of." Zorp chimed into Salbuk's mind message. Stating, while grinning ear to ear. "You ain't seen nothing yet."

Things were happening, so fast, Jakka started to chatter and then quickly dug down deeper into the tote bag. Jakka had never seen such a large beast before. Especially this close.

With a big grin, this magnificent glistening golden creature flew higher into the air and with incredible speed, flew directly at the Krug Dragon. Zorp's Dragon, Dymma, bit the tale of the Krug's Dragon and the two Dragons flew off in a nasty mess.

Smarge the Krug who was sitting on the other Dragon's back when Dymma, started her attack, had managed to jump safely to the ground just as the two Dragons began to fight. With incredible speed for a Krug, Smarge ran toward them, zigzagging. He was very fast for a Krug. Smarge was dodging arrows from Hagjel's bow, when all of a sudden and without any warning, the attacking Krug jumped into the air and swiftly threw his shield, like a saucer, at Hagjel.

The blow was so strong that it knocked Hagjel out, with a deep gash to his forehead. When Hagjel went down it must have stunned Jakka, who was still in the tote bag, chattering to himself.

Then Smarge was onto Salbuk so fast that Salbuk because his magic powers were weak, from the earlier fighting, couldn't put up a mind barrier fast enough, nor strong enough. The Krug hit Salbuk with his fist and the blow was so hard, that the blow cracked three of Salbuk's ribs. Salbuk was smashed to the ground, stunned and moaning in pain.

Bobbiur noted that Hagjel wasn't moving at all.

Zorp had quickly ran and hid behind a large tree. "Go get em 'Rocco'!"

Bobbiur heard this from behind the tree where Zorp was hiding. It almost sounded like the old man was enjoying this battle.

Things were happening so fast that Bobbiur was just able to get his sword up before Smarge was onto him.

A vicious and fierce sword battle began between Bobbiur and Smarge.

Smarge was much bigger than most Krugs, in fact Smarge was the biggest Krug that Bobbiur had ever seen. Smarge was much taller than Bobbiur, much bigger, but both fighters were almost equal in strength. The battle was going to be long and hard on both of them, as their skills were almost equal. The battle had been going on for quite some time and it seemed that no one would ever win. Bobbiur was starting to get tired and he thought that he had better finish the fight real quick, so he mustered all of his power and went in to finish off Smarge.

Bobbiur dodged and went for Smarge's side but to Bobbiur's surprise, this Krug was very fast, and parried. Bobbiur went for a head attack, but Smarge parried this also. Before Bobbiur could recover from his attack, Smarge swung at Bobbiur's ribs. The swing ricocheted off Bobbiur's armor, yet the blow was still strong enough to also crack some of Bobbiur's ribs.

Then Bobbiur made a stupid mistake due to his tiredness from his previous battle and the cracked ribs. He lunged at Smarge and missed by three inches. Before Bobbiur could draw back, Smarge bent over and pulled a dagger out of his boot and stabbed Bobbiur in the ribs.

It must have been one of the missing Darmonarrow weapons, for it cut right through Bobbiur's armor as if it were butter. Before he collapsed Bobbiur slashed into the Krugs arm. The slash on the Smarge's arm seemed to make him quite angry, at which time he gave a low vicious growl. Smarge turned and looked at Bobbiur on the ground. Then in a very determined mood, because he knew he had won this battle, Smarge started a deep throated roar, just like the savage beast he was. Smarge had opened his arms wide and then viciously roared at the sky.

Bobbiur had hit the ground very hard, and was laying there stunned and defenseless for a few moments. His sword had been knocked out of his hand and was lying on the ground, just out of his reach. Smarge's dagger was still sticking out of Bobbiur's side.

Deep down inside, Bobbiur knew that the battle was over and he was about to die.

Smarge took a step closer towards Bobbiur. As he stood over Bobbiur ready to finish him off, Bobbiur out of the corner of his eye saw Jakka run up quickly and quietly behind Smarge. Jakka must have gotten free of the tote bag carried by Hagjel and it appears that Jakka had figured things out quite well. Smarge was raising his sword high into the air, in order to cut straight through Bobbiur when he heard the most dreaded sound in all of Adjemir.

It was the attack cackle of a GymmKat. "Ka, Ka, Ka, Ka, HaWussss."

Jakka hissed in a rapid fashion from just behind Smarge.

Smarge halted all movement and just froze where he was. There was a look of absolute fear in his eyes and on his face. The fear was showing at the sides of his face armor. His eyes looking unblinkingly straight forward, where wide open. Smarge never moved, not even in the slightest.

Bobbiur in considerable pain, notice that Jakka was standing straight legged, tail straight in the air, with his back hunched up and was staring, unblinkingly at the center of Smarge's broad back. Bobbiur then heard Jakka making the attack cackling sound again. This time in a much quicker hissing fashion. "Ka, Ka, Ka, Ka, HaWussss."

Jakka blinked three times and then it just happened.

All these things were happening very fast, but for Bobbiur it was like slow motion and dream-like. Jakka had sent his stinger.

Bobbiur noticed that a bright narrow green light had just zapped out from Jakka's eyes. At the very end of this narrow green light, was a small orb of brighter light. The ord, which was no larger than a hen's egg, Bobbiur thought, must be the JymmKat's stinger. The shot blasted directly into Smarges broad back, just at the second when Smarge was starting to turn to see where the dreaded GymmKat sound was coming from.

Jakka was only about ten feet from Smarge when the sting had been sent and Smarge got a full dose of power from the sting. It was a direct hit. When Jakka's stinger hit Smarge there was a instant green energy which immediately surrounded the entire body of Smarge.

Bobbiur had never seen anything like this before in his life. A huge powerful Krug like Smarge, was knocked to the ground and reduced to a screaming mess, in the blink of an eye, by a GymmKat the size of Jakka. After being knocked to the ground by Jakka, the green energy from the contact of the stinger, started to be absorbed by the now screaming Smarge. The screaming from Smarge started to grow even louder, that is once all of the green energy had been fully absorbed.

Never mind the practical joke which was played on Bobbiur earlier with Jakka. Hagjel and Salbuk were right, it did not seem to be all that difficult to start to feel good about Jakka.

Shortly after the stinger from the GymmKat had been sent at Smarge Bobbiur thought to himself. "This funny little animal had just saved all their lives."

At least Bobbiur had thought this thought was kept to himself. But Salbuk who was getting up from the ground, quickly sent a simple message which was almost like a laugh, to Bobbiur's mind, saying. "We told you so."

Bobbiur looked over to see Salbuk getting up off the ground and was holding his side with both hands. Even though it was evident that Salbuk was in severe pain Salbuk had a large grin on his face.

"Sorry you lost your thunder Bobbiur but it looks like you needed some help." Zorp snickered as he peeked out from behind the tree.

"Saved by a GymmKat." Then with a teasing laugh and with a huge grin, Zorp asked. "How will you ever explain this to your grandchildren?"

At his own humor Zorp started to laugh out loud. Zorp had a twinkle in his eye and was smiling ear to ear. "How did you know my name?"

Bobbiur managed to spit out this question while grimacing in pain. Then Bobbiur, quickly, before Zorp could answer the question went on. "Why didn't you help us? You must have some kind of magic power?"

Without giving Zorp a chance to answer, Bobbiur who was somewhat mad, quickly followed these questions with yet another question. "You have this Dragon with you, who also seems to have magic powers, so why didn't you help us?"

Staggering somewhat, Bobbiur who was still in severe pain had asked this in a demanding tone, while holding his side where the cracked ribs and the knife wounds were located.

"Oh you don't know the half of it." Zorp said chuckling and then he spoke further. I know a lot about you three and your renegade city, of Darmonarrow. Anyways." Zorp paused, while squinting and rubbing his chin, before going on as he changed the subject.

"You shouldn't be expecting me to do your fighting for you, now should you?" Zorp had said this, with both arms held wide and bent over in a half bowing motion.

Then standing quickly erect Zorp added. "Oh, and by the way."

He clapped his hands. "You and your friends' wounds are healed and I think Dragon's got something for you." He was actually quite business like at this time, as he was speaking matter of factually, while glancing up into the sky.

Bobbiur had been looking down at his wounds which were gone, as were Hagjel's and Salbuk's. This amazed him. Then Bobbiur heard something, and he quickly looked up to see the Dragon coming in for a landing, right in front of them.

"I believe these belong to you." The Dragon, smiling, placed on the ground a number of boxes, which contained all of the Garriton's weapons shipment.

"Thanks." Said Bobbiur, somewhat puzzled as he quickly said. "Goodbye."

Because Zorp had started to quickly walk away headed towards the Dragon. Zorp was chuckling as he yelled over his shoulder. "You will never have to worry about Smarge again."

In a confident tone Zorp went on. "I promise you this. After he comes out of the sting from your friend Jakka he will never fight again. I can't tell you anymore than that."

Bobbiur was quite puzzled by this and he looked over to see Smarge still withering on the ground in severe pain. Zorp, shaking his head spoke further. He yelled over his shoulder as he continued to walk towards the Dragon. "Don't kill the Krug. The pain is good for his likes and maybe he will send a message to the other Krugs about leaving travelers alone."

Zorp hopped onto the back of the Dragon and they flew into the air. They hovered above Bobbiur and his men for a few moments before Zorp yelled.

"Have a nice day and good luck."

Then without saying anything further Zorp and the Dragon Dymma simply flew away. The three men looked at each other. "What was that?" Bobbiur felt in his mind.

Bobbiur glanced over to see Salbuk staring at Zorp and the Dragon as they flew away.

"You mean that guy?" Bobbiur replied.

"Yes. What was he besides a little crazy?" Salbuk mentioned this in both Bobbiur's and Hagjel's minds.

Then Hagjel said to both Salbuk and Bobbiur. "Kind of a funny old guy. Never seems to take anything serious."

Jakka was back in Hagjel's tote bag was chuckling in his GymmKat fashion.

"I don't know." Bobbiur said this while looking off into the direction where Zorp and Dymma had flown.

Then Bobbiur said. "But he sure had some powerful magic and he also had his own talking Dragon for a friend."

At this last comment Hagjel broke in. "If he had that kind of power then why didn't he help us in the fight with Smarge?"

Bobbiur just shrugged again while saying. "I don't know."

Salbuk had been listening to Hagjel and Bobbiur talking and when he got the chance, he sent a mind message to both Bobbiur and Hagjel. "I sure would have liked to see those two Dragons fighting."

Then Salbuk sent a further mind message in the form of a question. "I wonder what happened to the other Dragon?"

Both Hagjel and Bobbiur turned towards Salbuk and nodding in his direction they both agreed, the Dragon fight would have been interesting.

With a boyish grin on his face Hagjel added. "It's to bad they flew completely out of sight before they finished their fight."

Pausing while changing the subject Bobbiur said. "Well let's get these weapons to Garriton."

Hagjel then interrupted as he was bending over to inspect the boxes of weapons. "I wonder if we will ever see him again?"

When Hagjel was finished Bobbiur said in a quiet tone. "Yes. Your right Hagjel. I also wonder if we will ever see him or his Dragon again."

Then Bobbiur said. "This place might not be that safe."

Glancing over his shoulder with a worried look on his face, Bobbiur commented. "There may be more Krugs around."

So the three men loaded the boxes of weapons onto the Spaggidons and started to walk back towards the road. As the three men trudged back towards the road Bobbiur and Hagjel heard Salbuk in their head.

"You know that Zorp was kind of a funny guy. I'm very glad he was on our side."

Then the group laughing disappeared down the road towards Garriton.

Darmonarrow is Attacked

Just before the attack on Darmonarrow the guards by the main gate were just about finished their tour of duty, when they saw something in the sky.

There was something there but it did not seem real. It was like a small cloud but it wasn't a cloud. It was more like a glistening sphere. It hovered silently above their heads, shinning and expanding but they could see right through it. It seemed to stay for a few minutes, moving about slightly, then it seemed to disappear.

The guards looked at each other and just shrugged their shoulders like they may have been dreaming that they saw something, which was realy nothing. This thing which did not seem real, made no noise and it just seemed like it was a figment of their imagination. Then poof, as they guards turned away, they instantly lost all memory of what they had just seen.

A little later Ram stepped out of his house to get some fresh air but mostley just to get away from his work for a short while. Also he was getting quite hungry.

Ram wore a heavy black hooded cloak with the hood down. On his belt he carried a golden handled dagger, the best the Darmonarrow forge could build. The dagger on his belt was one of his few luxeries in life. Ram did not wear any jewelry. His long graying hair was tied back in a pony tail and it hung half way down his back. Ram had very intense and piercing green eyes.

Under his arm he carried a large leather bound book. He walked slowly down the road towards his favourite tavern. He was aware of everything around him Every sound and every movement. His keen, light green eyes glanced in all directions and missed nothing.

Bobbiur Salbuk and Hagjel had been gone for about two hours and no word on their progress had come in yet, but Ram was not worried. The group he had picked to get the weapons back was very capable.

"Yes." Ram spoke softly to himself. "Very capable indeed."

Although Hagjel and Salbuk were relatively new to Darmonarrow, when Ram had first met with them to see if he would allow them to live in Darmonarrow he had entered their minds to see if they were telling the truth and also to see if they could be trusted. After he had completed the mind search he was more than satisfied that they could both be trusted.

Ram smiled to himself when he thought about just how capable these two new recruits realy were. Then he wondered to himself. "I wonder if they have driven young Bobbiur a little crazy yet?' Then with an uneasy feeling he thought, as he continued walking towards the tavern, that there was something, like a light shinning behind him. But when he turned to look, there was nothing there. Or was there? This feeling gave him an uncertain and uncomfortable feeling, but the uneasiness soon disappeared as he turned and continued walking further.

As he walked down the street he stopped occasionally to greet people who stepped out just to see him. Finally he turned and stepped into the noisey tavern at the end of his street, not far from the front gate. As Ram entered the room, the bar went deadly silent.

"Eat, drink and don't mind me."

Ram said this loud enough for all to hear as he walked over to an empty table. He set his book down and took off his cloak.

The bar noise quickly returned as soon as Ram was seated.

When he was comfortable he opened his book at the page which he had book-marked. He read for only a few minutes when he was approached by the barkeeper, who interrupted by saying. "Your usual sir?"

The Barkeep who was an Elf placed an already prepared tray on the table. On the tray there was a bowl full of delicious smelling Elfs stew, a small loaf of bread, two sticks of cheese, a small salad, and a pint of Dwarfen ale. Ram had always liked Dwarf ale. He did not especially care for Dwarfed food, but Dwarfen ale was some of the best in all of Adjemir.

"Thank you." Ram said, looking around and glancing out the window, as he asked in a friendly sort of way.

The Nine Moons of Adjemir

"You wouldn't happen to know why I saw no woman or children, anywhere in Darmonarrow, on my way down here today would you?"

Ram had asked the Barkeep.

"I would sir." Said a funny looking old Dwarf with a grey beard, sitting off to Ram's right with two Krugs. The Dwarf was wearing a large flat hat with a large fluffy bird feather stuck into the brim.

"It was such a nice day for a picnic, so the woman took the children and a large lunch and went to the falls near the bottom of the hill."

The Dwarf paused, smiled knowingly and then said. "They have six guards with them."

Smiling, the older soft spoken, friendly Dwarf then said to Ram and the barkeeper. "It's the kids day off, from school, you know."

The old Dwarf seemed to understand that Ram was a very busy person and did not get out much so Ram probably did not know that the kids had the day off from school.

"Good, good." Ram said nodding his head and smiling. Ram then turned to his steaming food, tore off a piece of bread and dipped it into the stew as he started to read while occasionally sipping his ale.

Ram was just finishing his meal when he heard a sound. It was a noise that Ram did not recognize. A loud wailing noise which he had never heard before and it was getting louder all the time. He quickly hurried out the door of the tavern. He could still move remarkably fast for an older man. The sound was becoming louder and he could tell that it was coming from a distance away. The noise was a high pitched wailing sound, but he could still not identify what the sound was.

He ran down the street towards the city wall. Ram was about twenty meters from the wall when he heard the attack whistles being sounded by some of the guards in the towers. Ram could also see the guards firing arrows at an enemy. Ram raised his hands in the air and uttered a few words at which time he quickly flew into the air. He hovered just above the wall and was able to see what appeared to be about fifteen warriors, riding something which looked like very large, big headed lizards charging the main gate.

These large lizard type animals Ram was to find out later, were actually called Kilpacx. These Kilpacx were big, green, fierce animals. They had a very large head with a short, but powerful looking jaw bone. The teeth in these animals were actually razor sharp. They had

43

beady little, yellow eyes, which looked straight forward, from the center of their head. The Kilpacx had short round ears, which could be swivelled in any direction in order to hear better. The tail on these animals were fairly long, with a yellow spike ball at it's very end. This spike ball had very sharp quills sticking out of it. Clearly the Kilpacx tail could also be used as a killing weapon.

Ram noticed that these Kilpacx were about three times the size of the largest Darmonarrow Spaggidon and were just about half the size of the average Adjemirian Dragon. He also noticed that these Kilpacx were not using their short front legs to run, but they were still able to run fairly level with the ground. For a big animal they were able to move quite fast and they were actually able to move smoothly without much jarring. The speed which these animals could move was incredible for such a large animal and in an open field, Ram guessed their speed would just be slightly slower than the speed of the average Darmonarrow Spaggidon.

There was a set of humps on the back of the Kilpacx, where the warrior who was called a Haddron, could ride without a saddle if they wanted. There were no reins and the signals to the Kilpacx were given through mind messages. Sometimes the messages to the Kilpacx were given through signals from the use of the warrior's knee. Ram had never seen these type of animals before but clearly they were not Adjemirian Dragons. These animals were something completely different.

The gate archer, knowing that Darmonarrow was being attacked, although he was not sure who these people or things were, shot an arrow into the chest of one of the attackers. The arrow stuck into the riders chest, who momentarily seem to be in pain but suddenly the shaft just turned to dust and fell off. The warrior only laughed.

The archer continued to shoot his arrows but with little or no effect. Unknown to the guards on the gate a complete protection shield, would soon be in place and soon the arrows which were being fired would just bounce off.

Some guards who had picked up arms were heading for the gate. Other guards were climbing into the gate towers and were getting ready to defend Darmonarrow. Some of the guards had seen that Ram was present and this gave them confidence, because they all knew how strong and capable, a fighter Ram was.

One of the attackers raised a yellow flag, or something like a flag above his head. This warrior waved this flag slowly three times

The Nine Moons of Adjemir

in a circle and then it happened. Almost immediately a very powerful magic spell, in the form of a great energy ball of flame came from behind a large earthen mound, which was situated by the road just behind the charging warriors. This magic fire ball was headed straight at the gate at an incredible speed.

Although the gate had been attacked by various different means in the past, from Humans, Krugs, Elves and Dwarfs, it had never been hit with this much force. The power from this enormous fire ball was tremendous. The gate was not made to withstand this kind of force and with a loud crashing sound the gate was instantly turned into charcoal and splinters.

Now there was nothing left except the guards and Ram, to stop the apparently powerful and oncoming charge.

The explosion from the gate was so strong that there was considerable damage. Some guards were injured and some were dead. The guards who weren't dead, or injured ran for cover. A large number of archers took cover in huts and opened fire on the attackers. These arrows either bounced off the attackers or had little or no effect.

Ram flew down towards the first attacker, who had entered through the burning and smashed front gate. He then quickly put up a weak, temporary protection shield around his body. As he found out later he should have put up a much stronger protection shield.

It soon became obvious to Ram that these warriors had considerable power and Ram knew instantly, that these powers could not have come from anywhere in Adjemir.

As Ram attacked the first enemy through the gate he fired his most powerful fireball. He did not take aim at the animal, on which his enemy was riding. When the fire ball hit the attacker, it was not able to penetrate the enemy's protection shield. The enemy attacker quickly emerged untouched, but Ram saw instantly that the animal had been temporarily stunned by the force of the blast.

The attacking warrior retaliated with his own fire ball and to Rams surprise, his own protection shield was shattered. But the shield had absorbed most of the energy of the fire ball and Ram had not been hurt. Ram was not knocked off of his feet, but to his surprise he had been staggered back a few paces.

By this time the two combatants were very close and Ram, knowing his enemy would need some time to cast another magic spell or to send another fire ball. Ram knew he had to act quickly. Ram was certain that the enemy's protection shield was only able to stop magic spells and fire balls, and possibly some ordinary weapons. But Ram felt the enemy's shield could not stop a physical attack, especially if a physical attack was with a temporary magic energy penetrating tool.

Ram would put an energy point onto his fist and break the protection shield which the attacker had surrounded himself with.

Ram for an old man could still move very fast in a fight and he still maintained a young man's strength. Ram had but one chance too win. The large Kilpacx animal which the enemy was riding, was still staggering around somewhat stunned by Ram's earlier fire ball. So Ram was not very concerned about the large animal. Ram was moving really quickly and from the side, he lunged towards the enemy warrior. Ram threw his best punch which was led by the magic penetrating tool.

The penetrating tool had been made quickly by a magic spell and it looked like it was nothing in particular, but it was made by some very powerful magic. It was a bluish transparent, glove type weapon with an exceptional ability to bust through protection shields, easily.

Ram broke through the protection shield. Both the penetrating tool and the protection shield shattered at the same time. Ram's fist forcefully slammed into the nose of the enemy. Through all this Ram was moving at such an incredible speed, he seemed like a blur. Ram had caught the enemy warrior completely by surprise. Ram knew that the punch was a good one and that the protection shield, which was protecting the attacking warrior would remain temporarily broken. He was right and as the enemy was slipping off of the animal and before he had even hit the ground, Ram had another magic power spell ready.

Ram very quickly cast a simple empowering spell to give himself extra strength. He punched the attacking warrior in the face again, to ensure that the enemies protection shield spell remained open. The enemies nose started to bleed and Ram knew instinctively that he had definitely disabled his enemy's protection shield. Then Ram threw the enemy, face down onto the ground with considerable force. He then leaned over and quickly punched the enemy twice in the back of the head. The enemy, was knocked unconscious.

Without looking up Ram knew, in the back of his mind that the other enemy warriors were very close. So he quickly went for the kill. With his magic power being temporarily enhanced he commanded eight razor sharp rocks to jut upwards, with considerable force from the ground, and slam deep into the strange looking warrior's chest, killing the enemy instantly.

Ram was getting weak because of all the magic spells he had been forced to use in such a short time. And he also knew that the other enemy warriors were now very close. Without even looking up, he teleported immediately to the Forge. It was just in time, because the incoming warriors were aiming spells at him. Ram disappeared just as the first fire balls, from the attackers were striking the spot where Ram had just killed the enemy warrior.

After he had quickly teleported to the Forge, Ram quickly put in place, with most of his remaining magic powers, his strongest protection shield to protect the Forge and those who were still inside. This huge and very powerful protection shield, took almost all of his remaining powers.

Ram wanted to go back out and fight the invaders but he knew that he would lose to these attackers. Especially after his original protection shield had been shattered by the power of the enemy he had just killed. Plus he knew his magic powers were getting very weak and also because he was becoming very tired. Ram also knew because his powers were getting so weak, his magic powers could only be renewed by a long rest.

From inside the protection shield which he had placed around the Forge, Ram was then able to see all of the destruction throughout the town of Darmonarrow. He had never seen this kind of power before and he knew instinctively that this was not an attack by any of the peoples who lived in Adjemir.

These warriors resembled somewhat both Humans and Elves, but they were not the same. In his mind these warriors were not Krugs or Dwarves either. These strange warriors who were attacking Darmonarrow, had heavy eye brows and their eyes seemed to be sunken farther into their heads than Humans and Elves, but in all other aspects they looked similar.

Ram had a lot of questions in his mind but the answer to these questions would have to come later.

The incoming warriors on these large Kilpacx were smashing everything. These Kilpacx were attack animals and if somebody tried to resist them, Ram noticed these huge animals would kill them with their powerful jaws.

When the Kilpacx had the time they would gulp down any fallen enemy, with just a shake of their enormous head and a few gulping swallows, armor and all. While this was happening the warriors on the back of these animals, would just sit on their Kilpacx and laugh.

These Haddron warriors enjoyed killing that was for sure.

Ram had no power left to stop the destruction of Darmonarrow therefore he could just watch.

Men were being killed. Towers were being toppled with spells of magic fire balls, not as powerful as the one that blew up the main gate of Darmomarow during the start of the attack, but these magic spells were very strong just the same. Houses were being torched by the fire balls from the invading warriors. Some houses and other buildings were being smashed by the use of the tails of the large Kilpacx.

Ram thought that it was a good thing that the women and children were away from the town for the day. He hoped that they were all safe. Ram saw some of the attacking warriors heading towards his house, so he knew that the treasures in his safe would be taken.

There were still some of his own warriors in the forge, so after the protection shield, had been made strong enough, Ram ordered all of these men into a well known escape tunnel. Ram told them to go find the women and children, and bring them to the Temple of the Ancients.

These were very loyal men so he also told them that he would also be going to the Temple.

Then Ram turned to watch from the safety of the protection shield, which was strongly in place around the Forge, to see what was happening outside of the protected area. The fire balls which were directed towards the Forge had no affect on the strong protection shield which Ram had magically constructed.

Ram noticed when a Kilpacx was to swing it's enormous tail in the direction of a soldier, which, if it did not immediately kill the soldier it was powerful enough to knock the soldier senseless. At this time the Kilpacx would finish killing the soldier. Ram noticed that the warrior riding the Kilpacx would easily finish off any injured soldier in a quick fashion, if the kilpacx didn't finish the job.

Just then out of the corner of his eye, Ram saw a soldier running out from a burning building and was immediately chased by two Kilpacx. Not surprising to Ram these large animals could move quite fast. Not as fast as a Spaggidon, but very fast just the same. The first fast moving animal, easily caught the escaping soldier, with it's powerful jaws.

The soldier was almost immediately cut in half by the powerful jaws of the Kilpacx. The first animal quickly picked up half of the torn soldier's body which it swallowed in a gulping fashion. Then as this animal, was reaching for the other half of the soldiers body, the second Kilpacx finally caught up. At this time the first Kilpacx, who had caught the soldier started to hiss loudly at the other Kilpacx, over the dead soldiers remains.

While the Kilpacx was making this loud hissing sound, the animal had reared up as tall as it could on it's rear legs and balanced it's huge body, partly on, the rather large fighting tail. Then the Kilpacx put it's large round ears forward on it's large head, to make itself seem larger than it actually was. Rather quickly the animal hiss, grew into a very loud and aggressive roar. The first Kilpacx won the hissing and roaring dual.

Smiling, the warrior who was riding on the second Kilpacx who really didn't want these large beasts to fight, gave an order to his mount. The second animal, lumbered slowly away looking for another soldier for it's next meal. Ram was disgusted, not only by what he had seen but also by knowing that there was nothing he could do to help. He finally had to look away.

Ram then saw another movement from the corner of his eye which was up a street and away from the main gate. It was good to see that some of his men, had made it up the wall and were escaping over it. Ram was very saddened by all the killing but he was unable to help out, because even if he was able to fight, he would have to drop the protection shield around the Forge. Ram knew that everybody who was still inside the Forge, would be killed by the strange warriors or by the large number of enemies killer Kilpacx.

Ram could not remember ever seeing any animal, which could kill as fast and as efficiently as these Kilpacx. At present Ram was not exactly sure how to kill them, especially when they were present in the numbers which the Haddrons had brought to Darmonarrow. With the last of his remaining power and after all the soldiers from the Forge had left, Ram sadly teleported off to 'The Temple of the Ancients.' This was his favorite spot in all of Adjemir, for rest and for meditation.

Also at this time he would have to rest in order to rebuild his magic powers. Ram knew he would be safe at the Temple because even though it was very close to Garriton, it was off the main road and somewhat hidden. When his magic powers regained their full strength he would go after these killers.

The Temple itself was just off of a rarely used secondary road, just a little further than halfway between Damonarrow and Garriton. The Temple was somewhat closer to Garriton than it was to Darmonarrow. When he got all of his men safely to the Temple he could form a plan on just how they were going to fight the attackers but for now his first concern was to get as many of the people from Darmonarrow, to safety, as he could.

Shortly after Ram had left Darmonarrow Zalghar entered the smashed city, riding on his own Kilpacx. Zalghar wore no armor and other than the color of his cloths, he looked very much like the other Haddron warriors. The Haddrons themselves resembled the Adjemirian Humans very much. The only real difference was the eyes of the Haddrons and the narrowness of their faces. The eyes of the Haddrons were sunken more deeply into there heads than Humans and the faces of the Haddrons were somewhat thinner than the faces of the Human's. But you had to look very closely to see these differences in the features.

Zalghar rode in slowly looking around at the destruction in the city and he was pleased. As his men gathered around him, he noticed that there was a warrior missing. Zalghar asked about the missing warrior and he was told that Ram had killed the first attacker through the gate. To this Zalghar said nothing but his men saw that he was deeply troubled and he was apparently quite angry. Zalghar then turned and saw there was still one building remaining intact.

This building had not been touched by any of his warriors, so he asked with a raised eye brow. "Why is this building still standing? I thought I had said to you before the attack that everything in this city must be destroyed."

Zalghar had not been speaking to any individual in particular but was speaking to all of the warriors at the same time. When one of the nearest warriors told Zalghar that this structure was protected by some form of a magic circle of protection. Zalghar just made a disgusted look.

Zalghar, just to make sure that the destruction of Darmonarrow was complete, rode over to the Forge. Then from a short distance Zalghar sent one of his most powerful magic spells which was a large fire ball, directly at the Forge. The fire ball in a very large explosion just bounced off the protection shield, which was magically still in place.

The Nine Moons of Adjemir

Not wanting to get closer but still wanting to send another spell at the Forge, he took a deep breath and then Zalghar sent another spell at the Forge. This time the magic spell was similar to a powerful lightning bolt and as before, with a huge explosion it just bounced off.

Zalghar said to himself as he was viewing the Forge from where he was standing. "This leader of Darmonarrow must be more powerful than I had first thought. But I will find him and I will personally deal with him later."

In a determined tone Zalghar had made this statement to himself out loud and with certainty. "I will have to destroy him myself."

At this time Zalghar had a mean and vicious look in his eyes. Then he turned to his men as he said. "Take anything with you which you want from this town."

He wanted to see the treasures from the leader of Darmonarrow's house. So he had one of his warriors open the boxes which contained the treasures. Zalghar took a short look at the contents of the boxes and with a slight smile he said to his warriors. "Good work my freinds."

Then looking over his warriors who had gathered around him Zalghar said. "Make sure you bring lots of food with you."

Quietly Zalghar had given these orders to the Haddrons, as he abruptly turned and was moving slowly back towards the place where the gate of Darmonarrow was before.

Then he paused, turned, and he said to his men. "We will leave this place as soon as you all have gathered enough food for travel, for a number of days. As I said earlier, I will deal with the leader of Darmonarrow at a later date."

Zalghar had been referring to Ram. Then turning back to his warriors Zalghar said. "The next city we will destroy will be a place these Adjemirian people call Garriton. I will wait for you all outside."

After this last statement had Zalghar rode his giant Kilpacx slowly out of the destroyed and burning town of Darmonarrow.

The Spirit Eye Over Darmonarrow

Prior to the attack on Darmonarrow, Zalghar had been watching the town for a few hours and just before the attack, he had even sent his spirit eye to do some spying for him and his warriors. The information which he was to receive from the spirit eye was very useful. From what he could see, Darmomarrow could be conquered very easily. The only real power in Darmonarrow, from what the eye had seen, was that of Ram, the sorcerer. But from what Zalghar observed, Ram was old and the attack on Darmonarrow should remove this old sorcerer from being any problem.

His warriors had also known about the war axe, with the Rune on it, which had been spirited into Darmonarrow the day before. They also knew that somebody in Darmonarrow had it. This particular Rune, had a very powerful evil magic spell contained within it which would be activated by Zalghar when the time was right. As it turned out Zalghar had not seen any sign of the war axe, during the battle, nor had he felt it's presence when he entered the city. The axe, should have been in Darmonarrow, but this was not going a problem and he knew he would find it later.

In order to use his spirit eye, Zalghar would to go into a very deep trance, so that his spirit eye would have all the power from Zalghar which it needed, in order to go where Zalghar was to send it. Zalghar would gather his Haddron warriors around him in a fairly tight circle. This was done because he could not defend himself while he was in this trance like state. The soldiers would sit on their Kilpacx, facing outwards. They would stand guard, armed and ready until the spirit eye had completed it's mission. Before Zalghar would go into his trance, he would stare at the area or put an image of the object in his mind, where he wanted the spirit eye to investigate. Then he would simply nod and quickly go into his trance like state. His men would have to be very quiet, so that the trance would not be broken, before the spirit eye had finished doing it's work.

The spirit eye was nearly a completely invisible orb and to anybody who did see it, because of it's magical powers, they would forget all about seeing it within a few minutes. Zalghar wanted to ensure that there were no hidden dangers in Darmonarrow so before he had sent his warriors into Darmonarrow he had made absolutely sure, there would be no unforseen problems.

After the eye returned from Darmonarrow and when Zalghar was certain that there were no hidden dangers, it was with this knowledge when he had prepared his troops. Zalghar was no coward but why take chances when there was a battle to fight. So he had instructed the troops on what he wanted done. He had told them that he would remain behind the hill and if he was required, he would enter the battle after the first major attack. He told his warriors he would send a powerful fire ball to smash the front gate just before the warriors reached the wall. Zalghar instructed one of the Haddron warriors to wave a flag when the attacking warriors wanted Zalghar to smash the gate to Darmonarrow.

Only seeing the one danger, Zalghar had told the warriors that the only real threat inside the walled town of Darmonarrow was the old sorcerer Ram and he could be found in his office, or his house. He had told them what he looked like and that Ram was old. The warriors had also been told about the location of the money and gold which was in the safe in Ram's attic. Also some of the riches and the jewels of Darmonarrow were hidden in a secret steel closet in Ram's office.

The spirit eye, had seen everything.

Weapons Delivery to Garriton

Bobbiur and the group walked their Spaggidons slowly down the winding road towards Garriton. They were traveling alone not knowing that Darmonarrow had been attacked and destroyed just after they had left Darmomarrow the day before. Bobbiur and the men were feeling really good despite the fact that they must now walk. It was a sunny afternoon and they were not more than about two hours from Garriton.

"You know that the Humans in Garriton absolutely hate Elves." While walking along Bobbiur had said this to Hagjal, just so Hagjel would not be surprised by any the behavior of the people of Garriton.

"Yes." Said Hagjel. "I passed through there once and they didn't seem too friendly to my kind."

Salbuk sent a mind message to both Bobbiur and Hagjel. "I used to live in Garriton for a short while before I became friends with Hagjal. If the residents of Garriton start to bother Hagjel then I should be able to assist, as I still have many friends there."

After Salbuk had sent this mind message to both Bobbiur and Hagjel. He proceeded to float in the air because his feet were getting tired, which also meant that his magic powers were starting to return and were getting much stronger.

Eventually they could see the flagpole of Garriton fluttering in the wind and within a few minutes they could see the rest of the town. Although Darmonarrow had been constantly attacked by some of the Human cities from elsewhere in Adjemir, Garriton had never been amongst the raiders. There had always been a good relationship between Garriton's leaders and the leaders of Darmonarrow.

The group approached the large wooden gates of Garriton slowly and when the three looked up they could see a line of men positioned around the walls.

"Open the doors." Called Bobbiur. "We have your weapons' shipment from Darmonarrow."

Then he added. "Sorry the shipment is late."

"Who goes there?" One of the men on the wall yelled. He looked like a Captain or something like that.

"I am Bobbiur of Darmonarrow. These two are my companions, Hagjel and Salbuk."

Bobbiur spoke loudly in a perfectly calm and confident tone, while continuing to look upwards.

"And I believe these belong to you."

He motioned to Salbuk and Hagjel to put down the boxes and open them. Salbuk, with the use of magic powers, lowered some boxes, from the Spaggidons, then he knelt beside them. They opened the boxes revealing the weapons.

"Are they from Darmonarrow?" The Captain asked.

"Yes, some of the best." Replied Bobbiur.

Then the Captain on the wall in an abrupt fashion yelled. "Darmonarrow has been destroyed."

Then the Gate Captain made a growling sound as he gruffly yelled even louder. "Leave the boxes and get out of here."

Bobbiur, Hagjel and Salbuk stood there looking at each other with puzzled looks on their faces. Then in a puzzled tone Bobbiur yelled up to the Captain. "That can't be true, we just left Darmonarrow yesterday and everything was all right when we left."

"No." Came a strong deep and commanding voice from inside the city. "Let them in. They have our weapons and they probably don't have anything to do with the destruction of Darmonarrow."

Then the voice added. "We can trust them. Salbuk is with them and besides we have many men armed and ready, that is if they are lying."

"General Yauddi." Said the Captain. "I'm sorry. We'll let them in."

The Gate Captain pointed at two soldiers standing beside the gate as he said.

"You two. Open the gates."

When the gates finally were opened the three men entered the town of Garriton, at which time they saw a large group of armed soldiers gathering around them.

"What do you mean Darmonarrow was destroyed?" Bobbiur asked in a commanding yet bewildered voice. "It is impossible for any of the four enemy armies to over-run Darmonarrow!" Bobbiur was being very clear as he demanded an answer. He was looking straight into the General's eyes.

The General was quite tall, had a short beard and a very large mustache. He had on his fighting armor and carried a large sword, which Bobbiur recognized as being made in Darmonarrow.

Just then a loud voice came from the back of the soldiers and towns people who had gathered near the front gate. "It wasn't an army made of any of the four races of Adjemir. There were only about fifteen of them and they looked Human." Then with a deep growl to his voice, the speaker said. "But apparently they weren't." The loud voice continued on. "They weren't Elves, Dwarves, or Krugs either. But I can tell you they were pure evil."

This loud voice was coming from a short strong looking Dwarf. This Dwarf was wearing a brown Dwarf made leather armor suit and he was carrying a very shiny and very new, double bladed war axe with a golden colored Rune emblazoned on the handle.

This Dwarf had fiery red hair and had a long red beard, which was tucked into his belt. His eyes were dark and set close together. His face was stone cold. The fact that he was middle aged and had many wrinkles on his face, implied that he didn't laugh much and probably lived a life of hardship.

The Dwarf was getting closer and was pushing himself through the middle of the crowd. The way he pushed himself through the crowd showed just how strong this Dwarf really was.

"And just who the hell are you." Hagjal said to the Dwarf and getting himself between the Dwarf and Bobbiur. Hagjel was ignoring the crowd of people, who were gathering around him and hissing. "Pointed ears."

Hagjel was thinking to himself that if the crowd got too close, he could always let Jakka raise his head out of the tote bag and that would get everybody back in a hurry.

Salbuk sent a mind message to caution Hagjel against this idea. "Hagjel, if you let Jakka show himself these people might panic and somebody might get hurt. If you let Jakka out, he may get shot with an arrow, because everybody is very close. Besides I am with you and I will not let anybody bother, or hurt you."

Salbuk, with a sly almost boyish grin on his face and a twinkle in his eyes sent another message, to Hagjel. "I can set up a protection shield for Hagjel, if you want me too?"

Hagjel knew that Salbuk was teasing him about the protection shield and he promptly gave Salbuk a scowling sideways look, which probably meant he wanted to be left alone. Salbuk then turned to Bobbiur to ask about the Dwarf. When Bobbiur understood Salbuk's mind message, he said.

"Don't worry." Bobbiur said to both Hagjel and Salbuk. "I saw him in the Forge one day, he's one of us."

Then turning, Bobbiur asked the Dwarf. "Where you there when Darmonarrow was attacked?"

The Dwarf said. "I was near the Forge. I saw everything. Ram used some of his most powerful spells and killed one of them. But that's it."

The Dwarf went on. "Whatever these beings are they were very strong. When Ram was starting to run out of powers he went into the Forge and did something. And then he just disappeared into the shadows." Said the Dwarf.

Then the Dwarf added with a smile on his wrinkled face. "By the way my name is Obmar."

Bobbiur asked quickly. "How many of these attackers were in this battle and how many survivors were there?"

"As I said earlier there were about fifteen of them by my count." Said the Dwarf as he continued. "And they rode some sort of creature, just like a large lizard."

Obmar, scratching his head continued and even as he was telling the story of the attack he did so without showing any signs of emotion.

"I was on the wall near the Forge when the attack started. Some tremendous magic power came from down the road from somewhere just behind the warriors and this magic power just blasted the front gates open. I am not sure where the power had come from but it was very strong."

Then Obmar added. "I'm not sure how many survivors there were. Myself and some of the guards had shot arrows at the attackers but these attackers seemed invincible."

Then as an afterthought, Obmar added. "Our arrows did nothing."

Bobbiur was scratching his head with a puzzled look on his face as he started to speak in a stumbling, mumbling fashion. He seemed very confused. "Only about fifteen warriors. That's impossible."

Bobbiur had a look of disbelief which remained on his face. Then the Dwarf called Obmar continued. "I was the only survivor that I know of. I escaped through a secret tunnel leading from Darmonarrow to here. I'm not sure if Ram is still alive or not."

There was a frown on Obmar's face and his voice was getting louder as he was trying to make Bobbiur understand.

Speaking to Hagjel and Salbuk, Bobbiur said.

"Salbuk, Hagjel. Give them the weapons." Bobbiur said this with a worried look on his face as he pointing towards the General and his men.

"You there. What's your name? I seem to have forgotten your name." Bobbiur said turning towards the Dwarf.

"Obmar Axehammer." Stated the Dwarf. Then the Dwarf said to Bobbiur. "I know who you are. I've seen you around Darmonarrow."

Obmar said as he continued talking. "If you want to see Darmonarrow for yourself I can get you back to Darmonarrow the fastest and safest way possible."

"How?" Asked Bobbiur

"Through a secret tunnel built by Ram." Was Obmar's whispering reply as he added. "But you cannot take the Spaggidons. They will have to remain here at Garriton. We Dwarfs really like digging tunnels and Ram wanted it kept secret, so it is probably the safest way to get back to Darmonarrow."

"I don't think it would be safe to travel back to Darmonarrow by road. Not with those things running around." Obmar had meant the strange looking warriors with the large kilpacx, who had attacked Darmonarrow.

"Okay lets go Obmar. Show me where this tunnel is." Said Bobbiur as he turned back towards Hagjel and Salbuk. "Salbuk, Hagjal. Please distribute the weapons." Bobbiur ordered again because nobody was taking charge of the transfer.

Turning back Bobbiur said to Obmar. "Show me this tunnel."

"Follow me." Said Obmar and he pointed towards a building.

"It starts in the back of the tavern under a table and ends in my quarters back at Darmonarrow.

I figured that living in a place like Darmonarrow that I might need an escape route, so when Ram told me to build an escape tunnel. I didn't hesitate. It made a lot of sense." Obmar had said in matter of fact tone.

Then commenting further he said. "I made it tall enough for Humans to walk in but, as I told you earlier, you will have to leave your Spaggidons here."

"I understand. But I have to get back to Darmonarrow to see exactly what happened. I hope we will be safe in this tunnel." Said Bobbiur nodding to Hagjel and Salbuk, as he turned and followed Obmar towards the tavern.

While Bobbiur and Obmar were hurrying towards the tavern where the tunnel was, they saw General Yauddi coming towards them. The General approached Bobbiur and grabbed his arm pulling him aside and started speak softly to Bobbiur.

"We need to talk now that I am certain that you are Bobbiur of Darmonarrow." Said the General. "My name is General Yauddi." The General said as he was introducing himself. They stopped in the middle of the street as they looked at one another. Just as the General was starting to speak, Obmar tried to get himself into the conversation. But a sideward glance from the General caused him to back off. The General turned back to Bobbiur.

"I'm sorry the guards stopped you at the gate but they had to make sure that you were the men from Darmonarrow like you said you were." Spoke General Yauddi.

Bobbiur said as he shrugged his shoulders. "I understand why your men behaved like they did." Then Bobbiur said in a softer tone. "I probably would have done the same thing."

Quietly General Yauddi then said. "Earlier this morning I was approached by a strange looking older man who I hadn't seen around here before." Then General Yauddi said as he shook his head with emphasis. "He looked as old as dust." And he wore a funny hat and had a beard almost down to his knees."

Taking a deep breath the General continued. "And he called himself Zorp. Do you know him?"

To this question Bobbiur answered. "Well yes. Zorp's Dragon got the weapons back for us."

Bobbiur went on. "I didn't have any time to tell you the particulars earlier but the weapons' shipment for Garriton had been highjacked yesterday and we just got the weapons back. We had to fight a bunch of really mean Krugs from the Dark Storm Clan.

And in the end we had finally killed a large group of Krugs. Jakka, a GymmKat friend of Hagjel's, finally had to send a GymmKat stinger into their leader, called Smarge."

Bobbiur went on explaining the battle which he and the group had just had with the Dark Storm Clan. "Just after we had defeated the Krug camp, their leader Smarge had shown up on a Dragon and this Krug Smarge was winning against us."

Bobbiur noticed that General Yauddi was listening intently. "Smarge was just about ready to finish us off and this old man Zorp, must have sent a message or spell to Jakka."

"As it turned out, Jakka saved our lives."

Bobbiur went on. "Zorp had very strong magic and I think that he sent commands to Hagjel's GymmKat. I believe that Zorp gave Jakka a message and probably also released him from Hagjel's tote bag. That's when Jakka had sent his stinger into Smarge's back."

Nodding and speaking softly Bobbiur added. "This is just a feeling that I have."

Then shaking his head in a questioning way, Bobbiur spoke further. "I'm still not sure why Zorp didn't help us himself but he didn't seem to want to get involved, until we were losing."

"He seems very powerful. What about him?" Bobbiur had asked as his voice trailed off.

The General started to explain things to Bobbiur.

"Well." Said the General. "He came here earlier and told me that three men from Darmonarrow would be bringing a weapons' shipment today. I'm guessing that's you and your friends because no one else has come this way today."

Looking Bobbiur straight in the eyes the General continued. "Anyway he told me to tell you exactly what you're up against. You know bring you up to speed sort of. Zorp told me that you and your men would be meeting up with him later. Although you won't know where or when it will be. It will be soon."

Then with a furrow on his forehead as he was trying to remember all of the message the General continued. "He said that he's got a very dangerous job for you, and that he needs your help. He knows you will help because you've got nothing left in Darmonarrow."

Then the General said. "Zorp has been watching you three for a couple of days now and he said he was satisfied with you and your men about a task which he has for you."

Then the General Yauddi asked. "Would you like to go with him? I think it has something to do with trying to destroy the Haddron warriors who attacked Darmonarrow."

With a raising of his eye brow, Bobbiur stated flatly. "I'll need a little more information than this before I go anywhere."

Bobbiur then spoke very forcefully as he said. "Also, before me and my men go anywhere, I must return to Darmonarrrow to see if there were any survivors and to see if I can contact Ram. I must know if Ram is still alive."

Just then a young woman dressed in a soldier's armor, who Bobbiur had never seen before came running up to General Yauddi. "Father, Father. We need you at the front gate as some of the men need to be told just how you are going to prepare to defend the town."

The young woman was out of breath as it appeared she had been running a considerable ways.

Bobbiur could not help but notice that the General's daughter was quite tall and very beautiful. She had long curly red hair, big blue eyes, a small amount of freckles, with clear skin and high cheek bones. Bobbiur could not remember ever seeing a more beautiful girl in all of Adjemir.

The General said as he turned back to Bobbiur. "I'd like you to meet my daughter. This is Kirwynn."

"Kirwynn. I'd like you to meet Bobbiur from Darmonarrow."

Bobbiur gave a short bow which was not much more than a nod of his head and Kirwynn gave a short salute, while nodding in Bobbiur's direction.

General Yauddi then told Kirwynn to go back to the main gate to tell the guards and the soldiers, that he would be back with them shortly.

"I have some very important business which I have to finish with Bobbiur here and I will be right behind you." General Yauddi was holding his daughters arm as he asked her to tell the troops to be patient. Kirwynn nodded to both the General and Bobbiur, and without even making a comment, she turned quickly, and ran off on the direction of the front gate.

Bobbiur then looked down at his feet with a worried look on his face. He looked very tired. He started kicking the sand while thinking about the conversation the General and he were having before the General's daughter, Kirwynn had appeared.

Quietly Bobbiur continued by saying. "Well I think he did help in saving our lives and we owe him something. I guess."

Then Bobbiur said. "I will have to talk to him later that is if he shows up again and I must discuss all this with Salbuk and Hagjel, before I will agree to anything."

"All right? Then I'll give you some information that you'll need in making your decision." The General paused and took a deep breath and thought for a moment as he glanced towards the sky. "Zorp and Zalghar." General Yauddi paused again and continued looking at the sky while scratching his beard. Then the General began to speak haltingly.

"Zalghar is the leader of the warriors who attacked Darmonarrow. Both Zalghar and Zorp are from another land, which is very very far away from here." The General spoke even more quietly as he continued. "They both have tremendously powerful magic powers. Stronger powers than even the magic powers of Ram."

The General then said. "Zorp was sent here by the Elder's from a land called Haddron to capture or control Zalghar. He is trying to catch up to Zalghar right now. But he can't beat Zalghar and his gang of thugs by himself. And also the laws of their land will not allow Zorp to fight Zalghar in any land which is not part of their home land. Zorp can only advise and assist peoples from other lands."

"You see they come from a peaceful land but Zalghar as it turns out was a renegade and very destructive. He had started a gang which it seems was dedicated to destruction. The leaders of the land where Zorp and Zalghar came from attacked and surrounded him and his men. Zalghar and fourteen of his toughest and most loyal men, were the only ones who escaped."

Then the General said. "The rest of the members of the gang have been given very long prison sentences. Zalghar and his fourteen men came here to Adjemir and they will kill everything and everybody they see. Apparently they are really mean and very tough."

The General paused briefly before he added. "Just think of what happened at Darmonarrow."

Bobbiur continue do listen very carefully as the General continued speaking. "The men he brought with him, ride something like huge fighting lizards which I am told are very vicious. They call these beasts, Kilpacx. These animals are apparently quite large and very vicious when they attack."

Bobbiur stood quietly as the General continued. "I think that Zalghar wants to rule Adjemir. He will kill any people who show any resistance to him and his small army."

As he was finishing General Yauddi added. "They must be quite powerful I guess. Apparently Zalghar does not know that he is being followed by Zorp."

Then in a very serious tone the old General spoke further. "This information I am giving you must be kept a secret until the right time."

Bobbiur remained very silent and never said any thing as he glanced over towards Obmar. Bobbiur noticed Obmar was standing off in the shade of a building and Bobbiur could tell he getting more impatient by the minute. Bobbiur gave Obmar a nod and waved a hand, motioning that he should remain patient and sort of showing that he thought the General was almost finished.

General Yauddi then continued. "Zorp needs your help to stop them. As I said earlier Zorp is very powerful but he cannot do it alone. He has been following Zalghar and at the same time he has also been watching Darmonarrow and you. Zorp also told me that he was very impressed by the way Darmonarrow is governed, in a land like Adjemir where the four races continue to have wars."

In a softer tone the General stated. "He said that the only place where there is any real peace in all of Adjemir, is inside the walls of Darmonarrow."

In a solemn sounding tone General Yauddi said. "He is very impressed that all four races have been able to live together in Darmonarrow, for quite some time. Zorp told me that Darmonarrow, is governed very similar to Haddron, the land which both Zalghar and he came from."

Then with a slight grin on his face as the General continued. Pretty far-fetched this stuff, huh?"

General Yauddi said this and in a laughing tone the General also said. "Zorp even said that any information about his land that I have been instructed to tell you, would disappear from my mind."

As General Yauddi was finishing, he said. "And when I was done telling you Zorp said I would forget everything." I just said to him. What a crock of…"

The General all of a sudden went stiff in mid sentence and stopped talking. He just stood there staring at Bobbiur with blank eyes and then he began to sputter.

The Nine Moons of Adjemir

"Wha... Huh... Who..."

The general continued to sputter and he seemed somewhat embarrassed. "I was just getting ready to defend the city." The General was talking very rapidly. "Who are you? Where are you from?"

Then abruptly the General sputtered. "I have to go." Clearly he seemed very confused.

Then the General quickly turned and hurried away, scratching the back of his head. He stopped every few steps and turning back to look at Bobbiur, with an even more bewildered and puzzled look on his face.

Tunnel to Darmonarrow

Bobbiur gave out a weak laugh as he watching General Yauddi depart. Shaking his head while smiling to himself, he turned and ran to catch up to Obmar. Bobbiur thought that General Yauddi was very likeable. That is for a General.

Then Bobbiur said smiling to himself. "Sure has a nice daughter."

Salbuk and Hagjal had just finished handing out the weapons and moved quickly to catch up with Bobbiur and Obmar. The four men entered the empty tavern. Empty because all the people in the town were taking up arms.

They walked towards the back of the Tavern and headed in the direction a large table. There was a small trap door just below the table which was really hard to see. The trap door was well disguised so that it could not be detected easily. But Obmar knew exactly where to look.

Obmar opened the door and looked down into the darkness. Obmar then turned his head towards Bobbiur with a big smile and full of pride he pointed towards the hole, as he said. "Here we are." Then he added quickly. "You'll have to duck a little in order to fit into the tunnel, but not much. It's about five and a half feet tall." Looking at the group Obmar said with a serious look of his face. "So you will have to watch out or you will hit your head."

Bobbiur looked down into the hole as he turned he said. "Well lets go."

Pausing momentarily and looking around the room, Bobbiur saw Hagjel silently standing behind Obmar and Salbuk. Hagjel was standing beside the counter chugging an ale.

"Hey. Hagjel, we are here on a mission. What the hell are you doing?" Bobbiur demanded. Hagjel sputtered. "I was thirsty, and well,,, er,,,, there was umm,,, well,,,, er,,,, ah, well. Lets go."

Hagjal seemed very embarrassed as he put down the ale onto a table and quickly walked over to the hole. Obmar yelled back to Hagjel, telling him to close the trap door after he was in the tunnel. I'll go first because it's my tunnel and I know the way." Obmar said this when he jumped into the hole while carrying a lantern above his head. Then he started walking down the tunnel into the darkness. Over his shoulder Obmar hollered loudly again. "Hagjel make sure that you close the entrance behind you."

When Obmar heard the door to the entrance being closed he turned and started off at a very quick pace. Bobbiur was somewhat surprised that a short legged Dwarf could move as fast as Obmar could move.

Bobbiur had been the one who had jumped into the tunnel behind Obmar, followed by Salbuk. Then finally came Hagjal with a fresh mug of ale in his hand, which Bobbiur could not see, as the tunnel was not very well lit by the lantern carried by Obmar. Hagjel was behind everybody. Jakka could smell the ale and started to chatter softly in protest.

The tunnel was dark but straight and it had a smooth floor, so walking was easy.

The only one in the tunnel who could walk, without being slightly bent over was Obmar.

"Hey Obmar what exactly makes this tunnel so fast?" Salbuk asked with a scowl on his face. "Huh! What the hell was that!" Obmar had yelled. "Oh! One of you must be one of them mind 'mages'! Huh?"

"Yah. Salbuk is." Said Hagjal between gulps.

He had a mischievous grin on his face which nobody could see in the dark. Hagjel sure did like his ale and he had hidden another flask of ale under his tunic. He was at the back of the group so Bobbiur did not know that Hagjel had brought another flask of ale with him.

In an answer about the question from Hagjel about what made the tunnel so fast, Obmar stated. "Well the road is twisty and goes up and down but the tunnel is straight, fairly flat and is just slightly uphill. Its also much safer because nobody knows about this tunnel, except Ram and myself."

Obmar had told them this with a friendly grin on his heavily bearded face.

Now as they were traveling, everybody got quiet, thinking their own thoughts. Also because they were not sure if the warriors who had attacked Darmonarrow, had found Obmar's tunnel and set up an ambush. They walked for just under two hours before they saw light at the end of the tunnel. Obmar was the first to be aware of some light coming into the tunnel entrance as he whispered to the group. "Be careful I must have left the trap door open."

Then Obmar said in a whisper. "Either that or the door has been broken because of the battle." Obmar said this as he handed the lantern to Bobbiur at which time he walked ahead and peeked up through the hole. There was no trap door left at this end of the tunnel. Not anymore.

Obmar after only a few moments returned as he said softly to the group. "Welcome back to Darmonarrow, or what's left of it."

Obmar as he was climbing out of the tunnel, found to his surprise that his old quarters had been completely burnt away. Instead of coming out in the middle of his room he came out in the middle of a nearly completely destroyed city. The other three climbed up behind him and in a stunned silence they all began looking around. Only one building was still standing. It was the forge. They walked towards it and saw it remained untouched.

"What the... How the... It's impossible... What!?" Bobbiur was rambling on as he looked at the remains of the once strong and invincible Darmonarrow. Hagjal who it seems had one ale too many, walked over to the forge and reached out. Suddenly Hagjel flew back with a loud. "Bang!" He landed about eight feet back in a pile of ashes from a burnt out building. The three men who were still standing broke the tension as they all broke out laughing.

"So that's what Ram did to the Forge before he disappeared." Obmar was rubbing his beard with an understanding look on his face.

With a slight smile starting to show at the corners of Bobbiur's mouth he said. "This protective shield means that Ram is still alive and he must be hiding some place."

"Well, well, well. I see Zalghar that criminal has already been here."

Zorp with a shake of his head was walking through the ruins of Darmonarrow and was looking around as he headed directly towards the group. Bobbiur wondered why Zorp had a large green sack slung over this shoulder. Then Zorp with a smile of friendship towards the group, spoke softly.

"I see that they have done, what they do best." Still shaking his head Zorp added in a softer tone. "They like to destroy things."

Then Hagjel demanded in a terse tone. "What do you know about them? Who are they and what are they?"

Hagjel was a bit tipsy from the ale he had consumed while marching through the tunnel. Bobbiur looked at Hagjel with a stern look on his face.

"They are just like me." Said Zorp.

"And what exactly are you." This time it was Obmar's turn to ask the questions.

"Oh me. I'm Zorp. Well that's just my alias." Zorp started to laugh as he continued.

"Really my name is." Zorp paused for just a moment. "The King."

Then rubbing his chin and looking towards the sky, Zorp with a huge smile on his face added quickly. "The King of all of Adjemir."

"Not this again." Bellowed the voice from the ground below them.

Obmar looking at the ground was the only one who looked puzzled. The rest of the group was getting used to the Dragons voice coming from the ground.

"Actually I'm a secret Agent." Zorp continued with his chest pumped out as he was ignoring the Dragon's voice. Walking around slowly, Zalghar glanced towards the sky, smiling and rubbing his chin as he continued. "Adjemir's finest and I'm…"

"Zorp!" The Dragon had become quite angry and started to bellow even louder.

"Okay. I'll tell em. But you don't let me have any fun any more." Zorp said wagging his finger and speaking towards the ground.

Then turning to the group and in a serious tone Zorp said. "The fifteen who attacked your town and I, are like Humans but we live longer and are much more powerful with the use of magic."

Then looking upwards towards the sky again, Zorp continued on. "We come from a land far away. We are actually known as Haddrons and we have more power than your four races from Adjemir could imagine." Zorp continued. "Now the leader of this renegade group of warriors is called Zalghar and he...." Zorp fumbled for words. "Well he's.... He has been my enemy fore many years. He and his mean fourteen warriors are dedicated to death and destruction."

Zorp quickly went on. "The last world they attacked." Zorp paused for a second. "I tried to stop them." He was talking very slowly and glancing at the ground while shuffling his feet. "But I was too late." Zorp paused again and looked up, before adding. "This time I have you four lads." He had said this with a slight smile on his tired looking old face.

Bobbiur asked. "How can we stop them? Like you said your people are powerful and for us they are probably just like gods." Then Bobbiur in a pleading tone added while shaking his head in frustration. "And we are just ordinary people."

Then the old man said. "Your leader Ram killed one of these renegades already so Zalghar is down to a lean thirteen." Zorp said thinking out loud while scratching his head while glancing at the ground. "If Ram can defeat these warriors then so can you." Zorp said this with confidence, before he added. "I'm gonna…Well I'm going to give you stuff." Then with a knowing smile Zorp added. "Magical weapons to be precise."

At this Zorp proceeded to reach into the large green sack which he had brought with him.

Bobbiur noticed this old man Zorp must have considerable strength because he was able to carry this large bag of weapons, which must be quite heavy, with considerable ease.

"We already have strong weapons." Said Bobbiur. "The best which Darmonarrow could produce." Bobbiur had said this with considerable pride as he had placed his hand on the handle of his sword.

"Oh, but not like these." Said Zorp with a flourish.

He then pulled out three weapons with Runes attached to all of them. Bobbiur noticed that these Runes were just like the Rune on Obmar's new war axe.

Zorp produced a bow, a war axe, a sword and a strange looking, steel cube, which actually looked transparent. The group had never seen anything like this cube before. He gave the bow to Hagjal, which Hagjal examined and he found a scroll which was attached. Zorp also handed over a very beautiful and well crafted quiver of arrows, which had about forty enhanced arrows in it. Each arrow had a scroll attached to it also.

"What's this." Hagjal asked holding up the scrolls as Jakka had just raised his head up out of the tote bag blinking and was looking around.

"Those are the instructions. Read them, memorize them and then destroy the scrolls." Zorp said this while handing Bobbiur the sword.

Then he walked over to Obmar. As he went to hand him the axe Zorp realized that Obmar's axe was just like the one he was going to give him. Zorp had a very frustrated look on his face and he was getting noticeably nervous. A slight trickle of sweat rolled down his face. It was not especially warm at this time and Zorp had a very weary look on his face.

"I bought this war axe off a guy just outside Darmonarrow, a few days ago." Said Obmar with considerable pride. "It was expensive but I've never seen a better axe before and it seemed to fit my hand as if it was made for me. So I bought it." Obmar explained with a very comfortable and friendly smile.

With a look of uncertainty on his face Zorp spoke to Obmar. "Oh well, I guess its okay."

Then Zorp said, as he was becoming a little more quiet, with an intense look on his face. "Well we won't need this now will we?"

Zorp threw his own axe over his shoulder as he changed the subject. "Well Bobbiur don't you think this new sword is light?

Oh yes. Very much so." Replied Bobbiur.

"Well then you could hold another." At this, Zorp reached into his sack and pulled out another identical sword which he also handed to Bobbiur.

Bobbiur could not help but notice the Rune, emblazoned on the well crafted handles, on each sword, were identical to each other.

"Oh yes. Sorry Salbuk. I almost forgot you." Zorp walked over to Salbuk as he said. "Here is your upgrade." Zorp flicked Salbuk in the head with his middle finger at which time Salbuk winced. Zorp then touched Salbuk in the head with the transparent metal cube. "Ouch! What was that for?"

Salbuk had sent a mind message while rubbing his forehead as if he was in pain and he continued wincing.

"That was your upgrade. Now your magical powers are much stronger and you have enough magic to compete with the renegade Haddrons. But I must warn you Salbuk, you can compete with the

Haddron warriors but you will not be a match for Zalghar. Keep this in mind as Zalghar is very powerful and if you try to match him in a battle, you will certainly lose."

Zorp said this while watching for a reaction from Salbuk.

"Thanks Zorp. I can feel something." Salbuk was looking at his hands which were getting a slight reddish glow to them.

"Yes, thanks." Said the others at almost the same time.

Then Zorp said. "You have a little more time before you should depart. So read the books, test your weapons and get some practice. Good luck and I should always be close by in case you get into trouble, but there is no guarantee." Said Zorp wagging his finger.

"I must go now and talk to my Dragon. Its very important that I see Dymma now." Zorp said, in an old man fashion as he turned to walk away.

Hagjel grabbed Zorp's shoulder. "How do these new weapons work?" Then Hagjel said. "I think we need more information."

"Oh yes. Maybe so. Just read the scrolls." In a patient way Zorp spoke further. "In the scrolls there are pictures of Runes. Just like the ones on your weapons. Each Rune does something different."

Zorp continued on without stopping. "Except for the swords I gave you Bobbiur." Zorp said speaking to Bobbiur over his shoulder.

Turning back towards Hagjel and Salbuk Zorp went on. "Read the instructions to learn about these Runes and just speak the Runes name to activate them."

"Okay?" Zorp paused. "It's that easy." Zorp explained again to everybody. "Don't forget to destroy these instructions when you are finished with them."

"Yah. We got it."

Hagjal interrupted because he was now getting tired of this lecture.

Zorp turned and began to walk further away. He had a very worried look on his face.

Zorp Speaks with Dymma at Darmonarrow

Zorp walked through the burnt out ruins of Darmonarrow and after stepping over a heap of broken rocks he started calling for the Dragon. This was later when he was out of ear shot from the group and when he was certain he was out of sight. He sat on a fallen partly burnt timber.

"Dragon we need to talk." Zorp whispered to the ground.

The ground began to rumble and the Dragon Mist started to appear, swirling quietly around. With the loud crackling noise the mist started to thicken and slowly without any explosion a form started to appear. The beautiful massive golden Dragon stood right in front of Zorp.

"Hello Zorp I'm here." Then looking at Zorp and speaking in a much softer tone Dymma said. "Let me make this a little easier."

The Huge Dragon started shrinking and soon a normal Haddron body started to appear. When the transformation was complete, it had only taken a few seconds, there was an average sized very beautiful young Haddron woman standing in the place where the large Dragon had been, only moments before.

This beautiful woman was dressed in green robes, with silver sandals and a very shiny grey colored metal war helmet, with a small magic Rune on each side. She had long blond hair which was braided halfway down her back. She had thin eyebrows, long eyelashes, bright blue eyes with a very intense stare, and high cheekbones. All in all she was very pleasing to the eye. She walked with confidence and grace. She carried no visible weapons which indicated that she had some other way of fighting. This very beautiful young Haddron warrior woman walked over and sat beside Zorp on the same timber where Zorp was sitting. Dymma spoke first. "What would you like? Old Man!"

"Be nice Dymma you sometimes over grown lizard. This is serious."

Zorp muttered but was smiling just the same. These two had been friends for a very long time. There was a strong bond between them and they were quite comfortable with trading insults with each other. This was how their relationship existed. It had been like this for years.

"Okay, I'm listening." Dymma said. With a serious look on her face. Dymma was looking towards Zorp, as he began to speak and she could recognize that he was very worried about something.
"Dymma did you see the Rune on the Dwarf's axe?"

"Yes I saw it, through your eyes." Dymma spoke softly.

"I've told you to stay out of my mind… " Then Zorp said with a twinkle in his eyes and a slight smile starting at the corners of his mouth. "You know, I've had a craving for Dragon souffle for quite a while. So you had better behave."

Zorp said this with an even larger smile as he put his arm around her shoulder and pulled her towards him. Zorp continued to smile as he stared off into the distance.

"Anyway the Rune on Obmar's axe could be dangerous. Clearly the Rune is from Haddon and it must have been planted here by Zalghar." Still with the worried look on his face Zorp continued. "It may also have some spell on it. I also think the Rune axe had been sent into Darmonarrow, by Zalghar, before the battle of Darmonarrow. But before he could activate the Rune on the axe Obmar must have disappeared into this tunnel which Obmar talked about earlier."

Zorp paused but only for a moment. "The Rune would have been shielded from Zalghar's control once Obmar was in his tunnel." Zorp had added.

"Take the weapon away." Dymma suggested quietly as she also looked off into the distant sky.

"I don't think I can. I think if I so much as touch that axe, 'Zap, Bang, Poof,' I could be gone. It might be booby-trapped by Zalghar."

Zorp said as he turned. "I believe the same applies to you."

Then Zorp added. "I might be able to control some of the power within the axe if I am close enough when Zalghar sends a spell towards it, but I'm not sure about that either."

In a very serious way Zorp added. "It may be booby-trapped in such a way that if Obmar tries to throw it away, it may activate a spell and kill everyone who is close to it."

Dymma spoke in a helpful tone."Then it's best to just to ignore it until something serious happens. No point in scaring them." Stated Dymma in reference to Bobbiur and his men.

"Your right. We'll just continue our mission. If something goes wrong we will deal with it then."

Zorp changed the subject when he asked. "Do you think Zalghar knows that we may be here in Adjemir?"

Dymma just shrugged and said quite softly while looking down towards the ground at her feet.

"Probably not." She said softly.

Dymma leaned over towards Zorp and softly kissed his cheek before she stood up.

Temple of the Ancients

After the attack on Darmonarrow Ram had travelled immediatly to the Temple of The Ancients.

"Hello Ram. It's good to see you back here again." Said a small Human older monk who was sitting crosslegged on the ground in the open gardens in the center of the entrance to the Temple.

This Monk had a very shinny bald head. He wore black baggy clothes and sat cross-legged. The old monks name was Dhavden. The old monk looked very relaxed and comfortable sitting there and Bobbiur noticed the whispy, long, white beard of Dhavden, was curled up and resting in his lap.

Bobbiur could never remember this old monk ever cutting his beard and he also wondered how the old monk kept his beard so clean.

"Master. Did I interrupt your meditation?" Ram said with a respectable and a very low bow.

"Yes. But I don't mind my son." The old monk said as he solemnly nodded his head. "It's always good to see you." The old monk had a smile of fondness on his face.

"Master. Darmonarrow has been overrun and destroyed. I need to stay here for a while." Ram had requested.

"Sure. You can stay as long as you want my son." The monk offered. Nodding and slowly smiling.

Ram went on to say. "I will also have to dispatch some of the surviving Darmonarrow men to bring the women and children here."

Then Ram added. "It seems we are quite powerless to stop this invasion and I do not know were these warriors came from. And

I can't return the women and children to Darmonarrow until I know much more about this new enemy. I'm not sure exactly what I will have to do." Ram said before adding. "But I will need to use 'The Room of the Ancients'."

"What for my son?" Asked the monk.

"I need to see the outside world to know when it is safe to leave here. I also need to know who these enemy warriors are and where they came from."

"Fine. You may use, 'The Room of the Ancients', but there is time for that later." The old monk while saying this was nodding knowingly. "You look tired so now you must sit and meditate with me." The monk said. "You must relax and give your magic powers sufficient time to build back up."

Then in a very wise and cultured tone Dhavden stated in a serious way. "You will be no good to yourself or the people from Darmonarrow if you are too tired to fight, or if you are too tired to think clearly." Then the old monk adddded. "As your men from Darmonarrow start to gather here we will give them all a place to stay."

Smiling and nodding in a knowing fashion Dhavden continued. "Actually they are starting to gather outside right now."

The old monk Dhavden, continued to smile as he gestured. "Come sit. Come sit." The monk was tapping the ground lightly beside where he was sitting.

Ram knew that this old monk was very wise and was never in a hurry for anything. Dhavden was also, always very relaxed.

Ram was very worried about Darmonarrow but he was also concerned about just how well Bobbiur, Salbuk and Hagjel were making out. But the old monk was right about getting some rest and about the meditation. Ram knew that he had used a lot of energy in the fight at Darmonarrow and that he must let his powers return through rest and meditation. He would go to 'The Room of the Ancients,' later. He also knew he must get all of the remaining Darmonarrow soldiers together in order to protect the women and children and also in order to defend Darmonarrow from further attacks. That is if anything was left of Darmonarrow.

Then Ram remembered seeing the Temple of Ancients, the first time, when he was really very young. Ram had been brought here the first time by his step father, Alleek. At this time Ram was clearly

The Nine Moons of Adjemir

starting to feel more relaxed and yet he knew he had just arrived. It must be something about this place. It always felt like home to Ram and yet he didn't know why.

The Temple was located deep in some very dense forest, a very short distance from a large valley. The bottom floor of the Temple had a square base. There were six floors in all and all the floors were about seven feet tall. Each floor was set back about eight feet, from the floor below. This formed a balcony at each level. The balconies formed an outwards appearance of terraces, as the floors of the Temple had been built upwards.

On the very top of the Temple there was a watch tower constructed, but it was seldom used.

There was one main entrance to the Temple and it had a large wooden door which was almost never closed. Each level of the Temple had one large door to get out onto the balconies. The doors leading to the balconies allowed the monks to tend for the hanging gardens that surrounded the Temple on all sides, except for the front. The monks had very little area on the ground floor, in the Temple gardens, so they used the hanging gardens in order to save space.

The outside of the Temple was constructed of squares of plain brown rock. The inside walls were constructed with the same type of rock, but the floors on the inside of the Temple were made from a beautifal marble and this same marble was throughout the Temple.

Just inside the main entrance there was a large court yard, where the large flower garden was planted. Off to one side of the court yard was a large and deep well. This well was sufficient to produce more than enough water for all of the monks daily use and also for the hanging gardens around the Temple. Ram remembered sitting in the flower gardens for long periods of time when he was younger, thinking and meditating.

Besides the gardens which were on the balconies of the Temple itself there were trelleses between the Temple and some of the large trees which grew close to the Temple. The large trees also conrtained more hanging gardens, also for growing food.

All in all the Temple was actually a very beautiful place.

All of the gardens on the Temple balconies and the hanging gardens in the trees had to be watered daily by the monks. The monks had an ingeous way of syphoning water up the Temple walls and up into the tall trees which contained the gardens. Ram had always thought to himself, that the way which the water was syphoned up to the top of the Temple could only be done with strong magic, but he never said anything.

Before Ram went into his meditation period, he glaced around one more time, as he thought to himself. "This must be the most beautiful place in all of Adjemir."

Room of the Ancients

Ram was not sure as to how long he had sat with the old monk Dhavden in the Temple gardens and meditated, but he was feeling much better now. He also noticed that the old monk had already left the garden area because as he looked around he noticed that he was alone. It was starting to get late in the afternoon. The old monk, Dhavden, must be elsewhere in the Temple so Ram got up and headed slowly towards, the 'Room of the Ancients'.

Ram was very hungry but he would eat later. There were very many things he would have to do before he would have any time to worry about himself.

When he was walking towards the Room of the Ancients, he glanced down at his hands and he noticed that they were starting to get a soft pink glow. A sensitive tingling up and down his arms, was also becoming noticeable. Which from years of having sorcery powers gave him the knowledge that his magic powers were returning to almost their full strength. Ram could feel the power starting to surge up and down his arms. Ram flexed his muscles as he was heading in the direction of the 'Room of the Ancients'. This was good because he would need considerable power for the Room of the Ancients. It takes considerable magic power to see things by using the 'Pedistal of Light', and Ram was not sure how long it would take, to see all which he had to see while using the 'Spirit Eye'.

Ram's immediate concern was to see if Bobbiur, Salbuk and Hagjel were still alive. Ram also wanted to see what was left, if anything, of Darmonarrow. But most importantly, Ram wanted to study and learn as much as he could about the warriors who had attacked and destroyed Darmonarrow.

As Ram neared the 'Room of the Ancient's', which was on the ground floor of the Temple and was just off the side of the court yard. Ram started to open the door and he was instantly aware that somebody was already in the room. It was dark. It was always dark in the 'Room of the Ancients'. So as his eyes were getting used to the darkness Ram glanced around. It was the same as it had always been. There was no furniture, but only flat rocks for people to sit on. There were no windows.

As his eyes got better at seeing in the near dark room, he saw the old monk Dhavden, sitting off to his right. The Pedestal of Light, in the middle of the room was the same as it always had been, glowing slightly, giving off some light with a dull purple pulsating haze.

The Pedistal of Light was sitting upright on a similar stone, to that of the sitting stones. The Pedestal was about one meter long and was triangular at the top, but it was rounded and pointed at the bottom. Nobody could ever figure out what held it up, but it must have been some secret power which was contained within the Pedestal.

The Pedestal of Light had always been here and nobody, not even, monks, knew where it had originally come from. Maybe the Ancients knew where the Pedestel had come from and what held it up but nobody else in Adjemir had ever been able to figure out this secret.

Ram walked over to the old monk Dhavden and sat down beside him, nodded with a smile, as he said. "I am going to use the Room of the Ancients now." Then Ram said to the old monk. "I am not sure how long I will be but I will need a favour while I am in this room."

The old monk knew that Ram would be very occupied after he started to use the Room of the Ancients. So Dhavden, with a slight bow, said he would help if he could.

Ram started off by saying. "I will need to get a message to some of our men, that they should sneak back to Darmonarrow and get as many weapons and Spaggidons as they can find. That is if there are any Spaggidons still alive and only if it is safe to return to Darmonarrow." He then added. "I will also need some of the men to stay here to put up a defense, just in case those strange looking warriors attack the Temple."

The old monk said to Ram that this would be done, at which time Ram went on to say he also wanted two men to stand guard outside

The Nine Moons of Adjemir

the door of the Room of the Ancients, while he was in his trance using the Pedestal of Light. So that if the Temple was attacked somebody could interrupt the trance, and then he would be able to help defend the Temple. But unless the Temple was being attacked that he should not be bothered. When Ram nodded that he was finished and was going to start his trance, he told Dhavden, that he was not sure how long he would be in the Room of the Ancients, but the men should be patient.

Ram got up and bowed very low as the old monk was leaving the Room of The Ancients. Ram then went and sat on another sitting rock which was closer to the center of the room and which was very close to the 'Pedestal of Light'.

Before Ram sat down and got started to call upon the 'Pedestel of Light', to commence it's search, he remembered, when he had first learned how to use the 'Pedestal' and the 'Spirit Eye'. Ram remembered it had been Dhevden, the old monk who had first taught him how to use the 'Pedestal'. Ram had been very young then.

Ram could not remember whether or not he had ever properly thanked Dhevden, for time Dhavden had spent while teaching him how use the 'Pedestal'. Ram made a mental note, that when he had the time, he should properly thank the old monk Dhavden for all his time and effort in the training of himself in the use of the 'Pedestal'.

The Pedestal of Light

Ram sat before the Pedestal of Light. While staring deeply into the Pedestal, he slowly, in a relaxed manner, gathered his thoughts. In order to make his mind's eye, travel through the 'Pedestal of Light' and go out and search for whatever he wanted it to search for, he would have to place those images into his mind.

Because Ram had been well taught on how to properly use the 'Pedestal of Light', he did not need any help in sending out the 'Spirit Eye'. Ram began to breath really slow and at the same time he put an image of Bobbiur, Salbuk and Hagjel into his thoughts. He was sitting cross legged on his rock. His head nodded slowly forward and he fell into a very deep trance.

Slowly Ram's body started to glow in a slight pinkish colour and his cloths started to waver slightly around his body, as the energy was gaining strength. It was like there was a slight wind blowing, but there were no windows or doors in the 'Room of the Ancients'. Ram understood the movement of his cloths was because of some form of magic energy coming from the 'Pedestal'.

A pinkish glow which was coming from the 'Pedestal', started to gather around Ram's shoulders. Then when the light became more intense, it sprang gently upwards towards Ram's head. At this time his head started to be pulled gently in the direction of the base of the 'Pedestal of Light'. Suddenly without any warning and with only a slight crackling sound, a bright swirling energy, left the top of Ram's head and traveled slowly, through the air, downwards towards the base of the 'Pedestal of Light'. A visible energy coming from Ram's head continued to curl downwards towards the base of the 'Pedestal', and when the energy touched the Pedestal's base, there was a louder crackling noise. The energy from Ram went quickly inside the 'Pedestal'.

At this time the energy was now visibly swirling around inside the 'Pedestal of Light', and the Pedestal now was becoming much brighter. Then without any noises, the light from the Pedestal, began to pulsate. Only a slight line of a pinkish pulsating light, remained between the base of the Pedestal and Ram's bowed head.

Slowly the 'Pedestal of Light' seemed to grow more powerful. The purplish light grew steadily stronger and more intense.

Suddenly a loud crackling noise began and the energy from the Pedestal, instantly sprang upwards from the Pedestal and zoomed, at a tremendous rate of speed towards a slight hole in the ceiling of the room. All motion stopped as the beam of light from Ram's head traveled through the 'Pedestal', and was projected through the roof of the 'Temple of the Ancients'.

Only a slight purplish line from the 'Pedestal', pointed towards the hole in the roof where the energy had gone. Clearly the power was on its way to find Bobbiur, Hagjel and Salbuk as Ram had earlier envisioned in his mind.

After only a short while the 'Eye' discovered Bobbiur, Hagjel and Salbuk coming out of the tunnel at Darmoñarrow. The 'Eye' had stayed in this position, for a short while and it was during this time when the eye also observed all the destruction of Darmonarrow. The damage to Darmonarrow was considerable. This knowledge was being transfered back to Ram's completely motionless body in the 'Room of the Ancients'.

Then after a short while the 'Eye', viewed an old man who had had suddenly appeared from nowhere and had started a conversation with Bobbiur. The last observation which the 'Eye' was able to gather, was the distribution of the new weapons, for Bobbiur, Hagjel and Salbuk, by this strange old man.

When the 'Eye' had completed it's task, it quickly returned to the 'Pedestal of Light', and then to Ram. The energy from the 'Eye' returned the way it had come and traveled back through the 'Pedestal of Light'. The energy sprang from the base of the 'Pedestal' with considerable force in the direction of Ram's motionless and still bowed head.

Ram was pushed backwards as the energy from the 'Pedestal', slammed back into him. Then Ram himself seemed to lighten up for only a few seconds, just like the Pedestal had done earlier. With his

The Nine Moons of Adjemir

quivering eyes, still closed, his head was jerked upwards towards the ceiling of the 'Room of the Ancients', as the energy had hit him. Ram was still in his trance but now there was a smile on his tired face.

Then immediatly after as his head had been slammed into a raised position, it began to sag back to it's lowered position. Ram's head had now sunk back into the bowed position, just like it had been when he had first started to use 'Pedestal'. His chin was resting onto his chest and he remained sitting there.

In a few moments Ram came slowly out of the trance and then he began to frown, or maybe it was a smile. He knew that Bobbiur, Hagjel and Salbuk were still alive and everything with them seemed to be fine. His thoughts then turned to the old man with the pointed hat, as Ram wondered to himself, just exactly who this old man with the pointed hat was.

Ram sat there quietly and was thinking to himself as to what he should do next. He was going over the information about Darmonarrow, when his mind returned to Bobbiur and the old man with the pointed hat. The old man seemed friendly to Bobbiur, Salkbuk and Hagjel, but Ram felt he should know more about this strange old man. But at present Ram had more important things on his mind.

Ram's greatest concern was still very much the attack on Darmonarrow. Just who the strange warriors were? And how they had so much power? Ram decided that he must know much more about these enemies and therefore he must go back into his trance and have the 'Spirit Eye', gather as much information about these warriors, as was possible.

Sitting in the same spot Ram summoned up his powers and the same sequence of events took place. The energy built up and soon the 'Spirit Eye' was traveling onto it's next mission. The mind picture which Ram had in his mind when the 'Spirit Eye' was being summoned, was the image of the warriors, and the Kilpacx which had attacked Darmonarrow.

The 'Spirit Eye', traveled out on a search for the strange warriors, but this time it was no easy task for the 'Eye' to find the image which it had been recieving from Ram's mind. This time the 'Eye', needed considerably more time to complete it's task, but finally after a lengthy search, the 'Eye', found the enemy warriors.

The Haddrons it seemed were travelling towards the land of the Elves. Ram was to find out later that the strange warriors were actually in a more direct line to come upon Garriton. The information which Ram had received from the 'Eye', was very valuable because now he knew that these warriors were very powerful and the leader of these warriors looked mean and vicious. Ram had never seen an enemy like this before and clearly these enemies were not from Adjemir. Ram could not tell from the information from the 'Eye', just where these people had come from, but in the future, the leader of these invaders was going to be very easy to recognize.

When viewing the other warriors with this wandering band, the 'Eye', noted that these warriors did not talk much and they rarely smiled. It would appear from what the 'Eye', was able to see, these warriors meant buissness and they also seemed very discplined. These warriors, although not great in numbers, were a formidable force. Besides the strong magic, these warriors were well armed. The 'Eye', saw that the animals which the warriors were riding, were fighting animals. The giant lizard type animal looked like they would be quite hard to defeat.

All of the warriors, their leader and the giant lizard type animals had made Ram think that this fighting force was one of the strongest which has ever been seen in the land of Adjemir. Without any doubt.

When the information from the 'Eye', was brought back to Ram, he had to spend considerable time to absorb and understand this new enemy. The reason why the leader of these renegade warriors did not help in the attack on Darmonarrow, was still a puzzle to Ram but he would find this out later.

Some of the questions which Ram needed to have answered, were now answered, but he would have to get the other answers which he had in his mind at another time.

Once the information which Ram had recieved was complete and he had finished his search with the 'Eye', Ram came out of his trance. As before, as the energy returned to Ram's bowed head through the 'Pedestal of Light', Ram had been slammed backwards from the sudden return of his magic powers.

Slowly Ram stood up and noticed that he was quite stiff from all the sitting. Ram also knew he was very hungry and when he went to the door to talk to his guards, he found that he had been in the 'Room of the Ancients', for quite some time. It was late in the day. It was now completely dark outside.

He told the guards who were defending the door of the Room of Ancients that he would need a messenger and a very fast

Spaggidon. The messenger and the fast Spaggidon were to be ready on short notice, if and when Ram needed to send a message to Bobbiur. He went on to tell the guards that he wanted to speak to everyone from Darmonarrow but he would have to eat first.

    Ram wanted to speak to the people of Darmonarrow, in order to find out just who had survived the attack and just how well they were doing. He also wanted to let them know that he was planning to rebuild Darmonarrow and that he would build the new defences even stronger than they had been before.

The Portal to Garriton

Back at Darmonarrow and after Zorp had finished talking to Dymma, Zorp walked back to the speak with Bobbiur and his men. Dymma the Dragon went underground again.

Zorp hadn't noticed earlier but while talking to Dymma, the sun had escaped behind a hill. It was still light out but I wouldn't be for long. He walked up to the group and looked at them all individually. He smiled as he said. "Are you comfortable with your new weapons?" Zorp asked this while he was rubbing his beard.

"Yah sure." Said Hagjal with a grin.

Zorp with a knowing smile said. "Great. Well I got a feeling Garriton will be attacked next."

Zorp stopped and looked at a gold-plated watch which he had taken from his breast pocket. "About well... Err. Lets just say, very soon. So lets go." He had said this with a merry little grin on his tired looking face.

Zorp turned around and held his hand up in front of him. His hand was open and the thumb of his hand was pointed towards the ground. The air around his hand quickly turned red, started misting and swirling around. The swirling mist continued to grow until it was all the way from his thumb to the ground and the swirling mist was now as tall as Hagjal, who was the tallest one in the group. Zorp's hand was now raised high above his head.

Young Bobbiur who was amazed because he did not know what Zorp was doing and because he had never seen anything like this before. He got nervous. With wide eyes Bobbiur took a step back, as did Hagjel and Salbuk. Obmar scurried in behind Hagjel and peeked out to watch.

With a smile and a relaxing tone, Zorp said.

"It's a small portal to Garriton. A door. And you'll be getting there instantly if you go through here now."

Then speaking to Bobbiur Zorp said. "Lets go Bobbiur. Would you do the honor and go first?"

Zorp was bowing and pointing towards the portal which had now turned transparent with a blueish tinge in the middle. The portal was making a faint humming sound.

"I'll go last. And don't worry it won't hurt." Zorp said this while waving his hand through the entrance of the portal. In order to show the group that it was safe for them, Zorp then put his whole arm inside, and then he put his head inside.

Without questioning Zorp any further, Bobbiur, who was starting to believe in Zorp and also to show he was not afraid because he was the leader of the group, bent into the portal and quickly disappeared. The other three followed behind Bobbiur very quickly.

But before Obmar who was the last to enter and who was still somewhat unsure about the entire episode turned to Zorp as he said. "You coming with us Zorp?"

"You bet. I'll be right behind you." Said Zorp with a mischievous twinkle in his eye.

Obmar slowly and with a fair amount of uneasiness stepped through the portal and suddenly appeared with the others. The place where he found that he was, was with the others just behind the tavern in Garriton. The portal closed almost immediately right behind him. Obmar looked at Hagjal, Bobbiur and Salbuk then he just shrugged. While standing there, he started to look down, as he was checking to see that he still had all his arms and legs. Then he said. "I guess Zorp never intended to come with us. I wonder why?"

"I think your right Obmar. But we can find that out later." Said Bobbiur as he turned and headed in the direction of the main gate at the front of Garriton. Salbuk and Hagjel were nodding their heads in agreement with Bobbiur while they were both busy checking their weapons.

Salbuk sent a mind message to both Obmar and Hagjel. "Well, Zorp said Zalghar is gonna attack here soon so lets head for the front gate."

As they started to walk towards the front gate they turned the corner of the tavern when they saw, the whole town running around in every direction, getting ready with torches and weapons. It was now fully dark so Bobbiur and the others went over to a soldier who was handing out torches and grabbed his last three. Over all the yelling they could here a woman's voice giving orders.

"Light those lights. Get the rest of the women and children into the town hall. Double check the gates are locked. Man the walls." Then in a louder voice while clapping her hands. "Lets go people."

It was Kirwynn, General Yauddi's daughter, who was giving all the orders and she was doing so with a confident authority.

"What's going on here?" Bobbiur yelled to Kirwynn with a friendly smile on his face.

"Oh! Hey Bobbiur." She stopped yelling and walked over to see him.

"Our scouts inform us that the people who attacked Darmonarrow earlier today are coming here." She spoke softly while she was toying with a large dagger in her belt.

"Where is your father Kirwynn? Shouldn't he be taking care of the defense preparations?"
Bobbiur had said.

Kirwynn answered by saying. "He left town about a half hour ago with about fifty of his best cross-bow men." Adding to this she said in a louder and somewhat unfriendly voice. "He's going to ambush the Haddrons before they get here." She then went on to say. "They'll also be our early warning system."

Kirwynn then with her hands on her hips, because she was a bit mad at the statement from Bobbiur when he asked why General Yauddi was not in charge of the defenses. She went on to say.
"And I also believe I am perfectly capable of handling this situation." She said this in a huff. "After all, I am the General's daughter and I have completed officer training."

She had said this with a raised voice and a roll of hers eyes. She had also said this with an angry look on her face, as she waved her arm at nothing in particular. It seemed like Bobbiur had insulted Kirwynn without really meaning to. "Now get out of my way." She pushed past him as she said. "I have work to do."

After softly pushing Bobbiur out of her way she quickly walked towards the main gate. Bobbiur had a slight smile on his face as he stared after her. He was starting to like Kirwynn but he didn't want the others to know. So he removed the grin from his face as turned to talk to his men.

Glancing at the group Bobbiur replied. "Light those torches!"

Then Bobbiur nodded towards Hagjel, Salbuk and Obmar. "Come on lets go and find a spot on the wall by the gate because it's filling up fast." Bobbiur said as he motioned towards the gate. The four men moved towards the gate climbed up the ladder and then looked out onto the road leading from the front gate. It was almost pitch black by now. Suddenly with a low whooshing sound the road was instantly lit up. Bobbiur looked to see where the light was coming from.

What Bobbiur saw were several strange contraptions along the wall and he noticed that they were large curved mirrors about the same size as a man. A small fire in front of the mirrors which was contained in some sort of metal pot was what made the lights work. The entire apparatus was built on a swivel. These large lights could turn very easily and the soldier in charge of the light could point the light in any direction where it was needed.

Bobbiur saw Kirwynn lighting the closest light to where he was standing.

"What are those?" Bobbiur yelled pointing at the strange contraption. Because it was quite noisy near the main gate Bobbiur had to yell over to her.

"My father invented them." Kirwynn yelled back. It seemed that she was in a better mood now and this made Bobbiur feel a little better.

"They just magnify the light and we are able to point the light in the direction where it was needed the most." Kirwynn hollered. "He made them after a few night raids by Krugs. The Krugs were very successful because we could barely see them at night." The Kirwynn added. "But once we built these lights the Krugs got beaten back very easily and we have had very few problems since that time."

Then Kirwynn said in an urgent tone."Now we had better get ready. They'll be here soon." Kirwynn had stated this as she nodded towards the road in the direction where it was expected the enemy warriors would come from.

Bobbiur turned from the wall. He drew his swords, looked towards his men and he saw they were ready. He thought to himself that Ram had put together some good men to help him. He then turned to observe the road as he waited for the enemy to appear. He also thought he could see a few men standing in the woods not to far from the front gate, holding crossbows, but he couldn't be sure.

Bobbiur did not know that the enemy was so close, until he saw a barrage of crossbow bolts flying from the cross bow archers

The Nine Moons of Adjemir

who were stationed in the woods. The cross bow bolts were aimed at a target somewhere down the road. He could see the bolts from the cross bows because the bolts were made of metal and they had caught the light from the 'magnifying lights' which had been positioned on the walls of Garriton.

Following the direction of the flying bolts Bobbiur could just barely see a dozen or so men on the road, coming into view. They were all wearing black leather armor except one, who was wearing red leather armor. The one with the red armor, Bobbiur felt must be Zalghar himself.

The bolts aimed at the men hit something, just before they were to hit the Haddrons and just bounced off. A second barrage of arrows was shot towards the oncoming enemy and the same thing happened. They bounced off just like the first salvo and never hit the enemy. Bobbiur was sure that the warriors were being protected by some sort of powerful protection shield.

"Fall back!" Came a voice from the woods. It was definitely the voice of General Yauddi and it appears that he knew something was wrong. In the light from the walls of Garriton Bobbiur saw the rider who was dressed in the red leather armor suddenly hold out his right hand, with his three middle fingers pointed towards a large bolder which was lying beside the road, to the oncoming riders left. Then Zalghar turned and pointed with his right hand at General Yauddi and his cross bow archers, in the same fashion as he had pointed at the large rock. About this time the archers and General Yauddi had started quickly retreating back towards the walls of Garriton.

In a flash, a greenish colored energy flew from the end of Zalghar's hand and curved downwards in the direction of the ground, at which time the greenish energy from Zalghar's hand stopped momentarily. Then within only moments, the energy proceeded as it entered the ground in the area around the base this large rock. The ground around the base of this large rock suddenly started to rumble and shake violently. This huge piece of rock, about the size of one of the huge Kilpacx which the enemy Haddrons were riding, began to slowly lifted from the ground.

In the light from the large lanterns on the wall Bobbiur could tell that it was taking a considerable amount of energy and a great amount of force, because even at this distance, Bobbiur could see the concentration on Zalghar's evil face. Bobbiur saw this large rock started to glow in the same greenish color as the energy coming from

Zalghar's hand. The rock which had been lifted from the ground stayed at the same location, but now it started to glow in a yellowish color. The yellowish color then quickly started to turn to a bright reddish tinge. This huge boulder now started to travel slowly towards General Yauddi and the cross bow men who were now in full retreat back to the walls of Garriton. The men from Garriton now started to run in a hastier retreat to the safety of the walls.

When the large rock was moving more quickly got about fifty feet from the soldiers of Garriton, it suddenly exploded into thousands of small red thumb sized molten pieces. Then with lightening speed these small pieces of hot molten rock flew directly at the cross bow men and General Yauddi who was also now in complete retreat. Bobbiur heard blood-curdling screams coming from the woods, as nearly all the men with General Yauddi were mowed down, by these molten rocks.

Then instantly and as fast as it took Zalghar to shatter the rock and send the barrage of killing stones at the men from Garriton he changed his stance. Zalghar now calmly pointed the same three fingers towards the walls of Garriton and all the molten rocks which had not hit the Garriton archers in the field, were now being redirected towards the walls of Garriton.

Instead of hearing something like. "Get down." Coming from Kirwynn. Bobbiur heard. "Father no!" Then Bobbiur heard Kirwynn screaming. "Why?"Kirwynn screamed again as she jumped over the wall to the ground. "Father." She started running swiftly through all the smoke towards the woods. Running directly to where she had last seen her father and the men with the cross bows retreating. All the soldiers on the wall had ducked down for safety, as did Bobbiur. After the molten rocks had cleared the walls of Garriton and when it was safe to do so, Bobbiur looked into the battle field to see if Kirwynn was safe. Somehow, it appeared she had been missed by the incoming molten missiles.

Not all of the lights on the wall had been hit by the molten rocks and there was still sufficient light on the battle field so Bobbiur could see Kirwynn. She was still running in the direction of General Yauddi and the other archers. Apparently she had not been hit by any of the molten rocks which Zalghar had fired at the walls of Garriton. "Kirwynn. No don't!" Bobbiur yelled loudly as he too had jumped over the wall as he began chasing after her.

Kirwynn ran directly towards one of the lead attackers who had dismounted his Kilpacx and was walking through the smoke in order to finish off the wounded soldiers and General Yauddi. The enemy warrior turned and watched her pitiful attack towards him with a smile of amusement. But the Haddron did not see that Bobbiur was right behind her.

Kirwynn, as she neared the Haddron, jumped over a log and landed right in front of the black armored warrior and then swiftly she started swinging her dagger. With considerable speed she slashed at the Haddron, at least six times, but he was still protected by his protection shield so her knife would just bounce off without leaving a mark. The Haddron warrior only laughed.

The enemy warrior had just about had enough so with a mean grin on his face he reached through his protection shield and knocked her down. with a good swat. Just like a cat swats a mouse. Bobbiur only being seconds behind Kirwynn came upon the attacker, who apparently was still unaware that Bobbiur was upon him.

When Bobbiur saw Kirwynn on the ground, through the smoke, he thought she was dead and he instantly flew into a rage. As he was running he quickly spoke some words to the Runes which he remembered were on each of the swords and both swords instantly became engulfed in flames. Bobbiur quickly lunged in front of the attacking Haddron, so that he could be between the Haddron and Kirwynn. With a tight vicious grin Bobbiur then launched himself at the attacker. The attacker did not know the attacking Bobbiur had Rune enhanced swords. The Haddron was just starting to sneer and laugh at Bobbiur because he thought his protection shield would protect him.

It was too late. The swords were on their way with such force that the Haddron warrior was caught completely by surprise. Due to the magic Runes on Bobbiur's swords the swords were able to cut right through the attacker's protection shield. The first strike a parry from Bobbiur's right hand landed under the Haddron's arm and cut deeply into the side of his chest. Bobbiur let the first sword sit in the Haddrons side while he swung with the other hand. The next strike hit the Haddron on his other side and sliced deep into the surprised warriors arm.

Ignoring the Haddron's pleading cries which were in a language that Bobbiur did not understand, Bobbiur withdrew both swords. Then with his left sword he again stabbed deep into the enemy's chest. Almost in the same motion, with the other sword he sliced into the Haddron's thigh. Withdrawing quickly the sword which was in the enemies chest, Bobbiur viciously slashed diagonally down the Haddron's neck right into his rib cage. The warm blood splattered across Bobbiur's face. The surprised Haddron fell to the ground where he died very quickly from these severe wounds.

Another attacker who was near the front of the attacking Haddrons saw what was happening and charged Bobbiur with his Kilpacx. Bobbiur didn't have time to react before the Haddron warrior was within striking range and the Haddron warrior raised his arm and a bolt of energy started gathering around his hand. Bobbiur ducked, getting ready for the assault yet he was certain he was about to be fried. Suddenly looking up Bobbiur heard a piercing scream.

A Rune arrow from Hagjel's bow had sliced right through the Haddron's palm and stuck deeply into the Haddron's shoulder, pinning all movement. The attacker at this time was unable to send a power bolt at Bobbiur. It had to be one of the arrows with the Rune on it, which Zorp had given Hagjel at Darmonarrow. The protection shield around the Haddron had no affect on the arrow from Hagjel's bow. The Haddron screamed in agony and fell off his Kilpacx. Before Bobbiur could get to the Haddron and finish him off, the Haddron had quickly gotten up and in a panic ran swiftly back towards Zalghar's location.

Bobbiur didn't have to turn around but he knew it was Hagjal's arrow which had just saved him. Bobbiur quickly turned to his left to see the Kilpacx charging him. Then to Bobbiur's surprise another arrow from Hagjel's bow flew and hit this giant Kilpacx right between the eyes. But this arrow just bounced off of the Kilpacx strong skin and fell harmlessly, broken to the ground. Another arrow flew into the Kilpacx's underbelly. Again this arrow broke and fell harmlessly to the ground. The Kilpacx was getting closer and Bobbiur simply froze because he did not know what to do. There was no place to run for safety. To Bobbiur it looked like both he and Kirwynn were now going to be this huge beast's next meal.

Just then Bobbiur heard Hagjal yelling from the wall. "Stay still damn you." For Bobbiur, everything was happening so fast he had been completely unaware of anything, except his battle with the Haddron and this huge animal and Hagjel's raised voice coming from the walls of Garriton.

Just as the vicious Kilpacx was getting ready to bite down on Bobbiur, the large beast paused for just a second and this was all that Hagjel required. As Bobbiur was raising his swords to defend himself, he quickly glanced over his shoulder and saw Hagjel, standing high up on the ledge of the wall. Bobbiur saw Haggjel taking a very careful and steady aim. Bobbiur again wondered to himself that it seemed Hagjel's arrows were useless against these large Kilpacx animals and that Hagjel was just wasting arrows. Then as Bobbiur was preparing to fight the Kilpacx with his swords, Bobbiur glanced quickly, one more time towards Hagjel.

Bobbiur watched Hagjel shoot his next arrow. With tremendous speed and force, this arrow went flying slightly above and past him with a swishing sound. At this Bobbiur was completely amazed because this arrow slammed with considerable force, right into the Kilpacx's left eye. "Plunk." Instantly the attack on Bobbiur by this Kilpacx stopped. This great animal flung the huge head backwards, came to grinding and immediate halt. The animal started a loud and screeching, ear piercing roar of pain, into the night sky. Everybody on the battle field, Human's, Elves and Haddrons stopped all movement, all eyes remained on this incredible scene. The wounded Kilpacx, in tremendous pain, then started to frantically thrash about screeching so loudly, that everybody, even Zalghar himself remained motionless and powerless from what they were doing, just to watch. All eyes were transfixed.

The wounded animal, after trying to grasp the arrow with it's short front legs, which it was unable to do, began to run around in a tight circle, running to the left, in the direction of the injured eye. In tremendous agony this large screeching animal fell loudly to the ground and began scratching frantically at it's injured eye with it's huge back legs. Blood from the eye injury, and from the scratching of the beast's face by it's huge back claws, was flying all around.

At this time Bobbiur was aware of a cheer coming from the defenders of Garriton, but even hearing this, Bobbiur was unable to remove his eyes from the wounded beast.

An even greater surprise was about to unfold. Two other Kilpacx which were standing close to the injured animal, instantly, aggressively and viciously tossed off their riders. Too Bobbiur's complete surprise, these two riderless beasts swiftly charged directly towards the injured beast. The first Kilpacx, to get to the injured animal, smashed into the injured Kilpacx, which at this time was trying to get up off the ground, back onto the ground. The second larger Kilpacx, came at the injured animal from a different direction and viciously bit down with incredibly force on the injured animals neck. Then this attacking

Kilpacx, with a firm grip on the injured Kilpacx neck, started shaking the injured animal just like it was a rag doll.

The injured animal was being killed by it's own kind. Bobbiur was thinking to himself that these giant Kilpacx must do this whenever one of them gets hurt. It must be a characteristic of these large animals. They just become incredibly vicious and become cannibalistic when they smell their own blood. Bobbiur would have to keep this in mind in case he needed to use this as a tactic in the future.

Bobbiur had never seen anything quite like this but he had no time now to stay and finish watching. He knew he had to get over to Kirwynn, right away, because he saw out of the corner of his eye that she was not dead. She had only been knocked out. Bobbiur knew he had to get Kirwynn back inside the walls of Garriton and away from the battle field, before these giant Kilpacx finished with the vicious blood thirsty killing of the injured animal.

Zalghar Retreats

"Stop." Yelled Zalghar to the remaining Haddrons. "Fall back. We will regroup and continue on. This city is not worth the losses we are suffering." At this, the remaining attackers started to break away. The two Haddrons warriors who had been riding the Kilpacx, which were attacking the injured beast, on the battle field had to stay and watch these two aggressive Kilpacx until their mounts had finally finished killing and devouring the injured animal.

In the intenseness of the cannibalistic behavior by these two giant beasts, they now started growling and snarling at each other. It appeared like they may fight each other over the remains. But this was only some sort of Kilpacx behavior, as when they had finished snarling at each other, they then turned all of their attention back towards the feast laying dead on the ground.

Blood was dripping down their enormous faces as they seemed to immensely enjoy the meal laying lifeless on the ground. On occasion, while they were gorging themselves on the dead Kilpacx, these giant animals would place their heads straight into the night sky and howl aggressively, at the seven visible moons in the sky over Garriton.

The two Haddron warriors who had been riding these two vicious Kilpacx, knew that there was no way they could remount until these rampaging animals were finished with this cannibal type behavior. While all this was happening, Zalghar had sent a magic spell at all the remaining Kilpacx turning them somewhat instantly passive.

Before the Haddrons had started the attack on Garriton because he was aware of the archer's ambush, Zalghar had sent a magic spell into all the Kilpacx. This spell put these beasts into an even meaner, vicious and aggressive fighting mood. The plan by Zalghar was to send the Kilpacx into the woods against the hidden archers and completely destroy them all. It looks like his plan has worked against him and his warriors this time.

Zalghar was also now aware he would have to do something to protect the eyes of the Kilpacx, in future battles or he would lose more of these beasts, to the warrior on the wall with the bow. Zalghar had to admit the warrior on the wall could sure shoot a bow. Zalghar knew he would have to keep this in mind and therefore he would be ready for this archer next time.

Back on the battlefield Bobbiur bolted over to Kirwynn and although they were a good distance at this time, away from the Haddron warriors and the hungry Kilpacx, he was still quite anxious.

"Get up, he didn't hit you that hard." Bobbiur nudged her with his boot trying not to laugh at her. Kirwynn did not know it but Bobbiur was very relieved to see that Kirwynn was not injured too bad. The greatest damage to Kirwynn, Bobbiur thought to himself, would be her pride. He kept looking over his shoulder in the direction of the two Haddrons who were waiting and watching, until their cannibalistic mounts had finished ripping apart and devouring the dead Kilpacx.

Trying to stop from laughing Bobbiur looked towards the ground. "You wouldn't believe how hard he hit me!" She replied, groggily rubbing her jaw with a grimace of pain.

"You're right. I wouldn't." He said still grinning as he helped Kirwynn to her feet. "Now lets go get your father." She stood up very quickly, suddenly remembering why she had left the walls of Garriton in the first place. "Father!"

Kirwynn, instantly had a very worried look on her face as she quickly turned and started to run, as fast as she could towards the woods, where the injured Garriton troops were.

"Wait!" Yelled Bobbiur, as he ran to catch up to her. Then he said. "It could be very messy and I hate to say this but you must be ready because your father may already be dead."

When they got to the place where the main attack had been centered they realized it wasn't as bad as it first appeared. Which enhanced the chances of survival for those who were hit by the molten stones. As they walked through the area the injured were laying all around. Bobbiur glanced towards Garriton and saw rescue soldiers coming towards the woods. The barrage of rocks had literally ripped right through some of the archers. Some were dead. There was also a large number of severely wounded soldiers, but on the other hand from the sounds coming from the area, there were a number of uninjured fighters who were completely untouched.

Kirwynn was frantically looking for her father but she could not help but notice some of the Garriton archers who had been ripped apart. They passed a armless body and then they had to climb over a large fallen tree. They then both noticed another crushed body of a man who's arms had also been ripped off. Kirwynn, as they moved along pointed out an other Archer who had lost a few fingers. But worse than the battle sight was the cries of pain, the pleas and the moans for help, from the wounded soldiers. They passed three or four soldiers who had some minor injuries but generally they looked okay. Some uninjured soldiers were leaning over friends, giving comfort. Some assistance from Garriton was starting to arrive, when finally in a mess of bodies they finally discovered General Yauddi.

The General was in the area which was the hardest hit. Kirwynn quickly kneeling beside her father started to cry softly, but was thankful that he was still alive. He was in bad shape but General Yauddi, was still alive. The General was still somewhat incoherent as he mumbled. "We had no time. It happened so fast. We should have stayed in the Fort. What did they shoot at us?"

Bobbiur picked him up.

The General continued to mumble and Bobbiur was quite surprised when he found just how light the General actually was. Kirwynn had her hand on her fathers head and with the light coming from the walls of Garriton she was looking deep into his eyes, with a very concerned and worried look.

Bobbiur said. "Kirwynn we have to hurry and get the General back inside Garriton as fast as we are able to. These Haddrons could attack again at any time." They both turned in the direction of Garriton and to Kirwynn's surprise, Bobbiur was able to run as he carried her father towards the safety of the city walls.

Kirwynn and Bobbiur

Bobbiur paced up and down the hall of General Yauddi's house, wanting very much to see how the General was doing. Even Bobbiur was surprised that he could like the General this much, after only the one meeting. Bobbiur smiled to himself when he recalled earlier, the look of confusion on the General's face when General Yauddi was giving out the information about Zorp and the Haddrons. The funny part was when the General's memory had been instantly removed after the message about Zorp had been delivered.

Outside the General's bedroom door Kirwynn sat silently on a chair in the corner and was watching as, this strange young man, Bobbiur was pacing up and down. Neither Kirwynn nor Bobbiur talked very much and neither of them would look at each others eyes, as they were both pretending to be deep in their own thoughts.

After about one hour, the door opened and the Town Healer stepped out of the General's room and into the hall where he stood for a moment, looking very tired. Bobbiur spun around and started walking towards the Healer and Kirwynn jumped out of her chair, as they both rushed towards the Healer at the same time.

"Well he'll live. But he'll have a limp for the rest of his life." The Healer said while taking a deep breath, and looking towards, first Kirwynn and then Bobbiur. The Healer continued speaking while wiping his forehead on the sleeve of his shirt. "But I can tell you he won't be defending the town for quite some time."

"But he'll live? Right?" Kirwynn somewhat confused had asked with a trembling voice, as if she hadn't even heard what the Healer had already said.

"Yes he'll live." Repeated the Healer, as he was looking down at Kirwynn with a quizzical look on his face. Kirwynn began to feel faint and she started to slump down. Quickly Bobbiur put his arms around her so he could keep her from falling. She then tucked her face into his shoulder. Her body was trembling and to Bobbiur she seemed quite weak.

With considerable concern Bobbiur glanced over the top of Kirwynn's head and asked the Healer. "Can we see him?" At this time Bobbiur was looking somewhat uncomfortable but he never moved.

"I rather you didn't because he's sleeping now and he will need a lot of rest before he is able to recover." The Healer went on in a professional manner. "What you should do is let the General rest as much as possible. Let him wake up on his own. He'll feel a lot more like talking then."

The Healer nodded towards Bobbiur, who nodded back towards the Healer, showing he was in agreement. At this time Bobbiur could feel Kirwynn starting to relax.

"Fine. I guess." Said Bobbiur scratching his forehead, as the Healer was turning to go back into the General's room. As if by surprise, Bobbiur noticed that he still had his arms around Kirwynn and he was still holding her quite strongly. He had one arm around her waste. The other hand was behind her head and he was holding her into his inner shoulder with considerable force. All of a sudden to Bobbiur's surprise he found that he was very interested in her. He couldn't help but notice that she was holding him quite firmly also.

He became very aware of her perfume and then Bobbiur who was somewhat embarrassed, started to let go. He was aware that she did not let go of him right away and she continued to cling firmly to him. He didn't know why maybe because he wanted to comfort her, but he leaned slightly forward and slowly and softly kissed the top of her head. They both stood there quietly. Neither wanted the moment to end.

Without saying anything, Kirwynn started relax her hold on Bobbiur very slowly and as she looked up, Kirwynn very gently, reached up and placed her hand behind Bobbiur's neck, pulling his head down towards her. Without saying anything Kirwynn kissed Bobbiur very softly on the lips. The kiss was not very long, but it was very sweet and very gentle. At first Bobbiur was surprised and a little confused, but also he was very interested. After a short while, they both eased the firmness of their embrace, of each other at the same time but kept standing very close. Both noticed that the other one had very red cheeks. Kirwynn looked into Bobbiur's eyes for a short time and then they both looked down towards the floor. Without saying anything, Bobbiur and Kirwynn knew that something important had just happened.

Bobbiur said almost in a whisper. "Kirwynn, I have to go now. My men are waiting." Kirwynn nodded her head and without saying anything, she looked up at him with big eyes, which had just a slight wisp of tears in them. Bobbiur noticed that Kirwynn seemed more relaxed and she seemed a little happier now.

Bobbiur again whispered. "Kirwynn I have to go." Without saying anything further, Bobbiur turned and walked slowly down the hall towards the front door. He never looked back. Kirwynn watched him leave and then she slumped down in her chair to wait until she could see her father. She was very tired.

Even though her father was injured in the next room, Kirwynn could not help but continue thinking about this strange quiet young man from Darmonarrow. She had never met anybody as interesting as him before. Not in all of Garriton, and not in any of the Human cities in Chesfeld which she had ever been to. Kirwynn continued sitting there, thankful that her father was going to be all right, but also being very surprised that her mind could not forget the kiss with Bobbiur.

Then with a knowing, whimsical smile catching at the corner of her mouth, and while glancing at the door which this tall young man had just left from, her entire face broke into a complete and almost laughing type smile. The kiss had told it all. Kirwynn now knew that Bobbiur was as interested in her as she was in him. Where this feeling for Bobbiur had come from she did not know, nor did she care.

Still smiling she thought to herself. He could walk out that door not look back and make it seem like he was not all that interested, but Kirwynn knew better. Human Adjemirian girls and women, had a way of knowing when a boy or man was interested in them and deep down Kirwynn could feel the strong sense of interest coming from this good looking and strong young man. Kirwynn could not help but to continue smiling, as she said to herself while shaking her head. "Bobbiur you can run but you cannot hide." Then she wondered when she would see him again. Soon she hoped. She couldn't help it, as she started to giggle.

The Chase Begins

As Bobbiur had stepped out into the street and was starting to go in the direction of the front gate, there was determination in his step when something had caught the corner of his eye. Bobbiur spun around to see Zorp leaning up against the wall of the General's house.

"Good to see you again Bobbiur. Well done in the battle." Then with an even bigger smile on his wrinkled old face, Zorp said. "That must have been hard fighting Zalghar and his boys?"

With a questioning look on his face Bobbiur asked. "So what the General told me was true. Those were the warriors that you were talking about. Huh?"

"Yup. Those were Zalghar and the boys." Zorp said while slowly stroking his beard. "Now its time for you to be going."

With a pause Zorp said. "Go gather up the rest of your men and hurry." Zorp suddenly became somewhat anxious and he seemed very serious. "Oh, and by the way, your friend Hagjel is an awfully good shot with the bow." Without pausing, Zorp went on to say. "Normally I wouldn't have believed it but I saw the shot for myself. But keep in mind that Zalghar will not make the same mistake again so you should let Hagjel know that a chance of repeating the same kind of shot on one of the Kilpacx will probably never work a second time. You can expect that the animal's eyes will be protected by some kind of spell from Zalghar when you meet again."

Bobbiur had been standing quietly listening to what Zorp had to say and he nodded his head to show that he agreed with Zorp on this matter. Then Bobbiur said. "It was a very good shot and also it was a very lucky shot." Then Bobbiur also added as an after thought. "Lucky for me and Kirwynn also."

Changing the subject in somewhat of an anxious tone Zorp began speaking in a pleading fashion while shaking his head from side to side. "Bobbiur you must get going because time is getting short and you may lose the trail of these renegades. Enough of this idle chatter, you must push on. Chop. Chop." Zorp had said this while he had been clapping his hands together.

"Go where?" Bobbiur said. "We saved Garriton and now I have to return to Darmonarrow and help everybody rebuild the town."

Bobbiur took a step forward while he was trying to get past Zorp.

"Not so fast youngster." Zorp put out his arm blocking any chance of Bobbiur's escape while he was saying. "You ain't done yet. You still have to stop Zalghar and those Haddron warriors."

Looking directly into Bobbiur's eyes, Zorp continued. "I'll help when I can but I can't do everything you know. You've seen how bad Zalghar is and you must keep in mind that Zalghar will not let you rebuild Darmonarrow, in fact he will keep going until all of Adjemir is destroyed."

Then with a broad grin in his wrinkled old face and a twinkle in his mischievous eyes, in a knowledgeable tone, with his head tilted sideways while looking at Bobbiur, Zorp said laughingly. "You should also consider Kirwynn."

Bobbiur, with a quizzical look in his eyes, quickly turned to Zorp as he was wondering how Zorp knew that he had feelings for Kirwynn. Bobbiur's face was somewhat red but Zorp just continued on, in a pressing fashion, as if nothing was out of the ordinary. "This is the Zalghar I know and I can tell you he will not stop until he gets what he wants. He wants to rule all of Adjemir." Zorp kept pressing on. "If you want to rebuild Darmonarrow you'll have to stop Zalghar first." Zorp was looking directly into Bobbiur's face in order to see if Bobbiur understood exactly what would happen if Zalghar was not stopped.

Bobbiur noticed that Zorp who always seemed to be joking about everything, was very serious at this time about Zalghar. Zorp was not smiling, not even in the slightest. "Listen. I'll help you out a little more." With this Zorp broke into a chuckle.

"What?" Bobbiur looked puzzled.

"A little longer." Zorp continued laughing. "You really don't know what your getting into, do you?"

Without saying anything more Bobbiur finally pushed passed the 'Crazy Old Man,' as he began walking through town looking for Salbuk, Hagjel and Obmar. Bobbiur could never figure out why Zorp found everything so humorous all the time.

While Bobbiur was walking along, he was surprised to note, that his mind kept wandering back to the kiss from Kirwynn and he swore to himself that he could still feel her kiss on his lips. Bobbiur found that he couldn't stop smiling, whenever he thought about Kirwynn. At this he started to chuckle to himself. As he walked along, he then wondered to himself about Ram and just how well he was making out.

About fifteen minutes later Bobbiur found the group and there was a large number of people around them. Although it was quite late at night, these Garriton people were all interested in hearing the story from Hagjel about the shot he had made with his bow, which had hit the huge Kilpacx directly in the eye.

Bobbiur had to admit to himself, with a slight smile on his face, that the shot which Hagjel had made earlier in the night probably saved his and Kirwynn's life, not to mention everybody else who was outside the walls of Garriton at the time. The more Bobbiur thought about it, the shot from Hagjel's bow had probable saved all of Garriton.

Bobbiur thought about the change in attitude by the citizens of Garriton. Just a short while ago these same people of Garriton were calling Hagjel, "Pointed Ears." And other insulting names. Now Hagjel seemed to be the most popular person in all of Garriton. Bobbiur said to himself as he stepped towards the group of people who had surrounded Hagjel, Salbuk and Obmar. "Things sure can change awfully fast."

When the crowd had finally left, Bobbiur discussed with the group what they should do next. He started by saying Zorp wanted him to go after the Haddrons right away. As it turned out, everybody, after they had considering everything, agreed that they should all get some rest. It was still dark out. Bobbiur agreed with this decision, mostly because he felt the Haddrons would not return and the possibility of tracking the Haddrons at night would be almost impossible.

Besides, Bobbiur thought Salbuk would need his powers fully restored. They picked up their equipment and headed towards the nearest Tavern and asked for some rooms for the night. When the group arrived at the Inn, the Inn Master refused to accept any money for the use of his rooms. This grizzled old Inn keeper had been on the wall during the battle. The Inn Keeper had seen the way Bobbiur, Salbuk, Obmar, and Hagjel had fought for Garriton against the strange Haddron warriors.

Bobbiur also noticed that the Inn keeper had kept staring at Hagjel as if he was some kind of god or something.

As an after thought and in somewhat of an absent minded awe struck tone the Inn keeper, pointed to the back of the Inn as he said. "Stables are in the back." His eyes had never left Hagjel's smiling face, not for a second. Bobbiur was smiling to himself, thinking that one shot with a bow has probably changed Hagjel's life forever. The information about Hagjel's shot, which in the end killed the giant Kilpacx, would be all over Adjemir, by noon tomorrow.

Bobbiur shook his head, just smiled towards the floor, as he said softly under his breath. "A star is born."

Leaving Garriton

In the morning they all got up and after they had something to eat, they headed for the stables to get their Spaggidons. After Bobbiur had saddled his own Spaggidon he saw that Salbuk, Hagjal and Obmar, who had already saddled their Spaggidons, were in front of the stables with the old man Zorp, with puzzled looks on their faces. Bobbiur thought to himself looks like they were having the same problem he was having, and that was, concerning the reason why Zorp never stopped smiling.

When Zorp saw Bobbiur coming he turned towards Bobbiur with a raised eyebrow, the same old smile on his face, as he asked while rubbing his hands together. "Great! Now your ready to go?" Bobbiur noticed the grin on Zorp's face was the same grin he had the night before. Zorp continued rubbing his hands together in a somewhat gleeful manner.

But before he could answer Hagjel spoke up. "No we are not ready." Hagjel's voice was getting loud as he interrupted. "We don't have any supplies or anything." Then without giving Zorp a chance to speak Hagjel continued on. "Nor do we know what direction the Haddrons traveled in."

Hagjel had said this with very little change in his tone.

Bobbiur thought to himself. It looks like Hagjel was in a cranky mood this morning.

"Oh well. They went that way." Zorp said, pointing East. "Towards the Elves land of Volkjynn. Now you must hurry and leave, time is of the essence. Now lets go. Forward march!"

Zorp clapping his hands together started shooing Bobbiur and the men towards the main gate of Garrtion. Just as Bobbiur was starting to wonder where Zorp's Dragon was, Hagjel started questioning Zorp again. "Wait just a second. Why are you hurrying us this way?"

Then Hagjel repeated himself in a nagging tone. "We still don't have any supplies!" Bobbiur noticed that Hagjel did not seem very happy, at all.

Jakka, knowing that Hagjel was in an ugly mood, just stayed out of sight. But he was fully awake.

Then Zorp with a slight frown on his face said. "Well, if I have to do everything!"

Zorp turned and walked over to Hagjel's Spaggidon. While leaning up against the animal he started tapping his fingers on the saddle as he was continually glancing up into the sky. Just then the Dragon Dymma came flying into the sky over Garriton and zoomed in for landing, right in front of them. Zorp had a knowing grin on his face and as this was happening Jakka was poking his head up to watch this magnificent beast, as Dymma came in for a landing.

As before Bobbiur was amazed because in all his life this was the first Dragon he had ever seen who would, or could, actually smile.

Salbuk was then given a very large green colored sack, which Dymma laid at his feet. "This should be more than enough supplies to last you for a couple of days." Then Dymma said quite softly for such a large Dragon. "There is lots of food and there is also some clean cloths."

Zorp shrugged and made a sweeping motion with his hands towards the front gate, as he said. "Now you have all your supplies so just get on and go."

Bobbiur started to ask Zorp why he didn't fight Zalghar himself but Zorp had already began climbing onto the back of Dymma, as they were preparing to leave. Bobbiur was also starting to understand that Dymma and Zorp did not like long goodbye's.

Then Bobbiur turned and nodded to the group and without saying anything further the men started to sort through the supplies. Bobbiur noticed that Zorp and Dymma were hovering in the sky just over Garriton and Bobbiur was wondering why they were hanging around, but it was only a few minutes before they finally left.

The four loaded their supplies, then they quickly got on their mounts and started riding out of Garriton. But before the group had left the town of Garriton, Dymma and Zorp flew back over them and Zorp hollered down to Hagjel. "You should try to travel in the direction of Domerge."

Salbuk and Hagjel both knew where Domerge was located in the Elf land of Volkjynn, and they nodded to each other as Salbuk sent a mind message to Zorp thanking him.

The guards at the main entrance opened the gate for the group as they got close. The gate was closed immediately after they left and the group turned and waved to the crowd of people on the walls. Bobbiur looked back and while he was waving, he was also looking to see if Kirwynn was on the wall, but he noticed that she was not present. Bobbiur then turned his attention back to the task at hand which was the tracking of the Haddrons but he was quite disappointed because Kirwynn had not been present to watch him leave. Although he fully understood that Kirwynn would want to be with her father at this time, he was somewhat sad when he didn't see her. Then as he remembered holding Kirwynn in his arms a smile came to his face. Bobbiur smiled because he could still remember her kiss.

The group rode silently down the road in the direction Zorp had pointed in which was in the general direction of Domerge. All of them were somewhat quiet, and then the tracking by Hagjel began. They were heading in the direction of the Elves territory of Volkjynn and it wasn't long before Hagjal picked up on Haddron's trail coming out of the woods. They followed the huge and well defined Kilpacx's prints which had been left by these giant animals from the night before. Bobbiur had to agree with Zorp. At present the Haddrons were going in the general direction of Domerge but he was to find that this would change very soon.

As they traveled along the Spaggidons trotted down the road, as fast as Bobbiur would allow them. Spaggidon's could run quite fast but Bobbiur wanted to slow down just in case the tracks led off into the woods again. Bobbiur as well as the others were also aware that there may be an ambush by the Haddrons, especially if the Haddrons knew that they were being followed. To Bobbiur's way of thinking, it did not make much sense to be in too much of a hurry and therefore be ambushed by these powerful Haddrons.

They trotted the Spaggidons for quite sometime and it was later in the morning when the Spaggidons began to tire that Bobbiur signaled that they should slow up a little. Bobbiur said to the men. "We need to rest the Spagiddons for awhile and we need to let them get something to eat. We should also rest and have something to eat while the Spaggidons are resting."

Then glancing around, he said. "We'll look for a good place to stop."

Bobbiur had been very quiet since they had left Garriton.

Salbuk knew that Bobbiur's heart and mind was still at Garriton because of Kirwynn and Salbuk did not like the quietness of Bobbiur, so he decided to liven things up a bit. As they slowed down Salbuk with a smile on his face, sent a message telepathically, to only Hagjal and the message was. "Watch this!" Suddenly a small rock about the size of an arrow head, from near the edge of the road, flew into the air and struck Bobbiur in the back of his helmet

"Ambush!" Bobbiur had yelled back loudly as he jumped to the ground running and looking for cover. He was also looking for the enemy. In his panic he looked over his shoulder only to see that Hagjal and Salbuk had jumped off of their mounts and were bent over laughing, Obmar just sat on his mount as if nothing had happened. Dwarfs don't have much of any kind of a sense of humor.

"Very funny. But that hurt!" Bobbiur started to get mad, but when the others kept laughing it broke the seriousness of the moment and then soon he began to laugh also. As they were finishing off with the laughing, Bobbiur told them that they would have to be more careful now because they had just recently crossed the border into Elf Territory.

It was at this time the group decided to have a quick bite to eat, so they tethered the Spaggidons to some trees. These trees were close to some very rich looking green grass and other shrubs, so they let the Spaggidons loose before they themselves sat down to rest. When they had finished eating they gather up the Spaggidons and headed out in the same direction they had been traveling since they had left Garriton.

Soon after as the group had started to trot their Spaggidons down the road and just as they were starting to climb up a small hill on the road, a group of about twenty well armored Elves, who were mounted on horses rounded a curve just in front of them. About ten Elves already had arrows notched in their bows and it appeared that they were clearly on a hunt.

Bobbiur and the group came to a halt as the leader of the Elves slowly rode up a little closer at which time he said. "Well, well, what have we here?" Then the Elf leader answered his own question. "Looks like we have two new Human slaves, an Elf traitor, and what's this? A Dwarf." Grinning the Elf leader said. "These Dwarfs always put up a good fight."

About this time Obmar started to growl and he was peering at the Elf leader through tightly squinted eyes. The one who appeared to be the leader was laughing and looking over his shoulder while he had yelled to the rest of his men. Then as he was turning back to face Bobbiur he said. "The Krugs can wait."

The Elf raiding party started to gather around Bobbiur and his men and Salbuk saw big grins on all the Elves faces which caused him to start smiling to himself. Salbuk sent a quick message to Bobbiur and the rest of the group. Hagjel's mind message was that he did not feel the presence of any magic powers coming from any of the twenty Elves. Then in his mind message he added that he was preparing to put up a protection shield.

Bobbiur nodded and without even looking at Salbuk he sent a message. "This is a good idea Salbuk. Just be ready."

"Looks like you lost the trail. We haven't seen any Krugs around here." Hagjal said with a very forceful tone and Bobbiur noticed a slight smile was beginning to show at the corners of Hagjel's mouth. Bobbiur was wondering to himself, how Hagjel never got excited at times like this nor did he ever stop smiling. "Shut up traitor or your head will be on my wall!" The leader yelled back at Hagjel in a very vicious and aggressive tone.

As Bobbiur was getting off his Spaggidon he was drawing his swords and very quickly Salbuk and Hagjal followed. Obmar eventually jumped off his Spaggidon still growling in his Dwarf fashion. They all walked towards the Elves and as they got closer half the Elves also dismounted. The remaining Elves who were still on their Spaggidons were the ones with their bows and arrows already notched. "You don't want to try anything do you? We out number you five to one!" The leader said looking directly at Bobbiur.

Bobbiur started laughing. He threw back his head and looking at the sky he laughed some more. The Elves on the ground looked at each other with a puzzled look on their faces because of this strange behavior by Bobbiur.

Then the two groups lined up toe to toe as Bobbiur stopped laughing. Things began to get real serious. Salbuk, as he saw some Elves starting to pull back on their bow strings, sent a mind thought only to his group, as he started counting. "One. Two. three!" Just as the Elves arrows were being released, Salbuk very quickly set up a protection shield just in front of his group. The arrows as they were released by the Elves, bounced harmlessly off of the protection shield. Salbuk sent another message to the group, that as soon as the arrows were shot, he was going to drop the protection shield and that everybody should get ready.

Just as the shield of protection was brought down by Salbuk, Bobbiur who was starting to get quite mad, with lightning speed, punched the Elf leader in the face causing him to fall to the ground. Salbuk and Hagjal did the same to the two closest Elves. Then all four went in with their weapons raised. Obmar did not waste any time with punching the Elves, he had just draw his axe and using the flat edge of his war axe, he slapped a couple of Elves in the sides of their legs and the Elves fell to the ground screaming.

While all this was going on Bobbiur had used the flat side of his two swords and knocked down two more Elves. Bobbiur again with lightning speed turned to the Elf leader and put both of his swords up under the leaders chin, who was still lying flat on his back as Bobbiur said. "Tell your men to stop or I will have my men kill you all. I will be starting with you first." Bobbiur then asked without smiling. "Do you understand?'

Salbuk who had not moved since the battle had begun except for punching the one Elf, was watching the archers to see if they were going to do anything. He would have to be ready with a magic spell to form another protection shield in order to keep Bobbiur, Hagjel, and Obmar safe. This all happened so very fast even before the Elves had any chance to react. Bobbiur kept staring at the Elf leader on the ground and finally the leader told the other Elves to put their weapons away.

"Get the hell out of here. We have more important matters to deal with." Then in a very crisp tone Bobbiur speaking directly to the leader said. "Just for your information there is a very strong force of renegades from another land attacking cities and villages all throughout Adjemir."

Speaking in a softer tone Bobbiur said. "These renegades are from a land called Haddron and they are very powerful." Then Bobbiur added. "They attacked Darmonarrow yesterday." Bobbiur abruptly put his swords back into their sheaths.

The Elf leader just looked at Bobbiur without blinking and never saying anything. He was probable feeling lucky to still be alive. He was probably thinking that this group of warriors must be really tough because they showed no fear and they seemed very strong in magic powers. The Elves got up and quickly scurried back to their waiting horses. After the Elves had ridden a short distance away, they kept looking back over their shoulders wondering why they had not been killed, were not robbed, and they still had their horses. They were in such a hurry to leave that they had left some of their weapons where they had been dropped on the ground.

Once the group saw that the intruders had disappeared they put their weapons away and Bobbiur noticed that Obmar had stopped the growling, or whatever it was he was doing. Salbuk sent a mind message to the entire group. "I feel real good about my magic powers because since Zorp enhanced my powers everything seems to operate much faster."

Quickly the group mounted up and continued down the road. Hagjel took up the lead again and was watching the ground very closely for any signs of the Haddrons, or the giant Kilpacx. The group continued down the road for a short time and then picked up on some large Kilpacx footprints which were coming back onto the road. They followed the signs for another mile or so before the Kilpacx tracks turned off the main road again and continued into a very thick forest area.

Obmar said. "They might have an ambush up ahead as they probably know by now that we are following them." He then gave that same sort of growl. It was the same sound which the group had heard him make when the Elves were bothering them earlier.

Hagjal pondered for a while, he then suggested. "There's an Elf town up the road just a little ways and it's called WynnFred" Then Hagjel also added. "Maybe they got their Kilpacx off of the road so they don't draw too much attention to themselves." Then with a different thought in mind Hagjel said. "Wait a second if they got off the Kilpacx then maybe they are going to attack the next town." "They use those Kilpacx in battles, right?"

Then thinking in a different manner Bobbiur broke into the conversation. "Or if they took the Kilpacx into the bushes then they might have just wanted to go around the next town without causing any trouble." Bobbiur had said this while bending down beside Hagjal and pointing at the tracks.

"Don't jump to any conclusions. Do you here that?" Hagjal said while he quickly stood up and was looking down the road off into the distance. They had all heard the same noise at the same time, that is except Salbuk and Bobbiur.

"I don't hear any sounds." Bobbiur said while standing up with a questioning look on his face. "Sounds like screaming or yelling coming from up the road." Hagjal had said this with a worried look on his face. Hagjel because he was an Elf and had spent considerable time in this area before he came to live in Darmonarrow knew that there was an Elf Village just up the road.

"Lets go." Bobbiur quickly walked over to his Spaggidon and jumped on. They all rode down the road as fast as they could because everybody was interested in getting to the place where the noise was coming from. Sure enough when they got closer Bobbiur and Salbuk could now pick up the sounds of battle. Then as they rounded a corner in the road they all saw that the area was clear for quite a long ways and in the distance they could see an Elf Village with the main gate broken and burning.

As they rode closer they all looked through the gate very carefully to see Elves running around everywhere. Parts of the town were on fire but the Elves didn't seem to be trying to put the fires out. Instead they were putting bows to the sky and firing at something above them.

At first Bobbiur couldn't tell what it was because of all the smoke. Then Bobbiur looked up to see a large fire breathing Dragon flying through the smoke and over the town. Bobbiur drew his Spaggidon to a stop and was wandering what he should try to do next. Salbuk noticed that Bobbiur was watching the Dragon very closely.

The Dragon was about twenty feet long and it was a very dark blue. The Dragon had a very long tail which was red with black stripes. This Dragon had horns on its head but none on its back. But it was a Dragon which could also spout flames. Bobbiur thought to himself that these Dragons never bothered to attack villages, so something must had angered this Dragon. Then Bobbiur thought that maybe the Haddrons had put a spell on this Dragon which made it attack this Elfen village.

Bobbiur had an idea. "Hagjal look!" Bobbiur was pointing towards the Dragon as he turned towards Hagjal.

"Shhhhh." Hagjal already had his bow notched and was aiming an enhanced arrow at the Dragon.

"Wait! Don't kill it." Bobbiur was speaking quickly. "Just wing it or put a spell on it as we may be able to use this Dragon later. It's a lot faster than the Spaggidons. And we should be able to use it in battle."

The Nine Moons of Adjemir

"You can tame it with a magic spell. Can't you Salbuk?" Bobbiur said this as he turned towards Salbuk. Bobbiur was still talking very quickly and he was getting even more excited.

"I'll try." Salbuk said crossing his arms, leaning slightly forward and opening his mind to enhanced powers that Zorp had given him.

"Hurry Salbuk." Bobbiur said just as he turned to Hagjel. "Do you have a stunning arrow with you?" Bobbiur then turned and watched as the Dragon swooped down and set fire to another group of houses.

"I don't remember. Let me check" Hagjal said as he pulled out some arrows that Zorp had given him and started to look over them very closely.

As Bobbiur was watching Hagjel looking through his arrows he saw out the corner of his eye, an Elf who seemed familiar. Bobbiur said to himself. "This is the Elf who tried to capture us."

Just then Obmar pointed towards the Elf and Bobbiur quickly nodded to Obmar that he had recognized him also. Bobbiur kept watching as the Elfen villager's kept firing arrows at the swooping Dragon.

"Hurry up Hagjel these Elves will hurt the Dragon if we don't do anything really quickly." Bobbiur said this and he was also thinking to himself that the Elves arrows were having no effect on the Dragon.

Bobbiur, Salbuk and Obmar rode their Spaggidons closer and surrounded Hagjel, who was still looking for the arrow. They all kept an eye on the Elves just in case the Elves thought this was their Dragon and therefore they might start to attack them as they sat on their Spaggidons.

Salbuk, who was still worried about the Elves, sent a message to the group. "If it is needed I will be ready to put up a protection shield." They looked around at the Elves who seemed not to notice them being in their town. The Elves were very busy trying to fight the Dragon.

Hagjal, with a look of hesitation eventually began saying. "Yes. Here's one here. Says it'll stun 'anything,' for about five minutes. Is that long enough?"

Salbuk said to Hagjel in a mind message. "Five minutes is more than enough."

Quickly Bobbiur asked Hagjel with a quizzical look on his face. "Anything?" What Bobbiur meant was that this is a very large Dragon and maybe the arrow's spell may not be strong enough.

Hagjel said glancing up. " Yes. Anything. Even this Dragon."

Bobbiur then turned to Salbuk. "Is it possible to cast a magic spell on the Dragon so that it does not crash to the ground after Hagjel hits it with the stunning arrow?" Then he added. "Make it float to the ground if you can."

"Should be able to do that." Salbuk sent this message so all the group could understand.

Hagjal notched his bow and took aim at the Dragon just as it was swooping in for another attack.

Hagjal released the arrow.

As the arrow flew in the direction of the Dragon, Hagjel called out the Rune spell. The arrow from Hagjel's bow hit the Dragon square in the chest just in front of one of the Dragon's huge wings. Then surprisingly the arrow seemed to quickly vanish. After a very short time the Dragon's movements grew slower and then the Dragon started to fly very awkwardly, towards the ground. All of a sudden this huge beast stopped moving and began falling out of control, directly towards the ground. Very quickly Salbuk sent out the mind spell which Bobbiur had asked him to send. The Dragon started to slow down and then very gently, now under Salbuk's magic control, the Dragon began to float very slowly towards the ground below.

Salbuk sent a message to the group, that they must. "Surround the Dragon and keep the Elves away or the Elves might do the Dragon some harm."

Obmar nodded that he understood and he immediately jumped off of his Spaggidon and ran over to the Dragon with his war axe at the ready. Salbuk rode up to the Dragon and got off his Spaggidon. He walked over to the dazed animal, who's big eyes were intensely following him everywhere. The Dragon although unable to move, appeared to be totally aware of everything. While standing very close to this enormous animal, Salbuk began looking directly into the animal's eyes. Then he placed his right hand onto the Dragon's forehead, at which time he closed his own eyes. This was when some of Salbuk's energy entered the Dragons head. When the energy was passing from Salbuk into the Dragon, it was like a blue colored light which traveled down Salbuk's arm. The Dragon shook slightly as the magic energy was being transferred from Salbuk into the Dragon's head.

The Nine Moons of Adjemir

Bobbiur, Hagjel, and Obmar now surrounded both the Dragon and Salbuk because some angry Elves were starting to come closer. But at this time the Elves were only watching curiously. A few moments after the energy had left Salbuk's arm, Salbuk opened his eyes and took a few steps back. He waited silently while watching the Dragon. After a few moments the magic spell from Hagjel's arrow, which had made the Dragon harmless, was finally starting wear off. At this point the Dragon was still watching Salbuk very closely and it had a very evil look in it's eye. The Dragon tried to get up on all fours. But this large animal kept falling back to the ground which meant the spell from the enhanced arrow had not completely worn off.

Finally after numerous attempts, this huge beast was able to stand on it's own without shaking, but it was still not able to move. This magnificent animal was now shaking it's enormous head and was still staring straight at Salbuk, who was the closest to him. This large beast still had a mean vicious look in it's large eyes.

All the Elves who were watching this quickly hurried back to a safer position. The Elves had their weapons ready. Clearly at this time, the Elves thought that there was going to be a big fight between Salbuk and the Dragon. Salbuk did not notice the Elves, which Bobbiur and the group were now keeping at a distance, because he was so deeply concentrating on the Dragon's behavior. Salbuk, with a deep awareness had to be very vigilant and weary, because this Dragon was still very powerful.

"You gonna be good?" Salbuk sent a message into the Dragon's brain and through all this Salbuk had a knowing smile on his face.

The Dragon showed it's teeth, snarled loudly, hissed viciously and then the Dragon with all it's force, fiercely lunged at the still smiling Salbuk. Halfway through it's lunge the Dragon skidded to a complete stop, fell to the ground in severe agony and began moaning in pain.

"Thought he might try that." Salbuk sent this message to the others as he was continued watching the Dragon's every move very intently. Salbuk walked closer to the Dragon as he continued to stare intensely at the Dragon.

"What did you do to him?" Bobbiur asked with a genuine curiosity.

Salbuk answered with a mind message which he sent to all the group. "Just a light mind bolt of energy." Still watching the Dragon's every move and with the same smile, Salbuk's message was short and to the point. "He's okay. But it tells him who's in charge." Without looking away from the Dragon, Salbuk went on with a question. "How are the Elves behaving?" The Salbuk sent another message. "I can still put up a protection shield if you want, but I am running out of energy and I'll have to watch this Dragon for just a little while longer."

He went on. "The Dragon should be really good very soon and I hope he is no problem because I will have to rest soon."

Salbuk went on as he added. "Otherwise I will be completely out of power shortly.

"Great. Will he let us ride him?" Hagjal as he had asked this question had been looking at the Dragon cautiously but with an extreme interest.

Salbuk's next mind message was short and to the point. "Oh yes but not right away." I trained him magically and he will be just like any ordinary Human battle Dragon. It's a little trick I picked up a few years back but it'll take some time for him to adjust to us. You will have to be patient with him a little longer.

Hagjel could tell by the mind message from Salbuk that he was becoming very tired. Salbuk kept staring at the Dragon to make sure that he was not going to be a problem. Salbuk, while continuing to look directly into the Dragon's eyes, walked over and patted the Dragon on the head. This time the Dragon just stared at Salbuk and began nudging Salbuk's hand with the side of it's enormous head.

Obmar started to make his growling noise and Hagjel said to Salbuk that they might need a protection shield because the Elves were starting to close in. The leader Elf who attacked them earlier in the day was leading the Elves closer. Bobbiur's worries were soon put to rest, as the Elf leader showed no hostility. "Thank you for saving our village."
Said the Elf who was the leader with a quizzical look in his eyes. "My name is Pendahl and I believe we have already met." Then Pendahl added. "Our Village is called WynnFred."

The Elf was talking directly to Bobbiur but he also nodded to Obmar, Hagjel and Salbuk. The Elf leader had signaled to the other Elves to put up their weapons, as he stepped closer to Bobbiur and hesitantly, put out his hand as a sign of peace.

The Adjemir sign of peace was very simple. The person offering the peace sign would hold out their right hand, with the fist fully clasped and facing the ground. Just the thumb would be sticking out. The person offering the peace sign would then would touch their thumb to their heart. This was the peace sign for all of Adjemir.

The Nine Moons of Adjemir

"Is this your Dragon?" Pendahl, with raised eye brows turned and asked Salbuk.

Salbuk wasn't sure about sending the Elf a mind message so he just shook his head and nodded towards Bobbiur. Meaning Pendhal should talk directly to Bobbiur.

"No this is not our Dragon." Then Bobbiur went on. "It's to bad that he has nearly destroyed your village but I guess that I might have some answers for you."

Bobbiur walked over to the Dragon, turned and looked Pendahl straight in the eyes. Bobbiur began to speak in a very tired tone. "As I told you earlier today Darmonarrow has been destroyed." Then with a little sigh Bobbiur continued. "We are from Darmonarrow and we are tracking the people who are responsible for destroying, not only Darmonarrow, but they have also attacked Garriton yesterday."

"I think the attack on your village, by this Dragon, was done by the same warriors." Bobbiur then added. "These warriors are from another land far away and they intend to conquer all of Adjemir."

Salbuk quickly sent a mind message to Bobbiur alone, telling Bobbiur that when he had been inside the Dragon's mind he had found the Dragon had received a spell earlier from Zalghar. "The message in the Dragon's mind was that it should attack this village." Salbuk went on in the same message to Bobbiur. "I think that the Haddrons are now watching our movements as we follow them."

Speaking to Pendahl, after reviewing this message from Salbuk, Bobbiur said in a thoughtful tone. "I think the attack on your village was mostly to cause confusion in order to slow us down."

Bobbiur nodded towards Salbuk, thanked him in a mind message, and without saying anything more he turned his attention back to Pendahl.

"Where did the Dragon come from?" Bobbiur asked.

"I don't know." Pendahl responded. "The Dragon appeared right after we saw some strange Humans up on the hill above the our town."

As Pendahl replied to the question, he had been pointing at the ridge which was just north of the village. Then Pendahl waved his hand towards the Dragon as he asked Bobbiur. "You people have such strong powers! Where did you get these kind of powers' from?"

Bobbiur, with a slight smile on his young face shook his head slightly and placed his hand on Pendahl's shoulder. Bobbiur then told Pendahl. "Sorry. But I cannot tell you where these powers come from."

Pausing, Pendahl thanked Bobbiur and the group again for saving the village and then apologized for the earlier attack.

Bobbiur said. "You are not to worry. We are not the enemy."

Pendahl went on a little bit hesitant as he said to Bobbiur.

"I know you are a Human and we Elves have been fighting Humans for many years but if we can help in any way against these people from this other land. Just ask."

"Okay. I'll remember that." Bobbiur said and then he added. "This new enemy's name is Zalghar and he comes from another world called Haddron. But I don't think he will be back here." Bobbiur then said. "At least not for the night."

Bobbiur was getting more relaxed with Pendahl and he was now actually thinking Pendahl was not such a bad sort of Elf, after all.

Obmar, Hagjel and Salbuk were staying real close to the Dragon and all the Elves who were close by, were in awe of how fast the Dragon had become tamed by Salbuk's magic spell.

Jakka was starting to roust about in the tote bag and Hagjel reached in and rubbed Jakka's ears. Then Hagjel offered him some small fresh fruits. Hagjel thought to himself that there was no need to show Jakka to this crowd of Elves, because they had already seen enough with seeing the Dragon being tamed by Salbuk.

Bobbiur went on talking to Pendahl. "Does this town have an Inn?" Bobbiur asked. "And I think we will need a place to keep this Dragon over night."

Pendahl thought for a moment and then he said. "About a half of one now."

Pendahl had pointed to a half smashed building, which prior to the attack by the Dragon, was the Inn.

Hagjel who was still standing quite close, heard Pendahl talking about the half Inn which was still there, spoke with a smile on his face. "I hope that the part of the Inn which is not destroyed is the half with the ale in it. I could sure use some a big jug of ale about now." He smiled and rubbed his belly.

Obmar as he heard this chuckled, rolled his eyes back, with an amusing smile on his face, as he said to himself while glancing sideways at Hagjel. "You beer bellied ale lover."

Bobbiur who had heard Obmar's statement about Hagjel's beer belly had a slight smile on his face, mostly because he had never heard Obmar make any type of joke, or ever make any attempt at humor before.

Nodding with a slight smile Bobbiur said to Pendahl. "It'll do. Do you mind us spending the night at your Inn?" Bobbiur asked of Pendahl.

"You can stay." Pendahl started saying as he was looking towards the Dragon and watching the control over the Dragon that Salbuk had. Pendahl then turned to Bobbiur and went on with a smile. "I'm sure you can stay as long as you want."

"Thanks. But we'll only be here for the night. We'll have to leave early tomorrow or we may lose the trail of the Haddrons." Bobbiur had replied before saying. "Also there might be a messenger from Ram coming through here some time tomorrow and I would ask that he be given a safe passage through this area."

Bobbiur knew deep down that Ram would be trying to contact him and his group very shortly and he had only assume it would be done by messenger. Pendahl nodded his head as he was turning back to move closer to the area where the Dragon was now the center of attraction. As Bobbiur walked towards the Inn he was thinking that he did not need to rest and he did not think that Hagjel or Obmar were that tired, but Salbuk would need to get considerable rest in order to rebuild his magic powers back up, to the same strength that he had before he tamed the Dragon. Bobbiur was thinking that it must have taken a considerable amount of energy to tame a Dragon this large and in such a short amount of time. All of a sudden Kirwynn came into Bobbiur's mind and he smiled to himself as he walked towards the Inn. He hoped she was doing alright.

Salbuk, who was following Bobbiur, could not help but smile and laugh to himself. Salbuk who was very tired by this time, could not help but think. "Hagjel and I are going to have a lot of fun with this.

Before the Attack on WynnFred

After the attack on Garriton by Zalghar and his warriors, as they had rode away, Zalghar was more determined than he was before to put great fear into all peoples of Adjemir. As they were riding along Zalghar was thinking about different strategies. But he also was thinking that these Adjemir people were tougher and smarter than he had first thought. He also knew that these people of Adjemir were always at war with each other, so maybe he could use this knowledge to his advantage.

It was early the next morning, they had broke camp and had again been traveling, for a considerable time, steadily in the direction of Volkjynn. Zalghar had known that there was an Elfen village just up the road but he had not wanted to send his warriors into this village because he now had a different strategy.

A plan had started to form in his mind the night before. "Hold up." Zalghar had raised his right hand into the air and turning to his men he had said. "I want to use my 'Spirit Eye to see again, what is up ahead."

Zalghar had pointing in the direction of a small hill. "The men had followed Zalghar up the small hill where the Haddrons had then formed the Kilpacx circle, in order for Zalghar to send out his 'Spirit Eye.' At this time Zalghar had went on to advise his men that he would not be using the 'Spirit Eye' for very long because he had not wanted to use much energy. When he had gone into the trance he was not in this trance very long. While Zalghar had been using the 'Spirit Eye' he again observed a small Elf Village just a little further up the road from the location where he and his warriors were at the time. He did not know it but the name of this Elf Village, was WynnFred.

He had said to his men who were still mounted on the backs of the giant Kilpacx. "There is an Elf town right down the road so you can rest for a short while. If you want some of you can dismount because I will be a little while."

Zalghar, after speaking to the warriors again had turned to his warriors as he said. "Bring me the extra Kilpacx."

At this time one of the Haddron warriors had walked over to Zalghar leading the extra Kilpacx. The warrior was leading the large animal by holding a rope which was attached to the Kilpacx right front leg. Zalghar had then told his men to back up a short distance as he said. "I need considerable room because I am going to cast a very powerful spell."

After Zalghar was certain that all of his men were at a safe distance, he had turned and walked up closer to the waiting Kilpacx. While he was preparing the Kilpacx, Zalghar reached up and placed his right hand on the huge animals head. The animal only stood there, with it's eyes wide open, scared, and staring at Zalghar. Then when Zalghar was sure he had the Kilpacx complete attention, he began to slowly go into a magic trance. A slow moving bluish, glowing mist had then begun to slowly become visible. This mist surrounded both Zalghar's feet and the huge paws of the beast. This blue mist seemed to be coming from the ground immediately around these two figures.

As the blue mist had started to thicken, Zalghar became in complete control of this large animal. Now the Kilpacx's head had begun to get lower to the ground, as the magic was being forced into the animal's brain. The Kilpacx also seemed tired at this point. Then very slowly the large animals head bent even further forward, towards Zalghar. Within a few moments there was a loud crackling sound, coming from the head of the now terrified Kilpacx. The large beast had started to twitch uncontrollably. There was smoke coming out of it's ears and it's eyes were growing larger. The Kilpacx's nostrils were becoming quite flared and smoke was now flowing freely from the large snout of this huge beast.

Now this huge and fearsome beast was becoming even more frightened but by now it could not move. It was as if the Kilpacx feet had been glued to the ground. There was now a visible light coming not only from Zalghar but also from this large and very scared animal. This light was again, a bluish color. At this point the head of the Kilpacx started vibrating and pulsate at a very fast rate. The light which was now completely surrounding this huge beast and Zalghar, was becoming much stronger and much brighter. As the magic spell gained momentum the bluish light continued to get brighter.

Noticeably the huge head of the Kilpacx had started to change first. Visible horns started to grow from it's forehead, where no horns were before. Then the Kilpacx skin started to slowly turn a dark blue and it sprouted wings which were also dark blue. As all this was going on, the already large animal, had grown to almost twice it's original size.

Next the tail of the animal had started to grow longer and quickly turn red, with black stripes. When the the transformation was complete, there stood an animal which looked very much like a large Ajemirian Dragon. Zalghar had said to his men near the completion of this transformation, while he continued to look the Dragon right in the eyes, just as he was coming out of his trance. "Okay. Get ready. Lets go."

Zalghar had pointed in the direction he had wanted to travel, as he had spoken to the warriors. After the transformation of the Kilpacx into a Dragon was complete Zalghar looked and sounded very tired as he said. "There is a ridge just beside the Elves town and I want to go there now. By the way I want you all to walk your Kilpacx and place them in the forest over there." Zalghar had said this while he had pointed in the direction of some very dense bushes, a little ways off of the road.

"Why did we have to get off our mounts?" One of the Haddron warriors had asked. "Because we don't want any body noticing us until we are in position. I would like to have the animals tethered away from the ridge as far as possible. I have a plan and I will explain more in a few moments."

Then Zalghar had added in a quiet tone. "So we are going to have to walk the Kilpacx into the thicket over there, were we will tie them up until we have finished with this village. We have to move as silently as possible. Remember those Humans in Garriton. They were ready for us." The Zalghar in a confident tone spoke further. There was a slight smile on his evil face. "We don't want these Elves knowing that we are coming, now do we?"

Zalghar put his hand on his own Kilpacx neck and started walking through the bush heading for the thicket which he had talked of earlier. "Hurry up we can't waste time here." Zalghar had said this because some of the Kilpacx had started to graze on some of the grass which had been growing from the ground where they had been gathered.

The warriors had done as Zalghar had instructed and they all marched off in a single file to the place that Zalghar had pointed out. It took about one hour before Zalghar and the Haddron warriors were all positioned on the ridge above this Elfen town, called WynnFred. Zalghar had then ordered his men to show themselves to the Elves in the town below. To act like they were Human and not Haddrons. At this time Zalghar instructed his men to shoot arrows at the Elfen town below them. From this distance the Elves in the town below would easily believe that they were being attacked by a band vicious Humans. This had been the most important part of Zalghar's plan.

Zalghar told his men that once they were sure the Elves had seen them and believed that they were a Human band of warriors. He was going to order the Dragon to attack the town. Zalghar had went on to say to his men that before he would send the Dragon on it's attack of the town that they should go off a little further as he was going to use his 'Spirit Eye' to observe what was happening in the town when he had sent the Dragon on it's attack.

Just before departing and heading up to the top of the ridge to make the Elves think that they were being attacked by Humans, Zalghar had sent a mind message to the Dragon ordering it to stay exactly where it was. Later the Dragon would be receiving an order from Zalghar, when it was time to attack. With this done Zalghar sent a further spell into the Dragon which caused the Dragon to go into a partial trance. The Dragon looked very relaxed, after the spell was put on him. The Dragon looking somewhat tired, laid down and put its large head on it's front legs and rested.

Zalghar had then taken his men and walked to the face of the ridge, which put them in clear view of the Elfen Village. With some of the warriors pointing downwards and some of the warriors firing arrows at the village. The Haddrons had made themselves very visible, and in fact from this distance, they did resemble Humans. Once the Haddrons were sure they had been seen by some of the Elves who were pointing back in their direction, they moved off to the place which Zalghar had told them to tether their Kilpacx earlier.

When they all arrived back at the location where the Kilpacx had been tethered the band of Haddron warriors immediately circled their Kilpacx. As a few of the warriors formed a protection circle, Zalghar quickly and without saying anything further, went into his trance. The remaining Haddrons who were not part of the protection circle, went to the edge of the ridge in clear view of the village of WynnFred then they began firing more arrows.

Zalghar's first concern was to send the message to the Dragon to begin it's attack on the village. Once this was done he came out of this trance and with a slight smile on his face, he went immediately into another trance. This trance was the kind of trance which Zalghar needed to send out the 'Spirit Eye.' After the message had been sent from Zalghar to the Dragon, the huge and now vicious beast had quickly come out of the trance which Zalghar had placed on it earlier. This large Dragon had then suddenly went into an induced vicious fighting mood. The huge beast with a loud snarl, had flown into the air and had started flying downwards from the ridge to begin attacking the Eleven town below.

Zalghar had remained sitting down on the ground with his knees bent, with arms across his knees and he remained still deep into his trance. At this time the 'Spirit Eye' which had been sent by Zalghar, was just arriving at the Elf village.

The Dragon was just beginning it's attack as the 'Spirit Eye' arrived.

The 'Spirit Eye," saw the flames from the Dragon, smashing down and burning the main gate. Then the 'Eye' also observed the Dragon starting to burn houses.

The Dragon was actually trying to burn some of the Elves who were starting to shoot arrows at it. The 'Spirit Eye,' also observed that the arrows from the Elves of the village were having little or no affect on the Dragon.

Shortly after the commencement of the Dragon's attack on WynnFred and after considerable damage to the village, the 'Spirit Eye' saw an arrow, which seemed different. This different type of arrow had hit the Dragon deep in the chest. The message from the 'Eye,' being received by Zalghar, at this time was showing the Dragon beginning to slow up.

Then the 'Eye' had observed, just shortly after the Dragon had been hit by the strange looking arrow, the Dragon's ability to fly had been changed considerably. The Dragon soon started to weave and dip in the sky. This was just before this magnificent beast had started to come crashing towards the ground.

Then the 'Eye' had observed the Dragon's uncontrolled decent suddenly starting to slow. The huge Dragon seemed to just float very slowly to the ground. Then as the smoke had cleared out partially, the 'Spirit Eye' could then recognize some Humans and an Elf. These were the same Humans and Elf who where present when the arrow hit the Kilpacx in the eye the night before at the Human city of Garriton.

The Spirit Eye hovered over the town for a short while longer. The 'Eye,' remained in place and just after the Dragon was being trained by Salbuk the 'Spirit Eye' was ordered by Zalghar, to travel further. The 'Spirit Eye' had then been sent further down the main road to make a complete view of everything which was ahead of Zalghar and the Haddron warriors. The information at this time which had been received by Zalghar, would form a good deal of Zalghar's future plans.

As Zalghar was coming out of his trance he immediately started thinking of everything which had happened and which had been shown to him by the 'Eye.' He started to get very angry as he growled. "Leave it to a Dragon to mess everything up."

He had said this out loud but mostly to himself. "Those Adjemirians who had come to the aid of the people of Garriton and now this Elfen village are really starting to upset my plans." Zalghar was gritting his teeth in anger.

After the Attack on WynnFred

It had been at this time when Zalghar decided that he should not get mad, but he should get even. Zalghar, as he came out of his trance, while nodding his head in the direction of WynnFred spoke to his warriors. "Yes, we should get even."

The 'Spirit Eye,' had sent a vision back to Zalghar, showing both an Elf town and a Human town further down the road. These towns were of great interest to Zalghar. These two villages or cities, were considerably larger than the village of WynnFred and Zalghar knew that they must be very close to the Human and Elfen border. Zalghar had then thought to himself, this information would even make matters easier for his new plan to work. A strategy was coming into Zalghar's mind which made him smile and soon, while looking straight towards the sky he started to laugh out very loudly. He thought to himself that he should have thought of this earlier. His Haddron warriors all looked in his direction and they all knew that something important was about to happen.

Zalghar was thinking over the reasons why his original plan had not worked on this Elf village, but with just a few changes, his plan would surely work on these two larger cities which were just a little further down the road. Again he had wondered why he had not thought of this earlier.

Feeling real good about his new idea, Zalghar had then spoken out loud. "This plan is brilliant. Yes. Brilliant."

The 'Spirit Eye,' when it had traveled down the road and when it was viewing the Elf town on the boarder of the Human's territory had gathered some very valuable information. This town looked well defended and upon entering the town, the 'Spirit Eye' had observed a large amount of well armed and well disciplined Elfen soldiers. The 'Spirit Eye' also viewed a meeting with what looked like some very senior officers, in the middle of the garrison. This Elven town's name was Domerge.

The Spirit Eye, after only a short while at this Elfen city, had then flown across the boarder and then across a large valley. The 'Eye' had flown into the Human's territory where for a short time it observed the fairly large Human city. In this city there was very large castle, which was also very well fortified. This city was called LousBeckt. It was at this time that the 'Sprit Eye' had then spent some considerable time looking throughout all of the Human's Garrison.

The 'Eye' had entered the Castle grounds and spent some time hovering over some soldiers who where exercising in the middle of the garrison. When the 'Eye' finally went inside the castle the 'Eye, had observed a Human nobleman, who looked very important.

"Yes this is perfect!" Zalghar had said to himself, after the 'Spirit Eye' had returned to his body. He then told his men to make camp and get lots of rest. He also said to his warriors that the Kilpacx should get something to eat at which time he instructed which Haddrons should stand guard. Before the Haddrons started to bed down to sleep for the night Zalghar told his warriors he had a very interesting plan and he would tell them all about this plan in the morning.

Early the next morning Zalghar woke before the Haddron warriors were up and around. After Zalghar checked the guards on the perimeter of the camp he then turned back into the camp and he sat by himself, on a large rock in the middle of the sleeping warriors. It was early in the morning when he had spent considerable time rethinking the plan for his next battle. It was still very dark outside.

While he was alone at this time, he also took into consideration, the fact that he and his men were being followed by the troublesome and small group of mixed warriors. Zalghar knew these pests would have to be stopped very soon, but he would not turn to fight them yet. Zalghar knew he could set up an ambush later but right now he had bigger plans on his mind. Yet in the back of his thoughts he was wondering how the two Humans, the Elf and the Dwarf, who carried the war axe with his Rune symbol on it, had become so powerful.

The war axe had been a weapon placed in Darmonarrow by Zalghar himself, prior to the attack on Darmonarrow and Zalghar remembered not being able to utilized it during the attack. The axe had temporarily disappeared or at least it had been out of his immediate power range. He had been unable to activate the war axe by voice or even by a magic spell. He now thought everything would be all right, because he could use the war axe at a later time of his choosing. If the troublesome group got too close then the war axe could easily complete it's task.

Clearly, neither the Humans, the Elfen Archer, nor the Dwarf knew that they had an enemy war axe in their midst. Zalghar was convinced that he would have to pay more attention to this group who were following him and his warriors at a later time, but not right now. He had some very important war games to play, with the Human city and the Elf city which he had observed earlier with the 'Spirit Eye.' The band of warriors which were following them could wait.

The Plan

Just thinking about the plans he had for the day, brought an evil smile to his face and he began to chuckle as he walked slowly out to where the guards were. Zalghar was thinking to himself that this should be a very interesting day. And then he repeated his thoughts out loud. "Yes. This should be a very interesting day. A very interesting day indeed."

It was still dark as he told the guards to get all the others up at which time he went quietly and sat on the same rock which he had sat on earlier. He kept going over his plan in his mind. When everyone was up and about and while they were just finishing eating their meal he summoned them to gather around. "Okay here's the plan." Nodding his head as he began. "This is how it goes."

Waving his hand to his left he said. "You six. I will turn your Kilpacx into Adjemirian horses temporarily and you will attack a large Elf town just a short distance up the road." Zalghar did not know the name of the Elfen town which he was going to attack next but, the name of this town he would find out later was actually called Domerge. Zalghar then went on talking about his plan. "You must be dressed like Humans and make sure you kill enough soldiers in the town to really make them mad."

Making sure that he had his warriors complete attention, Zalghar paused for a moment as he looked over his men. When he was satisfied that all were still listening he continued. "There is also some very powerful looking Elfen commanders or something like that in the garrison. I will prepare some Rune enhanced arrows and make sure that you kill or injure some or all of these Commanders."

The men were nodding that they understood as Zalghar continued. "Remember. And this is most important." Again Zalghar paused to make sure that every warrior had understood. "While this is going on you must always appear to be Human." Then Zalghar also said. "I will add some more power to your protection shields so that no harm will come to you."

Then turning partly around Zalghar started on the next part of his plan. "You six." He pointed to the other six Haddrons to his right. "You will disguise yourselves as Elves and I will also temporarily turn your Kilpacx into horses. You will cross the boarder from the Elves territory close to where a Human city is. In this city there is a fairly large castle."

Zalghar was drawing a rough map in the dirt by his feet. "You are to attack the Human guards at the front gate but don't kill everyone. Okay?"

The Haddrons to his right all nodded their heads and they were starting to understand where Zalghar's plan was going to take this battle. Most were thinking that this was going to be a lot of fun as some of the Haddrons were starting to smile knowingly amongst themselves. Nodding again to the group at his right, the group who were going to enter the Human's city, he then told them the rest of the plan.

Zalghar said. "I will give you extra powers, so that you can send a very strong energy bolt at the front gate. I will also enhance all of your shields of protection." After a short pause Zalghar continued. "You must carry this plan out in a very short time because I will be using a tremendous amount of my magic powers, just to turn the Kilpacx into ordinary horses. Therefore I will be almost completely unprotected from all the magic which I will have to use, until these tasks are complete." Then in a deeper voice Zalghar repeated himself. "So all this must happen very quickly."

Then Zalghar went on explaining the main interest in the attack on the Human's city. "When you make your way into the town I want you to go directly to the castle. In this Castle you will find a old nobleman who lives there. He seems to be very important and he is also very well liked." At this time Zalghar slowly went on in a matter of fact tone. "Capture him and take him to the town square. Make lots of noise once you have left the castle."

Zalghar knew that he still had the complete attention of these warriors so he continued. "Be sure as many Humans as possible are able to see all this happen." Then he paused as he looked over these fighters. "Do you understand?"

The Haddrons on his right nodded showing that they understood all that was being said. "I want you to kill this nobleman right in front of the entire Garrison. Now if this works the way I think it should then both the Humans and the Elves will want revenge."

A slight but evil smile came to Zalghar's face as he continued. "If these two cities have such large armies as the 'Eye' has seen, then there should be a large battle between the armies of these two races."

There was a glint in the eye's of Zalghar while he continued speaking to these fighters. "It will make our job a lot easier. Let the Humans kill a bunch of Elves and at the same time the Elves will kill a large number of Humans."

Then Zalghar added with even a more vicious and evil grin on his face. "Maybe those Humans who are following us with the powerful weapons will get killed by getting mixed up in the war."

Then chuckling Zalghar added. "We shall see." In a business like fashion Zalghar continued on. "If the men who are following us do not get killed in the battle then I have another plan for them."

At this time Zalghar got back to discussing the strategy of having the two races fight each other. "Use no magic, especially Haddron magic. Or the disguises may not work."

Zalghar looked around and was waiting for any questions just in case some of the fighters did not understand all of the plan but there were no questions asked by any of the warriors. At this time Zalghar changed the subject a little bit.

Zalghar, speaking loudly to all the warriors ordered the Kilpacx to be brought to him. When all the Kilpacx, were brought in real close, Zalghar told all of the warriors to stand well back as he said. "I am going to use a tremendous amount of magic energy to make the changes to the Kilpacx and if something goes wrong you may get changed also." Then Zalghar explained things further. "If you get caught in this spell, I might not be able to change you back into your original form. So as I have said earlier, make sure you stand well back."

Zalghar nodded that he was finished as he said. "Now you can all step well back from the Kilpacx and I will change them all into Adjemirian horses at the same time."

The large Kilpacx were all brought into a very close circle surrounding the still sitting Zalghar. Once all of the Kilpacx were in place and Haddron warriors were well back, Zalghar started to bring his magic energies forth in order to change these huge beasts. First, there was a bluish mist which formed slowly around Zalghar. The group of large Kilpacx were watching Zalghar and this bluish mist with a interested curiosity. Then as the mist started to surround all of the Kilpacx and they were forced to breath in the mist, fear started to grow in their huge eyes. The nostrils of all these animals started to flare open, their eyes grew larger and they were all blinking rapidly. The closest Kilpacx tried to move away but part of the spell, had made them immobile and none of these huge beast was able to even lift a foot. Therefore none of the Kilpacx were able to move away. The ground around the Kilpacx started to shake violently.

    All of the Kilpacx slowly pointed their large heads upwards into the morning sky and started to roar at exactly the same time. The roaring by these large frightened beasts became so intense that even the Haddron warriors who were well back and watching the transformation, were forced to cover their ears. There was now a loud cracking noise coming from the ground immediately around the Kilpacx and the watching Haddrons, moved back even further. The Kilpacx had raised their heads higher into the sky and the roaring continued even louder. Sparks were flying all around this group of Kilpacx and the noises from these beasts and the cracking noises unbelievably became even louder.

    Then suddenly the Kilpacx started to change into Adjemirian horses. The blue mist was becoming thicker and it now it had completely engulfed all of the Kilpacx. The blue mist was starting to move around the group of Kilpacx like a large whirlpool. At this time the Kilpacx heads started to grow smaller and the sound of the loud roaring was being replaced with the loud whinnying of a horse.

    The mist which surrounded the entire group was now swirling at a very fast rate of speed. All the noises from these large animals and from the magic energy which was being used by Zalghar was now turning into a loud and thunderous roar, of Kilpacx sounds mixed with the whinnying of horses. The bodies of the Kilpacx changed next and quickly behind the changes to the Kilpacx's bodies, the gigantic tail of the Kilpacx was being reduced and replaced with the tails of Adjemirian horses. It seemed like a very long time but the entire changes to these huge beasts only took the matter of a few minutes.

    When all these changes were complete the blue mist instantly disappeared and there were now twelve Adjemirian horses standing in the space, which the giant Kilpacx had just occupied. All became quiet within seconds.

    Zalghar still had his Kilpacx tethered in the woods.

Attack On LousBeckt

It was early in the morning, just before it turned light outside and in order to be able to surprise the guards at the Human's city called LousBeckt six of Zalghar's Haddron warriors who were disguised as Elves, approached the main gate. Once the warriors were in position they shot arrows at the guards patrolling the walls. These arrows were designed to injure but not necessarily to kill. As it had been planned.

When the warriors, who were disguised as Elves had shot the arrows at the guards near the main gate and the Haddron who was in the lead smashed the main gate with a magic fire ball, the fight and the plan, were in full swing. The six Haddron warriors rode their Adjemirian looking horses's quickly through the front gate. The disguised warriors started to attack any remaining Human guards who had not been injured by the first incoming salvo of arrows.

There were not that many guards on watch at this time and therefore it made the attack on the front gate much easier. After the Human guards at the front gate were stopped and could not be of any threat to the attacking warriors and before the entire city woke up, the disguised Haddrons, as quickly as possible headed directly for the Castle of LousBeckt. As had been the plan by Zalghar, the Haddrons knew exactly where to search for the nobleman. All this did not take the warriors a very long time because the castle was situated very close to the front gate of the city.

As the Haddrons disguised as Elves, rode through the court yard and up to the castle itself, none of them spoke. The secondary gate was open and the six disguised warriors quickly rode straight through and continued following the directions which had been given to them by Zalghar. Five of the Haddrons dismounted and ran straight through the hall and turned left. One of the Haddrons remained mounted and watched their mounts outside.

Once inside the castle the Haddrons without any hesitation, ran up a spiral stair case to the second floor. The Haddrons found the Nobleman still in his bedroom, exactly where Zalghar told them he would be. The Nobleman was just in the process of getting up when the Haddrons entered his bedroom. The noise from the front gate had woken him and he was just going to go to the window to see what had made all of this noise.

The nobleman was an older man and was somewhat frail. He could not resist the attack by the powerful Haddrons and he was still dressed in his sleeping cloths. The nobleman raised his voice and said. "What are you Elves doing here?" Then the Nobleman quickly added while shaking his head in disbelief and asking in a questioning tone of disbelief. "We have a signed peace treaty with your people, so I don't know what you are doing here."

The disguised Haddrons said nothing, but just grabbed the Nobleman fiercely by both arms and with considerable force, they quickly pushed the old nobleman out the door. Then the Haddron warriors quickly turned and went rapidly down the castle stairs. Once the Haddrons were back with the warrior waiting outside with the horses and just before mounting, two of the Haddrons quickly tied a rope tightly around the Nobleman's neck.

The Haddrons then started trotting their animals back towards the front gate. The town square and the nobleman's castle were situated right beside the front gate. Therefore it was not a great distance for the Haddrons to travel back to the cities entrance. While all this was happening the Nobleman was able to run for a short distance behind the horses, but then he fell. The Haddron who was riding the horse which was pulling the nobleman, started to laugh out loud and he made his disguised horse run faster. The Nobleman with the rope still tied tightly around his throat was then dragged the rest of the way. The Nobleman's hands had not been tied so he was able use his hands to hold onto the rope, in order to keep the noose from getting tighter, around his neck while he was being dragged.

When the Haddrons had returned to the town square and were now very close to the main gate, the frail Nobleman although grasping for air was still alive. The nobleman who still had the rope around his throat was trying to loosen the noose. A large crowd was starting to gather but nobody could do anything because the Nobleman, was now like a hostage. None of the town's citizens or the soldiers, were able to attack these disguised Haddrons.

One of the Haddron warriors had quickly jumped from his disguised horse, ran over and pulled the mumbling weakened Nobleman to his feet. Viciously and brutally the Haddron warrior placed a very large dagger against the Nobleman's throat. The Nobleman while in great pain, was forced to stand on his tip toes in order to keep from being cut by the knife. All this was happening very quickly and a crowd of still half asleep citizens and some garrison soldiers from LousBeckt were starting to get even larger. It seemed that the entire city was now awake and everybody, although very sleepy were very curious. Clearly this Human city had been taken completely by surprise by these disguised Elfs.

Some of the towns soldiers from the garrison started to advance and the Haddron holding the Nobleman. With a very loud voice, using as best he could an Elf accent, the Haddron warrior warned the advancing soldiers. "Stay back or I'll kill him."

The Haddron, who continued to keep his knife up against the nobleman's throat, began moving slowly back towards the main gate. The other Haddrons went through the gate just before him, at which time they turned and pointed their bows back towards the crowd and towards the gathering LousBeckt soldiers. The Haddron holding the Nobleman slowly stepped closer to the gate, edging back step by step. By this time nearly the entire town, was awake and were watching. The Haddron with the dagger, pressed it hard against the nobles neck. Then without any notice, but with great force, the Haddron viciously and swiftly pulled the large dagger horizontally across the Nobleman's throat. It was brutal.

A large gasp came from the crowd and the soldiers of LousBeckt who were close enough to see what was happening. Warm blood gushed out of the nobleman's neck and onto the ground as the nobleman began to slump downwards. With every beat of the nobleman's heart more blood spilled onto the older nobleman's chest and onto the darkening ground.

The attacker dropped the nobleman quickly, turned and darted through the gate towards his disguised horse. His mount had been held by another Haddron. As Haddron warrior was quickly moving towards his mount, the disguised Haddron warriors immediately released all of their arrows into the crowd. There was considerable confusion by the citizens and soldiers of LousBeckt.

Then the Haddrons just quickly turned and rode swiftly away.

Most citizens and soldiers from LousBeckt had just woken up and were just starting to understand that a terrible thing had just happened. All of the people of this city were very saddened and also very infuriated by the killing of the nobleman Kurrest by the attacking Elves. But the sadness of the citizens quickly turned into a strong, vicious rage and anger. All the citizens and soldiers who had witnessed the killing of the nobleman were talking amongst them selves, about what had happened.

One senior Human officer, a Captain, yelled in a loud and angry voice. "We will get even with those Elves." Then in an even louder voice, so all who were present could hear. "We must get a message to General Karridhen, as quickly as we can."

At this last statement there was a complete murmur of approval. The Captain then turned to one of his aides and said. "Get me at least six messengers as soon as you are able too."

Attack on Domerge

Meanwhile, at just about the same time as the attack on the city of LousBeckt, across the border in the Elf city of Domerge, a similar thing was also taking place. The Haddrons who were disguised as Humans had snuck up to the main gate just before daylight and ambushed the guards who were guarding the wall. The main gate had been smashed by power bolts which had been sent by all the attacking Haddrons at exactly the same time. Poof there was no more gate.

The disguised Haddrons were able to enter the city, riding their disguised horses without any problem because they were protected by a very powerful protection shield, which they had created just before they arrived at the town of Domerge. These disguised Haddrons were able to go directly to the Elfen garrison and they were very safe in their attack. Once the Haddrons were inside the walls and when nearing the Garrison, they very quickly began firing arrows at the Elfen officers, who had been woken by the noise coming from the smashing of the front gate.

The Elfen officers were just starting to come out of their sleeping quarters in the Domerge barracks. The arrows shot by the Haddrons who were disguised as Humans were killing a few officers, but were also wounding many others. All this was happening very quickly and many other soldiers who had been woken up, were also killed in the mayhem. When there was total confusion throughout the city, the Haddron attackers started back towards the main gate but were still firing arrows at a rapid pace, at anything which moved. The arrows which were being shot back at them were having no real effect because of the protection shield which Zalghar's warriors had put in place prior to the attack. This was a special protection shield, where the Haddrons could fire outwards but the Elves could not shoot arrows back at he disguised Haddrons. It took a considerable amount of more magic energy to create this type of protection shield, but at this time it was needed.

When the Haddrons had returned to the main gate, the last Haddron turned to the oncoming soldiers, and yelled, in an very loud faked Human voice. "All you Elves deserve to die just like the stupid animals you are."

The Haddron warrior was waving his bow over his head, while yelling and sneering at the oncoming Elfen soldiers. Both of the attacks, on the Elf city and the Human city were designed to take place at the same time, and this had been accomplished.

Both groups of warriors were supposed to meet up with each other at a designated location on the road between the two cites at almost the same time and this had also been accomplished. When the returning warriors met, all of the warriors turned and formed a line across the road. This was done in order to stop any pursuit by any soldiers from either of the cities, and also they did not want to lead any pursuing soldiers, if there was any pursuit, back to Zalghar.

Even though Zalghar had been situated very close to the Human city of LousBeckt there was a plan to meet in a different location. After a short while the warriors began to relax as it appeared there was to be no pursuit. This fact was important because if there was to be no pursuit, it probably meant that the two cities would actually be planning for war. Just like Zalghar had predicted earlier when he had spoken of this plan. The Haddrons turned and rode slowly to the place where Zalghar said he would be waiting. They were all laughing because it was like Zalghar had told them earlier, it was going to be a lot of fun getting the Humans to fight the Elves. The plan seemed to be working out very well up to this point.

What surprised the warriors more than anything, was that, neither the Elves nor the Humans had put up any fight. Not even in the slightest. The early morning surprise attacks on the two cities had worked out perfectly.

The Haddron Mission is Complete

As the Haddron warriors traveled to the place where Zalghar was waiting, after the attacks on the Elf city of Domerge and the attack on the Human city of LousBeckt were complete, there was a strong feeling of gratification. All the Haddron warriors seemed happy with the plan's success. Zalghar's strategy seemed to be working very well and now they would only have to wait to see if the Humans and Elves would go to war, as Zalghar said they would.

The warriors neared the place where Zalghar said he would meet them and Zalghar slowly walked from his hiding place towards his warriors, looking very tired but showing that he was very satisfied. Zalghar had a relaxed grin on his face as he surveyed the returning warriors. All his men had returned safe and he could tell by the big smiles on their faces that the plan seemed to be working very well and they all seemed happy with the outcome.

Zalghar began by saying. "I need to speak to you all but before we speak, I must turn all these things." He was referring to the disguised horses. "Back into Kilpacx." I am running out of magic because my powers are getting weak and I will have to rest very soon but we need our Kilpacx back first." In a quieter tone Zalghar said. "We may need the Kilpacx to protect us. That is just in case you were followed and if the plan did not work."

All the men nodded towards Zalghar that they had understood. Zalghar continued and he seemed that he was in quite a hurry, as he went on. "Get all the disguised horses into a tight formation and I will turn them back into Kilpacx, again with only the one spell." And in a very serious tone Zalghar repeated what he had said earlier. "We must do this as quickly as possible."

The Haddron warriors did as they were told, and soon all fake horses were gathered together in a tight formation. But before Zalghar walked into the middle of the group of animals he ordered his fighters, as he had done prior, to stand well back in a safe place.

Zalghar did not want his men to be hit accidently with a spell which was meant for the horses, because if a spell which was meant for the horses accidently hit one of his men, he was not really sure what would happen. This spell was going to be very powerful and it might kill a warrior or change him so much that Zalghar was not sure that he could correct a mistake like this.

Once Zalghar was sure that his men were at a safe distance he walked in amongst the horses and sat on the ground in the exact center of the animals. Then Zalghar put his head down onto his crossed arms which were resting on his knees. Very soon, his body started to let out the bluish pulsating energy. As the energy was leaving his body, it quickly became a mist and started to travel towards all the horses. The disguised Adjemirian horses were now starting to gather around Zalghar, with a very curious interest. As the energy touched the horses, their muscles began to twitch and they tried to back away, but just like the Kilpacx earlier, they couldn't. It was as if their feet were made of a very heavy material, or that they were glued to the ground and although they tried, they just couldn't move away.

The blue mist started to swirl and soon the mist was traveling through and around the disguised animals. The eyes of the disguised animals were becoming very large and bulging. At this time the bluish mist was completely surrounding the horses and then the loud noises started again. The noise coming from these animals, was a loud kneeing and whinnying sound.

One by one all of the fake horses put their heads upwards straight towards the sky and next their tails began to flutter uncontrollably. All the fake horses now were letting out a very low screeching sound, as if they were in considerable pain but the Haddrons who were watching weren't sure if these horses were actually in any pain.

First the horses heads started to return to their original state, that of the Kilpacx , and then their front legs began turning back into the Kilpacx front legs. The bodies started to enlarge, to their original size and the tails were the last to return. The entire transformation only took a few minutes to complete. In the place of the fake horses now stood the original forms of the very vicious Kilpacx.

The Haddron warriors close by were able to notice that the Kilpacx after this spell was completing, knew instantly that the Kilpacx were hungry. For some unknown reason the spell had given the Kilpacx an enormous appetite. The Haddron warriors who were still watching from a safe distance seemed very impressed. The magic spell which Zalghar had to make, to change the horses back into Kilpacx, although took a much shorter time than it took to change the Kilpacx into Adjemirian horses, must have taken an enormous amount of energy.

Some of the warriors wondered to themselves, as to whether or not this tremendous use of magic energy might kill Zalghar. The Haddrons could see Zalghar's body shaking violently as the power for the spell was passing through him. Clearly those observing Zalghar while he was under this spell, knew that the reversal of the spell, which had turned the Kilpacx into horses, was now requiring considerable more energy. Probably because the Kilpacx are so much bigger than Adjemirian horses, there was more magic power required.

When all the horses had been successfully turned back into the original form of the Kilpacx and once the Haddron warriors were certain that it was safe, they cautiously came closer at which time they slowly helped Zalghar to his feet. All of the Haddron warriors could easily tell that Zalghar was getting very low on energy as he was looking really weak. Zalghar, while being helped up stood somewhat wobbly amongst his warriors, as he said. "Get me to a place where I can sit and rest."

The warriors closest to Zalghar looked around and then helped him walk slowly over to a large rock, so he could sit and rest while he was going to speak to them. Once Zalghar was sitting all the Haddrons gathered around him. The Haddrons with smiles on their faces who attacked the Human city of LousBeckt were on Zalghar's left. They began to tell their story about the attack on LousBeckt first.

Once they were finished, looking to his right Zalghar nodded towards the group who had attacked the Elf city Domerge. With great excitement these Haddrons told all that had happened in their attack on the Garrison.

After hearing from both of these groups of warriors, Zalghar spoke softly. "Great work. This went exactly as planned!" Then looking very tired, Zalghar nodding his head in acknowledgment quickly went on. "Now with a little luck they should play right into our hands." Zalghar exclaimed upon hearing the details of the attacks. "This should work out perfectly ."

Zalghar then quickly changed the subject. He went on to say as he was thinking, looking off into the distance and tapping his chin. "Its been a while since the Kilpacx were fed some real food. Right?"

Speaking softly Zalghar said as he was tiredly looking and speaking to the Haddrons closest to him. Zalghar had a distant look in his eyes almost as if he was speaking to himself. "Yes its been about three days now. Time for a real feeding."

In a quiet tired tone Zalghar said. "Help me up."

Speaking to a tall Haddron who had been standing very near to him Zalghar said. "We have some time to spare before the Elves and the Humans get ready for the possible battle between the races." Zalghar had said this in a somewhat cheery but tired tone. "We haven't tried our skills on those Krugs or Dwarves yet have we? We probably do not have time to do both but we can feed the Kilpacx and kill some Krugs or Dwarfs at the same time." Zalghar said this as he was starting to get a little more energy.

Some of the warriors could sense a little bit of excitement in Zalghar's voice. "Which will it be? The Krugs or the Dwarves?" He said to no one in particular.

"I think Dwarves. The short guys should make quite a meal and they probably can't run very fast." This was said by a Haddron who was standing farther back in the pack.

"I vote for Krugs." Another Haddron had spoken up. "They won't put up as much of a fight." Then he quickly added. "We have to save our energy. We don't want to go into a battle weakened by our leisure time, now do we?" There was a chuckle which ran through the warriors after this statement. Another comment came from another Haddron warrior from the back of the pack. "The Krugs will put up the least fight and we should be saving our energy."

"Very good point." Zalghar nodding his head as he agreed. "Now its up to the rest of you." Zalghar asked in a questioning way. "Krugs of Dwarves?"

"Krugs!" Almost all of the Haddrons said at once.

Zalghar was nodding his head with a slight yet evil smile on his face. "Very well there is a Krug village not very far from here."

The 'Spirit Eye' had seen it, when the 'Eye' was last used. In a tired but determined voice Zalghar said to all the warriors. "Lets go!"

Zalghar walked very slowly over to his Kilpacx and started to mount up, with the help from the closest two Haddron warriors.

War Cry, at Domerge

After the disguised Haddrons had left the Elfen city of Domerge, some of the Elders had gathered with all the population who had witnessed the attack. A senior Captain, by the name of Eeando, seemed to take charge almost immediately.

Captain Eeando was an average sized Elf, with plain features. Captain Eeando had extremely light green eyes, high cheek bones, with more freckles than any other Elf in all of Volkjynn. Eeando was very young for a Captain in the Elf army, but he had been well trained and came up through the ranks quite rapidly. Captain Eeando was already dressed in a green Elf officer's uniform, because he had been up early and had just been getting ready for a training session with some new cadets, when the attack on Domerge commenced.

Eeando had not witnessed any of the attack but he had been instantly briefed when he had made it to the attack location. This young officer was very angry as he started to give orders in a very rapid fashion and in a very aggressive manner. He directed his orders to some young messengers who were standing very close. He began speaking loudly but was also pointing at some Elves who were nearest to him. "We must go quickly now to Sorchell, Tarranel, Syvegonn, and WynnFred. We must tell them what has happened here." Then in a louder voice the young Captain said. "Tell the commanders of those cities that Domerge has been attacked by raiding Humans."

Speaking in an even louder voice, Captain Eeando continued on without any interruption. "Tell all that the truce with the Human's has been broken and get Elfen cities and Villages to gather the Grand Elfen Army, as soon as possible. Tell them that we will make the Humans pay for what they have done."

Then Captain Eeando added. "Make sure that the message to Sorchell is given directly to General Charranoid because we will need him to command all the armies. He is the strongest General we have left and he will be able to bring in all the best trained troops to the Red Valley, in the fastest possible way."

The Red Valley, Captain Eeando remembered, was not red at all but the cliffs surrounding this lush green valley, were a bright reddish in color and this is why it became known as the Red Valley.

Then Captain Eeando said in a slightly quieter tone of voice. "You three have our fastest horses so you are our best hope for alerting the other towns in the quickest fashion. Now you two messengers." He said pointing at two other Elf messengers who were standing in the back. "You will go to any Human town and tell them to meet us in the Red Valley within one day." With a very determined and aggressive sound to his voice he added. "Tell them if they do not come to the Red Valley tomorrow then tell them that we will march on their cities." Captain Eeando continued on without any interruption. "The rest of this Garrison will now pack up and march immediately to the Red Valley where we will start constructing our camp. Even if the messengers fail to raise all of the Army I still expect to be ready for battle in one day."

Then looking over his troops Captain Eeando then asked. "Any question?"

All who were present nodded in agreement and this included even the Elders who were present. Although none of the Elves who were present wanted to go to war, this attack on Domerge had to be avenged. About this there was no doubt. Somewhere in the distance from within the city of Domerge, some Elves started to beat their war Drums. All the Elves who were present started to chant. "War!" "War!" "War!"

Turning quickly the messengers were on their way.

LousBeckt After the Haddron Attack

General Karridhen was pacing back and forth. The General was a fairly tall Human with very broad shoulders and because it was early in the morning, he was plainly dressed. He wore a simple light brown tunic, with a large leather belt, synched tightly around his waste. In the sheath on his belt was a large dagger, which had been his father's. This dagger had seen many battles and was very old. The General had steely blue eyes, which when he was concentrating as much as he was at present, showed his intensity. The General's beard had just been trimmed and was very short.

Because of his age and importance he no longer took part in the actual battles, but the scars on his body showed that he had been in many campaigns. It was also known throughout the Human's land of Chesfeld that when the General was younger he had been a fierce fighter. The General it was said had honed his fighting skills at a very young age.

The most serious injury the General ever had was to his right shoulder, where there was a very large scar. This scar came from a spear which was thrown at him in his younger days, when he had been in a battle with a fierce group of Krugs. The injury had almost killed the young Karridhen. The injury had been so severe, it was said, that the spear could not be removed by pulling it out of the young man's shoulder, but could only be pushed all the way through his body and out the other side. All those who had been present at the time when the spear injury to Karridhen had happened and who witnessed the removal of the spear remembered. As the spear was being pushed through the young soldier, he had never even made a sound. Rumor through the Human's land of Chesfeld soon spread, as to just how tough this young soldier was.

When Karridhen had been a young soldier it was said that he had such an incredibly intense stare. This was true, even after he had been promoted to a General in the Human's army. The General's intense stare remained intensely strong. While he was pacing back and forth nobody who was present even looked up, or made a sound as he yelled. "I can't believe you men couldn't kill those Elves. They just rode into LousBeckt and killed the nobleman, Kurrest!"

All the soldiers from the Garrison had gathered around and most were shocked and embarrassed. They all had their heads hung down and they just continued to stare at the ground. The Human General continued bellowing at the guards. The General had not witnessed the early morning attack on LousBeckt because he lived in a place at the other end of the city and he never made it to the Garrison, until well after the attackers had departed.

General Karridhen had been pacing back and forth in front of all the men who had gathered after the attack, and he continued yelling at them. When he noticed that they had all hung their heads, he then realized that they were not to blame. It appeared that the Elves had been lucky with this surprise attack on LousBeckt. The General started to calm down but continuing to speak out loud he said. "It appears that the Elves have declared war on us."

The General paused and was looking off into the distance in the general direction of Domerge. Then he continued. "We must have a strategy and must gather a very large army as fast as we can."

All the citizens and all the soldiers who were present nodded their heads. There was some murmuring but nobody spoke. There was a quiet determination amongst all of the people at the gathering.

Just then a messenger came up behind the General and tapped him on the shoulder. The General quickly turned to the messenger, who, when he saw the General's scowling mood, just like a large Dragon gone mad, involuntarily stepped back a few paces and just stood there nervously. For a few moments General Karridhen glared at the messenger through squinted eyes. Then the General said in a calmer quieter tone. "What is it?" He asked questioningly. The General at this time seemed very tired.

Then the messenger said. "General there are two Elf messengers on the hill just south of LousBeckt and they said some Humans attacked their city of Domerge this morning." The messenger

The Nine Moons of Adjemir

paused to take a breath and the General thinking that the messenger was not finished, waited impatiently for him to continue. The messenger paused before finishing the message. He was looking at the ground, kicking at the dirt at his feet and scratching the back of his head, while concentrating on getting all the message correct. Clearly the messenger did not like giving this part of the message to the General and the young messenger was very uncomfortable. Then the messenger quickly blurted out the rest of the message. "Apparently the Elves are gathering a large Army right now and they will be in the Red Valley ready to do battle, first thing tomorrow morning." The messenger quickly went on as his voice grew louder and more excited. "They said if we do not meet them in the Red Valley tomorrow morning, then they will march their armies against our cities and our villages. They will start their attack on LousBeckt first."

After hearing this General Karriden stood quietly but only for a moment. It looked like he was going over the information which had just been delivered and then with a renewed energy he turned to his soldiers and began to speak. "I have no idea what the Elves are talking about and I do not know of any Human attacks on their city of Domerge. I think they are lying just to start something."

Then the General went on. "They are the ones who came in the night and killed Kurrest. If the Elves are looking to start a war." The General roared in an even louder voice while shaking his fist at the sky. "Then so be it." He went on with an even stronger voice. "They could have started a war without this attack on LousBeckt. Those Elves killed Kurrest in his bed cloths and this alone is very insulting." General Karridhen was pacing up and down in front of the soldiers and he was starting to get even redder in the face.

His men had never seen him like this before. The General continued to get louder until he was actually shouting so loud that he actually began to loose his voice. "This attack on LousBeckt must be avenged." The General waved a fist at the sky again. Almost immediately a roar of approval went up from the crowd. "I want all the messengers and scouts in the Garrison, to report to me right here, right now."

Speaking to all who were present, but the orders were directed towards the messengers. General Karridhen stated the following. "I want riders in pairs to ride to the towns Garriton, Divatz, and Shalatok. The message will be about this Elf attack on LousBeckt. Tell these other cities that the Elves have just murdered Kurrest. And these war challenges by the Elves must be delivered to those cities as fast as possible."

The General was beginning to get quieter but he continued. "Tell those in charge of those cities that we must be made ready for battle in the Red Valley, at daylight tomorrow. And we will need as many soldiers as possible, with full armament."

Then softening his voice even more, the General continued. "Now after you have delivered this message to these towns then I want you ride to every Village nearby to those cities and tell them what has happened."

The General added. "Im not sure just yet what to do but we must have a very large army ready as soon as we can get to the Red Valley. Be sure to bring them up to speed that there is going be a battle." Then as an afterthought the General said. "Tell them that the Fort from LousBeckt cannot field such a large Army. But we are going to the Red Valley and we will stop those damned Elves from attacking any Human Villages. This is war." With a wave of the General's arm the messengers started out on their assignments.

The Captains who were present turned and went directly to their headquarters to start the marching arrangements of the army, which was in the garrison. As he was walking away, in the back of the General's mind, there were questions. The questions which was nagging the General were.

"What made the Elves want to start this war? And why did some Humans attack Domerge?"

He had no knowledge of any attack being planned against the Elves. Not really knowing what had happened at Domerge this morning he just shook his head as he followed his Captains towards the Garrison's offices.

Zalghar Waits

After the attacks on Human city of LousBeckt and the attack on t he Elf Town of Domerge, Zalghar had known that he would have to rest. His magical powers would need considerable time to replenish. His body was tired and he also knew that his troops would need some rest also.

As the Haddrons started to travel towards Krugland, Zalghar recalled when his 'Spirit Eye' had been sent out the last time it had seen a Krug Village. The Krugs called this village, Theoris. The Village of Theoris is located in a Valley called Dorrall and it is in a very dark forest just inside the boarder of Krug land.

Thinking to himself Zalghar had felt all along that his troops would enjoy some fun. It had also been his thought that it was near the time for the Kilpacx to be fed. The Kilpacx could eat grass and grains while traveling, but it was meat that they really enjoyed the most. Besides fresh meat would give them extra energy. Fresh meat also made them better fighters. Zalghar also knew that any time now he would have to have a big battle which would put even more fear into the peoples of the land of Adjemir. So the Kilpacx would have to be at their best and a good feeding was what these large animals needed.

Zalghar's plans were going really well, except for losing the Kilpacx at Garriton and a few men along the way, he felt that there was not much opposition to his conquering all the races in this land called Adjemir. Except for the two Humans, the Elf and that Dwarf, who were following him and his Haddron troops, there was very little in Adjemir for him and his warriors to worry about.

He would deal with those who were following him very shortly and in good time, but at present his immediate concerns were to save energy and to rest his men and the Kilpacx. He would look after feeding the Kilpacx and resting himself as much as he could, but he was also rather anxious to send out the 'Spirit Eye.' Zalghar really wanted very much to send out the 'Spirit Eye,' mostly so he could see if his plan to get the Humans fighting the Elves, had worked.

Deep down inside Zalghar knew that the Dwarves would be easily conquered because they did not build big armies and had very little in the way of Dragons or machinery in which allow them to become a dangerous enemy. So he felt that he did not have worry very much about the Dwarves of Adjemir. Zalghar also knew that Dwarves did not have any magic so the Dwarves ability to fight him and his Haddron warriors would be very limited.

The Krugs did not seem to pose much of a problem and Zalghar knew that the use of the Kilpacx plus a little of his magic would make short work out of any type of Krug army that could be brought against him and his Haddron warriors.

"Yes." Zalghar said to the Haddron on his right as they were traveling along. "If my plan works the Humans and the Elves could easily cancel each other out. This whole thing could be very interesting. We may only have to mop up any stragglers."

The Haddron warrior just smiled and nodded in Zalghar's direction, meaning he agreed with this idea. Zalghar was also thinking as he looked down at his hands that this little rest was already doing him some good, as he was starting to feel his magic powers returning. After about two hours Zalghar and his men had just topped a small hill above a clearing. They were all looking down into a small quiet Krug Village. It was the Krug Village of Theoris. Zalghar looked towards his men and nodded. Without any strategy the twelve mounted Haddron warriors charged into the Krug village on the hungry Kilpacx. Using no magic and very little use of hand weapons by the Haddrons, the giant Kilpacx took care of most matters by using their powerful teeth and their long tails. There was going to be very little opposition.

Zalghar was watching the battle from above on the hill and he had a cruel and very vicious smile on his face. He noticed with satisfaction and pride that one of the larger Kilpacx, whom the Haddron rider had dismounted from was smashing houses with it's huge tail. Then as the Krugs tried to escape from their homes this Giant Kilpacx was viciously biting the Krugs in two. Swallowing the pieces with only a few shakes of it's gigantic head and a few powerful gulps. The escaping Krugs who were running away, were running with such fear that they were unable to protect themselves. The Haddrons who were on foot, seemed to be having fun practicing with their weapons.

Dead Krugs, mostly women and children were lying about all over the place. For the Kilpacx, the Krug villagers made a very easy meal. Deep down Zalghar understood after this Village of Theoris was destroyed, the Kilpacx would be well fed. Also his Haddron troops should be well rested and relaxed.

"Mission accomplished." He said out loud to himself.

After all of the Kilpacx had eaten well enough, some of the riders gathered them in and they started returning to the hill top where Zalghar was waiting. Zalghar told one of the Haddron warriors to take his personal Kilpacx down to the smashed village of Theoris and let him have some time to feed on the dead Krugs.

At this time Zalghar walked over to a large log and sat down to rest. After the last of the Krugs fled into the woods, the remaining Haddrons turned around and set fire to the remainder of this Krug Village. When Zalghar was sure that all of his warriors had returned to the hill above the village, Zalghar said that he now had enough power returned to enable him to use his 'Spirit Eye.' The Haddron troops obediently gathered around so Zalghar could utilize the 'Eye.' Zalghar wanted the eye to bring back information on just how well his plan to get the Humans fighting the Elves was working.

The information received by Zalghar from the 'Eye,' was good. The Humans and Elf armies had started to gather and both armies were traveling off to the Red Valley, in preparation for war.

The Grand Elf Army Comes to the Red Valley

After young Captain Eeando from the city of Domerge had sent off his messengers, he very efficiently set about gathering all the available troops and war machines which were available. Within the hour Captain Eeando and a formidable Elfen army were marching in column towards the Red Valley.

It was at the Red Valley where he would start setting up the headquarters in preparation for the arrival of General Charranoid.

A young Elf Drummer at the front of the column was beating out a marching rhythm on his war drum. All the Elf soldiers with the exception of a few, were very quiet. The march to the Red Valley would only take about four hours and all the troops were marching in a well organized fashion. Captain Eeando turned in his saddle and looked back on his men. The look on his face showed he was extremely satisfied because he knew that his men had been very efficient at getting ready for this hurried march.

Captain Eeando could feel the determination amongst his troops and was very satisfied regarding the confidence coming from all the soldiers who were traveling with him. He turned and looked forward as the column was coming onto a straight portion of the road and he could see the coordination of the marching rhythm. Deep down he felt pride in how well these troops had been trained.

Thinking ahead, Captain Eeando knew that once these troops arrived at the Red Valley they would be placed into fighting divisions by General Charranoid. Captain Eeando's, immediate concern was only to get to the Red Valley as fast as he could. At present the Calvary was in the front with a large number of foot soldiers and directly behind Captain Eeando's position where he was riding in the column, the remainder of the soldiers just marched wherever they fit in. The more well trained veteran soldiers were always placed in the front of the columns and this was a tradition which had been in place for as long as anybody could remember. In soldier terms, it was a sign of respect for the senior veterans to march at the front of the column.

As Captain Eeando turned his attention back towards the front of the column, he began to think about whether or not General Charranoid was already marching to the Red Valley. General Charranoid, Eeando recalled, had led the Elf Armies into battle for as long as Captain Eeando could remember. Captain Eeando smiled to himself, as he could still remember when he first saw General Charranoid. It was when the General entered the Garrison in Syvegonn many years ago, where Eeando had been traveling with his father. Eeando was very young at this time.

The entire place had become completely quiet. It was as if some mighty god had just entered. All Elves in the land of Volkjynn held General Charranoid in the highest regard and although General Charranoid never showed any emotion regarding the esteemed position he held in the army, he appreciated and respected all of the confidence which was bestowed upon him from all the Elves in general population. It was known throughout the land of Volkjynn that no greater General had ever led the Elfen Grand Armies into battle. About this was no doubt.

While Captain Eeando was marching his troops to the Red Valley, some of the messengers at just about the same time were starting to arrive at the different locations. Once the messenger from Domerge arrived at the Elfen city of Syvegonn and with the urgency of the information about the attack on the city of Domerge, the messenger had been sent directly to General Charranoid's office, which was situated in the Garrison at Syvegonn. At the time of the arrival of the messenger from Domerge the General was going over some documents which were on his desk. When the knock came to his door the had General glanced over his reading glasses and said, in a slightly gruff voice.

"Enter." To his guards.

A guard entered the room and in excited tones, gave the information about the attack on Domerge to the General. General Charranoid stood up calmly and asked the guard, to bring him this messenger immediately.

The Nine Moons of Adjemir

The General was a tall good looking Elf with a long grey hair, sunken cheeks, with very broad shoulders for an Elf. He was dressed in his Generals uniform, which was a well tailored, hand crafted, but plain suit of chain armor. His eyes which were a steely blue, could stare so fiercely, that his enemies usually, could not look him in the face. His helmet which was also hand crafted, but which was also very plain, sat on the corner of his desk. He had very large hands for an older Elf and he also had a very strong grip. He always walked and talked with a great confidence.

When the messenger entered General Charranoid's office, the messenger immediately and quickly bowed to the General. Then the messenger walked quickly towards the General who was now sitting at his desk. In his excitement and from the long ride the messenger from Domerge, started to talk so fast that General Charranoid had trouble completely understanding exactly what the messenger was trying to convey. The General stood up and slowly stepped around his desk towards the messenger. While placing his right hand on the messenger's shoulder with a firm grip, the General said calmly.

"Please." You have to talk slower and give me just the information of what has happened at Domerge so that I can make an accurate assessment of what must be done." With a softening of his voice, the old General tried to make the messenger relax. "I only want the facts and not your opinion. So now, please continue and please try to talk more slowly." The messenger nodded his head, swallowed and waving his left hand in the air, signaled that he understood, swallowed again and took another deep breath. The messenger began to speak in slower softer tones, making sure that he never forgot anything. General Charranoid listened intently to the information as it was given to him. The General never interrupted the messenger, he just stood quietly while looking into the messengers eyes and not showing any emotions at all.

When the General was sure that the messenger was finished, he then asked if the messenger was sure that all the information was accurate and if the messenger was sure that he had not forgotten anything at all. The messenger then thought over everything that he had said to the General, very thoughtfully. Shook his head and said. "I am certain that all the information has been given."

General Charranoid put his arm around the shoulder of the young messenger and while walking him to the door he spoke to the messenger. The General said. "I will want you to go get something to eat and then report back to me within the hour. I want you rested and I will probably send one of my guards with you." Then thinking further the General added. "I will be getting the entire garrison of Syvegonn ready to march to the Red Valley and I will also need some information sent to Captain Eeando. I will not be sending any strategies with you but some other information can be sent with you which might interest Captain Eeando." Then as an after thought the General said in an even softer tone. "I also want to thank you for bringing this message to me and I will ask Captain Eeando to let you fight in my personal guard when we enter the Red Valley."

The messenger knew that this was indeed a great honor, to fight in the General's personal guard and smiled broadly as he thought to himself. " The soldiers back in Domerge will be green with envy."

Then the General said. "Go now. And I thank you very much."

Then the General repeated what he had said earlier. "And be sure to be back to me within the hour."

The General then turned to his personal guard as he said to him. "Bring all officers into the War Room and I want them all here within ten minutes." Then as an after thought General Charranoid went on to say to the guard. "The captain who is in charge of the Ballistas should take fifty soldiers and start transporting all five machines to the Red Valley immediately." Then in a quieter tone he said. "I want these machines to be ready to depart Syvegonn within thirty minutes."

General Charranoid then added. "I will also want all messengers outside the War Room within five minutes." The guard stood quietly and only nodded his head as he was receiving these new instructions. The guard was always amazed at how quickly General Charranoid could start making plans and how fast the army under the General's command could get into action.

The General's personal guard had been with the General for quite some time and he clearly understood that the army of Syvegonn was very efficient, because the General has spent so much time training and retraining the troops. In all of the Elf kingdom of Volkjynn the best trained troops came from the Garrison at Syvegonn.

Repairing WynnFred

Sleeping late at the Inn in the Elfen Village of WynnFred Bobbiur was completely unaware of the morning attacks on the Elfen city of Domerge and the Human city of LousBeckt. When Bobbiur woke up he found the sun was already high in the sky above the Valley, and sun light was shining brightly through his window. Both Salbuk and Hagjel knocked and entered his room. Hagjel shaking his head said. "Wake up sleepy head we are all ready to go."

Hagjel spoke directly at Bobbiur as he said. "Salbuk has already fed the Dragon and Obmar is presently feeding the Spaggidons."

Bobbiur slowly rolled over he opened his eyes completely and he saw Salbuk standing over him with a big friendly smile on his face.

"No." Bobbiur said to Salbuk and Hagjel as he was sitting up in his bed.

Bobbiur was rubbing his eyes to remove the sleep, probably because he had slept so deeply the night before. He stretched and yawned as he moved his feet off the bed to the floor before he spoke. "I had a strange dream last night and for some reason it made me want to stay here and help these Elves to clean and repair the damage to this Village."

"Well how long will that take?" Hagjal turned from where he was looking out the window at the Village below. He was chewing on a piece of very smelly cheese and at the same time he was feeding some small pieces of cheese to Jakka. Bobbiur also noticed that Hagjel had a small pint of ale in his hand.

"I don't know how long we should stay." Bobbiur said. "But we still have to catch Zalghar and the Haddrons, so we shouldn't stay too long."

Then Bobbiur said to Hagjel. "I really wish you would leave the ale alone Hagjel."

Bobbiur said this with a smile on his face knowing that Hagjel would just sneak away with the ale and drink it behind his back. Anyways, Bobbiur thought, it never seemed to bother Hagjel's ability to effectively shoot with his bow.

"So it was no big deal." Bobbiur had thought to himself, as he whispered and shook his head in a slight show of despair.

"It's just something that I must get used to." This thought in the mind of Bobbiur made Salbuk smile to himself. Because Salbuk had caught Bobbiur's thoughts about Hagjel's love for ale.

"You cannot stay the whole day." Said Zorp as he suddenly stepped into the room. "But I do like the fact that your agreeing to stay and help these Elves to do some rebuilding. In fact this was also my idea. Quite the coincidence right?"

Then Zorp went on in a quiet tone. "Builds friendships. If you know what I mean?"

Zorp was just speaking absent mindedly, out loud and to nobody in particular. He was just rambling on and before anybody could say anything, he started talking again. "But you cannot stay very long. You must catch Zalghar as soon as you can. But with the Dragon you should be able to help these Elves quite a bit, fixing their village, in a very short time. As soon as you get some of the big jobs done you will have to go. Is that understood?"

"Okay Zorp." Bobbiur said, smiling over Zorp's head as Bobbiur looked towards the door. "I know you work in strange ways, but for some strange reason I really want to help these Elves to try to fix some things up."

Bobbiur patted Zorp on the shoulder as he was passing him on his way towards the hall. Bobbiur was thinking. "This room is really starting to get just a little too crowded." Bobbiur was rubbing his tummy and speaking to nobody in particular turned into the hall. "I have to go and find something to eat."

"Bobbiur, I know you think I work in strange ways." Zorp said mockingly following Bobbiur down the hall. "But it is all for a good reason and you will start to understand more as time goes along."

Then as Bobbiur turned to say something more to Zorp he saw Zorp put both hands up to his head, as he touched two fingers

The Nine Moons of Adjemir

to both sides of his forehead. Bobbiur noticed that Zorp had pressed his fingers into the sides of his head with considerable pressure and as Zorp winked, he just disappeared. Nothing Zorp did surprised Bobbiur anymore. Bobbiur just shook his head with a slight smile showing at the corners of his mouth as he turned and walked down the hall towards the stairs.

After Bobbiur had finished his breakfast he wandered outside where he saw Hagjel, Salbuk, Obmar, and the Dragon doing a great deal of the heavy work, which he knew the Villagers would have been unable to do, that is without considerable effort. On his right he also noticed a large group of Elfen children had gathered around the Dragon so they could watch this mighty beast, doing some very heavy tasks.

The Dragon, to Bobbiur's surprise seemed to be smiling and between tasks, the Dragon would snuggle up to Salbuk, at which time this huge beast would pester Salbuk until Salbuk would rub the Dragon's ears. Sometime the pestering by the Dragon would become so playful and overpowering the huge beast would actually be nuzzling Salbuk around like a dry leaf blowing in the wind. Bobbiur could not help but notice the huge grin of friendship on Salbuk's boyish face made Salbuk look like he had just gone to heaven. For a moment Bobbiur could not help but compare the friendship between the Dragon and Salbuk, with the relationship between Jakka and Hagjel.

Turning and shaking his head while grinning ear to ear, Bobbiur went to a place beside where Pendahl was assisting a large group of Elves to clean up a big pile of broken bricks. Bobbiur noticed the entire population of the village was hard at work.

A Young Elf Prepares For Battle

Tynek, a tall middle aged Elf with light tan colored hair and chestnut shaped eyes, walked across his living room over to a large mantle which held a blazing fire. He stood by the mantle paused and looked around. "Where is it!" Tynek said to himself as he looked frantically around the room. His eyes stopped as he peered across the room and into the hall, where in the dim light he could see his son Raydhen, sheathing the small dagger. He also noticed the missing bow from off the mantle was slung over his son's shoulder.

"Just where do you think your going!" Tynek yelled across the room.

"A message has been sent." Raydhen paused briefly. There will be a battle in the Red Valley tomorrow." Then Raydhen quickly added. "It's against the Humans." Raydhen now speaking rapidly and loudly said. "I'm going to the Red Valley to fight with the Grand Elfen army."

Raydhen had again paused briefly, looking through squinted eyes for a reaction from his father before he went on. "Domerge has been attacked by some Humans and the Humans' must be made to pay for this."

Quickly Tynek, with a bit of a panic sound in his voice spoke in a sputtering way. "Your not going anywhere. Your not old enough to fight in these kinds of battles." The older Elf was rubbing his forehead with the back of his hand.

Raydhen with a pleading voice said. "Father I am nineteen years old. I think I'm old enough to fight in this battle."

At this time Tynek tried to sound forceful as he said. "No your not old enough. I will not let you!" Reaching out the Tynek said.

"Give me the bow Raydhen!" The older Elf was shaking his head as he started crossing the room towards Raydhen. With an out stretched hand, which had a slight tremble, Tynek reached for the bow.

"You can't stop me father. I'm a grown Elf now and I can make my own decisions." The young Elf started to turn.

"Don't walk out that door Raydhen." In a pleading way, Tynek tried again to stop Raydhen. "I'm your father and I know what's best for you."

With a crisp snapping voice the young Elf spoke decisively to his father. "Just watch me father!" Raydhen quickly walked out the door.

Tynek limped to the door and just watched Raydhen leave. He saw his son's departure with mixed feelings. As a father he was greatly worried.

Raydhen had walked out of the yard and as he was just starting to climb the small hill in front of their house, when he turned and waved.

Raydhen yelled. "Good bye father." To Tynek.

Tynek with a tear in his eye, waved back and yelled. "Good luck my son." But Tynek was sure that Raydhen did not hear him because he was walking quite fast and was probably just out of hearing range. Tynek had to admit to himself that since Raydhen's mother had died, he had become overly protective of his only child Raydhen. At the same time, he could not help having a strong feeling of pride which was coming on because his son Raydhen had volunteered to go into battle against the Humans. His son was showing that he was fast becoming an adult Elf. Tyneck then thought to himself that if he did not have this limp then he would go with his son and help in the up and coming battle. But his injury was such that, he would be of little help on the battle field and he knew this only to well.

As he saw his son walking down the road and just as he was starting to disappear over the hill he remembered when he was his son's age and how he first went into battle. Tynek started to feel an even greater pride for his son.

All he could do now was hope that during this battle his son Raydhen would be safe.

A Young Human Prepares For Battle

Aldor stepped out onto his back porch. He was a short well built Human who walked stooped over and could only sort of shuffle along. "Bronell I need to speak to you right now!" Aldor had yelled across the field to where his son was working.

A tall broad shouldered, good looking young Human boy, with long red hair and blue eyes, looked up and with a friendly smile waved. Aldor watched his son with mixed feeling as he came running up still smiling, to the back porch.

"Yes father." And then he asked. "What would you have of me?" Bronell had asked a little out of breath.

"Son." Aldor went on. "Messengers have come. First one came talking of an Elf attack against LousBeckt and then within an hour, a second messenger came by saying the battle will be in the Red Valley tomorrow morning." Aldor had said this in a very grave voice.

"What does this have to do with us father?" Then, before Aldor could answer Bronell quickly asked. "Your not going into the battle are you father?" Bronell had asked these questions, with a worried, yet concerned, look on his young face.

Slowly Aldor began to speak. "Well son I would like you to take my place and fight for me in this battle. Your old enough now and my back still hasn't healed since the accident."

Aldor said haltingly while looking down at his feet. "I'm sorry son." Aldor slowly looked up as he went on. "My back will keep me out of this battle and you will have to take my place." A few weeks back, Aldor had been working on the roof of the barn, when he had slipped and fallen off the roof. The injury to his back was quite severe and he still needed some time to get back to his original state.

"But father I'm only sixteen years old." Bronell protested with a worried look on his face as he went on. "I'm too young."

Aldor with a reassuring tone added. "Son I was fourteen years old when I first fought in a battle."

With a reassuring smile and a nod Aldor continued. "My first battle was also in the Red Valley. I think your plenty old enough." Aldor was firm but gentle as he thought. "This must be a very scarey thing for Bronell." Aldor was very aware of this. "Now go into the living room where I have placed your new armor and equipment." Aldor said, as he nodded his head and pointed into the house. "The troops are right now gathering in the Villages of Garriton, Divatz and Shalatok, and you should go directly there to one of these towns."

Aldor followed his son into the house. He helped Bronell putting on the equipment and the armor. Once all the armor and equipment was in place on Bronell, Aldor stepped back and he was very impressed with what he saw. His son Bronell stood straight and very tall. With the new armor and equipment on, Bronell looked just like a fully grown soldier.

Aldor said. "Bronell you must hurry." Then Aldor said. "I can tell you Bronell that you look very impressive. Bronell I am very proud of you."

Aldor took a step forward and hugged his son. Aldor thought to himself that he could not remember when he had last hugged his son and then he wondered to himself. "Where had all the time gone?" His son Bronell was now a fully grown man and his growing up seemed to have happened much to fast. Aldor did not want Bronell seeing his face as he had tears in his eyes.

Bronell did not want to leave his father alone on the the farm and go off to war, but he knew he must. He also knew that this was what his father wanted and he would never do anything to disappoint his father. Still deep inside Bronell was scared and did not want his father seeing how scared he was, so he put on his best face, gave his biggest smile, stepped back, when he asked in a confident tone. "Father do I look all right?"

Aldor nodded and never said anything. Aldor hugged his son one more time and then Bronell slowly turned him towards the door. This was probably the toughest thing that Aldor ever had to do. No father likes to see his son go to war but all male Human children are well trained in fighting at school and all Human children must go to war when they are called to assist.

Aldor unknowingly wiped a tear from his eye.

Closer To The Up and Coming Battle

"We don't stand a chance." General Karridhen said to some of his captains as he stood looking over some messages and maps on his desk. The troops were starting to gather in the Red Valley and General Karridhen had set up a command tent above the battle ground, were all the other Human Generals in the past had stationed their headquarters. As long as anyone could remember, all differences between the Elves and Humans had been settled in this Valley, in this fashion. This is how grudges between the humans and Elves were settled. There was no other way to do things.

"We have an estimated five thousand soldiers and we are expecting two thousand more." Talking out loud to nobody in particular the General continued as he paced the floor. "Our scouts estimate the Elf army at seven thousand soldiers already and more are coming all the time. First they attack LousBeckt, kill the nobleman Kurrest, then they challenged us to this battle." Then the General said. "I wish we had more time to build a bigger army, he added slamming his fist on the desk. "We had no time to call in all the army regulars and at best, all we have is a bunch of volunteers."

General Karridhen kept pacing back and forth and was more or less continuing to talk out loud to himself. "These Elves have probably six Ballistas hidden just out of sight and we don't even have any War Dragons. The Elves had always brought Ballistas to every battle for shooting down our War Dragons and we don't even have any Dragons."

General Karridhen just shrugged his shoulders as he continued to passionately address his captains. "Although all the volunteers are equipped, we have no heavy infantry and very few cavalry." He said pleadingly to his Captains. "We better hope that the Elves don't plan on attacking for another day at least."

It was now late at night and with a worried look on his face the General stood up straight then quickly walked over to the tents entrance and took a breath of fresh air. He looked out over the Valley. First to the left and then to the right. This is where the battle would be fought in the morning. He looked back to his left and then again to right. Then he just shook his head. He was amazed at how fast the Army of Elves on the other side of the Valley had grown. Camp fires could been seen as far as the top of the Valley and continued to both ends of the Valley. He had been in big battles before but this battle was probably going to be the biggest. Clearly as things stood as they did his troops were already greatly outnumbered.

General Karridhen grew quiet before he turned and walked back into the tent. With his head hung downwards he moved closer to the large table which had maps on it. Just then his name was called from the entrance of the tent. He turned back slowly towards the entrance of the tent where he saw a young messenger, who had just stepped past the guards and came into the light.

"Sir." The young man said as he entered the tent.

"What is it? Can't you see we are preparing for the battle." A senior Captain standing on General Karridhen's right had snapped at the young messenger.

"Yes Sir but something important has happened." Then the young messenger stammered as he tried again to speak in front of all of the army officers. The young man stepped further into the tent and ignoring the Captain he walked straight towards General Karridhen whom the messenger easily recognized.

"Well what has happened?" General Karridhen had an inquisitive look in his eyes.

Tired, worried and looking like he had already lost the battle the General with slumped shoulders, took a step closer the young messenger. Starting hesitantly the messenger began to tell his story. "Well Sir the brother of nobleman Kurrest, who himself is apparently very rich, has sent us five Battle Dragons, fully equipped and also some of his personal guard."

There was an instant murmur from the officers in the tent. Very quickly the messenger looking directly at General Karriden, continued. "He said these men are all well trained in Dragon combat." "He also sent enough money which is intended to be spent on Dwarf mercenaries. He says there should be about eight hundred Dwarfen mercenaries close to here right now."

Then the young messenger said. "I almost forgot that there is also about five hundred regulars coming." The messenger quickly went on. "Or at least they will be here and ready for battle early in the morning." The command tent had become very quiet as the messenger had given out his information. The messenger also noticed as the information was being given that some of the officers were starting to relax. Some were starting to smile and nod their heads while listening to him speak.

The messenger feeling a little more comfortable although quite tired by this time, because of the long ride and also it was very late at night, added. "Kurrest's bother knows that the Elves killed Kurrest and although he is to old to join in the battle he is not to old to recruit troops who can assist in the battle."

"He will send more troops if he can." The young man finished with a very large smile.

"Excellent." The General said with a confident smile before he continued. Then speaking to the messenger in a solemn tone General Karriden spoke further. "Now you will have to go because we still have a lot of work to do. And we all thank you for the information you have just given us." The General then said this with a friendly smile, as he walked the young messenger to the tent door. "Now you should go and get some rest because you look very tired. And get something to eat."

General Karridhen with a smile which had replaced the wrinkles on his face, turned back towards his officers with a renewed energy. While pointing at the map on the desk he started giving orders in a rapid fashion. "We can use the Dwarf mercenaries in the front, for a concentrated hand to hand attack."

All the officers in the tent knew quite well, with this many Dwarf mercenaries in the middle of the battle that it would be hard for the Elves to be very effective. Dwarves with their war axes and war hammers could be very vicious, especially with such a large group.

The General went on talking and basically thinking out loud. "Now there are a lot of these Dwarves and if they were schooled well in the fighting. They should do alright without to many direct commands. But we will give the Dwarfs one of our Captains, if they come here without an officer." There was a slight pause as General Karridhen was thinking over some strategies. Then he went on. "Now the Dragons." The General paused briefly and then went on. "We will fly three Dragons directly over the middle of the Elves Cavalry. The other two Dragons should be able to strike the Elf Ballistas from behind. The attack from overhead and behind the Elves Calvary should hopefully break the Elves' lines. After the Elves' lines are broken then the Dwarves could flank the Elves foot soldiers. If the timing is right then the volunteer's casualties will be low."

    The General while explaining these things out loud to the Captains grabbed a peace of paper, and started sketching out the remainder of the battle plan for all the other officers.

Bobbiur Prepares To Leave WynnFred

Bobbiur, Hagjel, Salbuk and Obmar, with the help of the captured Dragon had spent the better part of the morning helping Pendahl and the Elves, of the destroyed town WynnFred in cleaning things up. With the assistance of the Dragon they were able to help move some large damaged objects out of the Village.

Salbuk approached Bobbiur and asked with a mind message. "Bobbiur I can be of great assistance to the Villagers if I am able to use my magic powers. Should I use my magic to help rebuild some houses or some other buildings?"

Bobbiur thought about this very briefly and was thinking to himself that he was getting quite used to Salbuk's mind messaging. He saw Salbuk looking at him with a friendly but amused smile, which meant Salbuk was in his mind right at this time, but it didn't bother him at all. Bobbiur quickly replied with a mind message. "I would like nothing better than to use all of your powers to help these people rebuild but then you might not be strong enough to fight the Haddrons."

Bobbiur went on. "We will be leaving WynnFred in a short while and should we meet, or catch up with the Haddrons, after we leave this place and you might not be of much help if your powers are weak."

Bobbiur then added. "The Dragon is doing a wonderful job at moving the larger pieces of damaged and broken buildings and every one of us is helping as much as we can."

Salbuk sent a message to Bobbiur that he understood. Salbuk then turned and went back over to where Hagjel was working. Bobbiur watched Salbuk returning to help Hagjel and Bobbiur could not help but note that Hagjel even when he was doing manual labor, never ever put down the tote bag which held Jakka.

Bobbiur and his group were all sweating and were able to do some very good work for the Elves of the village of WynnFred, when Bobbiur walked over to Hagjel and asked. "Hagjel why don't you let Jakka out so the Elf children can see him?"

Hagjel with a smile looked at Bobbiur with a look of respect but said knowingly.

"If I let Jakka out then we would have such a large crowd around us so fast, that it would be impossible to get any work done."

"Better just to let Jakka remain sleeping for now and when we leave WynnFred he can come out and get some fresh air."

To this Bobbiur nodded and said. "I understand and I keep forgetting how interesting it must be for any individuals in any place in all of Adjemir, to see a fully grown pet GymmKat up close." He turned and walked away as Hagjel returned to work with the other Elves who had been working close to him. Bobbiur then wondered to himself, if any of the Elves close by to where Hagjel was working ever asked why Hagjel never put down his tote bag, especially when some of the heavy work was being undertaken.

Bobbiur spoke out loud to himself and said. "Strange!" And while walking back to the place where he had been working, he glanced to his left and saw the Dragon of Salbuk's doing most of the heavy work. Bobbiur thought he saw the Dragon smiling. He wondered to himself if Dragons actually smiled? Then he remembered the Dragon of Zorp's and he remembered seeing Dymma smiling when the weapons were being returned, which was just after the fight with Smarge and the Dark Storm Clan.

As he was returning to his work place he briefly thought of Kirwynn and wondered how she was doing and also how General Yauddi was feeling now? Then he went back to work.

After a short while Bobbiur stopped work while some giggling Elf maidens brought him some water and a small snack. During this time he glanced over his shoulder and was amazed and somewhat impressed at how strong Obmar actually was. Obmar was moving objects, which in the estimation of Bobbiur, it would have taken six strong Elves to move. Obmar had actually gathered a crowd of onlookers, which was mostly children. The children were all beaming and giggling. Bobbiur thought he even saw a slight smile on Obmar's grizzled old face, but he wasn't sure.

It was midmorning, when Salbuk finally walked over to where Bobbiur was helping some Elves remove a large bunch of broken masonry and he noticed that Bobbiur was sweating a great deal. He noticed that Bobbiur's cloths were actually drenched in sweat. Salbuk thought to himself that Bobbiur was a hard working individual and this in itself spoke volumes as to the type of individual Bobbiur really was. Salbuk then thought to himself. "This Bobbiur is a good person and it is no wonder Ram was not afraid to put Bobbiur in charge of such an important matter, as chasing down the renegade Krug band."

Salbuk also thought to himself. "Bobbiur really doesn't treat anybody any different. He treats all Adjemir individuals the same." Salbuk went on in his own mind. "It makes no difference whether or not the individual is Human, Elf, Dwarf, or Krug."

Another thing which impressed Salbuk about Bobbiur, was the common sense which Bobbiur has shown. Such as the taming of the Dragon. The helping the Elves here at WynnFred. The release of the Elves under Pendahl's command when Pendahl had attacked them on the road to WynnFred.

Any other commander would have killed all of the Elves who had been present during the attack, but apparently Bobbiur saw things differently than most other Humans or Elves would. At the time, Salbuk had thought to himself that releasing those Elves after the attack was a big mistake. But now he could see some of the value placed on Bobbiur's decision to release Pendahl and his Elfen soldiers.

"Clearly Bobbiur has made a friend for life." Salbuk sent a mind message to himself while thoughtfully nodding his head. "Smart move Bobbiur." "Smart move."

When Salbuk got closer to Bobbiur and before Bobbiur turned around, Salbuk sent a mind message to Bobbiur. "Bobbiur, we should get moving." The next message from Salbuk showed his urgency. "The trail of the Haddrons may start getting too old for Hagjel to follow."

Much to Salbuk's surprise, Bobbiur, without even looking up because he was quite occupied with a small task, put a thought in his mind which Salbuk caught right away. "Your right Salbuk." Then Bobbiur still looking down, with a mind message said. "Your right Salbuk we should not delay much longer." Bobbiur then added. "I will go and get Hagjel ready."

Bobbiur had a further thought in his mind for Salbuk. What surprised Salbuk the most is how fast Bobbiur has become accustomed to using his mind messaging ability. Bobbiur's message to Salbuk, was concerning Obmar. "Although Obmar seems to be having a lot of fun showing off his strength you should go and see if you can get him moving."

Bobbiur went in one direction and Salbuk walked towards Obmar. While walking Salbuk sent a message to Obmar about getting ready to leave WynnFred.

A short while later as Bobbiur and the group were preparing to leave WynnFred, Pendahl and some of the villagers walked up to them with some food and gifts. Pendahl, with a smile of gratitude shook all the groups hands while repeating what he had said earlier. "If you ever need any help from me or any people from our village of WynnFred then do not be afraid to ask."

Continuing to speak to Bobbiur Pendahl said. "I'm not sure why our races fight all the time but I hope that our truce is never broken." Then looking directly into the eyes of Bobbiur, Pendahl said. "Our races have been fighting for so long they probably have forgotten why they started fighting in the first place."

Bobbiur just nodded towards Pendahl and his people knowingly, as he said. "Pendahl, I think you might be right."

Then with a slight bow of his head and a nod towards the entire group, Pendahl said something which surprised even Bobbiur.

"You." Pendahl paused briefly. "With your tremendous powers could have killed me and my soldiers on the road yesterday, but you didn't."

Pendahl continued. "You did not have to stay and help clean up this mess left by the Haddron's Dragon, but you did."

"The Village of WynnFred could have been completely destroyed by the Dragon and you did not have to risk your own lives to help us." Pendahl with a slight smile then said. "But you did."

"You are not like other Humans."

Pendahl turned and looked over his people and then turning back to Bobbiur, he went on. "I will speak to some higher Elf members at the next Elders meeting. I will tell them what you have done here at WynnFred and maybe they will learn to trust not only Darmonarrow, but also trust all Humans more. Possibly for the future we can make a greater and longer peace between the races." Pendhal nodded a she said. "I promise to do this." Pendahl paused again and with great conviction, he repeated what he had just said. "I promise."

The Nine Moons of Adjemir

Just before Pendahl turned away he said. "By the way Bobbiur the villagers have a new name for you. They are calling you." Pendahl paused for just a second, turned and looked at the villagers and then turned back to Bobbiur. "They call you." He spoke quietly. "Y'honitor." Pendahl was smiling.

With this being said Pendahl shook Bobbiur's hand one more time, nodded towards Salbuk, Hagjel, and Obmar as he said. "Thanks."

Then he turned and walked back to his people. He looked very tired but very relaxed.

Bobbiur helped Obmar onto the Dragon's back and because Obmar was a Dwarf, he did not seem to be very comfortable which only made Bobbiur smile to himself as he looked away. Salbuk then jumped on the Dragon's back and sat in front of Obmar.

The plan was to have Salbuk and the Dragon fly above Bobbiur, Hagjel and the Spaggidons, in order to watch out for them. If anything looked out of place they were to report back to Bobbiur and Hagjel right away.

"You know Bobbiur, there are only two of us and it's such a big Dragon, it might be possible for all of us to ride on it's back." Salbuk had been looking down at Bobbiur when he had sent this mind message. Bobbiur hopped onto his Spaggidon's back while saying. "That's okay at least for a while we will able travel faster and safer, with you flying over us as an outlook. The Dragon will be a great help to us, but we still need the Spaggidons with us to carry supplies and weapons. We will also have to fight the Haddrons when we catch them and if we are all riding on the same Dragon, then we would be one easy target."

Bobbiur went on in a matter of fact tone. "If we are on our Spaggidons then we can attack the Haddrons from different directions and if we have to retreat then we can move away more quickly." Bobbiur said. "I would like you to fly quite high because we don't know how powerful the Haddron's magic is. You should try to stay out of range of their magic, if it is possible."

"If you think you have spotted the Haddrons then put up a mind barrier as fast as you can and come back and get us. Don't try to kill any Haddrons by yourself." Bobbiur continued. "We don't know how strong their magic is nor how far they can send their magic spells, so I want you to be very careful."

As Salbuk was sending a mind message to Hagjel and Bobbiur that he understood, Bobbiur was nodding to Hagjel knowing that Salbuk would catch his mind message that they should proceed. Bobbiur turned and waved to Pendahl and the Villagers. Bobbiur was still somewhat tired and as Salbuk was getting ready to command the Dragon to fly upwards, Salbuk caught Bobbiur thinking about the Elfen people of WynnFred.

Salbuk sent a mind message to Bobbiur. "Your right Bobbiur these people of WynnFred are very nice, very gentle and this actually surprises me." Salbuk's mind message then went further about how Salbuk actually felt about the Elves. "We have been brought up to hate Elves and we have always been told that we cannot trust the Elfen population in general. Other than Hagjel I have never felt very comfortable around large groups of Elves." Then Salbuk added. "Village people of WynnFred are just like Human village people. We should rethink how we feel about the Elves." Salbuk finished his message by adding. "Pendahl seemed very sincere. I agree he is a very likeable Elf."

Bobbiur just nodded that he agreed.

Just after they left the village of WynnFred, they headed in the direction of the place where they had last thought the Haddrons would have been traveling. Nobody in Bobbiur's group knew that the Elfen city of Domerge and the Human city of LousBeckt had been attacked by the disguised Haddrons, during the morning while they had been busy helping the villagers of WynnFred.

About the time that they were getting out of sight of WynnFred, Bobbiur turned to Hagjel and he asked. "Pendahl called me 'Y'honitor." And with a slight smile on his face and a quizzical look, Bobbiur asked. "What does Y'honitor mean?

With a smile on his face and his head tilted a bit to the side, Hagjel peered sideways at Bobbiur as he said. "Y'honitor, means. In the Elfen language. Hagjel paused. "Savior."

Nodding his head Hagjel added. "Quite a compliment."

Hagjel noticed that Bobbiur was a little red faced. Hagjel slowly smiled and just look straight ahead at the road. Both Hagjel and Bobbiur rode onwards and both became silent.

Zorp Wakens Bobbiur

Very early in the morning in a small camp not more than about two hours travel from Wynnfred Bobbiur, Obmar, and Salbuk slept soundly, just like little babies. Hagjel was on guard at the perimeter of the camp. It was still very dark as it was only about two hours after midnight. Bobbiur had wanted a guard established because they could be fairly close to Zalghar and his warriors, and he did not want the camp caught in a surprise attack. A guard had to be established while the others slept even with the protection shield in place.

With his keen ears and keener eyes Hagjal looked out into the woods around them. Nothing was out there that he didn't know about. Hagjal was paying strict attention for movements and sounds and his senses told him that there was absolutely nothing near the camp. Besides if there was any movement, the Spaggidons would have been instantly awakened because they are such light sleepers.

Suddenly a hand reached out and grabbed his shoulder. Hagjel had been so intent on watching the forest for intruders, that he was given such a fright he almost came out of his skin.

Hagjel was so surprised all he could do was give a short scream. "Yeek." At the same time he spun around and he held a large dagger in his right hand. He jumped back and stood in a defensive posture, while staring at a very old slightly short strange looking individual.

Standing there right in front of him was Zorp. "Well Youngster. A little jumpy are we?" Zorp was asking this with a grin which stretched from ear to ear.

"I didn't hear you." Hagjal said with a bit of a blush and then he went on by saying. "You startled me Zorp. I was sure there was nothing in the forest that I didn't know about."

Hagjel was still blushing from the surprise and the embarrassment, when Zorp said. "Its good thing that it was me who was surprising you youngster and not Zalghar or his renegades." Without saying anything further Zorp turned and walked over to the tents where the other were still asleep. Zorp peered into the tent.

"Well we better wake these sleepy heads, up." Zorp said this as he was looking down at Bobbiur. Bobbiur felt a quick sharp jab in the ribs. He jumped up and sat up under his blankets, rubbed his eyes while looked dazedly around.

"Good. You're finally awake." Zorp was looking around to see the others were also waking up and rolling over. "You have to pack up now. Get all your things ready and you have to leave as soon as you are able too."As the men were rubbing the sleep from their eyes Zorp went on. "You must head for the Red Valley. Something big is going to happen in the Rad Valley later today." With a flourishing hand movement Zorp said. "Now go!" Zorp said this as he left the tent and was pointing in the direction of the road which was just a few yards from the camp.

Bobbiur in a raised voice argued with Zorp about his men needed more sleep. "What are you talking about. It's still dark and it will be for another couple of hours." Bobbiur had argued further. "The Dragon has poor night vision and we all need more sleep. Zalghar might be setting an ambush for us."

Quickly Zorp said. "No!" And then he quickly added. "Something big has just happened." Zorp raised his voice slightly and then he spoke with conviction and emphasis. "Yesterday unknown to you and your group, Zalghar set up an attack at the Elf city of Domerge with some of his warriors disguised as Humans." After pausing briefly Zorp continued on. "Zalghar at the same time sent some of his other warriors into the Human city of LousBeckt dressed as Elves."

Zorp continued to bring Bobbiur up to understanding all that has happened and gave him all the information which he should know about. "These disguises have had a drastic effect." Then in a louder voice Zorp went on. "Both the Human race and the Elfen race believe that they have been attacked by their old enemy and that whatever truce there was between the Elves and Humans has been broken."

Stroking the beard on his chin Zorp continued speaking directly to Bobbiur. "They are going to war with each other in the early morning in the place you Adjemirians call. I believe the Red Valley."

"Bobbiur only you can stop it." Zorp finished with his voice becoming soft and quiet.

Sounding somewhat confused Bobbiur asked with a sound of frustration creeping into his tired voice. "How am I supposed to stop a war."

Zorp looked Bobbiur straight in the eyes and with a slight smile said. "You'll think of something." Then Zorp quickly added. "You always do." Glancing down the road Zorp had an even bigger smile on his face as he added. "There are lots of people relying on you." Then as Zorp stood there he clapped his hands together as he stated. "You must leave now and you must travel as fast as you are able too. You can sleep later but now you have a war to stop." Showing no emotion Zorp stated. "Traveling will be slow but the more distance you cover before sunrise the better." Zorp seemed to be in a hurry when he added. "We would help you but Dymma and I are needed somewhere else." Quickly Zorp said in a raised voice. "Now go!"

Without saying anything more Zorp again waved his hand at the road and then he just disappeared.

Bobbiur knew that there must be some battle planned for the Red Valley as this was all the Valley was used for. All differences between Elves and Humans were settled in the Red Valley and he should get there as fast as he could to see if he could stop it. He was not sure exactly what he would do to stop the up and coming battle but Zorp might be right, while traveling he would probably think of something.

The four packed up as quickly as they could. Then set out down the road. The going was slow at this time because it was still dark and they were all very tired. The Dragon had to be led by hand, every step of the way. They trudged on down the road, tired and hungry, for a few hours never seeing anyone or anything on the way.

Later as the sun rose they didn't even stop to eat. They just nibbled on some loose food bits which were in their tote bags. The men could ride their Spaggidons now and were able to pick up the pace a little because the Dragon could now see a little more clearly.

Jakka was wide awake and looking up out of the tote bag to see where they were and made a clicking sound to get Hagjel's attention. Jakka wanted some small fruits and nuts. They couldn't use the Dragon for flying because they packed all their equipment on it's back and it would be faster just to walk instead of un-packing the Dragon. Besides only two of them could fly on it's back at one time. So they walked on only stopped once or twice along the way to get water at a stream, to rest their feet and to let the Dragon roll on some grass which was growing beside the road.

"Do you know what we are going to do when we get to the Red Valley Bobbiur?" Obmar asked while trying to keep up with the Bobbiur's large strides. In a tired voice Bobbiur said. "I don't know." Then Bobbiur added with a troubled look on his face. "It's just up the road a few more miles and maybe I'll be able to think of something before we get there. All I can tell you is that huge battles are fought there every once in a while between the Human race and the Elfen race."

"I've never been there myself." He looked down at Obmar as he smiled a little friendly smile.

General Charranoid Prepares for Battle

In the early daylight after the smoke from the campfires and the early morning mist began to fade away, General Charranoid and Captain Eeando from the Elfen side of the Valley looked across the Valley at the opposing Human army. It was the largest Human force that General Charranoid have ever seen. And although he had a great dislike for all Humans he had to admire the Human's ability to field such a large force in such a short time.

"Captain Eeando." General Charranoid spoke gravely. "I see a large Dwarf mercenary group and it looks like they will be in the center of the action. The General went on. "Generally arrows shot into the air are useless against them because they are able to form, an overhead protection with their shields."

General Charranoid had a worried look on his face as he went on. "They do this by placing their shields over their heads and then standing very close together. I have seen this done before. By simply putting all their large rectangular shields together over their heads when they see a large group of arrows being launched they are able to deflect all or most incoming arrows."

Then the General continued on without pausing and it was almost like he was talking to himself as he looked out at the Human's huge army. "I am told that they are taught this in cadet school and the Dwarfs are very good at it."

The old General now paused for a moment and then he said. "As they are in a tight formation when the command is given they immediately put their shields together over their heads and all you can see from above is a solid impenetrable plate of shields. No arrows can get through to the Dwarfs below. Captain Eeando without saying anything, nodded that he understood.

General Charranoid had a plan to cause considerable confusion for the Dwarves when this came about. He did not comment to Captain Eeando about his idea but if it worked the way he planned, his strategy could be very successful. General Charranoid had personally trained a full regiment of Elves, to fight with a new weapon, called the Jonzar.

The Jonzar is a three pointed disk type weapon which would boomerang back to the thrower, if it did not hit it's target. What was most interesting about the Jonzar, is when it would return to the thrower and as the speed of the Jonzar decreased, the cutting edges of the weapon would close. When the weapon was thrown with considerable force, the cutting edges would open wide. When the Jonzar was thrown, and as the cutting edges opened, this new weapon would also make a loud screaming noise. This screaming noise should put terror into the opposing troops.

General Charranoid thought to himself that if this manoeuver worked the way he wanted it to, then the effectiveness of the Dwarfs should be reduced. Still the size of the Dwarfen Regiment, if his plan to smash the Dwarves with the Elite Jonzar force did not work, could cause the Elfen troops some huge problems. The use of the Jonzars during the battle was planned, to be a timing matter.

The Jonzars would be launched by a signal and at the same time the Archers would be firing their arrows, in mass. This way if things worked out as planned the arrows should be arriving at the same time as the Jonzars. Therefore the Dwarves would not be able to have their shields in the air protecting against the incoming arrows and at the same time, in front of the Dwarves to protect against the incoming Jonzars.

General Charranoid planned to have the Jonzar regiment follow the first wave of Elfen foot soldiers but they would not throw their Jonzars until the signal was given. When the signal was given, three things would happen at exactly the same time. Firstly, the Elfen foot soldiers in the advancing group, who where facing the Dwarf regiment, would instantly flatten themselves to the ground. Thereby making an easy target of the Dwarf regiment, for the Jonzar throwers. Instantly the Archers would let fly with a full volley of arrows and the Jonzars would be launched almost at the same time, but slightly behind the overhead volley of arrows.

The Nine Moons of Adjemir

The Jonzar's were a new weapon and had never been used in any battle before. The Jonzar's cutting edges, are so sharp and well crafted, that they can slice right through any ordinary light fighting armor. General Charranoid said to himself. "These Dwarf mercenaries could be in for a big surprise."

Then General Charranoid became quiet for a few moments as he was trying to ponder some of the strategies of the Human officers across the Valley. "I can tell you." General Charranoid commented to Captain Eeando as he was looking across the valley. "Although it does not appear that the Humans have any Battle Dragons in the field, you can be quite sure that there will be Battle Dragons in this battle. General Charranoid went on talking to Eeando. "The question which bothers me the most is. Just how many Battle Dragons the Humans were able to gather on such short notice?" Then General Charranoid asked Captain Eeando in a questioning fashion. "I hope all the Ballistas are in good working order?"

As things went on the General was mostly commenting to himself, sort of thinking out loud, but Captain Eeando nodded and said. "The Ballistas have just returned from doing field practice and I have been advised that all the Ballistas are in really good condition. The Ballistas have been practicing for the last hour or so just over the hill there. Eeando had said this while pointing to a location where the Ballistas had been kept.

Captain Eeando made these comments in order to have the General understand that the Ballistas were in good working order. The information of importance in this matter was information about the field practices which should assist the General understanding the condition of all the battle Ballistas. Captain Eeando went on in a quiet manner. "In fact I have just recently returned from watching the Ballistas in field practice and I can tell you General the Ballistas crews are as good as I have ever seen them."

General Charranoid thought about this for a very short time and without saying anything more, slowly turned and went back into the headquarters tent.

General Karridhen Prepares for Battle

Across the Red Valley in the Human camp General Karridhen stepped outside of the command tent and looked across the Valley at the incredibly huge Elfen Army. The Elfen army, just like a huge monster, in the early morning light seemed to cover the entire opposite side of the Red Valley. General Karridhen with a worried look on his face stared out at the battle field as he spoke softly to himself, while shaking his head slowly. "This Elfen army is huge."

Earlier when he had been addressing his Captains in the war tent the troops from Garriton had arrived. As he was now back inside the command tent after observing the Elfen army, he just shook his head as he said to himself. "Today is going to be a tough day for our side." He turned again and went back to the tent entrance to take one more look at the large imposing army on the other side of the valley. Shaking his head the General was just turning back into the tent to take another look at the maps showing the opposing forces. This was around the time when Kirwynn was leaving her troops to walk up the hill towards General Karridhen's headquarters. The old General saw her coming and waited near the entrance of the tent.

The old General was surprised to find that General Yauddi was not in charge of the Garrison from Garriton. So he had some questions on his mind. To the General's further surprise, in General Yauddi's place his daughter, Captain Kirwynn had brought the Garriton troops to the Red Valley. Also and even more surprising, he was to find out later, was the Captains from Garriton did not seem to mind that this very young girl was in charge of the entire Garrison.

When this young girl was approached him he very quickly had to hide his surprise. With a questioning look on his face General had quickly asked Kirwynn, as she walked up to him. "Where is General Yauddi?"

This young woman, without saying anything had reached inside the breast pocket of her uniform and handed the General a sealed letter, as she said. "My father General Yauddi said I must give this to you and explain a few things."

Then she went on. "My father has been injured and he is presently very weak." Kirwynn paused before proceeding. "We." Kirwynn paused. "I mean. Garriton was attacked two days ago by some strange warriors."

Looking up at the General who had a questioning look on his face Kirwynn added. "The warriors which attacked Garriton were very powerful." Haltingly she slowly continued. "These warriors who attacked Darmonarrow first and then they attacked Garriton are not from Adjemir. I have been told that they come from a land called Haddron."

Kirwynn then added. "I do not know what is in my father's letter to you but just so you are aware." Kirwynn pausing, looked away momentarily, towards the troops from Garriton, then she turned back towards the General and resumed the conversation. "I have completed Cadet school. I have also taken Officer training and I am a presently Captain in the Garriton elite reserves." Then she added. "When we go into battle you do not have to worry about me or any of the troops from Garriton."

The old General remained quiet while listening intently to Kirwynn as he continued reading the letter from General Yauddi. Looking up when he was sure that Kirwynn had finished General Karridhen began to speak in a commanding tone. "Your father General Yauddi has given strict instructions that you must not directly take part in the battle. He said you must conduct your troops from the command post. He has also said that you will send your orders into the battle by messenger only."

With a slight smile on his face, with a wrinkle across his forehead and while looking directly into the eyes of Kirwynn he asked somewhat sternly. "Is that clear Captain?"

Kirwynn understood immediately that this was not a request but a direct order. Because of her advanced training as a Cadet and an officer she understood, that an order is an order. Although she nodded towards the General with a hurt look on her face, Kirwynn said in a somber tone.

"General I understand completely."

General Karridhen, could see an intense disappointment in Kirwynn's eyes and then he said somewhat abruptly. "Good now let me return to the tent. Come with me and I will introduce you to the rest of the officers."The General put his arm around her shoulder and said as they walked towards the command tent. "I traveled to Garriton to visit your father and to inspect the troops of Garriton. You were only a child then. You probably do not remember me but that is not important."

He then added. "It's good to see you have grown into a very beautiful young lady."

The general quickly corrected his mistake by saying rather quickly as he, with a red face, fumbled and bumbled around in a rather rapid fashion. "I'm sorry I mean a young officer."

Kirwynn glancing at the General, saw that he had a slightly red face and she smiled to herself. As they neared the tent and just before they entered the General stopped Kirwynn and said. "I hope your father is going to be all right." Then the General added. "In past battles he would be with me at the headquarters and he would assist me with the strategy as the battle progressed."

The General had removed his helmet and was carrying it under his right arm as he opened the flap of the tent. "I want you to take his place as one of my aides. Will this be all right with you and your Captains?"

Kirywnn knew that this was a great honor and a very good chance to see some of the strategies which were taught in officer school working in the field. But before Kirwynn could answer, General Karridhen turned inwards to the tent, as he said to Kirwynn over his shoulder. "Come. Come inside and I will introduce you to the Officers."

General Karridhen had a very soft voice at this time and he also had a look on his face similar to her father when he was happy with something she had accomplished. "I must tell you that some of these officers will be in the field and some will be with me at the Command post."

Kirwynn nodded her head as she said. "When we finish here I will have to go and prepare my troops for the battle."The General spoke over his shoulder as they approached the officers at the planning tables in the command tent. "Your right of course. It is nearly light and the battle should be getting started very shortly."

Without saying anything further the General turned and started introducing Kirwynn to all the officers who were present at the command post.

Zalghar Views the Battle

In the Early morning after the mist was starting to clear away, in a place which was hidden high above the battle field, Zalghar and the Haddrons watched and waited. When the mist started to clear away at the far end of the Valley away from where the Haddrons were hidden, Zalghar saw the two large armies facing each other.

On Zalghar's left the Humans were in position. The Human troops were in a very tight formation.

On his right was the larger Elfen Armies and although they were in a fairly tight formation there was somewhat more spacing between the different formations.

Because of the Haddron's vantage point Zalghar was close enough so that he could distinguish between the different types of troops on both sides of the battle grounds. What he saw was very impressive and as he sat there he thought quietly to himself. "The plan was working better than he originally planned."

Some of the different kinds of troops were wearing different colored uniforms and different types of uniforms. On the Human's side of the valley he also noticed a large group of Dwarfs, which had been situated directly in the middle of the Human's position. These Dwarfs seemed to be heavily armored and all seemed to be carrying large war axes just like the axe he had implanted the magic Rune onto. Then Zalghar wondered to himself. "Where is the axe now?" He still had some plans for it's use but he had been unable to see the Rune's presence since before the attack on Darmonarrow. He would have to spend some time after this battle is over in order to find the war axe. The axe was like a secret weapon and if he was within range of the axe, Zalghar could unleash the incredible magic powers held within it. This powerful axe could destroy any enemy which could be placed before it. But right now Zalghar would not worry about where the axe was, because wanted to concentrate on this large battle between the Human and the Elf army which he has created.

Zalghar confidently put these thoughts about the axe out of his mind. He would search for the war axe with the Rune attached to it, by using with his "Spirit Eye,' at a later time. He rubbed his hands together as he spoke to himself. "Let the show begin." Then he leaned back into a more comfortable position.

Zalghar had found a very good place to view the battle from. It was a good location at the end of the valley on the edge of a cliff, with a clear view. There was a good spot higher up at the top of the cliff where the Kilpacx could rest. There was food present for the Kilpacx to graze on and a fresh water spring close by. This place was well out of sight. Even if they were not clearly out of sight from the Valley below he would be putting up a, camouflage shield right in front of himself and his warriors, so that they could not be detected from anybody below on the battle field.

There was also at this location some big boulders which they could use for seats and which they could also hide behind, if needed. They were almost impossible to see from the battle ground below and as he looked around he noticed that his men seemed very relaxed. They all had smiles on their faces. Still he wanted to post guards so he mentioned this before he turned all of his full attention to the Valley below.

Almost immediately after Zalghar was settled down he started to see movement from the armies on the valley floor. He saw what looked like officers on both sides of the valley giving orders and positioning troops. Shortly after this and with a little more shifting of troops the Human armies, started to take the field.

He continued looking over the field and saw farther to his left a large group of grey and silver. This Zalghar assumed was the Human cavalry, who all seemed to be riding on grey colored horses. These troops were moving into position just behind the Dwarfs. The Dwarfs at this time, were starting to come down the Human side of the Valley. This Dwarf regiment was in large numbers and as they moved slowly down the Human's side of the alley, with their shinny armor, they resembled slow moving shimmering water.

Marching just beside the Dwarfs there was a large number of Human foot-soldiers. Their shields and breast plates were shining clearly in the bright early morning light. They slowly moved into the Valley to wait for the battle to begin. As this large number of moving soldiers with the shining armor were taking the field, it made Zalghar think of heat waves in a desert. As these troops moved down the Human's side of the valley, these foot soldiers were moving in rhythm from a steady, yet solemn, beating of their war drum. This war drum was stationed just in front of a tent which Zalghar knew the Officers of the Human army were stationed. When these large groups of foot soldiers moved in rhythm like this, it appeared that the whole valley was moving, just like a slow moving river.

The steady beat of the Human's war drum rolled over the valley floor, reverberated through the troops, which is what was causing the troops to march in unison. The sound of the drum passed through the troops and finally ascended the valley walls to the place where Zalghar and the Haddrons were waiting and watching atop the cliff. The Haddron warriors noticed the sound of the war drum, brought a small but satisfied yet evil smile to the face of Zalghar.

Behind the sound of the war drums was the slow rumbling sound, from the rattle of the battle armor which the soldiers were wearing as they marched along. Zalghar could tell from the sounds coming from the valley below that all the Human soldiers seemed to be also chanting, cheering and using their swords to strike their war shields in unison. It would appear with the beating of the war shields, the Humans were doing this, Zalghar thought, in order to get pumped up and ready to fight. The Humans moved in unison in a loud crescendoing sound. "Clash. Clash. Clash!"

As this was all done in time with the beating of the war drum, and the clashing of the swords against the steel of the shields, more and more troops kept marching over the top of the hill, just like free flowing water, which could not be stopped. The echo from all these noises was getting louder and now it was actually making the side walls of the canyon rattle. Because of the amount of troops which were moving at one time the rhythm and the sounds kept growing even louder.

As the marching continued on the Human's side of the Valley. Zalghar was guessing that this was probably the largest group of soldiers ever brought to this valley and as they continued to move into position it looked just like the whole hillside was moving. The march on the Human's side of the Valley, although noisy, was well organized and deliberate.

Some of the elite troops started to appear. Towards the farthest end of the Valley, Zalghar could see a very large troop of Human Archers dressed in bright blue uniforms. These Archers were slowly and quietly moving into position. Half of these Archers carried long bows. The rest of the Archers carried Cross Bows. This troop of Archers also had a small troop of Humans with them, equipped with war axes and swords. Zalghar thought that this troop of heavily armored soldiers, was there to protect the archers from a flank attack by Elfen foot soldiers. He would have to watch this portion of the battle, once the battle commenced in order to see if this was true.

Zalghar looked higher on the hill on the Human's side of the Valley. In this position, which would be just out of sight of the Elves, he noticed that the Humans had brought five, very large Battle Dragons into position. These Battle Dragons seemed very anxious because they knew a large battle was about to commence. All of these magnificent beasts were pawing at the ground and swinging their large heads from side to side in a rhythm with the large war drums. Even from this distance Zalghar felt these large animals were well trained.

Also Zalghar could see the platforms on these large animals backs and he estimated, these Dragons could probably carry as many as twelve soldiers with full equipment, at one time. These platforms of airborne soldiers, would be, he guessed, excellent positions with which to shoot arrows from. The idea that arrows could be shot from above, into the ranks of the Elves was a very good strategy. It would cause considerable confusion to the ranks of Elves in the battle field below because all targets could be chosen at random.

Zalghar just as he was about to turn his attention to the Elves side of the Valley also noticed, a very large group of soldiers coming up over the hill just beside the Battle Dragons. This must be the Human's reserve forces. Zalghar could tell that they were very heavily armed and they were probably going to be used later in the battle to help out in any weaker positions which might be spotted from the Human's Command Post.

These soldiers coming onto the field just out of sight from the Elves side of the battle field, who were close beside the Battle Dragons, must be the veterans. Which meant that they had probably saw many previous battles and were very well trained. Zalghar could not help but notice the precision in the movements of this large force of veteran soldiers. These troops moved about like a well oiled machine. Even at

The Nine Moons of Adjemir

this distance Zalghar could hear the troops movements and it appeared like this entire force of soldiers moved as one. The sounds coming from the group of these veteran troops at this distance, reminded Zalghar of the munching sounds of his giant Kilpacx, as it munched on grass. "Gwrrummpa. Gwrrummpa. Gwrrummpa. Gwrrummpa."

As this troop finally moved into position an unknown order must have been issued from the commander of these soldiers,and suddenly all movement stopped. Silence from these troops was instant. Then nothing moved.

Zalghar did not realize it but his entire evil face had an evil grin of satisfaction, as he viewed the Human's side of the Valley. The Haddron warriors had seen this evil grin on their leader's face and although nothing was said amongst them, they all seemed to share Zalghar's enthusiasm.

At this time, Zalghar still with his evil grin, now turned his complete attention over towards the Elf armies side of the Valley.

Viewing the other side of the valley he could see a small stream flowing swiftly down the Elfen side of the Valley slope. The stream turned slowly, at the valley floor, as it continued to flow down the center of the valley and out of the other end of the battle field. Zalghar noticed huddled on the bank, beside this stream a large group of Elf soldiers who were well armored. This group of foot soldiers, covered a very large portion of the Elf's side of the Valley. They were very heavily concentrated directly in front of the position held by the Dwarf mercenaries on the Human side of the Valley. These Elves, were all dressed in green and they seemed to blend entirely into the, still green grass on the valley sides.

To the right side of these ground troops and slightly behind at the top of the hill, out of sight of the Human side of the battle field, there was three large rectangles of Elfen troops. At this time Zalghar noticed these troops had no armor whatsoever and it appeared that they only carried daggers with them. As he was watching these soldiers a frown came to his forehead. He saw one of the groups being approached by what appeared to be an officer. Once the officer came in contact with these soldiers one of the three groups divided in half and then these halves, moved slowly into a position with the other two army groups. Now there were only two larger segments of these unarmored troops.

Once this movement had been completed the group which was closer to Zalghar's end of the Valley, moved over and took up a position directly behind the Elfen Foot soldiers but still out of sight from the Humans. They all remained just over the hill. This is where they would remain, for a short while, until the actual battle would begin. This position was just on the left side of the main Elfen ground troops.

    Zalghar also noticed that these troops were dressed in bright green uniforms and he could only wonder why these soldiers came to this battle with no armor. As they marched over onto the left side of the ground troops and just out of sight of the Human army, it was such a large movement of soldiers, to Zalghar, they looked just like tall grass blowing in a gentle wind.

    These particular troops seemed wispy and frail and to Zalghar's way of thinking, they seemed all very thin, even for Elves. This seemed strange so Zalghar thought that this part of the battle could be very interesting so he made a mental note to pay strict attention to these groups of Elfen soldiers when they finally entered the battle.

    What Zalghar had been watching moving into position was the elite and fearsome Eeasker's Elf regiment. These troops were not frail at all but they relied heavily on their speed. Therefore the Elfen commanders did not want these troops slowed down with heavy armor. Each and every Eeasker soldier, could not make the rank of the Eeasker detachment, unless they were incredibly fast, strong, yet agile. The Eeasker troop's primary reliance was their speed. But in order to break into the Eeasker detachment, the Elf soldiers who were trying out for this detachment must also possess a certain amount of strength. As Zalghar was to observe during the battle. These fighting qualities were impressive and very important in the way the Elves would do battle with the Human's.

    At this time Zalghar also noticed that the war drum which was beating for the troop movement on the Elf side of the valley, actually made a very different sound than the Human's war drum. This war drum had a crisp, clear, echoing cadence. Not like the Human's war drum which was making a much deeper sound. The rhythm of these war drums, caused an echo to reverberate up the sides of the valley, to where Zalghar sat and these echoing sounds gave Zalghar a warm fuzzy feeling deep down inside himself. The feeling of satisfaction was intoxicating. The plan for Zalghar and his Haddron fighters was working out really well.

    With a grudging admiration of his plan Zalghar now turned his complete attention back onto the movements and the positioning of the Elf troops. On the left side of the foot soldiers and slightly behind these troops was a tremendously large group of Archers moving down the valley slope in preparation. Zalghar noticed that these Archers had no armor at all and he also found this quite strange. This again was something which Zalghar would have to pay attention to in order to understand why these soldiers had no armor. As it turned out, Zalghar would later find these Elfen Archers, just like the Eeaskers detachment, would be able to move around the battle field, almost unrestricted because of their speed.

For the strategies of the Elfen Officers, speed was a very important component on how Elves fought their battles.

Just like the Human army, the Elves seemed to be saving the big weapons until the very last. What Zalghar was actually now seeing, was the Ballistas. There were five or possibly six of them in total. Zalghar would find out later, that some of these Ballistas would shoot very large spears into the sky and if required large stones could also be loaded for use against the ground troops on the Humans side of the battle field. As it turned out the main purpose of the Ballistas was to try to destroy the Human's Battle Dragons as they would begin to fly over the Elfen ground troops.

Zalghar thought to himself that these weapons seemed well made and he nodded his head in satisfaction because he wanted to see these machines in action. At this Zalghar also noticed that there seemed to be Human slaves with these machines. The Human slaves were chained at the ankles and Zalghar could tell even from this distance that the ankle chains contained some form of a magic spell, because of the slight bluish glow which was emitting from them. The Human slaves Zalghar noticed, were moving about, slowly and ghostly, just like zombies.

Then Zalghar saw a new group of soldiers moving up slope from behind the Elf army, towards the top of the hill. These new soldiers had no armor at all, just like the Eeaskers detachment and were only dressed in black tunics. These soldiers dressed in black had no visible weapons, but they each carried a large black sack on their backs. These new soldiers did not march in any rhythm at all but when they moved they were so close together that from this distance, to Zalghar it seemed like a large blob, of black oil sliding along the surface of the ground. This movement was more like a slither, than a march. There was absolutely no noises coming from these new troops.

Zalghar thought to himself that this group of soldiers must be some form of a special force and it would be interesting to see what they would be doing in this battle.

Tyler Dhensaw

Unknown to Zalghar at this time, he had been watching the newly trained Jonzar troops.

The Battle of the Red Valley Begins

Both of the two groups of Eeaskers had just moved closer to where the large group of heavy Ballistas were located, just over the top of the hill and out of sight from the Human side of the battle field. The position where the fearsome Eeaskers were located was basically right behind where Elfen foot soldiers had stationed themselves for the start of the battle. But the Eeaskers would remain out of sight from the Human side of the valley until General Charranoid decided it was strategically important for this troop to attack the Human's army.

Some form of signal must have been sent back to the Elfen Headquarters. All troop movements from the Elf's side of the valley stopped at exactly the same time.

All Zalghar could see at this time was large squares or rectangle of groups of Elfen warriors. The Elves were in position. There was absolutely no movement at all on the Elf side of the valley. Everything became very quiet and very still. The different groups of soldiers on the Elves side of the valley were separated in such a fashion and with the different colors, the valley seemed like large colored patches of woven material which somebody might use as a cover for their bed. To Zalghar this was beautiful. The plan was on time and working perfectly.

"Life is grand." The grin on Zalghar's face was infectious as he had whispered this to himself.

Turning his attention back onto the battlefield Zhalgar did some quick calculations. At this time Zalghar estimated that the Elfen foot soldiers numbered about four to five thousand. The two groups of the elite Eeaskers would number about two thousand in total. The

Archers who were on the field, in manpower, would be upwards of about two thousand. Including some of the other groups of support troops at different locations around the valley. The Elf army, from what Zalghar saw, was quite large.

Zalghar then turned to view the Human's side of the Valley. A quick estimate on his behalf, showed that the Elves clearly out number the Human's army, but not by very much.

From Zalghar's vantage point he noticed the Human General, was accompanied by a young woman who was dressed in an officer's uniform, which Zalghar found quite strange. The Human General was looking across the field to his left and then to his right. This was just about the time when the main body of Dwarf mercenaries were getting into position. The Human archers were just closing up on the place where they would station themselves for the commencement of the battle. It was just as the Human General was pointing things out to the young female warrior, when Zalghar instantly and surprisingly recognized her.

This was the young woman who ran out onto the battle field at the town of Garriton. He remembers seeing her try to fight one of his warriors. This made him laugh to himself. He also remembered the communication between her and the tall Human. It was the presence of these two on the battlefield outside of Garriton which caused the archer from the wall at Garriton to shoot the arrow which hit the Kilpacx in the Eye. He then thought to himself that he must watch her very closely, in order to see if the tall Human warrior was nearby.

At this time Zalghar saw the Human General turn and look back up the hill to where the Battle Dragons were stationed just out of sight from the Elfen side of the Valley. There must have been a signal relayed to the Human General, because he nodded in the direction of the Dragons and then turned his attention to his heavily armed reserves. Again a signal must have been received by him because he again nodded in the direction of this large group of soldiers.

A messenger came riding up the hill towards the Human General and there was a short conversation. As the conversation drew to a close the messenger turned and rode back down the hill to rejoin his companions in the Human Calvary unit. From what Zalghar could tell both sides, the Elves, and the Humans, seemed ready. The entire valley at this time had become very full of soldiers and yet everything became eerily silent.

Again Zalghar viewed the Elf's side of the battle field and saw that there was no visible Elf Calvary in sight on the battle field. He

The Nine Moons of Adjemir

thought to himself that the Elf calvary must now be held in reserve and therefore must be hidden somewhere just over the top of the ridge. Maybe the Elfen Calvary was behind the long line of Ballistas.

Zalghar just shook his head and said to no one in particular. "This is not the way I would have done things." Then shaking his head again he said to some of his warriors who were close enough to hear. "I don't think these people really know how to fight."

Zalghar then spoke in a menacing fashion as he spat at the ground in a disgusted way. "These people the Humans and these Elves, fight with too much honor. Both sides are too civilized."

The warriors close to Zalghar nodded in agreement and continued watching the battle preparation below.

"Well maybe we will learn something here today." Zalghar followed this statement with a short comment before the battle began. "It seems that the plan to have the Humans and the Elves has worked out better than we had expected." Zalghar now became very silent as he knew that the huge battle was just about to commence. He had a very evil look in his eyes and could not help but smiling broadly and laughing as he said to nobody in particular. "These two races think that they are so clever but a simple plan like ours has caused these to races to enter into to this great battle and possibly a complete war." Then he added quickly. "These people of Adjemir are really not very intelligent or well organized."

Just as Zalghar finished this last statement he could see the two Generals on both sides giving the signals to commence fighting. What Zalghar viewed next was both Generals place their swords into their hands and by raising their swords high above their heads, they signaled to each other that they were both ready.

Zalghar did not know that in Adjemir the raising of the sword by the senior officer of an opposing army, was to show absolute respect to the forces of the other army.

General Karridhen had always had the utmost respect for General Charranoid of the Elves and General Charranoid had the utmost respect for General Karridhen of the Human army. These two Generals had faced each other in many battles, many times in the past. These two old Generals had they not been sworn enemies would probably have been the best of friends.

Then General Karridhen pointed his sword straight in the direction of General Charranoid, who returned the same signal to General Karridhen. Unknown to Zalghar, both Generals were smiling.

Once this part of the ceremony was complete both Generals touched the handle of their sword up to their forehead and both Generals bowed his head towards the other army. This was a show of respect for the opposing troops. It was then when the Generals waved their swords over their own troops in front of them, that the battle began. The war drums had the started the battle march cadence.

The two armies which were already in formation for the battle, then started their opening movements. Both the Human foot soldiers and the Human calvary started, in a loud cascading noise, marching further down the Valley slope. The Foot Soldiers walked in unison, close to one another and again were in time to the beat of the large war drum. These soldiers also started to beat their shields with their swords, with each step.

The sound of this large drum seemed to fill the entire Valley with the steady, "thump, thump, thump." When this movement of soldiers was seen by Zalghar, it looked just like slow running water was flowing slowly down the hillside.

There was a steady murmur amongst these soldiers and as they neared the floor of the Valley, this murmuring sound, as it echoed up the Valley to the position of the Haddrons soon became a loud thundering screaming. This screaming became so loud and so strong that the whole valley seemed to be shaking and rumbling. The Human Soldiers in the first opening attack, appeared to be trying to put fear into their opponents on the other side of the Valley. It would be soon when these Human soldiers would brake ranks and charge the slow moving Elfen formations.

Just to the right of the advancing Human Foot soldiers, the Dwarfen mercenaries moved along in a mechanical fashion. These Dwarfen mercenaries, as they moved along, moved at quite a fast pace. Never did one Dwarf fall behind nor would any other speed up. These troops had practiced this march, and all of these Dwarf soldiers had learned these war skills in school when they were still young children. These soldiers moved like a well-oiled machine. Every time they stepped forward they, just like the Human foot soldiers, in unison they would strike their shields with their swords, war axe or war hammer, in a loud crashing noise. Out of all of the sounds coming up from the valley floor towards Zalghar, this sound by far was the loudest.

The Human calvary immediately moved down to the lower levels of the Valley they wanted to be ready to move instantly after the main battle began, whenever the proper signal was given.

On the other side of the Valley a large group of Elfen foot soldiers waited patiently for the Humans to get within range. In the ranks of the archers some Elf archers who were in place beside the main group of foot soldiers had already lit their torches. These Archers had stuck these flaming torches in the ground, beside where they were positioned, so they would have fire at the ready. Already a slight film of smoke was starting to form in the valley. When the Humans got within range the first group of Archers would let loose a heavy barrage of flaming arrows. A cloud of these arrows would fall upon the Humans and create considerable damage and confusion.

When these two armies were in direct contact arrows either on fire, or not were difficult to use, because of the mix up in troops. The Elf archers were always given strict orders, that being, when the hand to hand fighting was in progress a target had to be seen clearly to ensure that Elf arrows did not hit other Elves in the center of the battle.

As soon as the Human Captains saw that arrows were being launched by the Elfen Archers, they would place their shields over their heads for protection. Without stopping of even slowing down the Human soldiers would take this first blow of arrows and keep up their steady rhythm. They would lose very few men to this first barrage of arrows and they would just keep charging in the direction of the main group of Elfen foot soldiers.

Bronell who had for some unknown reason been placed by a captain, near the front of the first group of Human soldiers, continued to march down the field with his shield above his head. None of the arrows from the first attack hit him or his shield. He felt good. He really didn't want to be here in this battle but he had survived the first arrow attack. Confidence and a new form of energy, was building up inside him. He didn't know why.

Bronell was now starting to get very excited as the fever of battle, was slowly becoming part of his being.

The next group of Elfen Archers lit their arrows from the torches on the ground beside them, and notched the flaming arrows in their bows. "Fire!" A deep voice bellowed. The red wall of arrows, arced into the sky, just like a huge red fiery demon and fell onto the Human foot soldiers and Dwarf mercenaries shields. Some of the shields being made mostly of wood, took quickly to fire.

Bronell's shield when it was hit this time had instantly caught fire. His shield had been very dry due to the fact that it had been on his father's wall for so long and it was very easy to catch on fire. Being as new a recruit such as he was, Bronell panicked and dropped his shield.

A seasoned warrior who had been marching beside Bronell quickly picked up his shield. The seasoned warrior slammed the shield onto the ground and broke off the flaming arrow. Then the older soldier turned to Bronell and in a very strong, barking and commanding tone, while he continued marching stated the obvious. "You must keep your shield with you at all times." Then in a softer tone and with a slight smile on the old warriors face the veteran soldier said. "Hang onto it as it may save your life."

Bronell who was always polite and quite likeable, nodded his. "Thanks." With a weak sort of smile.

The seasoned veteran marching beside Bronell glancing sideways could not help but smile at the young man marching beside him and he only said. "Young man you will learn many of these things in a very short while. All by yourself."

The older veteran beside Bronell then turned his attention back to the battle, which was now just in front of them. They continued walking as another hail of arrows came over them. None of these arrows even came near Bronell. With each salvo of arrows Bronell seemed to get more confidence and he was becoming more relaxed. The sick feeling in Bronell's stomach was finally disappearing. The arrows just kept coming. Another hail and then another. The Elves were now just shooting arrows at will.

Panic must be setting in on the Elfen side of the field Bronell thought to himself. They must be just as afraid of this battle as he was. The closer the Human's got to the Elves the faster the arrows began to fly. Some of the arrows were now being launched horizontal to the ground as Bronell and his fellow soldiers neared the enemy ranks. The overhead barrage had finally ceased. Most arrows were now just normal arrows, as it seemed the Elves did not have as much time to light the arrows on fire, as they had before. Because the Humans were getting very close to the Elfen ground troops Bronell drew his sword at the same time as all the other soldiers with him had done. Bronell looked at his sword with some pride. This sword had been a gift from his father. He held his sword by the hilt in his right hand and touched the blade to his helmet. Bronell did not know it at the time but this was also a habit that his father had always had. His father always touched his sword to his helmet just before the actual hand to hand fighting was about to commence.

Then Bronell got a cold, determined and serious look on his face. He looked straight ahead, towards the Elfen column. His walk became trance-like as he continued marching towards the Elfen column. Now there was hand to hand fighting all around him.

Bronell now felt a fire burning deep inside himself. He marched on holding his sword high above his head and he heard some very loud screaming war cry. He did not realize at the time, that the loud screaming war cry, was actually coming from his own lungs.

All of a sudden, before he reached the front line of the Elfen troops, his war scream stopped. He felt a great sickening stinging pain in his left shoulder and down he went. He noticed that his left arm had been struck with an arrow which had somehow managed to just skim pass the corner of his shield. Bronell dropped his sword as he knelt down on the ground. The other Humans soldiers just kept marching past him. He looked at his arm and saw a shocking sight. The arrow was stuck deeply his shoulder. Gingerly he started to try and pull the arrow out of his arm. The arrow was lodged in his shoulder very strongly and it would not budge. He was screaming from the pain. He almost fainted.

Then an energy seemed to come from nowhere and Bronell became very determined. With a tremendous amount of effort, which was much more effort than before while gritting his teeth, he gave a huge pull, which again almost made him faint.

The arrow with this extra effort let go and this time it came all the way out. Momentarily Bronell looked dazedly at the arrow and although he felt sick to the stomach, he just threw the arrow disgustedly to the ground. He stood up weakly and grabbed his sword. Bronell moved back into position in the column. It seemed to Bronell that forever had passed and he still had not made it to the Elfen positions. Bronell felt warm blood running down his left arm. He felt faint and thought that he might get sick to the stomach even before he made it to the Elf column.

Bronell noticed that the arrows had suddenly stopped. Bronell stopped and looked around to see what was happening, but the rest of the volunteers just kept marching. Then he saw the Human Calvary started to make it's first move.

The Calvary of Humans started to pick up speed and Bronell noticed that they were making a deliberate but steady move directly across the field, mostly right towards the Elfen Archers. One of the Elfen columns noticed this move and the Archers from this column who had been firing at Bronell and his companions, started directing their arrows towards the fast and steadily advancing Human Cavalry. Bronell noticed out of the corner of his eye that the Human calvary had very large but light silver colored shields which they held high above there heads. But while stopping the arrows which had been shot into the sky and which were coming down onto the calvary, from above. These overhead arrows were created another problem.

    This strategy of placing the shield above the Human calvaries head, made the horses an easy target for the Elfen Archers, who were at this time picking out individual targets. The horses of these calvary units did not have any battle armor. Battle armor was not being used because the weight of the armor for these horses would slow the speed of the calvary's battle charge.

    The cavalry advancement was taking some hard hits from the arrows, so the command was given and the Human calvary quickly picked up the pace. The calvary which Bronell now saw, was at a charging speed. As they were charging into the Elfen column of foot soldiers and Elfen archers, the charging calvary was suddenly getting twice the fire which they previously had.

    Most of the concentrated fire against the Elfen archers was now coming from the Human archers but the concentration of fire from the Elfen archers remain steadily directed at the Human calvary. It appeared to Bronell that all of the battlefield was fully enveloped.

    On the Elfen side of the battle field, confidently Raydhen stood firing arrows as rapidly as he could at the charging Human cavalry. The arrows had already been very effective against the oncoming cavalry charge but it could not stop the advance against the Elfen foot soldiers or the corner of the Elfen archery troop. Nor did the rapid shooting of hundreds of arrows which was causing havoc to the charging Human calvary, even slightly slow the charge. Although the Humans were the opposing force and they were on the battle field to kill as many Elves as they could, Raydhen could not help but admire the courage of these Human riders.

    Raydhen wondered to himself why he was shooting so many arrows? As the oncoming Calvary had been moving at such terrific rate of speed that the possibility of hitting his target was greatly reduced. But he still continued shooting at the Human cavalry with all the speed he could muster. He wasn't able to shoot as fast or as accurate as the older Elves around him but he still tried.

At the head of the cavalry a young Human Sergeant rode at full stride, galloping down the field as fast as his poor war horse could run. This young sergeant was fighting and riding into this battle in a courageous and fearsome way. This young fighter was such a good calvary rider he was riding his mount bare back. This young Sergeants name was Shantok. With his right hand Shantok held the reins for the horse and his shield. With a firm grip with his left hand he held his shiny sword high above his head. There were already three arrows piercing through his shield. The young sergeant was more than lucky that none of the arrows had been able to pierce more than an inch through his shield. "The gods must be on my side." He thought to himself

He then looked over his shoulder. His men which were behind him, although they had been hit very hard by the Elfen archers, most of them were still in formation. With a quick calculation, Shantok figured he still had about four hundred men left. He turned and paid his attention to the Elfen foot soldiers and the Elfen archers. There where some Human soldiers in front of him and a bit towards his left, who were already in hand to hand combat with these two units of Elfen soldiers. The young Sergeant had looked back at the remaining charging calvary, who with his leadership would also be in hand to hand combat with the Elves very shortly. Shantok was very proud of his men and hated losing any of them in this battle. But war was war.

Just beside the Human calvary, Bronell continued closing in on the Elfen soldiers, who were in the front of the Elfen line. It made him feel quite ill from his injury and also from seeing the Calvary being ripped apart the way that it was. But his made him completely forget about his pain and his own fear. He did notice that the charging Human calvary was taking a lot of the pressure off of him and the other soldiers who had marched into battle beside him.

"How are we ever going too win this battle." Bronell thought to himself as he just shook his head. "Everything seemed so hopeless." Then suddenly some large shadows passed over him and the men who were fighting beside him.

The shadows passed over him very quickly as Bronell looked up at the sky. What he saw gave him hope and put a smile on his face. He was seeing three very large, fully armed, War Dragons, flying high above them and headed directly towards the Elfen Archers.

"Dragons! Dragons! The Dragons!" Shouted Bronell.

"Shhhhh! Kid." Said the warrior who was now next to him, who appeared to be a veteran of many battles. Bronell saw some very large deep scars on this man's face and Bronell noted that he was missing an eye on his left side. "Our job is to march in there and kill the Elves." "Not to tell them what we got and what we are doing."

It took a few moments for Bronell to understand that this seasoned old warrior was only joking with him. Smiling and laughing gently at Bronell the man hit him in the arm. Bronell could not help but understand how young he must appear to this old soldier. Bronell smiled at the old veteran and as he turned towards the battle, he stepped forcefully forward in order to match the stride with the old warrior beside him.

Above the battlefield General Charranoid as he was watching from his headquarters, the development of the battle, sent the message to bring the Ballistas to the top of the hill. General Charranoid had fought against the Human's General Karridhen many times in the past and he knew that three Battle Dragons had just been ordered to enter the battle. Only question in his mind was. "How many more Battle Dragons does Karridhen have at his disposal."

General Charranoid turned to Captain Eeando and talking slowly, while rubbing his chin, as he was thinking he said the following. "Eeando send a message to the remaining Ballistas that they should also come to the top of the hill and get ready for the battle." Then he also added. "I want the catapulting Ballistas brought up next and any remaining Ballistas should be brought to the ready."

As Captain Eeando was turning to leave, General Charranoid made a further statement. "I am not sure how many Battle Dragons the Humans have. But if I'm figuring Karridhen's manoeuver correctly he is about to dispatch some of his reserve troops very shortly."

Captain Eeando stood patiently for General Charranoid to finish. "I want you to give a clear message to the catapult Ballistas to concentrate completely on those veteran reserve troops as soon as they enter the battle field." Then he quickly added. "This is very important." General Charranoid then said in a crisp tone. "I want you back here as fast as possible."

Then with a slight smile on his aged old face the General said. "I have a surprise for the Dwarf mercenary which I'll want you to see."

Captain Eeando nodded that he understood and said. "General I'll be right back."

General Charranoid smiled to himself as he thought. "Some day this young Eeando will make a very good replacement for me as a new commander. I'm getting much to old for these types of battles."

As General Charranoid turned back to the battle he noted that the earlier progress by the Dwarf mercenaries was having a drastic effect on the main group of his foot soldiers in the center of the battle. He thought to himself. "These Dwarf mercenaries are really well trained so when Eeando returns we will see just how good these Dwarfs really are."

On the other side of the battle field General Karridhen had climbed slowly up to the top of the watch-tower, near his headquarters so as things developed, he could get a clear view of the entire battle below. He turned and motioned to Kirwynn that she should follow him. General Karridhen had instructed his engineers to build this tower the night before in preparation for the battle. Once they were in position at the top of the tower, General Karridhen pointed to the battle below and said to Kirwynn. "It's a good thing that we were sent the Dwarf mercenaries by nobleman Kurrest's brother. Because if we did not have them in the middle of our forces we would surely be losing this battle."

Kirwynn said without showing much emotion. "I think you're right General." "This troop of Mercenaries is launching the brunt of the attack against the Elfen formation and they seem to be winning."

Then she asked. "General. When will you send in the rest of the Battle Dragons?"

General Karridhen turned towards Kirwynn with a twinkle in his eyes and said to her. "Good question." With the same twinkle in his eyes, becoming more noticeable the old General went on. "I have fought against General Charranoid many times and I know that he always has a surprise or two so I will not let him know how many Battle Dragons we have at our disposal." He then added. "We must keep our wits about us because that old Charranoid can be quite inventive." Speaking quite loudly above the roar of the battle the General said. "I must anticipate some new surprises every time we do battle with the Elves. I have two more Battle Dragons ready to go. On short notice."

Glancing and pointing up over the hill behind him he said. "And right over the hill just out of sight we have another full regiment of veteran Foot Soldiers' at the ready. The three Battle Dragons which we have just sent into the battle should get Charranoid to show just how many Ballistas he has. The progress shown by the Dwarf mercenaries should make Charranoid show us his surprise tactics, very shortly."

Then General Karridhen added as an after thought. "That is if that old 'war horse' has any surprises to show." The General made a quick laugh as he said. "But he always does. I'm betting he will want to concentrate his next strategic moves against the Dwarf Mercenaries. Wait and see if I am right?"

While looking down onto the battlefield, Kirwynn said in a thoughtful tone. "I think I understand General. And I think you are right."

Down on the battle field, on the Elf's side of the valley, Raydhen had heard a bunch of commotion and yelling behind him. Raydhen turned around and saw a group of very large Ballistas, just being pushed over the top of the hill. The chanting from behind continued. These spear Ballistas were pointed directly up into the sky in the direction of the huge incoming Human's Battle Dragons.

Back on the Human's side of the valley, Kirwynn could, through the smoke of the battle, see over onto the Elfen side of the Battle field and there was a different type of Ballista also being brought to the top of the hill. She would find out later these new machines were the catapult Ballista.

Raydhen would soon find out when the Human reserve unit was starting it's march down the Human's side of the Valley that these different Ballistas were large catapults and he would see later that these catapult Ballistas would be concentrating mostly on the Human reserves.

A short while later Raydhen looked over at the nearest Ballista. He saw that some Elves were loading it and getting a few Human slaves in place to make ready for loading of the next large spear. All in all Raydhen thought that there must be close to six Ballistas in total. This gave him a strong feeling of security, as he turned his attention back to the battle which was now fully developed just in front of him. Behind Raydhen he could hear, quite loudly, an order being yelled by the officer in charge of the Ballistas. "Fire."

Raydhen quickly looked up and followed these large spears slicing through the sky. He could not help but notice that these large spears seemed like lightning going through the sky. They were traveling at a tremendous speed but unlike thunder bolts, these missals were, deadly silent. They all missed their targets. Then only moments after this first salvo of giant spears, he saw a second set of spears which had just been launched. Again they flew over Raydhen's head, in complete silence, but it appears this time, with a deadly accuracy.

The Nine Moons of Adjemir

Raydhen turned and watched the intended targets. Three Battle Dragons had been flying above the Elfen archers and the twelve Human archers on the backs of the Battle Dragons had been shooting arrows down at the Elfen archers below. The Dragons were high enough that the archers below could not hit them and therefore were defenseless against this attack from above.

These Battle Dragons had successfully dodged the first salvo of giant spears which had been launched from the front Ballistas. But as it turned out one of the battle Dragons was not successful at dodging the second salvo of giant spears. The huge Dragon Raydhen noticed seemed to come to a grinding halt as the huge spear sunk deep into it's chest. The injured beast seemed to shudder in mid air and gave out a tremendous roaring bellow of pain. Almost immediately this enormous beast started to fall from the sky. Clearly Raydhen could tell even from this distance that this large Dragon had been mortally wounded. An instant cheer erupted from all the Elves on the Battle field as the mighty beast began plunging, at an ever increasing speed, towards the ground.

Raydhen saw about a dozen Humans soldiers jump off of the already dead Dragon, just before it hit the ground. The Human soldiers whom had jumped from the dead Dragon's back, before it hit the ground, rolled around and as they tried to stand up were almost instantly cut down by a barrage of arrows fired at them from the closest Elfen archers unit. Death at this time for these warriors was sudden. Raydhen spun back around to see the crews who were working on the Ballistas had already reloading the Ballistas for another salvo.

Back at the Elfen command post just after the Battle Dragon had been shot from the sky, Captain Eeando returned to stand beside General Charranoid. "Congratulations General." Captain Eeando had a large grin on his face as he stood close to the General. The General turned towards Eeando and said. "Now you will see the Dragons change their tactics. They will now fly very close over our troops so that we cannot effectively use our Ballistas effectively."

The General then added, nodding his head with a show of confidence and knowledge. "It is just as well because now our advanced archers will have the Dragons in their range. The Human soldiers on the backs of those the Human's Battle Dragons have very little cover." What he was referring to was the platforms on the back of the Dragons were very shallow, because of weight restrictions and therefore could not offer much protection for the soldiers on the back of the Dragons. Sure enough the Battle Dragons, now started to swoop down very close to the battle ground and began to attack the center of the Elfen formation. The Soldiers on the back of the Dragons continued shooting their arrows with a definite accuracy but they were also receiving some injuries because of their closeness to the elven archers.

    Behind Raydhen six large Human slaves started turning the Ballistas towards the new Battle Dragons which had just been sent into the Battle by General Karridhen. They tried to aim the Ballista, but a Battle Dragon landed first. This Battle Dragon had landed just at the back of Raydhen's unit.

    General Charranoid was looking over the battle field and besides the fact that the Battle Dragons had landed troops behind his main group of foot soldiers he also noticed that the Dwarfen mercenaries were gaining momentum against his front line troops. He turned to Captain Eeando and said. "I promised you a little surprise. Now watch this."

    The old General turned and nodded to a messenger with a large horn who was standing off to the General's left, as General Charranoid very quietly said. "Now is the time."

    The young messenger put the large horn to his mouth and he gave off three short distinctive bursts on the horn in a very rapid fashion. Captain Eeando turned his attention down onto the battle field and what he saw surprised him. The tales being talked about around the Elfen garrisons were all true. General Charranoid always had a surprise or two ready for any Human army which he had to face.

    Things on the battle field started to change very quickly and Captain Eeando could not help but wonder how the precision seen on the battle field, by the Elfen troops could be this organized. In all of the confusion of the fighting he was actually seeing definite signs, of a well thought out plan. Eeando knew that General Charranoid had been giving special attention to a large group of soldiers from his own garrison but what Captain Eeando was about to see, really surprised him. What surprised him the most was that everything about this strategy and the training behind this military move had been kept a complete secret. Keeping his attention on the battle field what Captain Eeando saw not only surprised him but it seemed to surprise every body, even the Dwarf mercenaries.

    When the three blasts on the horn had been sounded, everyone around Raydhen stopped firing arrows and almost instantly, the large group of Elfen foot soldiers who held the position directly in front of him, instantly flattened themselves to the ground. Raydhen had been told this might happen just before the attack had begun and he was very curious to see what else was about to happen. Raydhen had to use all of his courage, not to fire any arrows at the Dwarfen Mercenaries. Raydhen quietly stood there with an arrow notched in his bow and just looked around. He was very surprised at what he was about to witness.

The fearsome Dwarf Mercenaries were taken by complete surprise. They just stood there. In fact all of the fighting on the entire battle field, at this moment, came to a complete standstill. The entire Battle field, instantly became very still and very silent. Curiosity was abundant on both sides of the battle field. This was because everybody on the battle field knew that something important was about to happen but nobody seemed to know what it was. The battle field for a few seconds remained eerily silent.

Immediately after the Elfen Foot Soldiers had flattened themselves to the ground with their shields placed above them another three blasts on the horn was sounded. When this signal was sounded, Raydhen knew his unit had been ordered to send an overhead salvo either directed at the Dwarf Mercenary unit or towards the large group of Human foot soldiers who had been fighting right beside the Dwarfen mercenary.

Raydhen looked over at the other Elfen archery unit and saw that same order had been given to them. Both archery units sent a large overhead salvo of arrows at the same time.

Raydhen glanced at the Dwarf mercenary and the Human units of foot soldiers. It was no surprise to see that signals were being given by the commanders of those units, ordering those soldiers to instantly raise their shields above their heads, in order to stop the incoming salvo of overhead arrows from doing too much damage.

What was happening, Raydhen saw was happening very fast and clearly this maneuver by the Humans and the Dwarfs was very well organized. The unit which was lightly armed and which Raydhen did not understand why they were there because they did not carry any visible weapons, went into action.

This unknown unit was situated directly behind where the Elfen foot soldiers, were positioned. Raydhen would find out later that this new Elfen unit was called, the Jonzars. This new unit never carried spears, swords, war axes, or any of the ordinary standard fighting weapons, which were being carried by all of the other Elfen army units. Instead they all carried on their backs, a large black sack of a disc type weapon. This new weapon was called the 'Jonzar'.

The horn from the Elven headquarters now sounded another three short blasts and this was only seconds after all of the Elfen foot soldiers had fallen flat onto the ground. With a quick command from their leader the front half of the Jonzar unit, opened fire upon the front of the Dwarf mercenaries and the front of the Human foot soldiers.

These new weapons, the Jonzars, which had just been released from the Jonzar unit hit the front lines of the Dwarf mercenaries with an incredible and noisy impact. The front line of the Human foot soldiers, were also hit with a devastating impact. The front lines of Human soldiers and Dwarf mercenaries were immediately cut down. The surprise which General Charranoid had told Captain Eeando, was just beginning.

Each Jonzar warrior carried at least twelve Jonzars with him and the warrior who had just released his Jonzar immediately flattened to the ground as the second line of Jonzar throwers went into action and immediately released a second barrage of Jonzars. There was still very little time to react by the Dwarf mercenaries and the Human Foot Solders. The front line of both these units took another direct hit. As before, it was devastating to both these units because their shields were still held over their heads to protect themselves from the over head salvo of Elfen arrows. The entire attack by the new Jonzars and the overhead salvo of Elfen arrows only took a matter of seconds, but the outcome to the Human and Dwarfen columns was significant.

Immediately after the initial surprise from the Jonzars, the commanders in charge of the front lines of Dwarfen Mercenaries and the Human foot Soldiers, ordered the new front lines to lower their shields, to guard against the next salvo of Jonzars.

But the damage had already been done. Arrows kept flying into the ranks of the Dwarfs and the Humans. Jonzars were now being thrown at an ever increasing pace. Just like the waves in the ocean, the Jonzars, in a screaming fashion, just kept coming. Some of the harder thrown Jonzars were able to slice right through some of the shields held by the front line soldiers.

On the Human side of the battle field General Karridhen took the Elfen surprise in stride and then ordered his own surprise. The General leaned over to Kirwynn and said calmly and confidently. " Watch this."

General Karridhen then quickly nodded to a messenger who was sending signals to certain units. The messenger turned and facing

The Nine Moons of Adjemir

the reserves sent a message for the reserves to start into the Valley. At the same time a message was also being sent to the remaining Dragons to enter the battle.

The instructions to the Battle Dragons commanders was to fly over the battle field and concentrate mostly on the new units of Jonzars. The surprise by General Charranoid was over and now the Jonzar units who did not carry any ordinary weapons or armor would have to face all of the fury from Battle Dragons and would almost be powerless to fight back. The Battle Dragons had also been ordered when possible to fly low and use their 'dragon fire' on the Jonzar unit.

The larger unit of Human reserves had been instructed to concentrate on the Elfen front line and to assist the Dwarfs who had taken on the greatest amount of casualties from the Elfen archers, and the surprise from the Jonzars. Kirwynn noticed that almost immediately the two remaining Battle Dragons had lifted off, complete with fully armed troops in the basket on their backs and headed directly into the center of the battle directly towards the Jonzar units. From her vantage point on the observation tower Kirwynn saw the Elves who had flattened onto the ground, to let the Jonzar unit start the Jonzar throwing, had to get back on their feet to assist in the fight against the incoming Battle Dragons.

Now the effectiveness of the Jonzar unit was vastly reduced. The Elfen archers were now opening fire on the Dragons. The Jonzar unit had to move quickly from behind the Elfen ground troops and make their way around the Elfen Foot in order to have a clear shot at both the Human soldiers and the Dwarf Mercenaries. Clearly the battlefield was becoming crowded.

Kirwynn also noticed that the Dwarf mercenaries could now continue their forward movements, as well as the Human foot soldiers. Momentum on the Human side although they had their numbers reduced by the surprise of the Jonzar attack started to make some forward progress.

As soon as the Dragons were in range of the archers and the Jonzar recruits, the troops who were on the backs of the Dragons started firing arrows and throwing their spears. One of the larger Dragons landed directly behind the Elfen Foot soldiers and shot out a great fire ball, at the back of the Elves main unit. Then while recharging for another fire ball the Dragon just stood there with a fierce look in it's eyes and stopped the free movement of the Elves fighting units. The riders who had been riding on this Dragon were wearing heavy armor and were able to jump off the Dragons back set up a perimeter and commenced with hand to hand combat. The commander in charge of the Dragon was the only Human to stay with the Dragon. He continued to fire arrows. The Elves fired arrows at this battle Dragon and the Humans without much success. The arrows bounced off the Human heavy armor as well as the Dragon's thick scales. The Ballistas were not able to shoot at the Dragon which was on the ground, because if something went wrong, they may hit the Elfen soldiers in the nearby surroundings.

    At a different location on the battlefield the Sergeant of the Human cavalry, Shantok, drew ever closer to the Elfen foot. Even though the Calvary had taken some very heavy casualties he estimated he still had nearly three hundred and fifty men left. The arrows had almost stopped thanks to the Dragons entering the battle at this time. So having no need for his shield to be held over his head he was able to manoeuver his attack horse into a better attack position.

    Shantok quickly turned to his men as he was signaling them to follow him. It was his plan to attack the Elven archers, as soon as he could. But from his position he must first battle through the Elven foot soldiers, who were situated right in front of him and his men. As Shantok broke away from the unit and the men who were closest to him he charged fiercely into the thick of the battle.

    Charging ahead as fast as his mount could carry him he smashed into the awaiting Elfen foot soldiers. From his military training he knew that he should lead by example and that the prime objective was to take out the officers of the enemy first. Jumping to the ground and using his sword with considerable force he stabbed right through an Elfen Sergeant. Shantok then quickly pulled out his sword from the Elfen Sergeant and then turning to his right slashed into the neck of the Elf, who was coming to the aid of the fallen Sergeant. A slash across of the belly of anther Elf spilled the Elf's insides over the ground. Having killed the Elves closest to him he jumped back onto his mount and spared a moment to look up to see his men smashing into the center of the Elfen Foot. They were showing good forward movement. The Elves were being torn apart by the impact from the calvary charge but the ones in the front who had been killed or injured, were quickly replaced by others from behind.

    Shantok spun quickly around and stabbed another Elf and then lobed the head off another. He gave a quick low whistle to his

The Nine Moons of Adjemir

horse in order to calm the animal down. He then began trotting back to where his men were attacking the main Elfen army.

From his vantage point at the Elfen headquarters, General Charranoid did not like the way the battle was turning. He turned to Captain Eeando and said. "Send a messenger to the Eeaskers unit." The General paused for a moment and then he continued. "Tell them it is time to enter the battle."

Before Captain Eeando could turn to the messengers, General Charranoid also said. "I also want all of the remaining Ballistas to get involved with their catapults." Then he quickly added. "As before, have them concentrate on the Humans reserves but unless they can get a clear shot at the Dragons they should not be shooting any more spears."

From the Humans's side of the battle field, General Karridhen leaned in the direction of Kirwynn and pointing in the direction of Sergeant Shantok said. "You can see the courage being shown by that young Sergeant Shantok and the calvary. It appears they have turned the battle in our favor." Kirwynn without saying anything, just nodded.

The General went on. "The Dragons are really keeping the Elves pinned down. And look over there our heavy armored soldiers are being very affective."

Then had he turned and mentioned to Kirwynn who had been listening intently. "That old 'war horse' Charranoid is about to send in his Eeaskers unit." And then the General added. "These Eeaskers you will notice, have incredible speed." Kirwynn looked towards the General and spoke quietly. "I have heard how ferocious and effective the Eeaskers are and how much speed they have. My father used to speak about them. He also said that sometimes the Eeaskers alone could sometimes decide a battle."

General Karridhen's mind seemed to be operating at a very fast speed and he was very intent. He then turned to another messenger and instructed him to get a message to the Dragon commanders, as fast as possible. He said to the messenger. "The Dragon commanders should concentrate on the Eeasker units completely when those units enter the battle. In a commanding tone with some urgency he added. "Go now quickly." The messenger turned and went off with this new message.

Back on the battle field Raydhen looked around. The heavily armored Humans where cutting down his fellow Elves and the Battle

Dragon was getting ready for another fire ball attack. The Humans fell back behind the Dragon, as some of the Human archers from the Dragon opened fire with their bows. Then the Dragon blew an enormous fire ball and some of the Elves broke and turned to run.

Raydhen turned just in time to see a Human unit of foot soldiers charging right into the middle of his group of Elfen archers. The Humans were yelling and chanting at the top of the lungs and when they weren't actually fighting, they would slap their swords on their shields to make an even louder noise. Raydhen sheathed his dagger and then pulled another arrow over his shoulder. He glanced back, over his shoulder, looked into his quiver and saw only one arrow remaining. Raydhen glanced over to the other unit of Elves which had been fighting right beside his unit during the battle. The charging Humans were now entering the middle of the front of the Elfen lines.

Young Raydhen also noticed these Human soldiers were screaming like some sort of wild animals. These loud screaming war cries were being made as these barbaric Humans launched an enormous sword and spear attack right into and through parts of the Elves front lines. Hearing a commotion to his right, Raydhen looked to see a large group of Dwarves mercenaries were now charging into the Elf flank.

The clashing noises of smashing armor, sword on sword, axe on spear, dagger on armor, and helmet to helmet of the combating forces, plus the screaming of the injured warriors all around him, brought a sickening feeling to Raydhen's insides. Silently and to himself he wished he were at home where it was always safe. Raydhen was learning first hand that the business of war was an ugly and an unfriendly place to be in. Maybe he should had paid more heed to what his father had been saying to him.

Things were now happening so fast that he was having trouble understanding who was actually winning this battle. But it appeared that the tide of battle was starting to favor the Human army. Raydhen wondered to himself, while looking at Elfen ranks being smashed by the Humans. "When General Charranoid would send in the feared Eeaskers to help his unit out?'

Raydhen looked to his right, just in time to see a young charging Human soldier, with an older battle worn notched bow coming right at him. Raydhen did not know, nor would he ever know but this young Human warrior's name was Bronell.

Both of these young first time warriors, at this time were only about six feet apart and this far into the battle, their actions were becoming mechanical. Both were acting with some form of pure instinct. With the best warriors scream that Bronell could muster he reached down and took out his father's war axe. He then with speed, threw his father's old war axe, with as much force as he could. Raydhen, while staring Bronell straight in his eyes, let loose the last arrow, which he already had notched in his bow.

The war axe thrown by Bronell, had found it's target. Bronell's chest armor had been pieced.

The arrow which was shot by Raydhen, hit Bronell directly in the throat, with considerable force.

Both the young warriors then sank slowly onto the cold ground of the battle field.

They lay very still in the middle of the battle and were staring into each other's eyes. For these two young soldiers, all was becoming very quiet. For them the battle no longer existed.

Both these very young warriors were to die like this. Alone, cold and unnoticed.

Back in the middle of the battle field the Dwarf mercenaries were now flanked by the front line Elves. The fearsome Elfen Eeaskers who had just entered the battle were attacking the front line of the Human foot soldiers and were also attacking the front lines of the Dwarfs. With great success.

The Humans with the heavier armor and heavier swords with stronger swings had cut down the first lines of the Elves. But the speed and grace of the Eeaskers was proving to be very useful tool against the heavy hitting but slow Humans and stout Dwarfs.

One of the advanced Ballistas finally got off a clear shot and killed another one of the attacking Dragons. When the injured Dragon fell in amongst the Human foot soldiers it caused considerable damage.

The Human Cavalry which had been attacking the Elf Foot continued the vicious hand to hand fighting.

Then the Elfen Calvary who had just entered the battle started to clash with the Human calvary. This made the Human calvary, turn their attention away from the Elfen foot soldiers and onto the Elfen calvary, with it's full force.

By this time all of the reserves and extra soldiers from both sides of the battle field had been committed to the battle. The entire valley was full of soldiers of all types. Dragons and Ballistas included. The Dwarves with their heavy, almost impenetrable armor kept marching forward and were trying to go right through the Elfen front lines.

The front lines of the Dwarf mercenary with their great double bladed war axes were cutting down the Elfen front line as they kept advancing deeply into the Elfen army. The advancing line of Dwarfs would cut down the Elfen foot soldier in the front line and the front of the Dwarfen attackers would just step over them, to get at the Elves who were in behind the advanced front rows of the defenders. The front line of Dwarfs would just swing their axes at any part of the Elfen defender, be it their legs, hips or sides. Then the other Dwarf mercenaries who were behind the front line, would with a mechanical efficiency, finish off the injured Elf.

And so it was the Dwarves with this forward momentum quickly found themselves, deep inside the middle of the Elves foot. Instead of marching right through the Elfen foot soldiers, the Dwarves had moved ahead too quickly and now found themselves stretched too thin. The Dwarf mercenaries were now completely surrounded by the entire Elfen foot.

The Dwarf mercenary had to go on the defensive and were now fighting to get out. At the head of the Dwarfen unit was an old stout Dwarf warrior by the name of Mhendha who had a great war hammer in his hands. This aged Dwarf warrior had a war hammer which was very old and which had been handed down, from father to son, for as long as anyone could ever remember. There were names of every Dwarf on the hammers handle, who had ever possessed this killing machine. It had been his father's, and his father's father, and all the fathers' before them. This aged war hammer was truly ancient and in Dwarf society, very famous.

With mighty swings this aged Dwarf would strike down Elves with a single stroke. Now that this old warrior knew that he and his men were completely surrounded by the closed Elfen foot, he started to swing this faithful old war hammer even more fiercely and harder. One hit in the chest from this war hammer when swung by Mhendha, could instantly kill a fragile elf.

The old Dwarf started to snarl, as he was trying to get his troops to break free from the entrapment. With a mighty sidewards swing to the shoulder of a Elf soldier, the powerful blow from Mhendha's war hammer, sent this Elf smashed and bleeding into another Elf and they both went down in a tangled pile. The two Elves were still alive and struggling to get up and the Elf soldier on the bottom, was strong enough to continue the attack, so the Old Dwarf swung down with his enormous strength killing them both. A loud growl of victory came from deep within Mhendha. Then out of the corner of his eye the Old Dwarf saw an Elf charging towards him and he noticed this swift attacker was moving at an incredible speed.

He said to himself, in a snarling fashion. "This must be one of those Eeaskers." With a growl Mhendha snarled. "I'll fix him."

But as he turned to meet this new attacker he found out why the Eeaskers were so fearsome. The Eeasker's speed proved to be to much for this old warrior. The double dagger swinging Elf with this incredible speed, was able to stab the old warrior Dwarf in his shoulder. The stabbing by the Eeasker Elf was so powerful that the dagger went right through Mhendha's heavy armor. The injury to the old Dwarf was located in his shoulder, at the joint in the armor, right were the shoulder plate meets the breast plate. The Eeasker's dagger slipped right through the joint in the old Elf's armor and was imbedded, with force, deep into Mhendha's shoulder.

The old Dwarf screamed in agony. The Elf jumped back out of swinging distance of the old Dwarfs's war hammer. The attacking Eeasker with lightning speed, quickly grabbed his bow from his shoulder while notching an arrow.

The tired Old Dwarf because of all his skills from all his fighting years, quickly, with his good arm and incredible speed for an old warrior, reached down to his belt grabbing a small throwing axe. With all the force he could muster in his heavy suit of armor, with limited flexibility, plus his injury, he threw the small throwing axe. The axe soared with such speed, making a whistling noise as it traveled through the air. Just before the surprised Eeasker could release his arrow, the axe hit him directly in the middle of his chest. The light weight Elf was hit with such force from the axe that he flew backwards screaming, and knocked down three other Elfen soldiers, in a tangled mess. The Old Dwarf glanced sideways when he saw some help coming to his aid. Turning back to face the injured and almost dead Eeasker. Mhendha spoke in a growling fashion, directly at the Eeasker.

"Let this be a lesson to you. Never bring a dagger and a bow. To an axe fight."

With this statement, the old Dwarf knelt down slowly on one knee wiping the Elf's blood from his axe and muttered painfully to himself while tiredly shaking his head. "I'm becoming too old for these types of battles." Again shaking his head and still muttering to himself as he was looking around at his fellow warriors, he gave himself the same lecture once again. "I have to retire and leave all this nonsense to these young fools. I really am getting too old for this sort of stuff."

Then his fellow Dwarves slowly surrounded the old wounded warrior to keep him safe from other attackers. All the younger Dwarves knew that Mhendha was far too weak to fight off many more of these vicious fast moving Eeaskers. These younger Dwarves who always had the utmost respect for Mhendha when he needed help, came to his assistance immediately. In Dwarfen society Mhendha was very esteemed and very respected.

In the thick of the battle the Human Cavalry who were now fighting right beside the Dwarves, was also cutting right through the front lines of the Elves. Sergeant Shantok was stabbing downwards at the Elves who were right in front of him. From his mount he could tell that the Battle Dragons had been very successful at pinning down not only the new Jonzar troops, but also most of the Elfen Archers.

It was at this time when Shantok saw them. A troop of skinny Elves wearing no armor at all were swiftly moving in the direction of his calvary unit. He noticed that besides these Elves wearing almost nothing, they had their faces painted red and they also had much longer hair than most Elves. These warriors were moving with incredible speed and they seemed to move effortlessly. This group of Elf warriors, were moving like an unrestricted wind, swirling and spinning in the morning light.

The only weapons which most of these warriors carried were two long thin daggers. The odd Elf in this group also carried a bow, but it seemed that the weapons of choice for these fighters, were the double daggers. One weapon in each hand, glinting and shining in the sunlight, with the swiftness of the swirling motions.

These Elves were screaming in a very high pitched, trembling, ear piercing scream. The closer they got to Shantok's calvary unit, the louder they screamed and the faster their arm movement became. This screaming and the swift arm movement with the daggers catching the light, was a scare tactic, used by the Eeaskers. Shantok had never seen any Elf with war paint on nor had he ever heard any Elves use any type of battle scream before. This was a first. Then Shantok smiled as he wondered to himself.

"Would these Eeaskers scream even louder with my sword slicing through them?"

The Nine Moons of Adjemir

"Eeaskers!" The young Sergeant muttered under his breath. Then Shantok started to yell as loud and strong as he could to his men. "Sword Dances. They have Sword Dancers!"

He had yelled to his men in the more common name for Eeaskers. Although the Eeaskers fought mostly with daggers they were called sword dancers. Mostly because on the nights before a big battle these fast moving Warriors would dance their special dance. This dance was done over red hot swords which had been placed on the ground. This is why they were called. 'The Sword Dancers.'

Shantok had never been present when a battle was taking place with the Elves, where there were Eeaskers present. But Shantok and all of the men in his unit, knew that these Eeaskers were the most fearsome of all Elfen warriors. The scream from these fast moving vicious troops was sending shivers up even Sergeant Shantok's spine.

The Eeasker who was the closest to Shantok was moving in at full speed when the Eeasker jumped upwards towards the young Sergeant's head. This Eeasker was spinning through the air and he easily reached the height of Shantok who was still on his mount. With daggers crossing over each other in the whirlwind killing fashion, the attacking Eeasker warrior with a piercing scream, flew directly at the Sergeant.

Only a quick parry saved Shantok's life. But the force of the blow from the Eeasker was so strong that it sent the young Sergeant flying backwards off of his horse and onto the ground. The young Sergeant quickly jumped to his feet but the Eeasker was upon him immediately. Screaming even louder than he was before the Eeasker leapt towards the sergeant. Quickly thinking Sergeant Shantok jumped away to his left. Turning quickly around the young Sergeant was confronted again, by this fast moving, smiling, screaming Eeasker.

Ducking, parrying, jumping away from attacks of the fast moving Eeasker, was all the Human Sargent could do. Finally Shantok's chance came and he swung with all his might in a horizontal slashing fashion, at the waist of the attacker. Shantok was surprised when the Eeasker was no longer there. With incredible speed the Eeasker had jumped high into the air. High enough to jump clear over the sword which Shantok had swung. The Eeasker landed and immediately went into an attack position.

Because Shantok had swung his sword so hard, the momentum carried him partly through a complete turn. His defenseless back was now partially towards the enemy Eeasker. Then Shantok felt a kick to the back of his head and he started to go down, but luckily he only stumbled as he was turning around to face his enemy. As Shantok finished turning around, he saw crouching down on the ground the Eeasker enemy. With lightening speed the Eeasker lashed out both of with both his legs and tripped Shantok. This time Shantok went down hard.

    Lying on his back partly stunned Shantok found he was looking groggily upwards at the bright blue sky. Then a shadow was quickly cast over his body and he saw the Eeasker standing over him. The Eeasker was pulling back both his daggers for the kill. Shantok knew he was about to die. In this position Shantock knew he was powerless to stop the vicious, incredibly fast, screaming killer Eeasker from finishing the fight.

    Just then as the Eeasker started to plunge his daggers into the dazed Shantok's chest the killing scream from the attacker stopped. To Shantok's surprise the fearsome Eeasker could now only give a feeble cry. Then to the further surprise of Shantok, the attacking Eeasker started to slip sideways towards the ground. The Eeasker was trying to turn in order to see where his new attacker had come from but he was dead before he hit the ground.

    The dead Eeasker who landed right beside Shantok, died in a pathetic heap.

    Sergeant Shantok looked up and over his feet to see a very young Human Calvary fighter on his horse. It was one of his men. This smiling young warrior who had just saved Shantok's life, yelled down to Shantok who was still laying, somewhat stunned, on the ground. "These Eeasker Elves they are very, very fast, but these Eeaskers Elves, are also very, very fragile."

    Then the young soldier, still smiling jumped down from his horse and helped, the still somewhat dazed Shantok to his feet. This young soldier seemed very happy and was showing absolutely no fear at all. He was so relaxed he continued to joke around. Even in the middle of this huge and prolonged battle, this young warrior found humor. The young soldier with a twinkle in his eye, while wiping the blood from his throwing axe. Said in a laughing manner. Something very similar to the old Dwarf warrior who had just killed the Eeasker with his axe had said.

    "Yep. Just like an Eeasker. Brings an knife to an axe fight."

    The young soldier, still laughing, bent over with even a bigger smile, chuckling to himself as he had pulled the daggers out of the hands of the dead Eeasker. He spoke, still smilingly and nodding towards Shantok. "Souvenirs." Then this young soldier repeated again what he had said earlier. This young calvary soldier spoke with the same slightly boyish grin still on his face as he was shaking his head back and forth as he repeated. "Yep. These Eeasker are very, very fast, but they sure are very, very fragile."

He quickly wiped the sweat from his forehead with the sleeve of his tunic then he swiftly ran towards his horse and using no hands, jumping clear from the ground and landed right into his saddle. Then still smiling this young soldier yelled to Shantok, just before kicking his horse in the sides which was his signal to go forwards and back into the battle. "My name is Alandaugh, but my friends just call me Aland."

Shantok only had time to yell. "Thanks." To this young warrior who had just saved his life because Alandaugh had turned so quickly and went back into the fray of the battle. Shantok thought to himself. "This young soldier seems to move almost as fast as the Eeaskers." Shantok had found the speed and the courage of Alandaugh somewhat strange and he would have to keep this in mind.

From Alandaugh's behavior, it was very easy for Shantok to conclude that this young man had courage, speed, and great confidence in himself. All in all, Shantok had thought to himself, that this young Alandaugh seemed like a very reliable warrior.

Shantok again vowed to keep this in mind. Shantok softly chuckled to himself when he remembered the joke which was told by this young Alandaugh. Shantok repeated the joke to himself as he was returning to the battle. "Just like an Eeasker. Brings a knife to a Axe fight." He would have to remember that saying. He couldn't help but laugh to himself as he also turned back into the center of the battle.

The Sounds of Battle

After Zorp had woken everybody up and they had marched for a couple of hours, Bobbiur was still not sure what he would do when he got to the Red Valley. They were making much better time now since the Dragon was able to see properly with the coming daylight. As it turned out, it would be about another hour before the group would finally hear the sound of the battle. Hagjel would hear the sounds of battle first, even before Jakka was aware of anything.

It was just after Jakka had woken up when he would hear the sounds of battle. He had his head poked up out of the tote bag and was just taking in the scenery while munching on some fruit which Hagjel had given him when he also heard the sounds of the battle. The pace of Bobbiur and the group had quickened. Jakka was immediately in a raised and intense sense as he looked up at Hagjel, probably for some sign of reassurance. This was mostly because Jakka was not sure what this new sound was. He had never heard this type of loud noise before. The GymmKat was clearly very tense.

Hagjel knew that Jakka had never heard this type of sound before, so he reached down and patted Jakka's head in a reassuring gesture. Jakka had been in battles with Hagjel before, prior to this battle, but this sound was not even close to anything Jakka had ever heard before. This was not just one simple sound. It was more like a giant roaring waterfall. The rumbling, crashing noise seemed completely out of control. Hagjel again looked down at Jakka and continued patting his head to comfort him. Hagjel could feel the tension from Jakka and thought to himself that this must be an awfully scary noise for such a little animal.

Salbuk looked over and sent a message to Hagjel. "This is probably true." Then Salbuk concluded the mind message with a short statement. "All animals are scared by noises which they have never heard before and Jakka is no exception."

Hagjel nodded in the direction of Salbuk, meaning that he was probably right. Then they both looked to the front where Obmar and Bobbiur were leading, and started paying more attention to what was about to happen. Jakka, who was still nervous, dropped further down into the tote bag. He actually hid his head under his paws and tried to cover his ears as best he could. Just then, Hagjel spared a moment and looked into the bag where he saw Jakka covering his ears.

"Everything will be all right little guy." Hagjel had said with a smile while continuing to rub Jakka's ears.

The group broke out of the walking pace as the entire group sped up a little bit, in order to see what was happening in the Valley which lay just ahead. It was a very short time before they got to the top of the ridge at the Valley's edge and they all looked over.

What they saw was quite amazing. It was almost beyond comprehension and quite scary at the same time. The entire Red Valley was fully engulfed in an enormous conflict as the Human and Elfen armies were attacking each other with a tremendous effort from both sides. What the group was witnessing took their breath away. From this position on the hill. none of the group could actually tell which army was actually having more success.

Salbuk sent a message to the group which made a lot of sense. "It appears that no side is winning."

With considerable emotion in the next message, Salbuk was shaking his head in disbelief. "They are smashing each others armies for absolutely no reason." Hagjel added to Salbuk's message. "It appears that there will no winner on this battle field today."

Bobbiur noticed that on their far right, was the Human camp and the Elf camp was on the hillside to their left. In the middle of the Valley was a battle which was so huge, the thought running through the group was that neither Bobbiur, Hagjel, Salbuk, or Obmar had ever seen anything this large before.

Bobbiur asked himself while shaking his head in a bewildered fashion. "How can anybody ever be expected stop something this huge?" Every soldier on the field was committed to some form of combat. Their were missals from the Ballistas being shot, large rocks were being catapulted in a rapid fashion from the Elves side of the Battle field and falling into the field of combat. Over head the group could see the large War Dragons from the Human side of the battle field, were having great success. The warriors on the Dragon's back's were using spears, arrows and burning liquids to smash the Elfen soldiers below. Large flames were coming from the remaining Dragons in an ever increasing manner.

These two great armies had smashed right into each other, right in the middle of the Valley, where almost everything was now becoming hand to hand combat. It looked as if nothing could ever stop this battle. Dead and injured soldiers were scattered across the field. Two large War Dragons had been shot down by the Elves Ballistas. These two large magnificent Battle Dragons were lying lifeless, at the far end of the combat area, in the battle field below. Everything was a mess.

"We have to stop this." Bobbiur said with a worried look on his face as he looked back at Salbuk, Obmar and Hagjel. "But I don't know how. Zorp said I would think of something, but I can't think of any possible way as to how we can stop this battle." Then in a louder voice Bobbiur added. "Looks like they just got to the peak of the battle but if we are able stop it we could save some lives."

Bobbiur had exclaimed these last thoughts with a completely defeated look on his face as he looked downwards into the valley below, at the continuing destructive battle. Then Bobbiur asked of the others in a pleading fashion. "How does Zorp expect me to stop something this big?"

From behind Bobbiur, Obmar spoke up. "Bobbiur I have an idea." Obmar had dismounted from the Dragon and was walking directly over to Bobbiur so he could speak about his idea. Salbuk interrupted with a mind message. "And what is your plan?"

Obmar had heard Salbuk in his head and turned to see Salbuk had dismounted and was also quickly walking over to where Bobbiur was standing. The Dwarf turned towards Salbuk and waved his left hand towards to battle ground, as he spoke to Salbuk in the way of a question. "Salbuk why don't you use that mind power of yours to make the Generals sound a retreat?"

Bobbiur had turned his full attention on Obmar and Salbuk, during this exchange of ideas and he was listening intently. With what Obmar had just said Bobbiur had a very hopeful look on his worried face.

"Well I'm not sure they would even pay any attention." After this message Salbuk quickly sent another message. "I'm not even sure if I could get into the two General's minds at the same time for that matter." Then Salbuk sent a further message as he was sort of thinking in line with the idea which Obmar had spoken of earlier. "But I could make a suggestion in their minds. I guess. And we can see what would happen."

Both Bobbiur and Obmar could tell from this mind message from Salbuk, that the mage was not completely confident Obmar's idea would work. But at least he was willing to give it a try. Salbuk slowly turned to Bobbiur and asked with another mind message. "If it is all right with you Bobbiur. I could try Obmar's suggestion."

Then Salbuk quickly added. "But I'm not guaranteeing anything." Looking straight at Bobbiur Salbuk's tone seemed to take on a little more confidence as he spoke to the matter. "I've never tried anything like this before and the Generals are quite a distance from us, but maybe with the additional powers which Zorp has given me....?" Salbuk's questioning of Bobbiur seemed to tale off.

Bobbiur just remained silent as he was thinking of how this idea might work when Salbuk continued on. "It just might work because of the extra power that Zorp has given me and at least it's worth a try." Bobbiur was looking at Obmar with a smile of gratitude and praise when Salbuk, in a tone of gratitude sent a message to Obmar. "Good idea Obmar. Thanks."

Again Salbuk asked the same question of Bobbiur. "Do you want me to try Obmar's idea?"

Hagjel, who had been listening intently and paying a considerable amount of attention to the flow of conversation and messages spoke up. "Bobbiur I don't see how it could do any harm!"

Bobbiur then nodding his head while observing the battle, speaking very quietly as if he was not sure that Obmar's idea would work but felt that he must try something said. "Salbuk if you think you can send a mind message to both Generals at exactly the same time then I feel we should go ahead and try." At this time Bobbiur quickly added. "But this mind message must be sent to both Generals at exactly the same time. If not then one of the armies may be placed at a disadvantage. Then he added. "That is if either General calls the retreat, and the other side doesn't. If one side keeps on fighting we may be hurting one of the armies. We must be very careful." In closing Bobbiur said quietly."We cannot under any circumstances place either army in compromising position which might decide the outcome of this battle."

Without saying anything Salbuk turned and walked over to a big rock as he looked down into the valley at the two huge armies. Salbuk then turned around and looked at his companions with a worried look on his face. Abruptly Salbuk sat on the ground and leaned his back against the rock.

For what seemed like only a few moments he studied the headquarters on the Human side of the battle field. Then for a few moments, Salbuk turned his attention to the Elfen side of the Valley. Behind him Bobbiur was watching Salbuk's back as he sat on the ground. Both Hagjel and Obmar had walked back to the animals to keep them quiet while Salbuk was going to try to get into the minds of the two opposing Generals. While Salbuk was sitting on the ground leaning up against the large rock, he slowly closed his eyes and then he remained very still.

Within only a few minutes Salbuk was able to send out a spell and reach into the mind of the Human General Karridhen. General Karridhen did not even know that Salbuk was in his mind. All of a sudden and for no apparent reason the General had an itchy sensation in the scalp, at the back of his head. Breaching the mind of the Elfen General Charranoid, was somewhat more difficult for Salbuk. This was probably because the General was an Elf and Salbuk was a Human, or maybe because the old General was in such a testy mood. Then with a little more effort Salbuk suddenly broke through.

Bobbiur as he was watching Salbuk who was deep in his trance, noticed that, although he seemed to be deep in his trance, Salbuk appeared to be mumbling something to himself. From where Bobbiur was standing he could not tell what Salbuk was saying, but he found out later that Salbuk was actually going through the actions of speaking, as he was forcefully sending, 'Sound the Retreat.' Messages into both Generals minds at the same time.

Keeping in mind what Bobbiur had instructed him to do, Salbuk at this time was sending the mind message to both Generals to sound the retreat, at exactly the same time. Getting the instructions to the Generals at exactly the same time, proved to be somewhat easier than Salbuk had first thought. The entire matter, although it had seemed longer, once Salbuk was in the minds of both Generals, was over in only a few seconds.

When the message was sent, Salbuk's entire body had gone completely rigid and his head had been thrown backwards with considerable force. Yet after only a few seconds Salbuk's head, suddenly fell forward into a more relaxed position with his chin resting on his chest.

Bobbiur was sure that the message had been sent and while watching the battle ground intently, he walked slowly over to Salbuk and helped the mind mage to his feet. Before Salbuk was even able to get back onto his feet, things started to happen on the battle field. The idea from Salbuk which was placed into the heads of both Generals at the same time, was. "Sound the retreat!" This was done without either of the Generals knowing anything about what was going to happen.

The Human General Karridhen at the time had been looking over the battle field with a very confident and satisfied look on his face. He was very satisfied with how well the Human armies had been progressing. Thinking to himself the Human armies were going to win this battle, he turned and nodded with satisfaction to Kirwynn. He was about to say that the battle was going well, when he stopped abruptly.

Then while turning back towards the field of action his body went stiff as a board. With his hands waving, his body started to quiver. Quickly, General Karridhen spun back around facing the messengers and the buglers. "Sound the retreat! Sound the retreat! Sound it now! Get our men off of the field! Quickly."

The old General was yelling at everyone around him as loud as he could. General Karridhen had a strange and distant look on his face and everyone close to him, including Kirwynn, was wondering what he was doing. Everyone around him thought he must be going mad. But an order is an order and they sounded the retreat anyway.

No one knew exactly why but the full retreat was loudly sounded.

On the other side of the Valley the Elf General, Charranoid, with a satisfied look on his face, was just about to speak to Captain Eeando as to how he thought the battle was starting to swing in favor of the Grand Elf Army. When all of a sudden he seemed to go stiff and looked straight at the sky. His eyes were wide and his jowls were shaking.

Captain Eeando who had been intently watching the progress of the Jonzars, the success of the Ballistas, and the encirclement of the Dwarves, turned as he noticed the sudden change in General Charranoid.

Captain Eeando had just been thinking to himself and getting very excited as he started saying. "We're going to win this. We're going to win!" Then to Captain Eeando's complete and utter surprise he heard the strangest order which he thought he would never hear, coming from the General.

"Call a retreat! Call it! Call it now!" In a louder tone the General commanded. "Get ever one of our Soldiers off of the battle field and back to our camp as fast as you can."

The General was speaking quickly and loudly with an increased urgency in his voice. The more orders he gave the louder he got, until he was actually yelling somewhat hysterically. Captain Eeando noticed the old General had a weird and wild look on his face. All the captains and others around him were baffled and confused but they called the retreat anyway.

Zalghar who had been watching the battle intently from the end of the Valley had been very excited by all the fighting, killing and the blood letting. He couldn't get enough of it. He had an infectious, half crazed, grin on his face, which went ear to ear. Then suddenly, to his complete surprise, all the fighting stopped. There were loud drum beats and trumpet calls and at exactly the same time, both the Elves and the Humans command posts had sounded the retreat. The soldiers on both sides of the valley suddenly just stopped fighting.

As a loud horn had been blown from the Elf side of the battle field the Elves had almost instantly dropped their bows and other weapons to their sides. The officers on the Elf side had turned and looked at their headquarters to ensure that they clearly understood that the retreat horn had been blown and they were also checking to see if the retreat flag was flying. It was.

The remaining Human Battle Dragons took off. They had all landed behind the Elfen lines and had been flame throwing. When all of the Dragons soldiers returned and had gotten onto to the backs of the remaining Dragons, these magnificent beasts swiftly flew back to the Human encampment.

The Dwarves not fearing the Elves just turned there backs to them and grumpily walked back to the Human side of the field. Both the Elfen and Human armies were very confused by the commands to retreat, right in the middle of a battle. And there were loud muttering's and complaints from both sides of the valley as the troops retreated.

On both sides of the field of battle grounds, soldiers were stopping on their way back to their camps to help the wounded. Other than the Dwarfs, all soldiers slowly backed away from their enemies. This was done without taking their eyes off the other opposing army. When the armies had gotten about a hundred yards apart, the Elves turned around and walked away. Just as this was happening the Elf ambulances and the Elf Healers were approaching the battle field to help and assist the injured. The same thing was taking place on the Human side of the battle field. Both Generals had given the orders to their special guards,to go and protect the perimeter of the battle field in order to stop any Krugs from robbing the wounded or from stealing any weapons which had been dropped during the battle.

There was a long standing agreement between the Elves and Humans that there would be no magic used on the battle field by either side, in any of their battles. Also, all the magic powers from both sides, was to be used only to help and repair the wounded soldiers from the battles. This was the honorable way which these two races had fought their battles for as long as anyone could remember. No magic from either race had ever been used on the battle field by either army.

Keeping in mind, this rule had been in effect for so long this practice had never been broken by any Human or Elfen General. Sending out the special troops to guard against marauding Krugs, or renegade Dwarves from robbing the wounded or dead, had also been a long standing agreement between the armies. Immediately upon the call by both armies to retreat, all the Healers, ambulances, and the special guards to protect the area of the battle field, even before the orders arrived had been instantly on the move.

Zalghar's Plans Falter.

Up on the hill at the other end of the Red Valley, amongst the large red rocks where the Haddrons were hiding, Zalghar was becoming furious. "The battle hadn't ended yet. There was still plenty of blood to be spilt." In a vicious sort of growl Zalghar became even more furious as he screamed. "There was still lots of killing still to be done."

Zalghar was standing now and while he paced about he had just kept yelling. A blood lusted look had came over his severely contorted face and as he started to calm down a little bit, he slowly walked away from the rock he had been sitting on. He moved towards his Kilpacx. Seeing the look on his face and knowing his rage, the Haddron warriors avoided eye contact, tried to look busy and moved as far from away from Zalghar as they could get. Clenching his fist with a tremendous strength, he was looking over his shoulder and watching the armies as they got farther and farther apart. Zalghar still had a very vicious and mean look on his face. As he neared his giant Kilpacx, his body tensed. Then to his surprise he looked down and noticed blood was leaking out from between his fingers. He opened both his hands and saw that he had actually dug holes in his palms with his long claw like fingernails, because he had been gripping so hard. Zalghar had finger nails which were like razor sharp eagles talons.

He looked at his hands with a disgusted look on his face. Showing very little interest, he waved one hand over the other hand, then he flipped his hands palm up. Then he started moving his right in a circular motion. Zalghar's hands started to appear normal and within only a few seconds both were healed.

Zalghar began to calm down as he spoke out to nobody in particular. "Why did these armies just get up and just walk away?" He continued speaking out loud to himself as he started again to pace back and forth. "They shouldn't just act like that."

Zalghar continued to pace back and forth. "Something made them retreat." Soon Zalghar slowed as he thought to himself for a second. Then with a voice which was half growl and half screech he said to nobody in particular. "Maybe they are just taking a break. I'll just watch and see what happens." Zalghar returned to his position by the large rock and he sat back down to watch the valley below.

After only a few moments when Zalghar had sat back down, he stood up and speaking in a calmer and more controlled tone, as he motioned in a circular movement with his hand, while showing his warriors. "Form a circle. I will send out the "Eye." To see what has happened.

Questions Are Asked

In the valley below on the Human side of the battle field, Kirwynn with a concern showing on her face wanted to know why General Karridhen had called the retreat. She approached him just before he left the watch tower and speaking in a very soft and questioning tone, she asked. "General. I don't understand why you called the retreat." Then she quickly said. "I thought we were actually starting to win the battle." Kirwynn was looking the General straight in the eyes as she spoke further, because she did not want to offend the General. She was careful how she chose her words. "I'm just curious is all."

The General without much hesitation and while scratching the back of his head spoke softly to Kirwynn. "Kirwynn. I'm not exactly sure why I called the retreat." Shaking his head and looking somewhat bewildered towards the ground the General commented further. "I can't even explain it to myself. But because I have called the retreat and since the troops are already here. Feed the troops and get them rested."

It had been at this time with a tired and sad look on his face he had said. "Send some troops out to help the ambulances, and to retrieve the dead."

Then General Karridhen mumbled. "We'll send the troops back into battle in about a half hour." Then he said gently as he continued to scratch the back of his head. "As soon as you have the ambulances and the Healers moving onto the battle field come directly to the tent as I will want to discuss strategies with all the officers present."

Kirwynn noticed that General Karridhen looked very tired, as she thought to herself. "It must be a terrible burden to lead such a large army and to send these men into battle when you knew that a good deal of the soldiers might never return." Kirwynn knew that there would be many Human soldiers whom would have to be packed home on their shields. Bringing a fallen soldier home on his shield, was the custom, and a show of respect for the Human casualties after a battle had been fought.

Back on the Elfen side of the battle field Captain Eeando was watching the Elfen General who for some unknown reason, kept rubbing the back of his head as he was walking back to the command tent. Just as General Charranoid was nearing the command tent, Captain Eeando timidly asked. "General why did you call the retreat when you did?"

Before General Charranoid had a chance to speak to the question Captain Eeando blurted out. "I felt quite strongly that the Elfen Grand Army was very close to having a great victory." Eeando had been thinking to himself that the General was getting to old to lead the Grand army and that the retreat should not have been called when it was.

General Charranoid turned abruptly to Captain Eeando and snapped with a fierceness in his voice. "I don't know why I called the retreat."

The General's voice grew more commanding as he said. "But send out the Healers, the ambulances, the perimeter guards and then come and see me in the officer's tent right away." Then in a slightly louder barking voice the old General said. "Also send a message to the troops to get some food and rest. As much as they can before we send them back into the battle." In a bitter tone General Charranoid mumbled as he turned away. "Damned Humans anyways!"

Then turning again back towards the young Captain, with his voice still rising as he stepped closer to Eeando. The General in a commanding tone almost yelling asked. "Is that clear?"

Eeando who was not familiar with this tone coming from the General just nodded, swallowed, signaling that he understood without saying anything. Then he quickly turned and hurried away.

Back over on the Human's side of the valley at the headquarters in General Karridhen's tent while pacing the floor, General Karridhen continually rubbed the back of his head. While the old General was waiting for the rest of the officers to arrive General Karridhen was making some general comments about what should happen in the very near future. "When more reinforcements arrive we will take the field again." Then he quickly added. "I am starting to think that the retreat may have been a good thing because now it will give us some time to revise our strategies and to rest the troops."

He was just turning to say something further to his officers when a messenger entered the tent. "Sir! You have to see this." A young officer came limping into the tent. The young officer held an arrow in his out stretched hand. "This arrow had this attached to it." The young officer reached out and gave to General Karridhen, a round piece of paper which had been wrapped around the arrow.

The young officer said. "It just came sailing into our camp." With a slight bit of hesitation in his voice the messenger added. "The arrow was moving too slow to have been shot. It looked just as if it was sailing across the air. Like a slow flying bird."

The young officer with a quizzical look on his battle weary face, shrugged his shoulders and said. "It did not appear to be harmful and it just slowly floated right up to me."

"Well this is very strange indeed." The General had said this as began unrolling the tightly wrapped letter. Then the General read the message out loud for all the officers to hear.

"It says." The General paused. "Meet us in the middle of the Valley and bring only one other person with you." The old General had a disgusted look on his face as he said. "Blah! This letter must be some new Elfen treachery" The General was waving his hand towards the Elfen side of the valley, as he squeezed the letter into a small ball before he threw it to the ground.

"But sir." The young officer said. "It's signed." The young messenger paused and spoke in a very soft somewhat pleading voice as he finished saying. "Bobbiur of Darmonarrow."

The young officer had partly turned and was pointing down onto the battle field as he spoke further. "And there's a Human and an Elf on Spaggidons from Darmonarrow waiting in the middle of the Valley with a large white flag." The young officer then protested. "General the Human in the middle of the battle field must be Bobbiur. He seems to be waiting."

General Karridhen paused before he said. "Hmm." The General paused again. "I'll think about it." The General, unknowingly had said this while rubbing the back of his head again, just like he and the Elfen General Charranoid had been doing earlier.

251

Kirwynn who had just entered the tent when the messenger was giving the letter to the General, stepped forward and approached the General saying. "General Karridhen." She took a few steps closer to the General as she said in a gentle tone.

"This Bobbiur and his men saved Garriton from an attack from some very powerful warriors two days ago when my father General Jauddi was injured. Maybe Bobbiur should be given a chance to speak." Then Kirwynn said softly with her head slightly lowered. "Bobbiur is not an enemy."

The Human General turned, looked at Kirwynn, seemed like he was ready to speak, but it looked more like he was searching for words. Then the General without saying anything further turned and walked to the tent entrance so he could look down onto the battle field. Again he involuntarily began rubbing the back of his head.

On the Elfen side of the Valley a similar thing had also happened to Captain Eeando. While he had been going about delivering the Generals orders to the troops, the Healers and the perimeter guards, an identical arrow had floated up to him with the same type of note attached to it.

Immediately after all the instructions which General Charranoid had wanted delivered by Captain Eeando were delivered, the young Captain turned and with a spring in his step, started back to the command tent. As Captain Eeando hurried back to the Headquarters tent he had the message gripped tightly in his hand. When he arrived at the tent he went directly to General Charranoid and handed him the note from Bobbiur.

The General had been talking to some of the senior officers about what should happen next in the battle but stopped briefly, rubbed the back of his head and then stopped to read the note. The General seemed to have forgotten the earlier incident which had made him angry, when he turned to Captain Eeando he asked. "Who is this Bobbiur?"

But before Eeando could answer the General, with a quizzical look in his eyes also quickly asked. "Is this Bobbiur Elf or Human?"

Eeando said in a quiet tone. "Sir. I am not sure but I have heard that this Bobbiur is from Darmonarrow and is very close to the Darmonarrow leader, Ram." Then shaking his head Eeando added further. "I think he might be a Human but I am really not sure."

General Charranoid looked down at the note and said. "This Bobbiur wants us to meet him in the middle of the Valley and this letter states that I should bring one person with me."

Then he went on speaking directly to Eeando as he asked. "What is your feeling about this?"

Captain Eeando pointed out of the tent at the battle field below as he said. "Sir. Bobbiur and it looks like he is with an Elf, with a white flag are on the battle field right now."

Then Eeando added. "It appears that General Karridhen must have gotten the same note." The General walked to the tent opening and both of them could see that two Human warriors were already coming down the Human side of the valley and were traveling directly towards Bobbiur and Hagjel.

In a snap judgement and in the hastiness of a required quick decision, it appeared that General Charranoid had returned to his former bad mood. General Charranoid without any further hesitation said with a growling and raised voice. "Captain Eeando. You will come with me."

"We are going down there right now so get a white flag ready." Then in a louder voice while shaking his head he said in a gruff voice. "I hate white flags."

The General continued giving orders in a rapid fashion. "You other officers should be getting back to your troops and get them ready for the next battle."

Then in a softer tone the old General said while nodding in the direction of his senior officers. "I want to thank you very much for all the hard work which you have done in this battle."

Then the General stated. "I will send messengers if I want you back here or at which time we will be proceeding into the next battle."

"What ever the decision will be I will contact you all by messenger." The tired old Elf General turned and left the command tent.

The Eye Observes Bobbiur and Hagjel

Up on the cliff at the other end of the Valley, Zalghar sat, in the circle which had been formed by his warriors. The 'Eye' was on it's way, to observe the situation. Before Zalghar had sent the 'Spirit eye' on this mission, he had been thinking a great deal about why the battle between these two armies had ended when it did?

When the 'Eye' was traveling into the valley it had caught a glimpse of two figures carrying a white flag, descending into the valley from the Human side. The 'Eye' also observed from the Elfen side of the battle field two Elfen officers entering the valley and traveling down through the battle grounds. These two officers also had a white flag. They were riding very slowly into the valley, directly towards the place where the two individuals on the Spaggidons were waiting.

The "Eye' moved farther into the valley and then hovered just above the two waiting figures in the Valley below. These two figures seemed to be waiting for the other riders from both opposing sides of the valley, to arrive. Getting even closer the 'Eye' with a slight enhancing of it's vision eventually enabled Zalghar to recognize Bobbiur and Hagjel.

Zalghar almost instantly came out of the trance. "It's that damn Human and his Elf friend who have been following us since Garriton." Zalghar was speaking out loud, mostly to himself as he stood up. The Haddron warriors close by just looked away.

"Those two riders must be the reason why the battle ended?" Zalghar paced around in a circle as he asked. "What are they doing here now?" Still searching for an answer Zalghar continued speaking out loud to no one in particular. "And where in this world would they get such powers which allowed them to stop a battle which was this big?" He had been whispering this last question to himself and then sat back down and watched the meeting taking place below him and his men.

Zalghar was very intent and seemed patient, but he was actually smoldering inside.

After a few moments Zalghar stood up and said to his men. "Circle around me. I am going to send the 'Eye' back out over the battle field again."

Quickly the Haddrons circled around Zalghar who was seating himself on the ground. The 'Eye' was sent back out. It went immediately onto the battle field and as before it hovered above the six figures who were still meeting on the battle ground.

On the battle field the Human General got to where Bobbiur was waiting just before the two Elves, General Charranoid and Captain Eeando arrived. To Bobbiur's surprise Kirwynn was traveling with the Human General. The General stopped back about twenty feet, raised his right hand and introduced himself. "I am General Karridhen and this young lady with me is Captain Kirwynn Yauddi from Garriton."

Kirwynn nodded to Bobbiur with a slight twinkle in her eye. Bobbiur could not help the small smile which came quickly to his face. Bobbiur said nothing but nodded his head mostly in Kirwynn's direction, in a slight bowing motion.

"My name is Bobbiur and this is Hagjel. We are both from Darmonarrow."

Then Bobbiur quickly went on. "I have already met Captain Kirwynn at Garriton. It was only two days ago when Garriton was attacked."

But before General Karridhen could respond the two Elf officers arrived. General Charranoid and Captain Eeando also stopped about twenty feet back and spoke directly to Bobbiur. "I am General Charranoid from the Grand Elfen Army. And this is Captain Eeando my assistant. You have sent a message that you wanted to meet with us." Before Bobbiur could respond and in a snapping tone the General said. "But we don't know who you are."

Bobbiur introduced Hagjel and himself, then he proceeded to explain why he had called both Generals onto the battle field. "Before I start. I should explain that we are on a mission which I will talk about later. I am only a Captain from the Village of Darmonarrow but I am under direct orders from Ram." Bobbiur paused glanced at

The Nine Moons of Adjemir

Kirwynn for just a second and then turning his attention back to the two old Generals as he added. "What I am going to tell you will only take a few minutes and I would ask that you be patient until I have finished. That is if you have any questions about what I am about to say."

Bobbiur again looked towards both Generals before he continued. "You will have to hear the entire story before you will begin to understand what has been happening." Bobbiur, as he saw that both the Generals were listening intently continued. "If you have not heard Darmonarrow was attacked and nearly completely destroyed only a few days ago. The very next day Garriton was also attacked."

Then looking directly at General Charranoid Bobbiur added. "And in case you are not aware." Bobbiur paused again and speaking directly to General Charranoid, while glancing out of the corner of his eye was intently watching Captain Eeando. "WynnFred has also been attacked."

Bobbiur then turned his attention back towards General Karridhen as he said further. "When Darmonarrow was attacked it was apparently attacked by some strange warriors, not from the land of Adjemir but from some other land." Continuing Bobbiur added. "I can tell you for certain that these strange warriors have tremendous powers."

"When Garriton was attacked, it was by the same warriors but they were not able to surprise Garriton like they were able to surprise Darmonarrow." Bobbiur slowed briefly and turned all of his attention back to General Charranoid. "WynnFred was attacked by an evil Dragon which was sent by the same warriors who attacked Darmonarrow."

Turning Bobbiur said. "If you look up on the hill you will see that Dragon." Bobbiur turned in his saddle and pointed up to the top of the hill towards Obmar and Salbuk. They had remained behind to tend the Spaggidons and the Dragon. "We have with us a young Human mind mage called Salbuk. With his magic he was able to tame this Dragon and save WynnFred from complete destruction." Bobbiur stopped for a second giving both Generals a chance to understand the intent of his message.

Thinking to himself, Bobbiur felt the Generals were starting to understand completely what he had been talking about but in order to explain further, he turned and faced towards General Karridhen. Bobbiur spoke directly to the old General. "Garriton was attacked by these strange warriors. They are called Haddrons and we were just in time to help out in the defense of Garriton." Then Bobbiur added. "You can ask Kirwynn about these strange warriors."

Bobbiur then turned all of his attention towards the Elf General. "General Charranoid if you want to talk to Salbuk about the attack on WynnFred. I can call him down from the ridge. You may also want to discuss the attack on WynnFred with your Captain." Bobbiur had said this with a calm conviction while looking directly at General Charranoid.

He then turned his attention back to General Karridhen and said. "If you want you should talk to Captain Yauddi. She can tell you about the attack on Garriton and also about the attack on Darmonarrow."

Nodding his head slowly Bobbiur then spoke directly to both Generals. "I will give you some time to discuss these things."

Bobbiur turned to Hagjel and asked in a soft almost whispering tone. "Do you think these people understand what I have just told them?" Before Hagjel could answer Bobbiur asked in the same whisper. "Do you think I forgot anything?"

Hagjel only said while thinking about what Bobbiur had already stated. "No. I think you have covered everything which is important and the Generals seem to be understanding things." Hagjel quickly added. "If nothing else Kirwynn will probably be able to have General Karridhen understand everything which has happened throughout Adjemirin the last few days." Then Hagjel quickly added. "But General Charranoid really looks like he is in a very ugly mood and it looks like he might be a tougher nut to crack." Hagjel finished up by saying. "We just have to wait and see if they understand."

Smiling and nodding Hagjel then said. "Bobbiur I think your doing a very fine job." Hagjel said this while nodding his head in the direction of the two Generals.

From up on the ridge Salbuk sent a mind message to both Bobbiur and Hagjel. "Bobbiur I think your job in convincing General Charranoid may have just got a whole lot easier." On the ridge where Salbuk and Obmar were waiting for the meeting to end they had heard a loud noise coming up from behind them. It was the marching of soldiers. As it turned out it was the soldiers from WynnFred. Pendahl was leading these troops. They were in a hurry as it seemed that they were reinforcements for General Charranoid.

The Nine Moons of Adjemir

Salbuk sent a mind message to Bobbiur. "Bobbiur Pendahl has just arrived with all of his garrison from WynnFred. It looks like they are reinforcements for the Elves."

All Bobbiur put into his mind was one word. "Good."

Bobbiur then turned towards General Karridhen as he asked. "Have you had enough time to consider the information which we have given you?"

General Karridhen was thoughtful as he chose his words well. "After talking to Captain Yauddi. I am able to agree that the attack on LousBeckt was probably not the work of Elves but was probably the work of these warriors you have talked about. Who were actually in Elf disguises."

Then nodded towards General Charranoid and Captain Eeando, General Karridhen continued. "If you can get General Charranoid and his troops to withdraw from the battle field then I am prepared to do the same." Then in a thoughtful tone with a slight tilt to his head the General spoke in a forceful sort of way. "But he must remove the Elfen troops from the Red Valley first." General Karridhen went on in a quieter tone of voice. "I say this because the Elves were the ones who initiated this battle. They said they would come here to battle us and if we did not meet them here in the Red Valley, then the Elves were going to attack our cities and villages. Therefore they must remove their armies from the Red Valley first."

Bobbiur never said anything . He only nodded and then he turned his complete attention towards General Charranoid and Captain Eeando as he asked in a quiet tone. "How does this information affect you and your army?"

General Charranoid was still in a rather nasty mood. With his lips curled upwards he spoke in a very harsh tone when he said. "We have no proof of what you have spoken. I have discussed what you have said with Captain Eeando and we have never heard any information about these attacks which you have talked about." Talking rapidly Charranoid continued in a forceful manner. "We don't know who you are, or what you think you are. We don't believe you." The General was starting to get louder as he continued. "We feel that this is a trick by the Humans because we were winning this battle. If you are actually from Darmonarrow, like you say you are then clearly this even more reason why neither you, nor those Humans, can be trusted."

General Charranoid during this statement had nodded and pointed towards General Karridhen and Kirwynn. Probably because of the bad mood General Charranoid was in he almost spat out his next words. "We think you are just trying to trick us into leaving the battle field. The Grand Elfen Army was winning this battle."

Then speaking even louder to Bobbiur the General viciously added. "We were beating these barbarians." He was saying this as he was swinging his arm and gesturing to the Human army camped on the opposing hill above.

"Further to that you have no army and as I said before you are from Darmonarrow." The Elf General had said. Darmonarrow in such a fashion, that he had made the name Darmonarrow sound like curse word. He had made a face as if it was giving him a bad taste in his mouth just by saying the word Darmonarrow. Then the old General spat on the ground in order to further emphasize his dislike for Darmonarrow.

Bobbiur just looked at the General. Showed no emotion nor did he say anything. The General of the Grand Elfen Army finished by turning and speaking to Captain Eeando loud enough for all of the others to hear him speaking by saying.

"These Human barbarians must be made to pay for attacking our Elfen Villages."

Bobbiur continued to sit quiet throughout this heated outburst from General Charranoid and then simply asked.

"General Charranoid. What will it take for you to believe that the attack on your Elfen city of Domerge was not done by Humans? But was actually done by these Haddrons which I have spoken of. Who as I have said were dressed and disguised as Humans?"

General Charranoid said in rather a loud voice as he started to turn his horse around as if to leave. "You people are all liars and you cannot be trusted."

Quickly Bobbiur spoke loudly. "If you will just wait patiently. I may be able to convince you in a matter of moments."

Without waiting for a response from the Elfen General Bobbiur put a thought into his mind for Salbuk. "Salbuk send Pendahl down here as soon as he can make it please."

The mind message from Salbuk was short and to the point. "Bobbiur Pendahl is on his way."

Within moments Pendahl had ridden down the hill side from the place he had been waiting, which was just out of sight from the Valley floor, where Bobbiur, Hagjel, and the Generals were waiting.

When General Charranoid saw Pendahl riding slowly down the hillside and was moving in the direction of Bobbiur, he said, in a bit of a shocked voice. "Lord Pendahl. What are you doing here?

Pendahl with a slight nod of his head and a slight smile on his face, only said. "Hello General."

Nodding again with the same smile on his face he said. "I will be with you in a moment General but I must talk to my friend Bobbiur first." With that being said. Pendahl rode directly up to Bobbiur and so all could see, he reached over and shook Bobbiur outstretched hand in the formal Adjemir fashion. Bobbiur smiling, gripped the arm of Pendahl with a firm clasp. Then he slapped Pendahl on the shoulder in a friendly way with his other arm, as he said. "It's good to see you and it appears that it could not have been at a better time."

Then in a questioning tone with a friendly grin, Bobbiur stated. "Pendahl I didn't know that you were an Elfen Lord." Quickly, before Pendhal could respond or change the subject, Bobbiur added. "I will bring you up to speed."

Pendahl listened intently as Bobbiur told him what has been happening since they had left WynnFred. "If you remember correctly, just before the attack on WynnFred, you told me you saw what you thought were Humans on the Ridge above your village. But in fact in the end you understood those people on the hill were actually Haddron warriors. The same ones we are chasing and they had been imitating Humans when they used the Dragon to attack your village." Bobbiur then went on. "Yesterday Domerge was attacked by what General Karridhen was told were Humans. At the same time LousBeckt was being attacked by Haddron warriors disguised as Elfen soldiers."

Waving his arm towards the carnage in the valley, Bobbiur continued. "It appears these imitations by the Haddrons has worked."

Then Bobbiur turned slightly and in a waving motion of his arm, Bobbiur pointed again towards the carnage on the battle field. "As you can see by the battle field both sides, the Elves and the Humans came here, to get even and settle this matter. I'm trying to stop the battle between these two armies. I have been able to convince General Karridhen, with some help from Captain Yauddi that the attack on LousBeckt was actually an attack by these disguised Haddrons to get the Humans fighting Elves."

Shaking his head Bobbiur went on. "But I am not able to convince Charranoid of this."

With a slight smile Bobbiur nodded towards Pendahl while asking. "Maybe you can help?"

Pendahl who seemed very relaxed considering he had just came to this enormous battle with the intention of offering reinforcements to the Grand Elfen Army, simply said with a friendly smile on his face while nodding his head slightly. "I understand completely."

Without saying anything more Pendahl quickly turned and faced towards the Elfen General. Pendahl at this time nudged his mount into motion. Pendahl nodded towards General Karridhen and Kirwynn as he passed right by them. As Pendahl neared the General he slowed his horse and then he got off. Pendahl walked the rest of the way. When Pendahl was close enough he asked the General to step down so that they could talk in private.

Pendahl knew Captain Eeando quite well because they had gone to the same cadet school in Domerge, but he wanted to speak only to the General at this time. "How are you General?" Pendahl said while reaching out to shake the old General's hand.

The General answered by saying. "I am fine and you are looking good Lord Pendahl."

Then Pendahl, with a slight smile on his handsome face started by saying. "General I know I cannot order you to stop fighting as you are in complete command of the army but Bobbiur is right, Domerge was not attacked by Humans. Domerge was attacked by Haddron warriors disguised like Humans"

The General asked. "How can you be so sure?" Then he quickly went on. "All the reports and messages we have received have been all been the same." Then shaking his head in disbelief the old General continued on. "Nothing was any different, all reports said that Domerge was attacked early in the morning by some barbarian Human soldiers."

Pendahl thought quietly for a few moments before saying. "General. I would trust Bobbiur with my life. Bobbiur and his men have tremendous powers and they could have killed me and my men when we were out on a search for some renegade Krugs. We attacked them and in the end Bobbiur spared us. When we got back to WynnFred the same day, the city was under siege by that Dragon on the hill."

Pendahl turned and pointed to Salbuk while at the same time waving his arm in the direction of the Dragon and Salbuk's location. "Salbuk tamed the Dragon and the Haddrons went away without attacking our village any further. I think the reason why the Haddrons left WynnFred, was mostly because Bobbiur and his men were there. Bobbiur and his men stayed with us that night and the next morning they actually helped us doing most of the repairs to WynnFred." In a softer tone Pendhal continued. "They stayed and helped us with the repairs of WynnFred and this was when they were supposed to be chasing the Haddrons. The Haddrons were very successful at destroying all of Darmonarrow. Bobbiur and his men are hunting for those renegade Haddrons right now."

In finishing this statement Pendahl turned and nodded towards General Karridhen who was waiting patiently beside Kirwynn. Speaking solemnly Pendahl said. "The Humans did not attack Domerge and in this instance they are not the enemy." Looking the old General right in the eyes Pendhal said. "These Haddrons may be the worst enemy the Elves have ever had, or may be the worst enemy for all of Adjemir, for that matter."

Before the old General could say anything Pendahl went on quickly. "I also think the Humans and the Elves should join forces in order to see that these enemy Haddrons are chased out of Adjemir. If not these Haddrons will conquer all of Adjemir and they will do it in a very short time. Bobbiur has told me that they have great powers." Nodding his head in a solemn thoughtful way Pendhal finished by saying. "I may even go with Bobbiur to help him fight the Haddrons."

The old General all of a sudden, began to look very tired. "Lord Pendahl I wish to thank you for the information and I understand what you have said. I am going to withdraw all the troops"

With this, the old General turned and got on his horse as he said to Captain Eeando.

"We are going to withdraw our troops and I will explain the reasons why as we return to our headquarters."

General Charranoid then rode over to General Karridhen and advised him that he had listened to what Pendahl had told him. The old Elfen General then said while nodding to General Karridhen. "I am going to withdraw my troops. I will ask you. General Karridhen. To do the same."

The two Generals talked for a short while and there seemed to be an agreement.

Both Generals turned and rode back to the waiting camps, but before he left General Karridhen advised Kirwynn to go over to Bobbiur who was waiting off to the side and tell him that there was an agreement between the two armies. "Kirwynn I want you to thank Bobbiur for stopping this battle as it really made no sense. Bobbiur holds no military rank so it is best that you thank him for me." Then the General said. "Tell him that there is to be a general Human withdraw of all of our troops immediately from the Red Valley.

Kirwynn nodded quietly but with a form of excitement. She turned from General Karridhen and rode slowly over to where Bobbiur was waiting. She was uncertain as to how she should behave in front of Hagjel and Pendahl, who were still waiting for Bobbiur. So instead of showing affection for Bobbiur she rode up close to his Spaggidon and just shook his hand.

Bobbiur felt the same feeling running up his arm as he had when he kissed Kirwynn back in the hall of her father's house, at Garriton.

Then looking Bobbiur in the eyes Kirwynn said. "General Karridhen has asked me to thank you for ending this battle."

Bobbiur answered by saying. "We got lucky, because of Pendahl's arrival or probably the battle would still be going on."

Kirwynn nodding, could not keep back the giddy smile from her face. Kirwynn understood the feeling which Bobbiur was having and the same electricity was running up her arm. This sensation just like Bobbiur's, was warm and tingly.

They stayed like this for a short time with their eyes locked together. With a little bit of embarrassment which quickly turned to a business like fashion. They finally separated their hands.

Kirwynn said to Bobbiur. "General Charranoid has agreed to withdraw his troops from the Red Valley and so has General Karridhen. It seems like your work here is finished."

With an even bigger smile Kirwynn then said. "My father would be proud of you."

"General Karridhen also told me to say, thanks to you all because you have probably saved many lives here today"

Bobbiur thought about this for awhile and then he said, as he tilted his head slightly to one side. "I am glad I could help out." With a slight smile Bobbiur added. "I have never done anything like this before and I can tell you, it feels really good."

Then Bobbiur, as an after thought said. "Kirwynn I want to introduce you to Pendahl. He is from the Elfen Village of WynnFred. And he is my friend." Bobbiur turned to Pendahl and said. "This is Captain Kirwynn from Garriton and she is the daughter of General Yauddi." Bobbiur then added. "General Yauddi was severely injured when the Haddrons attacked Garriton."

Turning back to Kirwynn Bobbiur said. "And of course Kirwynn you still remember Hagjel."

Smiling broadly Kirwynn gave a nod towards Hagjel as she said admiringly. "Oh yes. I still remember that shot. The one that hit

The Nine Moons of Adjemir

the Kilpacx right in the eye." Then she added still smiling. "I would not have believed the shot if I had not been present to witness it myself."

Then she added in a very soft yet admiring tone. "Very good shot Hagjel." Hagjel only nodded, and blushed.

They all shook hands and then Bobbiur said as he turned to her. "Kirwynn I have to catch up to the Haddrons before they get to far away and you should get back to your troops again."

Before Kirwynn could answer Bobbiur had turned to Pendahl and said. "Let me ride you back to your troops." Kirwynn who probably wanted to spend more time with Bobbiur but knew that she couldn't. She only said. "Bobbiur you be very careful when you chase the Haddrons and you must visit my father when you get a chance." Bobbiur caught the double meaning.

This last statement by Kirwynn was not lost on Hagjel and Pendahl. They both glanced sideways at Bobbiur with silly grins on their faces. Bobbiur just looked straight ahead and kicked his Spaggidon into a trot back up towards the top of the ridge where Salbuk, Obmar, and the WynnFred garrison were all waiting.

Salbuk had the same silly grin on his face as Hagjel and Pendahl because Salbuk had been catching the thoughts between Kirwynn and Bobbiur. "Boy am I going to have some fun with this." To Salbuk's surprise he caught himself mussing these thoughts to himself. Or so he thought. Bobbiur had caught Salbuk's mind message and this put a bigger scowl on Bobbiur's face.

Bobbiur would not look Salbuk in the face but his thoughts, had said it all. "Salbuk if you bother me too much I will do the same back to you when you meet some one."

Salbuk, laughingly sent one more mind message for Bobbiur only, and it was short. "Bobbiur. Isn't love grand?"

This put even a bigger scowl on Bobbiur's already stiff looking face and Salbuk almost broke out laughing. Traveling quite fast Bobbiur, Pendahl and Hagjal had just got back to the waiting troops at the top of the hill when a messenger from Ram arrived. The message from Ram was short and it read. "I have about one more day to rebuild the defenses of Darmonarrow and then I will join you. I will not bring any men with me. I will come alone. So you must send a message some time tomorrow morning as to where I should meet you and at what time."

It was signed. "Ram"

Bobbiur gave the information about the battle in the Red Valley to the messenger and told the messenger to also tell Ram. "The

Haddrons are more powerful and sneaky than we had first thought." Then he added. "I will send a messenger to Darmonarrow about where Ram should meet us on the following day." As an afterthought Bobbiur related to the messenger. "The Haddrons have been disguising themselves as Humans and Elves. This is what brought about the huge battle in the Red Valley." Bobbiur finished by saying. "Tell Ram that while he is traveling anywhere at all that he should not trust any stranger which he might meet on the road."

     The messenger nodded, turned his mount around and started off at a gallop.

Zalghar Forms Another Plan

Since Bobbiur and the rest of the men had been farther away from where he and his Haddrons were located, Zalghar had to pay more attention and use more power. He was able to see everything. He had seen what he wanted to see.

After the 'Eye' returned Zalghar spent some time thinking about what he must to do next. Zalghar was so angry at Bobbiur for stopping the battle, he decided that he must attack Bobbiur and kill him as soon as possible.

Speaking to himself Zalghar said. "The sooner the better." But what Zalghar was more interested in was the messenger who had just spoken to Bobbiur. Zalghar wandered why the messenger was in such a hurry and he felt that it was very important for him to see what this messenger was all about.

Zalghar spoke to the Haddrons who were closest to him. "The messenger who was just talking to the Humans who have been tracking us looked very interesting. I want to travel to a safe spot where I can use my "Spirit Eye' safely because I want to see where that messenger is going in such a hurry." Zalghar continued in his matter a fact way and then told the rest of his plan to the Haddron warriors. "What I wish to do is to watch and see where that messenger was going. Also in the near future I want to set an ambush for the group of warriors who have been following us."

Because he was in a hurry to use the 'Eye' Zalghar said. "So lets pick a safe place." Then Zalghar went on in a commanding tone. "We cannot stay here because surely that Human Bobbiur will be coming after us a soon as he can get organized. He is more powerful and more intelligent than I first thought because he was able to somehow stop this battle between the Elves and Humans. I don't know where he got the power from. But I will find out." In a softer tone Zalghar went on. "Maybe if I am able to see where the messenger is going it might give me some clue about where they are getting their powers from."

The rider after he had finished talking to Bobbiur started to retrace his path back to Darmonarrow because that was where Ram was now. The messenger rode full on, to the closest town and straight to the stables. Leaping off his Spaggidon he jumped on a fresh one and continued onwards at an incredible pace.

As was a custom in this land and usually it takes some talking with the stable owners, but a deal had been arranged a long time ago between Ram and most stable owners. In all of Adjemir a deal had been made by Ram regarding a Spaggidon exchange for the messengers of Darmonarrow.

This allowed Ram to receive information in a rapid fashion. This is why the messenger could make such good time when he was relaying information between Bobbiur and Ram.

It did not take very long for Zalghar and his men to find a safe place where he could use the 'Spirit Eye' and it was a good thing for him. Zalghar was in a hurry because the messenger was making such good time. The longer it Zalghar took to send out the "Spirit Eye, the harder it was going to be for the 'Eye' to find the messenger.

Except in this case Zalghar had a pretty good feeling that the messenger was traveling towards Darmonarrow. This is exactly where Zalghar sent the 'Eye.'

Bobbiur Leaves the Red Valley

When the Elfen army had started to leave the Elfen scouts had been dispatched out in front of the main Elfen column. Since most of the Elfen army was made up from volunteers the majority of them just packed up their tents and went off in their own directions.

Strangely, it only took a short while and Bobbiur noticed that most of the Human's army had also almost disappeared. When Bobbiur had walked slowly down the path he had come up behind Hagjel. "Ram and some of the survivors of Darmonarrow have been coming out of hiding and have started rebuilding the city." Bobbiur had also said to Hagjel. "Ram will be coming to help us some time tomorrow."

Just then Jakka had started to chatter at the mention of Ram. Both Bobbiur and Hagjel looked at each other with smiles on their faces. Hagjel said with a chuckle. "I think Jakka likes Ram quite a bit." To this statement Bobbiur just nodded while petting Jakka's head.

As soon as the armies had completely left the Red Valley, Hagjel had started wondering about finding the tracks of the Haddrons because he knew Bobbiur would be wanting to get back onto the trail of the Haddrons, as soon as possible. Sure enough Bobbiur turned and asked Hagjel. "Where should we start to look for signs of the Haddrons?"

Without saying anything Hagjel with squinting eyes, looking off into the distance he just pointed in a direction at the end of the valley, as he said. "I have a feeling about where they might be and there is where we should be heading."

Bobbiur turning in his saddle so he could face Salbuk and Obmar, as he said. "No point in chasing these guys to all ends of Adjemir. Hagjel has said we will start to look over there." Bobbiur was pointing to the same place where Hagjel had just pointed.

"So mount up and that is where we will start looking for the Haddrons."

"Good idea my dear friend." Zorp had instantly appeared. "Zalghar has been up there watching the entire battle."

"Oh Zorp I didn't see you there." Bobbiur had turned with a serious look on his face.

Zorp then said to Bobbiur. "Bobbiur we should talk alone."

So they had walked off a little distance. "Bobbiur I cannot spend very long with you. At present Zalghar is on the move and he cannot use his 'Sprit Eye' so he will not be observing you at this time. But you must always understand that Zalghar cannot know that I am here in Adjemir because that will bring out the worst in him."

Bobbiur then nodded towards Zorp, which meant that he had understood why Zorp did not want Zalghar to know that he was in Adjemir.

Looking off into the distance Zorp continued. "If he knows that I am here he will do even more damage." Zorp continued. "He is not really afraid of you at this time. Which is important. He doesn't really know where you got your powers from but he is thinking that you got your powers from Ram."

"Zalghar still thinks that he can beat you in a battle."

Zorp turned towards Bobbiur as he said. "He really doesn't know the extent of your powers."

He paused again for an instant, then he continued. "The fact that I am in Adjemir must be kept as a secret. I did not tell you this earlier but under the laws of Haddron I am not allowed to fight Zalghar in your land and he knows this. Therefore I am only able to assist and counsel you."

Zorp kept talking in a hurried fashion. "I must also tell you that Zalghar for sure is going to be mighty upset about you stopping the battle, so you must be even more careful."

It had been with a worried look on his face when Zorp had said as he had looked off into the distance. "I have to go now."

Zorp just vanished instantly.

When Zorp had disappeared Hagjel had gotten onto his Spaggidon and he seemed in a hurry. He then started off in the direction of where he thought he might be able to find the tracks left

by the large Kilpacx and where Zorp had said the Haddrons had been watching the battle.

Salbuk and Obmar got up on the Dragons back.

The Messenger Returns to Darmonarrow

It was later in the day when Zalghar with the use of the 'Spirit Eye' was able to find and watch the messenger arrive back at the first city in Adjemir, which Zalghar and his warriors had attacked and the city was Darmonarrow.

Zalghar had picked this city for his first attack because of it's strong military and also because of Darmonarrow's well built defenses. Zalghar had used the city of Darmonarrow as an example of his powers in order to send a message to all of the neighboring cities in Adjemir.

It was at this time back at Darmonarrow with the use of the 'Spirit Eye' when Zalghar saw what he sent the 'Eye' searching for. The old Human who had killed one of his Haddron warriors in the first battle at Darmonarrow was there to greet the return of the messenger.

This old Human was helping rebuild the city of Darmonarrow. This old sorcerer seemed to be completely in charge. This must be where Bobbiur and his men were getting their powers from. With the use of the information from the 'Spirit Eye' Zalghar thought to himself. "Somehow this old Human sorcerer has found a way to somehow make Haddron kinds of magic and Haddron weapons."

Continued to think to himself Zalghar thought it had to be this old Human sorcerer who sent out the warriors who had been chasing him and his Haddrons all around Adjemir. Zalghar spoke even while in his trance. He mumbled. "I will fix these warriors who have been following us and I will kill that old sorcerer."

When Zalghar came out of his trance he talked immediately to his warriors. The Haddrons warriors had turned their Kilpacx loose so these large beasts could graze on some of the luscious green grass which was growing close by. Once his warriors were settled down Zalghar spoke in very clear and determined tones. "The group of Adjemirians who have been following us appear to have come from the first village that we attacked here in Adjemir. I think they are very dangerous for us."

Then he added. "The old sorcerer who killed our Haddron friend during the first attack is in charge at Darmonarrow and he must be the one who has given extra powers to those who are following us." Then Zalghar went on in a definite tone. "The next plan as I see it is to ambush those who are following us."

With a vicious grin Zalghar spoke through clenched teeth. "We will kill them all and then go and kill that old sorcerer back in the town of Darmonarrow." With the same vicious grin on his face Zalghar went on sort of thinking out loud. "I also believe that the key to conquering this land is when we kill the old sorcerer back at Darmonarrow."

All of the Haddrons who generally don't talk much were nodding in agreement and they were getting somewhat excited about what Zalghar had discussed with them. It made sense to them.

After the Kilpacx had finished grazing on the lush grass, Zalghar then took his warriors a farther up the trail and showed the Haddrons where to set up an ambush. Hagjel and the Haddrons had left clear signs for Hagjel to follow. The place where the ambush was to be set up was in a very narrow spot just a short way into a rocky canyon. Some very large rocks which were in this location in the canyon were large enough for the Haddron warriors to hide their giant Kilpacx behind.

Zalghar thought to himself. "This place could not be better."

Feeling comfortable with the plan to ambush Bobbiur and his group Zalghar brought his warriors in real close to where he was and said. "I want to send out the 'Sprit Eye' one more time to make sure those who are following us are close enough to make this ambush work."

"If they have decided to set up a camp at another location for the night before they get this far, then we will backtrack and attack them at whichever location they have settled down for the night. Either way we will be rid of these nuisances. Forever." Zalghar seemed happy.

The Nine Moons of Adjemir

When the 'Eye' had been sent out, the area where the Haddrons were became very quiet. The 'Eye' traveled out from Zalghar's body and was back, almost in a flash.

"They are very near." Zalghar stated to his warriors after he had come out of the trance and he motioned them to find reliable hiding places to prepare for the ambush.

Zalghar without saying anything more to the warriors, gave a short magic spell by using his right hand. With his fingers closed and pointed at the sky, shoulder high, waving in a clockwise direction, a slight wind began to flow into the canyon.

The reason he did this was to create a draft to pull any smells from the Kilpacx further into the canyon and away from the incoming Darmonarrow warriors. If the scent of the Kilpacx was picked up by the Spaggidons which were being ridden his enemies then the surprise of the ambush would be lost. The Spaggidons would make a terrible fuss. His enemies would instantly know that an ambush was just up ahead.

While the Haddrons were placing themselves and the Kilpacx into proper hiding places in preparation for the ambush Zalghar made another quick spell. He did this by glancing for a only moment, at each of his warriors and at each Kilpacx. The purpose of this spell was to block away any thoughts, or sounds, which were coming from any of the warriors or from any of the giant Kilpacx.

Zalghar knew that amongst the men who were following him there was a very powerful Human mind mage and a Elf who had incredibly good hearing. Any thoughts or noises by his men or their mounts, would be picked up by this Human mind-mage or by the Elf. The surprise of the ambush again would be lost. At this time Zalghar was happy with how things were going and he was sure that all details for the ambush had been looked after. He watched his warriors making themselves comfortable in the ambush location and although he was somewhat nervous, because the group of warriors which were following him were quite powerful he could not help but make an evil little chuckle. He only had to use a very little amount of power on these two spells, so his magic power was in good condition and nearly fully charged. He reassured himself by looking down at his hands and when flexing his muscles. He could feel the energy in the veins of his hands.

Zalghar was certain that the men following him would not stop until they were completely through this canyon. He also felt Bobbiur and Hagjel would find the tracks leading up to the canyon quite easy to follow because the signs which had been left by him and his warriors coming from the Red Valley, into this canyon were in a straight line and well marked. The tracker would probably conclude that the men he had been following were traveling fast and without any purpose in mind. Knowing how trackers think, they would probably not need to do very much tracking through the canyon because the canyon was solid rock. A good tracker would want to be on the other side of the canyon in order to see markings, at the first light the next morning.

      Zalghar whispered to himself. "These fools are in for a big surprise. If we don't kill them in this ambush then we will kill them in their sleep. When and wherever they camp." Then he thought to himself. "Tomorrow we'll go back to Darmonarrow and finish the job for good." He wanted to laugh because of the ambush and also because he felt real evil right now. For him this was a good feeling. But he could not laugh because his sounds might be heard by Bobbiur and his men as the sounds echoed out of the canyon.

Haddron Tracks

After the battle in the Red Valley was finished and all of the armies had departed. Bobbiur and the group had easily gotten to the place where Hagjel and Zorp had pointed out and it was not very long before Hagjel had picked out a good set of tracks to fallow. Hagjel was also able to identify the general direction which was being traveled by the Haddrons. The group trudged on past the spot where the Haddrons had been watching the battle in the Red Valley and after a short travel they soon came upon a small forest.

This small forest caused some concern for Salbuk. He sent a message to Bobbiur, Hagjel, and Obmar, at which time he stated he wanted to spend some time before entering the forest to see if there was a possibility of an ambush amongst the trees and underbrush. He would do this by blanking out his mind, at which time he would be able to feel the presence of any thoughts by any Haddrons who might be hidden in the forest. When Salbuk entered this partial trance, which only took a few minutes all the others waited quietly, patiently and a short distance away from Salbuk. Then after only a very short time Salbuk came out of his trance. Salbuk then turning to the others and sent a mind message. "I cannot feel the thoughts of any Haddrons coming from within the forest." Then Salbuk added to his message. "We should be safe to proceed."

But Salbuk at this time had been unaware that they were being watched. The 'Spirit Eye' of Zalghar had been in the sky above them but Salbuk was not able to detect it's presence, because the 'Eye' did not send out any thoughts. It only observed what it saw.

Zalghar already had his soldiers at the ambush sight and he was now in a very good mood. He was happy because he would be rid of the nuisance which was following them in a very short time and also because, he just felt like having a really good fight. Zalghar was slowly rubbing his hands together in an evil anticipation.

    As they entered the forest Hagjal and Jakka took the point and began marching though the trees. Right behind them came Obmar, then Bobbiur. Salbuk who was now riding alone on the Dragon, came tramping in last behind everybody. The floor of the forest was mossy, the trees were quite large and these large trees were a good distance apart. The Dragon didn't have to do much maneuvering while edging it's large body through the forest.

    They had been traveling through the forest for about one hour when a strange mist started forming around them. It was starting to get late in the afternoon but the group continued on without resting. Hagjel had wanted to stay as close to the Haddrons as he could otherwise the tracks might get old and become difficult to find.

    All in all, Hagjel found the tracks through the forest very easy to follow. Salbuk continued seeking messages from the Haddrons who may still be trying to ambush them in the forest but he was not getting any thoughts from any Haddrons at all. Obmar said in a knowledgeable voice. "Shouldn't be much further till we are out of this forest." Obmar knew this because he was the only one of the group who had been in this forest before.

    Soon the group started to notice things were getting much lighter and brighter as the canopy of the forest began to thin out. When the group was clear of the last big trees they were now just starting to enter into a small, lush, beautiful very green valley. Everything was beautiful. Jakka was sitting up admiring this lush green place. All was very quiet and very peaceful. Hagjel pointed in the direction of the travel signs of the Haddrons at which time he turned to look at Bobbiur and also glanced back at Salbuk. "The Haddrons have turned and are now traveling in a direction towards the Dwarfs land of Axpen." This statement by Hagjel drew a deep throated growl from Obmar. Jakka hearing this rose up out of the tote bag and looked for a long time, unblinkingly, at Obmar.

    Hagjel had two questions in his mind which he wanted answers to. The first question was for Bobbiur, which was. "Should we continue on or should we make camp?" Then without waiting for an answer with an anxious sound in his voice, Hagjel added. "I would like to continue on if that is all right with everybody else."

The Nine Moons of Adjemir

Bobbiur speaking thoughtfully said. "Its up to the majority but I am willing to go a little farther, that is if everything in front of us is safe." Then as an afterthought Bobbiur had said. "We still have a little bit of day light." Hagjel, without saying anything further turned to Salbuk and asked. "Is there any Haddrons in front of us which you can detect?" To this Salbuk had sent back a mind message. "Keep everybody still and quiet and I will check a good distance in front of us to see if I am able to feel any thoughts from the Haddrons."

The group grew very still and remained as quiet as they could. In only a few minutes. Salbuk's message to them concerning the area immediately in front of them. It was clear. His message was that he could feel no thoughts other than their own.

The group moved into the small valley following Hagjel who had found he was able to follow the Haddron tracks with considerable ease. After traveling for a little while Hagjel had said loud enough for all to hear. "The Haddrons still do not know that we are following them because they have made no attempt to disguise or hide their tracks."

The sound of Hagjel's voice woke Jakka up, who had just fallen asleep and at this time he started to look around for some nuts and fruits. Hagjel opened his canteen and filled his hand with water for Jakka to drink. Bobbiur smiled softly as he was still somewhat amazed that these two could get along so well.

While Hagjal was looking down petting Jakka, Obmar, who was now riding beside Hagjel was looking ahead. The group traveled in silence for some time they were now starting to climb upwards towards a canyon entrance, and as they all went around a large rock outcrop, Obmar confirmed this by saying.

"There is a canyon coming up." The group had now come to a complete stop.

"What should we do?" Obmar asked Bobbiur. Bobbiur looked over all of the group and asked. "What do you want to do?"

Then Bobbiur added. "We can go through this canyon or we can camp here for the night."

Hagjel spoke first. "We should have Salbuk search the area ahead to see if the Haddrons are close and if so we should stay here. Otherwise I would like to get through the canyon as soon as we can and then I will be able to find the Haddron tracks much easier in the morning."

Before anyone could answer Hagjel had went on. "There will be very little if any tracks in the rock in the canyon so I would like to be on the other side of the canyon this evening. I should be able to find the location of some tracks on the other side of the canyon this evening before it gets too dark, then I will be ready to start tracking the Haddrons with the first light in the morning."

Bobbiur nodded in agreement and so did Obmar.

Salbuk had sent another message on the matter. "Let me search the area in front of us again so that I can see if any Haddrons are close by. If there are Haddrons close by, then I think we should stay here. If not then we should try to make the other side of this canyon before dark."

Salbuk then dismounted and walked a short distance away from the group, as he had always done and squatted on the ground. After Salbuk had searched the area in front of them for any signs of Haddrons the group proceeded into the canyon. There were no signs of the Haddrons being in the canyon.

The Hunters Become the Hunted

It was as Hagjel stated earlier. The rocky ground in the canyon left very little signs of the Haddrons. So the idea of Hagjel's, that should reach the other side of the canyon in order to get an early start the next morning appeared to be the right thing to do. As they traveled into the canyon a slight drizzle began and the group moved closer to each other. Jakka hunkered farther down in the tote bag and everybody placed their tunics over their heads. The Dragon actually seemed to like the rain. His huge tail was wagging quite vigorously for such a big animal.

The Spaggidon's didn't seem to like the rain much but they continued on obediently. Onwards and somewhat upwards into the mountain pass. As they traveled farther into the canyon a thin fog started to close in around them. They were moving very slowly. It was almost completely dark by now but there was still enough light to continue.

They were only about half way through the canyon and were just going around some big rocks, when Obmar yelled. "Ambush!" The Dwarf was yelling in a deep growling hoarse voice.

A large group of shadowy figures came riding through the fog. They had been hiding in amongst the large rock boulders which had made up the canyon floor. The first figure to emerge was Zalghar and he was right in front of the startled Hagjel. Hagjel had been concentrating on the ground and was not ready for the Haddrons to be this close.

Hagjel had an arrow already in his bow, which he had placed in the ready position since they entered the canyon, but it was not a magically enhanced arrow. Within the blink of an eye, Hagjel had let loose of his arrow and was aiming directly into the chest of Zalghar. The arrow did nothing and it just glanced off the protection shield which Zalghar had in place. Then the arrow simply turned to dust. In the instant that Obmar had yelled ambush, Salbuk in the blink of an eye had put in place a fairly strong protection shield. It was not his strongest protection shield but it was fairly strong just the same.

Unfortunately, in order to create a stronger protective shield Salbuk had to dismount quickly, at which time he was able to place a very strong protective shield between his friends and the Haddron warriors. The Dragon was too large to be kept within the protection shield and was left alone without any protection at all. The Dragon whom Salbuk had still not named was now very protective of him and when the Dragon had seen the enemy. The Dragon charged. The sudden charge by the Dragon, who was growling loudly while blowing flames at these enemies, took all of the attention of the Haddrons who had been momentarily caught by surprise. This charge by the huge Dragon was probably what saved all of the lives of Bobbiur and the group.

A very angered, growling, hissing, flame throwing Dragon, was bearing down on the Haddrons and was directing most of his attention in the place where Zalghar was. With a fiendish smile on his face Zalghar sent a spell which stopped the Dragon's ability to blow flames but the Dragon continued it's forward motion. The next spell sent by Zalghar was a freezing spell, which nearly completely froze the huge beast, right in it's tracks. The big beast at this time was coming to a complete stop.

Zalghar ordered the Haddron's to attack the now nearly defenseless Dragon, at which time all the large Kilpacx swiftly moved in for the kill. Snarling and growling these vicious beasts attacked the large and now completely defenseless, Dragon from all sides. Just as the blood thirsty Kilpacx moved in on the Dragon, the Dragon turned and looked back at Salbuk with a sad teary look in his large eyes. The Dragon some how knew he was about to die and there was nothing anybody, not even Salbuk could do about it.

Salbuk and the Dragon had become very good friends in a very short time. The Dragon knew that he was about to be killed and he wanted eye contact with Salbuk, as a way of saying goodbye.

With sudden tears in his eyes Salbuk quickly sent a mind message to the Dragon. "Goodbye my new friend." Then the Dragon turned his attention onto the oncoming attacking Kilpacx. But it was hopeless.

The Kilpacx who were such methodical killers attacked from all sides. Using their razor sharp teeth just like a pack of wolves the Kilpacx advanced further. The leading Kilpacx advanced directly towards the front of the now completely defenseless Dragon. The other Kilpacx came in from the sides, and from behind. The Kilpacx which had gotten in behind the Dragon clamped his enormous jaws onto the tail of the huge beast stopping most of the Dragon's movement.

That is when it happened. With lightning speed, with years of being attack animals with considerable experience, as if a secret signal had been given all the remaining Kilpacx attacked from all sides at exactly the same time.

Although the Dragon was much larger, it was no match. Not without the ability to throw flames could this huge beast compete with this large group of systematic killers.

Salbuk had considerable magic power, but if he was to use his powers, to try to save the Dragon, he would have to drop the protection shield. Salbuk knew if he was to do this he would be unable to stop Zalghar from attacking the others in the group.

Bobbiur ordered the group to start to retreat. "Back up people we cannot save the Dragon and we must get back where we can fight these Haddrons because we cannot fight them here."

The killing of the Dragon was not so short and it was not so swift. With this many attackers, there was no defense except for the Dragon's bite. It was horrible to watch. And as it worked out there was still enough light in the canyon for the entire group to observe the vicious Kilpacx attack. Clearly Salbuk, with a very worried look on his face was taking it the hardest. The Dragon before it went down was able to injure a few of the smaller Kilpacx but it could not stop the entire attack. Once the Dragon had been knocked down the blood lusting Kilpacx started lashing into the now completely defenseless Dragon's sides and throat.

Bobbiur had never heard a Dragon scream before but the death sounds coming from the Dragon, was hard for him to take. He could only imagine how hard the attack on the Dragon was for Salbuk. Bobbiur had seen the nearly instant feelings that Salbuk had for the Dragon. Salbuk had tamed the Dragon while making friends with it and Bobbiur knew that this big Dragon now felt the same way towards Salbuk.

While the group had been traveling together after the Dragon had been tamed, Salbuk had said he would name the Dragon sometime during the festival of the 'Eight Moons of Adjemir,' which would be happening very soon. There was already seven moons in the now dark Adjemirian sky. Bobbiur had remembered this being stated earlier by Salbuk. Then in an apologetic tone, Bobbiur as they were retreating yelled over to Salbuk. "We should have stayed out of the canyon until tomorrow morning and we would not have gotten ambushed like a bunch of amateurs."

When the attack on the Dragon began the group had been given a very short time to escape. The attack by the Dragon against the Haddrons and the attack on the Dragon by the Kilpacx had saved the group. Zalghar and the Haddrons were very occupied when the Dragon had charged. And this had allowed the entire group within Salbuk's protection shield to back away from the ambush.

Zalghar sat on his Kilpacx laughing in an evil laugh, as he yelled to his Haddron troops. "The hunters have become the hunted." Looking down at the dying Dragon and with a vicious grinning sneer on his face Zalghar watched as the Kilpacx were slowly killing this large beast. He then turned and started to apply his attention towards Bobbiur and the group.

Deep inside Zalghar knew he would have to speed things up if he was still going to be able to kill Bobbiur before they got away. So he raised his right hand high into the air and then he waved his open hand towards the Dragon. Although the Dragon was clearly beaten and dying, Zalghar wanted the Kilpacx to finish the killing as fast as they could. So the spell was designed to speed things up.

This powerful spell started to show signs of an instant change in the Dragon's features. The Dragon's eye's which were filled with fear and tears, while it's entire body was shaking became instantly blank. Small cracks quickly began to appear in the Dragon's thick skin. Red light jutted out of these cracks. Very quickly and as the cracks got larger, the red shining light grew brighter. Then suddenly the Dragon just literally flew apart, into hundreds pieces and fell all over the ground. It was quite a disgusting sight and it only lasted a few seconds.

Hagjal in anger as Bobbuir and the group was backing away from the Haddrons drew back his bow string and whispered the words to activate Rune's magic spells. The bow was being strung with Hagjels's most powerful Rune arrow. Encased with a spell smashing ability the Rune of Swift Death, was being aimed directly at Zalghar. The bow and arrow both started glowing a bright green just before Hagjel was starting to release the Rune of Swift Death.

"Ha! You think that can hurt me with this pitiful attempt, Elf?" Zalghar scoffed in a loud and vicious tone.

"I sure can." Hagjel yelled with determination.

Then Hagjel released the arrow just as the bright green of the arrow was starting to turn to a bright yellow. The arrow flew towards Zalghar and when it was about half way to it's target, it was turned to dust by a very powerful spell from Zalghar.

Zalghar then laughed out loud. "Is this the best you can do Elf?"

In a very loud and cruel voice Zalghar was yelling at Hagjel. "Do you actually think that you can stop me."

With a fiendish grin Zalghar then pointed a finger at Hagjel spoke some magic words. To Hagjel's utter surprise his bow instantly turned to a greenish dust right in his hands.

Salbuk was still looking over towards the spot where the Dragon had last stood. "Salbuk we have to get out of here fast." Bobbiur yelled. "Were no match for these Haddrons. At least not in this place."

Obmar with his axe at the ready spoke to Bobbiur in a very rapid fashion. "Bobbiur there is a tunnel just this side of the entrance to the valley." Then Obmar went on speaking rapidly. "If Salbuk can keep up his protection shield for that long we should be able to make it safely to the tunnel."

Quickly Bobbiur turned as he told everybody who had all remained mounted to head for the tunnel which Obmar had just told them about.

Bobbiur wanted to help Salbuk so he yelled towards Obmar. "Obmar you lead the way Salbuk and I will be right behind you." With this being said Bobbiur turned to get Salbuk. With the power being fully maintained on the new and stronger protection shield, Salbuk jumped onto the back of Bobbiur's Spaggidon. Then they all turned quickly to follow Obmar towards the tunnel.

Zalghar had then tried to smash the group with a spell but he was unable to penetrate the new protection shield which Salbuk had just reinforced.

When the group had left Zalghar suddenly remembered the Rune axe, which was being carried by Obmar. But by now Bobbiur and the Adjemirians were running away and the Rune axe was out of distance of his voice. Also Bobbiur and his men were now out of the distance of his magic spells so Zalghar was unable to command the axe to do anything.

Zalghar turned to his men. "Lets go. I want to smash those people who have been following us."

Then in a somewhat maniacal and frantic tone Zalghar yelled. "We have to move quickly."

The Haddrons obediently turned their mounts away from the spot where the Dragon had been killed and started to rapidly pursue Bobbiur and his men. The Spaggidons could move considerably faster but the Kilpacx were not that slow either and the race was on. Obmar led everybody in the direction of the location of the tunnel. Or at least to where he knew the tunnel was supposed to be but it was now starting to get quite dark. It took Obmar a few moments to find the entrance. The short time that it took Obmar to locate the entrance enabled the Haddrons warriors enough time to catch up.

The group had dismounted and as the group was entering the tunnel, Salbuk stood outside the entrance while maintained the full power of the shield of protection. A mind message from Salbuk said. "I do not want to drop the protection shield completely and it should only take me a few moments to make the shield small enough so that I can enter the tunnel behind you, with the shield still in intact."

Then Salbuk sent another message. "I will be with you shortly." Salbuk remained calm.

At the entrance to the tunnel Bobbiur quickly hollered over to Hagjel to go first.

A light was quickly given to Hagjel by Obmar. Obmar then turned to Bobbiur and said. "You will not have enough room in the tunnel for the Spaggidons so they will have to be left behind."

Obmar seemed to temporarily take charge as he said. "Let them loose." Then Obmar yelled at Bobbiur. "Bobbiur you should go next."

Turning to look back at Salbuk, Obmar saw the Haddons coming over the rise and then solemnly yet urgently, he said to Bobbiur. "You go Bobbiur and I will stay and help Salbuk to enter the tunnel."

Quickly Obmar ushered Bobbiur into the tunnel as he said. "We'll be right behind you."

Bobbiur glanced at the approaching Haddrons who looked mean and ugly, as he said to Obmar. "Hurry." After releasing his Spaggidon with a slap on it's hind quarters, Bobbiur quickly entered the tunnel, backing in with both his swords drawn and ready.

Over his shoulder Bobbiur said. "Hagjel, Salbuk and Obmar will be with us shortly."

Bobbiur was not sure why he asked. But he did. "How is Jakka doing?"

Hagjel had been waiting for the rest of the men just a short distance into the tunnel and he had a worried look on his face as he said to Bobbiur. "Jakka's doing fine but I'm not sure about those two." Meaning Salbuk and Obmar.

Then Bobbiur said. "As I said earlier they will be entering the tunnel very soon."

Bobbiur also had a worried look on his face but he tried to sound relaxed when he said with a slight smile at the corners of his mouth. "Not to worry Hagjel. Salbuk will be able to handle matters all right. Besides when Salbuk and Obmar are in the tunnel the Haddrons will not follow us because they will not want to leave their Kilpacx behind."

Then Bobbiur said further as an afterthought. "The Kilpacx are too large and cannot enter this tunnel. We will be quite safe after we are a short distance from the entrance."

As the Haddrons were coming over the small rise which was just before the tunnel entrance, Zalghar saw that the Kilpacx were starting to get tired. He was just about to call a halt to the chase when he saw Salbuk and Obmar standing alone at the tunnel's entrance. The Haddrons continued the charge. Zalghar had not seen Hagjel and Bobbiur enter the tunnel but he saw what he thought was a small hole in the side of the canyon wall. It was then when Zalghar saw the Spaggidons running off into the night.

At this time Zalghar said under his breath. "We have them trapped now."

Then Zalghar saw Obmar say something quickly to Salbuk. It was just as Obmar was turning towards the tunnel when Zalghar saw that Obmar still had the Rune axe on his back and he knew that Obmar was about to enter the tunnel.

"Stay there." Zalghar screamed. And much to Zalghar's surprise Obmar stopped momentarily to see what the yelling was about. This was all Zalghar needed as he was close enough to Obmar to be able to voice command the Rune on the war axe. Zalghar instantly knew that there was going to be some fun. He had a mean looking evil smile on his face. So what if he couldn't break down the strong protection shield which Salbuk had in place. He didn't care. These people clearly did not know about the Rune which was attached to the axe.

Some Haddron riders started to close up to the protection shield and were going to strike at it with some magic spells when Zalghar gave a command. "No. They won't get very far." Then looking straight at Obmar Zalghar spoke the magic words to the Rune. "Ajellada. Ajellada. Ajellada." Which was the magic Haddron word which meant. "Obey the voice." But instead of sending a voice command, Zalghar had sent a mind message in the Haddron language instead.

Instantly the Rune began to glow in a bright blue pulsating light.

Just as Obmar was about to enter the tunnel he had Heard Zalghar yelling. For some unknown reason Obmar had stopped dead in his tracks and turned towards Salbuk. Obmar's eyes grew quite wide and he had an instant fiendish look on his face. His lips curled back and there was a deep growl coming from deep down inside him. Salbuk who had saw Obmar turn towards him sent a mind message to Obmar. Then Salbuk turned back around to watch the Haddrons as they were dismounting from their giant Kilpacx. The mind message to Obmar had been. "Obmar we have to move fast. So back up." Salbuk still didn't know about the control of Obmar by the Rune on the war axe.

Salbuk started to back towards Obmar and the tunnel entrance. While never taking his eyes off of the Haddrons he sent a very urgent mind message to Obmar. "Obmar we do not have much time. Now get going. Fast."

Salbuk continued to watch the Haddron warriors closing in on the protection shield and all of his attention remained completely on them. Salbuk was not going to be ready for what was about to happen next.

Zalghar who was standing back a little ways knew that Salbuk's protection shield could stop spears, swords, and magic, but it could not stop, voice commands, nor thoughts. Because Zalghar was a foreigner to Adjemir, it took a little while for Salbuk to fully understand the mind message from Zalghar to the axe. The message to Obmar through the Rune axe was in the Haddron language.

It was too late for Salbuk as the message had already gone through the protection shield, through the axe and was now entering into Obmar. Salbuk after he fully understood the message which was sent by Zalghar through the axe and into Obmar, now knew that he had enemies at both sides of his protection shield. But it was already too late.

The Nine Moons of Adjemir

The command from Zalghar in the Haddron's own language, was very short and very clear. "Kill the Human." Obmar was powerless to stop the axe from taking control. Obmar's eyes showed the same intense evil, just like the eyes of Zalghar. The control over Obmar by the Rune axe was instant and powerful.

The power surging through the axe was so great that there was nothing Obmar could do. He was under the complete control of the axe and Zalghar. Zalghar was now in complete control of the axe and therefore in complete control of Obmar. Just as Salbuk was turning around to defend himself from Obmar and the Rune axe, Obmar's swing, hit Salbuk on his right arm.

The axe sliced right through Salbuk's right arm and the axe was imbedded deeply into Salbuk's right side. Poor Salbuk never had a chance. The mind mage, in extreme pain and bleeding from the enormous wound was knocked viciously to the ground. The severe pain from the axe wound caused Salbuk to almost faint and it was at this time that he lost complete control over his protection shield. Salbuk now lay on the ground and was completely defenseless. Even his protection shield had disappeared.

The Haddrons showing no fear then moved in for the kill. Salbuk who was now bleeding heavily, was completely at the mercy of the advancing Haddrons. Salbuk turned and in a great deal of pain watched the killers advancing. Salbuk's eyes were wide with fear but he never lost his composure. Quickly Salbuk sent a mind message to Hagjel and Bobbiur. "Hagjel and Bobbiur it has been wonderful knowing you but you must get away as fast a you can. The Haddrons have gotten some kind of control over Obmar and he has turned against us."

Salbuk continued the mine message. "My protection shield has been broken and I am about to die.There is too many of them and their power is great."Then an additional worried message was sent from Salbuk's mind to Bobbiur and Hagjel. "If you come and try to help me you will also die. So I am pleading with you to get away as far as you can."

The next message was Salbuk's last message. "You must flee as fast as you can. And goodbye my friends."

These messages from Salbuk had been very short, as things were starting to happen quite rapidly back at the tunnels entrance. Salbuk sent no more messages to either Hagjel or Bobbiur. When the message from Salbuk had been received by Bobbiur and Hagjel, Hagjel turned instantly and was starting back to help Salbuk. But

Bobbiur stopped him in the tunnel. It took all of Bobbiur's strength to stop Hagjel but Bobbiur knew better than Hagjel, if they were to return to help Salbuk then they would also be killed.

The entire episode of the loss of Salbuk was to be very difficult on Hagjel because Salbuk and Hagjel had become like brothers over the years. Hagjel and Bobbiur were soon going to feel Salbuk's intense pain, as the Haddrons were killing him. Bobbiur who was holding Hagjel by both arms while standing between Hagjel and the direction towards the caves entrance knew he had to stop Hagjel, even if he had to knock him out.

Through clenched teeth Bobbiur said some things which seemed to make Hagjel listen. "Hagjel. Salbuk is already dead." Softly and slowly Bobbiur added. "There is nothing you can do for Salbuk now. If we go back then the Haddrons will kill us also."

Bobbiur kept talking through clenched teeth but in a calm and steady voice. "Salbuk knew that you were his best friend but to return to the cave entrance and be killed by the Haddrons will only make things worse." Just before he was about die, Salbuk had heard the command over the noise of the Haddrons. It was from Zalghar. "Stop! This Human is mine."

In a very commanding voice which was more like a growl Zalghar said. "You men guard the caves entrance in case those other warriors try to attack us." Zalghar had pointed towards four warriors who were closest to the entrance.

"You others." Zalghar was pointing towards a different group of warriors as he said. "Pick him up and bring him over here away from the entrance."

The Haddron warriors who were closest to Salbuk knew he was powerless because Zalghar had just placed a spell over him. The powerful spell by Zalghar had removed all of Salbuk's ability to use his magic powers. Salbuk had already been nearly completely weakened by the blow from the Rune axe swung by Obmar. The once powerful mage was now completely and utterly defenseless as he lay bleeding on the ground surrounded by these evil warriors.

The swing from Obmar's axe against Salbuk had been very evil and forceful. The spell from Zalghar which had entered Obmar, through the Rune on the axe had nearly completely turned Obmar into a Haddron slave, not only in the use of language but now also in Obmar's way of thinking.

Obmar now had the same evil look on his face as Zalghar, and he was smiling at the thought of not only of killing Salbuk but

The Nine Moons of Adjemir

also about chasing Bobbiur and Hagjel. Knowing that Obmar wanted to chase Bobbiur and Hagjel into the tunnel Zalghar said calmly to Obmar. "Not to worry my little friend."

Smiling an evil smile Zalghar then said. "I know exactly where those two will be going. I have gotten that information from your old Adjemirian mind already. We will have a big surprise waiting for them." Zalghar had continued in a confident tone as he patted Obmar on the head. "The Kilpacx were much too large to go through the tunnel. So we will have to go around this mountain and we will catch those two later." Then in a very confident tone Zalghar said. "But catch them we will."

Zalghar was now nodding his head towards Obmar in a fiendishly yet friendly fashion. When the spell had been sent by Zalghar through the axe and into Obmar's brain it allowed Zalghar to instantly know all about Obmar plus all of Obmar's thoughts. All of Obmar's thoughts except the thoughts of the strange little old, grey haired, individual by the name of Zorp.

Unknown to Obmar, or any of the others in the group who were with Bobbiur, Zorp had placed a mind barrier into Obmar's mind. This mind barrier would stop any thoughts about himself or Dymma if Zalghar or the Haddrons were ever to capture Obmar. This was a safety measure Zorp needed in order to keep his presence in Adjemir as secret as possible. Especially knowing that Obmar carried the Rune axe from Zalghar. The mind barrier had worked. No thoughts about Dymma and himself had been transferred to Zalghar when he had taken control over the mind of Obmar.

When Obmar did not enter the tunnel, both Bobbiur and Hagjel knew for sure he had been placed under the complete control of Zalghar. It would not be until later when they would find out that he had actually been turned into something very similar to a Haddron. Not in body but in mind. Obmar would still have the same outward appearance to others, except now he would have a different look in his eyes. It would be a piecing haunted look of evil, very similar to that of Zalghar himself.

With a fiendish smile Zalghar now quickly turned his total attention towards Salbuk, who was still lying defenseless on the ground moaning and withering in severe pain. While continuing to smile evilly at Salbuk, Zalghar waved all of his men and Obmar back too a safe distance. Although the Kilpacx were very interested in the bleeding Human on the ground, they backed away as well.

As Zalghar approached. Salbuk showing no fear at all sent a mind message to Zalghar. "I know that you are going to kill me but in the end my friends will kill you and all of your warriors." Then in a commanding tone Salbuk sent the last mind message he would ever send to anybody. "You would be better to leave Adjemir as soon as possible."

At this Zalghar just laughed out loud howling towards the night sky. Zalghar then looked down at the defenseless Salbuk with a ugly sneer on his contorted face. "Your people are nothing. I will control all of Adjemir in only a few days."Then in a vicious tone and through gritted teeth Zalghar screeched loudly in a hateful manner. "But you will not be around to see any of this."

Zalghar was looking at Salbuk right in the eyes. Machine like and not saying anything Zalghar then got even closer to Salbuk. Then Zalghar, making a snarling sound, knelt down on one knee. At this time things at the tunnels entrance became eerily quiet. With a fiendish and very evil look Zalghar continued staring deep into the eyes of poor defenseless Salbuk. Then it started. In a flash of light, a giant green magic arm and a talon like claw, extended outwards from Zalghar's right hand. This magic talon flew directly at Salbuk. The magic claws, with force, slammed right into poor Salbuk's chest, and grabbed onto Salbuk's spine. Slowly the giant magical hand began to squeeze tightly. Just like a vice.

Zalghar continued his evil stare, and his eyes during this time seemed to come right out of his head. These were the killer eyes of the most evil person to ever come out of Haddron.

All poor defenseless Salbuk could do was scream. Poor Salbuk was pinned down and dying in incredible intense pain.

Salbuk had no magic powers left. He was completely held to the ground by the force of the evil magic hand. Salbuk couldn't even roll away.

The evil look on Zalghar's face became even more evil looking as he was smiling in extreme pleasure. Zalghar's eyes bulged outwards even further and the veins in his forehead and neck grew very large. There was a vicious and uncontrolled growling sound which sounded more animal like, than Haddron, coming from deep within Zalghar. Some of the Haddron warriors took a few more steps back. Even they were somewhat unnerved by the vicious killing instincts coming from Zalghar.

The Nine Moons of Adjemir

The giant Kilpacx were not bothered by Zalghar's behavior. They were standing very close by, licking their lips because they knew that they would be given a very tasty meal, from the remains after Zalghar was finished with Salbuk.

Then in an instant, a narrow stream of green light came from both eyes of Zalghar and burned directly into the forehead of Salbuk. Salbuk screamed even louder. There was only a little smoke coming from the place in Salbuk's forehead at the location, where the magic ray from Zalghar's eyes had burned right through skin and bone and right into poor Salbuks's brain.

Viciously Zalghar then began to try to remove all of the magic energy from the dying Salbuk. Zalghar was actually finishing off Salbuk by sucking all of Salbuk's life's energy and magic away.

Zalghar wanted the energy from Salbuk and he also wanted all of Salbuk's magic powers. But unknown to Zalghar he could not take Salbuk's magic, because no magic in the land of Adjemir could ever be transferred by force. Then in a matter of seconds, Salbuk still screaming, died a horrible death. His body sank lifeless onto the cold ground and poor Salbuk was never to move again.

Zalghar with a fiendish look on his face after finishing off Salbuk, while still kneeling on the ground, leaned back, faced the sky and he began to howl like a wolf. Bobbiur and Hagjel from deep within the tunnel, had heard this strange sound.

The vicious Kilpacx moved in and within seconds, the poor lifeless body of Salbuk was viciously torn apart. Salbuk was no more.

Both Bobbiur and Hagjel had fallen to the ground in the tunnel because the incredible pain felt by Salbuk, was also felt by Bobbiur and Hagjel. The pain, luckily for both Bobbur and Hagjel, only lasted for a few moments. It was then when they both knew the killer Haddrons had finally finished Salbuk off. Bobbiur noticed from the light coming from the lantern that Hagjel had tears in his eyes.

Bobbiur had gotten up first and in the light from the small lantern, through his tears, while still kneeling on the tunnel floor, Hagjel saw something which sent chills down his spine. Hagjel had known Bobbiur for only a short while but there was such a fierce determination and viciousness on Bobbiur's face, Hagjel knew instantly, that the killing of Salbuk and the pain which was felt by both himself and Bobbiur, had somehow changed Bobbiur. Possibly forever.

Even before Hagjel had risen from the ground he also knew, deep inside, that Bobbiur would be a power to reckon with.

Hagjel was really going to miss Salbuk as Salbuk had been his best friend and companion. Salbuk was more like a brother to Hagjel and the pain felt by the loss of Salbuk would bother Hagjel for quite some time. But he would have to grieve later because they were still very close to the tunnel entrance. To Hagjel and Bobbiur's surprise, Jakka had also felt the pain of the attack on Salbuk, as he had been rolling around and moaning inside the tote bag.

Although the Haddron's Kilpacx could not be driven into the tunnel, Bobbiur and Hagjel still had to worry about the Haddrons. The enemy back at the tunnels entrance may still chase them on foot. They still had to escape. They must, as quickly as possible, get back to Darmonarrow and seek the help of Ram. Bobbiur never did get the chance to send a message to Ram outlining a meeting place but that did not matter now. Bobbiur knew they would be in Darmonarrow sometime early in the morning anyways. The wildness in Bobbiur's eyes, seen by Hagjel, was sufficient for Hagjel to know that the Haddrons would have to pay dearly not only for the death of their friend Salbuk, but for all the killing by the Haddrons on the peoples of Adjemir.

Both Bobbiur and Hagjel went swiftly through the tunnel headed towards the tunnel exit, which was supposed to be near to where Darmonarrow was. Neither Bobbiur nor Hagjel knew exactly where the tunnel would come out at but at least they were safe for now and they also knew this tunnel was in the general direction of Darmonarrow. They moved along, quickly, silently and without talking.

Bobbiur and Hagjel traveled quietly through the tunnel for quite some time and just before they were able to get to the end of the tunnel, they saw a dim light, smelled something and heard noises. Both Bobbiur and Hagjel knew that they must be near to the exit of the tunnel, because besides the smoke, they could also smell the fresh air coming into the tunnel entrance.

Cautiously Bobbiur put out the lantern's light. Hagjel thought that Bobbiur would want to discuss what they would do next. But this didn't happen. The noises which they had heard was coming from a band of Krugs who were camped in the entrance and these Krugs were actually blocking the exit of the tunnel. Hagjel was not sure what they would do now because they were not sure how many Krugs were blocking the exit of the tunnel. Hagjel noticed in the dim light coming from the Krugs camp, that the look which Bobbiur had on his face, was the same look which he had on his face when the Haddrons had killed Salbuk. The look was still there.

Hagjel heard Bobbiur mumbling something to himself in the near dark. Hagjel was to find out later that it was the voice commands to the Runes on the swords which Bobbiur carried. Before Hagjel actually knew what was happening and without saying anything, not even waiting for Hagjel Bobbiur started to rush the Krug encampment all alone. As Bobbiur charged towards the Krug's camp he was yelling in a fierce, ear piercing and blood curdling charge. For Hagjel it seemed the entire episode was happening in slow motion.

All Hagjel could do was watch and to follow Bobbiur into the Krug camp. Hagjel was surprised because he found himself screaming almost as loud as Bobbiur. This was strange as Hagjel had thought later because he was always of the idea that only Humans screamed as they entered a battle. Not Elves! Later, Hagjel thought this war scream of his must have been because he had been friends with Salbuk for such a long time. At the time when Hagjel gave his war scream he could feel Jakka tensing up because Jakka had never heard Hagjel scream before. Hagjel could also feel Jakka getting ready to assist in the fight. Jakka's back was beginning to arch upwards which was a clear sign that little Jakka also wanted to fight.

At full speed Bobbiur entered the Krug camp. Even before Hagjel could get fully ready Bobbiur was smashing down Krugs. As it turned out there was almost no need for Hagjel or Jakka to be there because Bobbiur was fighting the Krug guards with a complete abandonment. Hagjel also noted that Bobbiur seemed possessed. Bobbiur had killed the three Krug guards in a very short time. Bobbiur then swiftly entered the center of the camp and his furry, his rage seemed to increase.

The other Krugs who were just getting up to do battle with Bobbiur, never had a chance. The Rune swords, with their spell, when swung at full force would become magically longer and could kill an enemy about eight feet away. The Krug swords were very short in comparison to Bobbiur's magic swords and the Krugs could not reach Bobbiur. Also when the Rune swords were activated, they became as light as a feather. Bobbiur being as strong as he was and in his rage, mowed the Krugs down as fast as they could get up from off of the cave floor where they had been sleeping.

These swords could also be ignited at their tips but for this fight with the Krugs, Bobbiur only wanted the extra length. The only way that the Krugs could have fought Bobbiur effectively would have been with a bow or by throwing an axe or with a spear. Bobbiur just never gave the Krugs a chance to effectively get ready for battle.

    Not one spear or axe ever got thrown at either Bobbiur or Hagjel. As it turned out there were only twelve Krugs in the camp and all of the Krugs were dead even before Hagjel could get into position. Hagjel knew that something had just happened to Bobbiur which even Bobbiur was not quite aware of. Hagjel had never seen any person fight like this before. No mercy had been shown. Not even in the slightest. As much as Hagjel admired Bobbiur and his fighting ability he could not help but notice that Bobbiur was behaving, a bit like a wild sort of animal. Hagjel knew that Bobbiur was now a fully matured fighting warrior. A week ago Bobbiur would have shown some mercy but since the killing of Salbuk, Hagjel felt that the showing of mercy by Bobbiur was going to be a thing of the past.

    This entire episode reminded Hagjel of how Bobbiur had been capable of showing mercy. Hagjel remembered how Bobbiur had shown mercy when they had been surrounded by Pendahl and the other Elves on the road to WynnFred. Clearly Pendahl and the Elves from WynnFred had been lucky on that day because if he had been in a fight with this new Bobbiur, Pendahl and his friends would all be dead now. Hagjel looked towards Bobbiur briefly and he could see his friend Bobbiur still had an intense look on his face. Hagjel could see the extreme fierceness coming from Bobbiur and it made him somewhat nervous.

    Bobbiur quickly turned and walked towards the end of the tunnel and without looking back, spoke through clenched teeth. "Come Hagjel. We have to get going. We have some important work to do."

    Bobbiur had not even broken a sweat yet he had single handedly destroyed the entire Krug camp. They quickly left the tunnel.

Dymma Listens

After Zalghar had killed Salbuk and the Kilpacx had finished fighting over the remains of Salbuk, Zalghar went off by himself and soon he found a place where he and his warriors could camp for the night. The place which he found for the Haddrons to camp for the night was just outside of the entrance to the canyon. It was in amongst some small trees. It was just starting to rain slightly so the trees would give them some shelter to the Kilpacx from the wind and rain. Once the Haddrons had began settle in Zalghar started to speak to them about what he had planned for the following day.

None of the Haddrons, not even Zalghar paid much attention to the small grasshopper which had flown stealthily into the Haddron's camp and was sitting just under the end of a log over at the edge of the camp fire.

Zalghar spoke in determined tones. "We have just killed one of their most important and powerful warriors and he was the one which had been giving us the biggest problems."

With a look of accomplishment Zalghar paused for a second, then he continued. "He was their young sorcerer. The others whom we chased into the tunnel earlier are from Darmonarrow." Zalghar paused again but for just a few seconds, then he went on in a confident yet evil tone. "The enemy which is causing us our other problems must be that old sorcerer from Darmonarrow." Nodding towards Obmar, Zalghar then said. "I have found out from the information which I obtained from Obmar's mind when I made him one of us, is that the old sorcerer's name which is Ram is very powerful."

Zalghar became silent for a short time as he looked off into the night. Then he continued, as he turned his attention back to his warriors. "I was not able to get as much information from Obmar as I would have liked and I am not sure why I was not able to but it must be something this Ram may have done to Obmar's mind."

Then while Zalghar was looking directly at Obmar he continued again. "The powers which the young sorcerer had who we just killed at the entrance to the tunnel must have been given to him by Ram."

Without Saying anything and being somewhat nervous Obmar nodded quickly in agreement. Obmar was not sure where Salbuk had gotten his powerful magic from and he couldn't tell Zalghar anything about this.

But something had happened to Obmar. Back at Darmonarrow when Zorp had seen Obmar with the Rune axe which Obmar had bought for himself just before the attack on Darmonarrow, unknowingly Zorp had placed a secret spell into Obmar's mind.

Any knowledge from Obmar's mind about himself, about Dymma, any knowledge of any magic given to Salbuk or about any weapons given to Hagjel, or Bobbiur, would be completely forgotten by Obmar should he be captured by Zalghar. Apparently old Zorp had been quite right about his worries of Obmar's Rune axe.

Speaking a little faster and without pausing Zalghar spoke about his idea of winning all of Adjemir. "We must find this Ram and kill him."

With a fiendish smile on his face Zalghar continued to speak in a matter of fact tone, while addressing the Haddrons. "He is the only one who I think can stop us now." Then continuing in a softer tone Zalghar went over what was bothering him the most. "I am sure that it is from Ram that these enemies of ours have gotten the enhanced weapons and the strong magic. The enemies who we are following us are called Hagjel and he is the Elf, who has an enhanced way of fighting with his magic arrows. The one they call Bobbiur has magically enhanced swords."

Zalghar reached over and rubbed his hand over Obmar's head in a feeling, as close to affection as Zalghar could get. Then he went on. "Obmar has been a great asset in my understanding of where we should be concentrating our energies."

At this Obmar smiled broadly and looked up at Zalghar, just as if he idolized Zalghar, but this idolization by Obmar was actually part of the spell that Zalghar had placed over Obmar.

"We will be traveling directly to Darmonarrow in the morning and we will find this old sorcerer. Tomorrow we will be having some fun smashing forever, the city of Darmonarrow. So I want you all well rested." Zalghar paused momentarily and then he continued in a relaxed tone. "In the morning I will send out the 'Spirit Eye' and then we will know exactly where Bobbiur will meet with Ram."

Zalghar added to this by saying. "The location of Ram is where Bobbiur and Hagjel are going to. About this I am certain."

Then looking up at the now darkened sky Zalghar then added. "They will lead us right to him."

All of the Haddrons warriors were listening intently as Zalghar started to talk with a greater confidence. "Once we are rid of this Ram then we will have no real opposition in all of Adjemir."

Then with a fiendish grin returning to his face Zalghar said. "This Ram will be no match for my powers." Zalghar chuckled out loud and all of the Haddron's including Obmar laughed openly.

The tiny grasshopper flew out from under a log and flew swiftly away into the dark. The sound of the flying grasshopper caught the attention of Zalghar and he quickly glanced directly at the insect. Zalghar thought it was strange that this small insect would be flying around at this time of night.

Zalghar had a moment of concern but he did nothing. He was not aware why he had a slight itching at the back of his head. His worries left him very quickly. Why should he want to worry about a simple and harmless grasshopper anyways?

With a yawn Zalghar stood up and waved his hand over all of the camp. Immediately the rain stopped because Zalghar had erected a temporary protection shelter which acted like a roof over everybody. The Haddrons began to settle in for the night. The Kilpacx who did not mind the rain were laying down and some were rolling over in the wet grass.

The grasshopper flew into the dark in a direct line into a thicker part of the forest. Past some very large trees and then quickly ducked below the attack of an ugly night bat. The tiny grasshopper never even slowed down. This grasshopper was considerably larger than most grasshoppers and it seemed very determined to reach it's destination.

An unknown magic spell had flashed with lightning speed from the grasshopper and the ugly but hungry night bat had flown swiftly away, howling in severe pain. Needless to say this particular bat would completely lose his appetite for grasshoppers, probably for the rest of it's natural life.

Then this determined looking insect flew onwards into the darkness of the night and it was as if the grasshopper could see really well in the forest's complete darkness. Flying swiftly around an enormous tree the grasshopper turned very sharply to it's right and then it followed the path of a small stream until it came to a small opening in the forest.

The grasshopper landed on a large boulder and settled down, right beside a slouched and worn out looking old man. "I see you made it back safely my dear." Zorp was grinning ear to ear as he spoke softly to the tiny grasshopper.

Right before his eyes the tiny grasshopper started to transform, back into her beautiful Haddron form. The tiny insect as it turned out was actually the beautiful Dymma.

"I see you were never worried at all you old grouch." When Dymma said this Zorp laughed softly. He knew that Dymma was aware that when she was on a mission like this he would worry himself sick. Dymma and Zorp had been together for such a long time and which ever one of them had to go away for some time the other one would worry until they were together again. The love between these two Haddrons was very strong.

With a wave of his hand Zorp magically brought some light into the forest. At which Dymma scolded him. Because he should keep it dark as it was safer for them if they remained hidden.

Zorp with a friendly smile of his wrinkled old face, just said softly. "Dymma I just had to see you for a moment."

Then he kissed her softly and instantly the forest returned to darkness.

Dymma then spent some time advising Zorp about the intentions of Zalghar to attack Darmonarrow tomorrow and his desires to also kill Bobbiur Hagjel and Ram.

Returning to Darmonarrow

Once the Krugs had all been killed they had left the tunnel. Bobbiur never looked back. He was moving at a very fast pace and Hagjel knew that Bobbiur should be getting tired, but this never seemed to slow Bobbiur down, not even in the slightest. Hagjel knew even though it was still very dark Bobbiur was in a hurry to get to wherever Ram was.

About this time Jakka was sitting up looking around and wondering where they were going in such a hurry. So Hagjel gave him a few nuts and small fruits to chew on as they went along. Hagjel was not exactly sure how far it was to Darmonarrow from here but even in the dark Bobbiur seemed to know exactly where they were and where they were going.

As they went around a corner in the path Bobbiur came to a sudden halt and in a mean mood, he drew his swords. Bobbiur gave off a noise which to Hagjel seemed almost seemed like a grow. Somebody was sitting on a log near the path just in front of them. This person or thing was sitting with his back to them and was not moving

Hagjel lit Bobbiur's torch and he saw what appeared to be a slight smile on Bobbiur's face. "Thanks. Hagjel you wait here."

Bobbiur walked up to the person who turned around just as Bobbiur got there. He could see Zorp concentrating, while holding a spent match. "Bobbiur I was trying to light my torch but this match was not strong enough."

Smiling Bobbiur just shook his head because he knew that Zorp was playing another game with him, as Zorp had strong magic and did not need a match to light any torch. Zorp's magic could put fire to anything. Bobbiur just asked softly and quietly. "What do you want this time old man?"

Bobbiur liked Zorp but he would never say it. Bobbiur did not know that Zorp had been inside his mind and Zorp knew everything. So Zorp just smiled to himself.

Squinting into the night Zorp started to chuckle as he spoke in a rapid squeaky old man fashion. "Good job on the Krugs Bobbiur." Then softly and with a genuine compassion Zorp said. "Sorry about Salbuk." Without changing his tone and in a questioning fashion Zorp asked. "How is Hagjel dealing with the loss of Salbuk?"

All Bobbiur could say was. "Hagjel does not show his pain but maybe the Elves don't feel loss like we Humans do. I would think he is dealing with the loss as good as can be expected."

With a quizzical look on his face Zorp said quietly. "You've changed Bobbiur."

In a crisp tone Bobbiur spoke. "It's a long story but Salbuk is dead. Zalghar killed him. But you already know this Zorp." In a quiet tone Bobbiur spoke softly. "Hagjel, Jakka and myself felt Salbuk's dying pain and it was not very comfortable. If I have changed as you have said it is probably because of this alone."

Then while gritting his teeth Bobbiur also added. "Obmar's one of them now."

With an urgent sound to his voice Zorp changed the subject. "You must get back to Darmonarrow now as fast as you can in order to get ready."

Zorp then spoke with a deathly pale sad and serious look on his face. "Dymma has been into the Haddron camp. They are camped near the end of the canyon just this side of the tunnel where they killed Salbuk. Dymma heard what they intend to do tomorrow. These renegade Haddrons intend to kill Ram, Hagjel and you. They will also be destroying Darmonarrow." Pausing slightly Zorp continued. "The Haddrons know that you are traveling back to meet with Ram and they are following you."

In a determined tone and very seriously Zorp said. "You must get ready for them quickly. So lets go." Bobbiur blinked. Hagjel, Jakka, and himself were now standing in the middle of the partially rebuilt Darmonarrow. Standing just behind him was the old man Zorp.

It was just getting light. "Thanks Zorp." Bobbiur said turning to face Zorp. "We were starting to get tired."

Then looking straight at Zorp Bobbiur said. "Zorp I wished you could help us fight Zalghar and his warriors. We could sure use

The Nine Moons of Adjemir

your magic powers." Bobbiur was looking at Zorp in a questioning manner and Zorp nodded his head and only repeated what he had said before. "Young man. I wish I could help you. Dymma has said she would like to help you also if she could but we are unable to fight our own people when we are away from the land of Haddron." Glancing into the early morning sky Zorp gave his explanation again as to why Dymma and himself could not get into the battle. "You see Zalghar and these warriors from Haddron have not broken any Haddron laws over here in Adjemir. Dymma and myself would actually be breaking Haddron laws if we attacked any Haddron's away from Haddron. It might be difficult for you to understand but we would be severely punished under Haddron laws when we returned to Haddron if we attacked Zalghar when he is away from the land of Haddron. We don't like it but those are Haddron's laws."

Then in a very sincere tone Zorp said. "Bobbiur I hope you can understand this. We can give you some increased powers, enhanced weapons and I can give advise, but we cannot fight Zalghar and the Haddrons away from our land." In a very quiet tone Zorp repeated himself. "This is Haddron law and I cannot change it."

Then in a more cheerful tone while changing the subject Zorp said. "Zalghar still does not know Dymma and I are here in Adjemir. So this is still to your advantage." At this Zorp looked very concerned and Bobbiur knew deep inside that Zorp would really like to help him fight the Haddron warriors but Bobbiur knew that this was not about to happen.

Continuing quietly Zorp went on. "One other thing Bobbiur you should try to understand these old Haddron laws. Both Dymma and myself know that the things which Zalghar has been doing to your people here in Adjemir is wrong but we cannot under Haddron law be the 'Judge and Jury'."

As Zorp was finishing up with this last statement, Bobbiur noticed that it was now early morning and as Bobbiur looked around he could see about fifty workers mostly women and children. They had just been starting work on some of the town's defenses and Bobbiur wondered to himself. "Is this all that is left of Darmonarrow and it's people?"

A very young, strong looking Human with short brown hair and wide shoulders, whose name was Fondrall, left the workers and slowly came up to Bobbiur and Zorp. He spoke to Bobbiur without any hesitation. "The Haddrons are coming back otherwise you wouldn't be here?" This was more of a statement than a question and Fondrall was glancing directly at Bobbiur. Then Fondrall quickly added. "I saw you at the battle of the Red Valley." To this Fondrall quietly added while waving his arm towards the remains of Darmonarrow before Bobbiur could say anything. "My parents were from here."

Fondrall was glancing around and again waved his hand at some of the ruins of the old town. Then Fondrall finished his statement. "They lived here in Darmonarrow. They moved here some time ago." Then to offer further assistance this young man added. "I have brought some men with me. We have actually just come from Garriton last night."

Bobbiur nodded his head in acknowledgment and he briefly thought of Kirwynn as he wondered how she was doing. He couldn't help himself when he practically blurted out. "How is Captain Yauddi doing?"

The asking of this question caused him to briefly go slightly red in the face as Zorp with a big grin had given him a sideways glance. Bobbiur gave Zorp a quick scowl as he had seen Zorp was starting to laugh to himself.

Fondall did not catch the humor which was pointed towards Bobbiur by Zorp. This young warrior continued. "Captain Yauddi is doing really well and General Yauddi is doing all right also." Then Fondrall added. "In fact the General has been up and about. Helping Garriton getting ready for another Haddrons attack. Should they return."

Then changing the subject Fondrall volunteered. "I'd like to fight these Haddrons." The young man had stepped closer and then he quickly introduced himself again. "My name is Fondrall from Garriton and I am a skilled swords man." There was considerable emotion in Fondrall's voice as he added. "Please let me help you. These Haddrons have killed all that was dear to me." Fondrall turned and again waved his arm at the ruins. "Some of my friends are here and as I said earlier they are also ready to fight for Darmonarrow."

A voice came from behind Bobbiur. "Fine. But first I'll need to see your sword." Zorp as he had said this stepped out from behind Bobbiur while reaching for Fondrall's weapon. "I don't have time to teach you or to make your sword exactly like Bobbiur's but I should be able to do something." Zorp as he was saying this took the sword and instantly disappeared.

The Nine Moons of Adjemir

While this happened Fondrall had a complete look of surprise on his young face. As if nothing out of the ordinary had just happened Bobbiur calmly asked Fondrall. "Where is Ram?"

Fondrall with a look of awe still on his young face slowly pointed in the general direction of the Forge as he said. "We just got here late last night and Ram has some temporary sleeping quarters in the back of the Forge." Then Fondrall added. "I'm not sure why he is not up yet but he may have worked late last night."

Then Fondrall asked. "I have a question for you Bobbiur." And without waiting for anything from Bobbiur Fondrall quarried. "Who is this Zorp person?"

Without showing any emotion at all Bobbiur thought about the question for a short time and then answered. "The best I can tell you is that he is here to help us. I cannot tell you much more but I can tell you he is a very good friend of mine." With a questioning look on his young face while shrugging his shoulders Fondrall only said. "Thanks, I guess."

Bobbiur only nodded as he saw Zorp reappearing.

When Zorp returned with the sword it looked much the same but now it was somewhat larger and it seemed to glow slightly. Zorp had a friendly grin on his face as he handed the sword back to Fondrall. "Now it will automatically slice right through the magic protection shields of the Haddrons, so they won't be able to block against you that easily. This will give you the element of surprise but don't rely on this completely." Zorp went on without any hesitation. "This sword will hit harder and with more force than before." Holding the sword up for Fondrall to see Zorp continued to explain how the sword would work.

Fondrall was reluctant and seemed a bit upset. "I don't think I can wield it anymore. It's much larger and it looks very heavy." Smiling with a gentle voice Zorp said. "Don't worry this sword will enhance your strength. I have placed a Rune on it so it will feel light as a feather in your hands."

Zorp passed the sword over and as he did so Zorp leaned into Fondrall and whispered into his ear. Zorp knew that Fondrall had lost his parents when the Haddrons had attacked Darmonarrow so he said in a compassionate and friendly tone. "Just say your parents names and the magic of the sword will take over. You should also practice with this sword before the Haddrons get close to Darmonarrow."

Fondrall stepped back a few paces and did a few practice swings. This was after he had whispered his parents names. A large infectious smile came to his face. Fondrall was instantly grinning ear to ear. Even as tense as Bobbiur was about the up and coming fight with the Haddrons, Bobbiur could not help but smile when he had seen the look of absolute delight on the young Fondrall's face.

Zorp saw Bobbiur smiling and as he walked over to Bobbiur he said. "Sorry to burst your bubble Bobbiur but it will be completely light out very shortly and I will have to disappear before Zalghar sends out his 'Spirit Eye.' If you know what I mean?"

Turning to Zorp Bobbiur as he was just starting to walk to the Forge, nodded and said. "Your right Zorp, follow me."

With a sideways glance and a quizzical tone Bobbiur asked. "Where is Dymma? I haven't seen her for awhile." Zorp looked towards Bobbiur and said. "Oh she's around somewhere. I think she is resting right now."

Zorp then went on. "It takes a lot of energy to do what she has to do when she changes forms, such as being a Dragon. Actually she tells me that it takes more energy to enable her to turn into a tiny cricket or grasshopper than what it takes her to turn into a huge Dragon."

At this Bobbiur headed directly to the Forge walking at a very fast rate. Hagjel who had gone off for a short time to talk to some friends caught up to Bobbiur and Zorp just as they were nearing the Forge.

Jakka who was as inquisitive as ever was quite busy taking in all the familiar smells of Darmonarrow. He had just woken as he poked his head up and was looking around out of the tote bag.

Ram was just risen and was stifling a yawn as he walked into the main part of the Forge from the small room where he had been sleeping just as the three were entering. Ram quickly glanced over the three then walked directly up to Bobbiur, nodded and put his hand on Bobbiur's shoulder. "Good work my son." Then he quickly asked. "Where is Salbuk and Obmar?"

Ram said this while he looked directly at Zorp and before Bobbiur could answer Ram asked. "And who is this?" Bobbiur glanced down at Ram as he said in a quiet tone. "Salbuk has been killed by the Haddrons and for some reason Obmar has joined the Haddrons."

Bobbiur went on as if to introduce Zorp but Ram raised his hand to stop Bobbiur for a second as Ram placed all of his attention towards Hagjel. "Hagjel. I am sorry to hear this as I know that you and Salbuk were such good friends." Then looking directly into Hagjel's eyes Ram asked. "So how are you doing Hagjel?" Ram had said this while he was reaching out to shake Hagjel's hand. Hagjel looking somewhat sad only said. "Salbuk saved our lives."

Then Hagjel added. "And I will miss him a lot but I still have Jakka. I will get over losing Salbuk but at present I am much more concerned about the coming of the Haddrons. I'll grieve later."

Nodded his head with understanding at what Hagjel had just said Ram then turned to face Zorp. "And this must be Zorp?" Ram had said this while glancing directly at the little friendly looking old man who was standing slightly behind Bobbiur with a friendly smile on his face.

Bobbiur could not help but notice as Ram was starting to move towards Zorp, he was thinking to himself. "These two old warriors should be sitting in the sun playing chess and relaxing. They should be retired not getting ready for battle." But then he remembered just how powerful these two musty old warriors really were.

Nothing was being said by either Ram or Zorp. All was quiet and very still for what seemed like only a few moments. At least this is what Bobbiur and Hagjel saw. But the two old warriors had unbeknownst to either Bobbiur or Hagjel actually entered each other's minds. While this was taking place everything around them seemed to go into slow motion. All who were present remained silent. No sounds were heard.

When the mind search was over both Ram and Zorp began to smile knowingly at each other at exactly the same time. It was as if they were reading Bobbiur's mind, because as Bobbiur started to introduce Ram to Zorp. Zorp and Ram had raised a hand at exactly the same moment and Ram said before Bobbiur could say anything. "Don't bother Bobbiur. We have already been introduced and Zorp, has already brought me up to speed on just who these Haddrons are."

Not speaking to anybody in particular Ram said as he rubbed his hands together. "Now lets get planning for the battle with the Haddrons." Without taking his eyes off of Zorp Ram spoke to Hagjel. "Hagjel please get Fondrall and tell him to bring every available soldier to us as fast as he can."

Still looking directly at Zorp it was as if these two old men were sharing thoughts Ram said. "Bobbiur. For your information a small troop is coming in from Garriton and you will be happy to know that Captain Kirwynn will be bringing them." Both Ram and Zorp had knowing smiles on their faces and Bobbiur looked towards the ground with a slightly red face. With stirred feelings Bobbiur only said. "I would prefer that she was not here when the Haddrons come."

The smile on Zorp's face got even broader. Ram chuckled out loud as Zorp who always seemed to be looking for a laugh started to dance around in a tight circle with his arms over his head, singing a simple song which was being sung way out of tune. "Isn't love grand?"

Then Zorp went into another little dance step which resembled a waltz and he imitated Bobbiur holding onto Kirwynn in a tight embrace. Bobbiur just stood there shaking his head and scowling at the large grin on Rams beaming face.

Bobbiur shaking his head while referring to Zorp could only say to Ram. "He does this to me all the time. He never stops."

After Zorp had finished teasing Bobbiur he instantly became very serious again and looking over at Ram he said. "Ram I am sorry that I cannot give you more magic but at least I can boost your energy levels." With a wave of the hand from Zorp Ram seemed to stiffen up, but only for a few seconds. Then nodding Ram looked down and studied his hands while he flexed his fingers just as Zorp said. "I have upgraded your energy and magic level to be equal to that of Zalghar."

Glancing sideways Bobbiur noticed that Zorp was as business like as he had ever seen him. Bobbiur knew that the Haddrons must be getting close because Zorp was hurrying things up. Wondering why Zorp was not concerned about the possibility of the 'Spirit Eye' from Zalghar. To Bobbiur's surprise Zorp said. "Not to worry Bobbiur." Then Zorp had quickly said. "Zalghar has not sent out the 'Spirit Eye' yet. And there probable won't be any 'Spirit Eye' until Zalghar gets closer."

Stepping nearer to Bobbiur Zorp explained things a little more clearly. "He already knows where you and Ram probably are and he is headed in this general direction." Then to allow Bobbiur to relax a little Zorp added. "Dymma is presently watching for their approach and she will tell me when they are getting close. The other information that you will need which will be very valuable is. On which road will they be traveling? I can tell you that Zalghar and his warriors will probably coming here using the road from Garriton."

In a serious tone Zorp said. "I will only be here long enough to give some powers and weapons to your troops. Zalghar is too close and I cannot be seen by him or the Haddrons. So the troops from Garriton will only be ordinary warriors as I will not be able to give them enhance powers or upgrade to their weapons." Then without hesitating Zorp added. "What I can do is give you and Hagjel some extra enhanced weapons for the Garriton garrison. But you must instruct the Garriton troops on how to use these weapons. I must tell you also that the Haddrons will be heavily armed and they also have the Kilpacz. Ram's magic will help you out quite a bit."

In a quieter tone and talking slower Zorp continued speaking to Bobbiur. "And again I apologize for not being able to assist any of you in the fighting these renegades but we have been over the reasons why a number of times before Bobbiur."

Explaining things further to everybody Zorp quickly continued. "It would be in your best interest during the battle that you keep a distance as far back from the Kilpacx as possible. I would suggest that you use your arrows against these beast if you want, just like Hagjel did at Garriton. The Kilpacx will not be under any protection shields but they may have eye protectors of some sort, on their faces. We will see later what Zalghar has done but I know how Zalghar thinks and he will not make the same mistake a second time like he did at Garriton."

Everybody was listening intently as Zorp continued speaking in a rapid fashion. "Zalghar will know that Hagjel is still around and he already knows that Hagjel is an incredible shot with his bow. I will discuss with Hagjel where he can place a shot which will have the best affect on the Kilpacx and that is just between their toes." Smiling broadly Zorp frowned as he said. "A well placed shot between the toes will not be as affective as the shot which Hagjel made into the eye of the Kilpacx at Garriton but it will still have a strong effect." Zorp continued. "Just for your information the Kilpacx are very sensitive in this area and they carry no armor on their feet. Before I leave I will be giving arrow enhancement to the rest of your troops. I am also able to give greater powers to any spear throwers which you may have with you." Commenting further. "What I will be doing is enhancing the spears which your troops have. I will be giving these special powers to your soldiers but they will have some problems breaking through the protection shields of the Haddron warriors especially if Zalghar remains strong."

Bobbiur had been listening intently. He was getting very tired from not getting any sleep when he stifled a yawn. It was as if Zorp had read Bobbiur's mind about feeling tired. All Zorp did was give a quick blink and a short wave of his hand in the direction of Bobbiur.

Bobbiur could feel instantly, a renewed energy running through his veins.

When Bobbiur looked up he saw Hagjel and Fondrall approaching. They only had nine other fighters from Darmonarrow with them. With Fondrall's friends they now had about sixteen defenders in all. Hagjel hollered to Bobbiur. "This is all the defenses of Darmonarrow which could spared. The others cannot be spared because they have to guard the walls."

Zorp turned and motioned Hagjel to come closer. Jakka was stretched up and was looking around. Jakka was quite curious because he seemed to know that something important was about to happen. Before Zorp did, or say anything more, he gently rubbed the back of Jakka's ears.

Zorp touched Hagjel on the shoulder and said. "You are one of the best archers I have ever seen and if these young men with you are good archers. Then you should do all right. Continuing on Zorp said. "Hagjel I must replenish your quiver. But before I do that let me help you with your tiredness." The old man then blinked and waved his hand just like he did to Bobbiur. All who were present could see Hagjel seemed to instantly perk up. Zorp then rubbed his hand over the quiver on Hagjel's back and he said to Hagjel. "There. You now have all the arrows you will need."

As he was finishing up he said to Hagjel. "Take care of this little fella." Zorp was petting the head of Jakka again. Hagjel could only say. "Thank you Zorp." Because Zorp had nodded and turned quickly to other matters.

Walking over towards the incoming soldiers, Zorp said. "Oh well now we'll see what we can do with this group." Zorp was rubbing his chin and looking over the men he had to work with. It was almost as if young Fondrall knew what Zorp was thinking when he started to defend the men he had brought with him. "Don't worry about these men as they may be young but they have seen many battles and they are some of the best."

Then Fondrall as an afterthought added. "I would like to be in a battle with these men at my side more than any of the other soldiers who were fighting at the recent battle in the Red Valley." Then Fondrall also added in a serious tone. "I would trust these men with my life."

Looking at Frondall with admiration Zorp nodded as he said. "You would trust these men with your life would you?" Then knowingly Zorp commented as he patted Fondrall's shoulder. "Very good Fondrall. Very good."

Zorp stopped, turned and said to the soldiers. "I will want all the archers first."

Quickly the archers stepped forward and Zorp walked up and touched each one of them separately on their foreheads and in turn he brushed his right hand over each archer's quiver of arrows. When he was finished with all of the archers he stepped back and said. "Your arrows are enhanced and all you have to do is say in your own language. Fly true. But you still have to shoot straight and acurate. In the end it will depend on your skills as to how effective these arrows will be."

Speaking further Zorp said. "These enhanced arrows will not stop the giant fire balls which Zalghar can throw at you but they can stop the strongest fire balls which are thrown by the other Haddron warriors." Zorp paused for just a moment to be sure that all the archers had understood these instructions. Then he proceeded. "When the Haddron warriors send their fire balls at you, you should fire your arrows a soon as you can because even though you might be successful in hitting the fire ball, its when the incoming fire ball breaks up that there might bee a danger to you. The explosion and the momentum of the smashed fire ball will continue in your direction."

Zorp continued. "Keep back as far as you can because of these fire balls. At the same time you must also keep out of the reach of the Kilpacx. If you are able too you can hurt the Kilpacx by shooting them in an eye but hitting them with an arrow between the toes is almost as good." Then Zorp added."The eyes of the Kilpacx may have some form of protection from Zalghar." With a smile Zorp said this because these types of shots were nearly impossible. "Although these are tough shots they can completely stop a Kilpacx. Because for a Kilpacx this pain is terrible."

Continuing Zorp pointed at Hagjel and then he told the archers what Hagjel had done at Garriton only a few days earlier. In a deep and loud voice so every one could hear Zorp said. "At Garriton Hagjel hit one of the Kilpacx in the eye and the Kilpacx went kind of crazy from the pain. When this Kilpacx went crazy with the pain the other Kilpacx became cannibalistic and attacked the wounded animal. But I have to tell you that the shot into the Kilpacx eye by Hagjel was one of the best shots I have ever seen. I hope you are able to do the same as Hagjel."

Just then Zorp looked up at the sky as he saw Dymma coming. He turned his attention back to the soldiers and said. "I will be telling you more about the Haddron fireballs next but we must hurry because the Haddrons are getting closer." Zorp went quickly on. "The more fire balls the Haddrons send at you the weaker their magic will become." Zorp paused again for only a second to make sure that he had every ones complete attention and then he went on. "The white fire balls require the most energy from the Haddron warrior. "They are the smallest. They move the fastest and they are also the most powerful. The yellow fire balls are a little larger but they move a little slower." Continuing, Zorp was starting to speak a little faster. "The red Haddron fire balls are the weakest of all and they move the slowest. If you are able to stay at a distance then this will be the safest way to fight the Haddron's fire balls."

Then changing the subject slightly Zorp spoke more about the Haddron's weapons. "These arrows on occasion, can penetrate the protection shields of the Haddrons but they will not penetrate the protection shield of Zalghar. But to break the protection shield of the Haddrons you must get very close. You will observe that the Haddrons will probably throw the white fire balls when the battle starts but as they start to lose their powers the fire balls will start to become yellow or red."

Nodding that he was finished Zorp then turned to the spear throwers and he did the same sort of things for the these soldiers as he had done for the archers. Each spear thrower had about six spears with them which Zorp rubbed his hands over. These spears temporarily glowed with a green transparent sphere. When the greenish hue had faded away Zorp said. "These spears will now penetrate the protection shields of the ordinary Haddron warrior but you will not be able to penetrate the protection shield which Zalghar has.

The spear throwers showed a tremendous interest in what Zorp was telling them and Zorp noticed, all the spear throwers were well developed and very muscular individuals. Then Zorp with a smile on his tired looking old face said. "You will find that the powers I have given you will enable you to throw your spears with tremendous force but you will have to practice in order to become fine tuned with your new powers. As I told the archers earlier these spears can penetrate the protection shields of the Haddron warriors but you would be better off, if you use these spears to concentrate on their fighting animals, the Kilpacx. If the Haddron warriors are without their fighting Kilpacx then they might be easier to beat."

The Nine Moons of Adjemir

By this time Dymma was landing and she started to beckon Zorp because she knew that Zorp had to get out of sight right away. "Zorp you must come because Zalghar is getting close and the Haddrons are headed directly for Darmonarrow."

Then Dymma quickly added. "The Haddrons have just passed by Garriton."

Zorp walked over to Bobbiur and Ram shook both their hands and then said. "You two will all have to fight the fight of your lives." Then nodding to all the troops he spoke loudly so all could hear. "Good luck."

Bobbiur feeling that Zorp might not be coming back only said. "Thank you Zorp." Then Bobbiur asked in a soft tone. "If we beat Zalghar will we be seeing you afterwards?" Zorp nodded before saying. "If you beat Zalghar I will be able to visit with you." Zorp was looking towards Dymma and he finished off by saying. "If not then for obvious reasons you will never see us again."

Ram broke in at this time and said to Zorp. "We will do all right but we must hurry. I don't want to fight Zalghar this close to Darmonarrow so we must meet him as close to the Temple of the Ancients as possible. Meeting these renegades near the Temple of the Ancients is part of my strategy."

Then turning Ram said to Bobbiur. "I might have some surprises for Zalghar. In Adjemir he has never had to fight magic spells as strong as mine."

To this Zorp said. "Do not underestimate Zalghar at any time because I can tell you he has tremendous powers. These powers are of the type which you have never seen before." Zorp wanted Ram to understand fully just how powerful Zalghar really was. Then Ram became very serious and he spoke in a deep tone. He was looking straight into the eyes of Zorp as he repeated. "I said I may have a big surprise for Zalghar." Zorp went stiff because he was receiving a very important mind message from Ram.

With an extremely sad look on his tired old face Zorp before turning towards Dymma who was waiting patiently turned back to Ram. Zorp nodded his head and bowed solemnly as he said. "That will be a very big surprise Ram but I hope you never have to resort to that."

To Bobbiur Zorp suddenly seemed even more sad and he wondered what the mind message between Ram and Zorp was. Zorp then jumped up onto Dymma's back and he only waved as did Dymma. Then they quickly flew away.

Turning so all could hear Ram raised his voice . "We will get our Spaggidons and ride out to meet Zalghar near the Temple of the Ancients." Then he added. "I do not want this battle to be to close to Darmonarrow because of the women and children. They will not be safe if we fight the Haddrons here." Then Ram said in a tired but determined voice. "So lets mount up and ride."

Hagjel had asked earlier for some of the workers saddle the Spaggidons and just as Ram finished speaking the Spaggidons were arriving.

The Devils Start to Travel Back to Darmonarrow.

The Haddrons had woken early the next morning and there was a good feeling through out the camp, mostly about the killing of Salbuk the night before. Zalghar had been in a really good mood because he now could see that the conquest of Adjemir was at hand. Once he had the troublesome Humans, Ram and Bobbiur and the Elfen archer Hagjel out of the way, he felt that there would not be much opposition to stop him from complete control over of all of Adjemir.

The night before he had said he would send out the 'Spirit Eye' early in the morning, in order to follow Bobbiur but his thinking this morning had changed. Instinctively he knew where Bobbiur was going and this feeling had been confirmed by the conversation he had with Obmar earlier in the morning. Bobbiur was traveling back to the sanctuary of Darmonarrow in order to be nearer to the strength of the old sorcerer Ram. Now Zalghar had a plan. This time he would completely destroy not only Darmonarrow but Bobbiur also. Smiling to himself he thought. "Ram will soon be dead."

The Kilpacx were off a little ways grazing on some lush vegetation and the warriors were just finishing eating when Zalghar called them all together. "Today we will march on Darmonarrow." Then speaking further in a confident and commanding tone he said. "This time we will completely destroy Darmonarrow. After we kill this sorcerer Ram his Captain Bobbiur and finish off the archer who shot the Kilpacx in the eye at Garriton then there won't be much opposition left to stop us anywhere in Adjemir." After a short pause. "We should be able to conquer the rest of the people of Adjemir at our leisure."

Looking over his warriors and after a short pause Zalghar with determination in his voice said. "I have seen the armies of Adjemir and they cannot stop my magic." Then with a knowing smile on his evil looking face Zalghar continued. "It may be a lot of work to conquer them but I know we can do this. After we have conquered all of Adjemir I have decided because of your hard work I will be giving each of you, your own city." Glancing over at Obmar Zorp said in a friendly way. "Obmar you have been of great assistance and I will be giving you your own city as well." This brought a smile to Obmar's wrinkled and now evil face. Zalghar smiled deeply for the first time in a long time. Every one of the Haddron warriors seemed very relaxed.

Then Zalghar said to Obmar. "You will be given the first choice of which ever city you want." Zalghar waved his arm in a sweeping motion over the land of Adjemir. "You my loyal Haddron warriors will be given a city each." Then tapping Obmar's helmet Zalghar added. "We will number each of the largest Adjemian cities and we will place all the names of those cities into Obmar's helmet."

Speaking in a softer voice Zalghar said. "You shall draw for which ever city you get." Then in a quieter voice Zalghar said. "I will be rebuilding Darmonarrow for myself." With this last statement Zalghar said to the Haddron warriors. "Get your mounts and we will travel straight towards Darmonarrow. These people of Adjemir are about to see what kinds of powers we really have." Then in a laughing way Zalghar said. "They will be no match for us after the Sorcerer Ram is gone."

The Haddrons broke camp and they started the long trip back towards Darmonarrow. They were all quiet but very determined.

General Yauddi Worries.

Very early that morning, it was still dark when General Yauddi had said goodbye to Kirwynn, as she was preparing to travel to Darmonarrow. It bothered the Old General that his daughter had to leave and go to Darmonarrow in order to help the survivors, defend Darmonarrow against the Haddron warriors.

Zorp had come to her room very early in the morning, woke her and told her that she should gather as many spare troops as she could get and travel to Darmonarrow. This was because the Haddrons would be attacking Darmonarrow shortly. Bobbiur and the defenders of Darmonarrow would be needing her help. She had twelve of the best trained soldiers that Garriton could spare with her and General Yauddi hoped these soldiers would be enough. If he still had his health then he would be going to help at Darmonarrow and then Kirwynn could have stayed at Garriton where she would have been safe.

The attack on Adjemir by the Haddrons has changed everything. The old General was wringing his hands in constant worry but at the same time he was proud of Kirwynn. H was thankful that she had grown up and he was satisfied because she was turning into a very good commander. He had gotten good reports back from his other officers who had been with her at the battle with the Elves in the Red Valley. The old General thought to himself. "Garriton has lost a lot of good men at the battle in the Red Valley but at least Kirwynn had made it back safe."

General Yauddi turned and shuffled slowly down the hall to his bedroom. He felt old. He felt weak. He even looked old but he knew that he must get as much rest as he was able to. Because if Ram, Bobbiur, Kirwynn with the troops from Garriton, were not successful against the Haddrons then he and all the other Generals of Adjemir would have to place as many men in the field as possible, in order to try and defeat these Haddron foreigners. The old General had only been back in his bed for about one hour when one of the night sentries banged on his door. The night sentry told General Yauddi that the Haddron warriors had just passed by Garriton. They were traveling in the direction of Darmonarrow.

    Then the sentry said. "The Haddrons are just behind Kirwynn and the Garriton troops. Captain Kirwynn doesn't know that they are being followed by enemy Haddrons." General Yauddi was instantly awake and started giving orders immediately.

    Suddenly the General seemed to be in a very bad mood. The sentry just stood there with a worried frown on his forehead. "Get all the troops up." Then the old General quickly said. "Tell them to saddle their horses and get ready. Tell them to hurry. I don't care if I am crippled and if I am old. I feel like fighting."

    Then in a forceful tone the old General almost growling said through clenched teeth. "Those Haddrons must be stopped. We are going to ride to Darmonarrow and help fight these no good low down Haddrons." As an afterthought General Yauddi said. "Get the fastest horse in the stable and send the fastest messenger through the backs woods to Darmonarrow. Tell Ram and Bobbiur that Kirwynn is just in front of the Haddrons and tell them she does not know how close she is being followed by the enemy."

    The young sentry nodded as the worried look which was on his face for some reason disappeared. He could not help but smile. As he bolted from the General's room he mumbled to himself. "It looks like the Old General was quickly becoming himself again. Tough and cranky."

    The young sentry said to himself. "Looks like the Old-Man wants a fight."

    The sentry's smile became even bigger as he ran towards the barracks. The sentry was feeling really good because General Yauddi was becoming himself again and it was about time. He couldn't get to the barracks fast enough so he could tell everybody that General Yauddi had woken up and was very mean, and very cranky.

    This was good news. This was going to be a great day. Since General Yauddi had been injured he had just moped around and he was looking older by the day. Then the sentry said to himself as he was moving at a rapid pace towards the barracks. "Damn it is sure good to see General Yauddi cranky."

Then the young sentry laughed out loud. He was thinking to himself as to how strange it must seem because he was getting so excited about telling everybody at the barracks that General Yauddi was cranky.

"The troops are going to be very happy. Yes indeed." The sentries pace quickened.

The Haddrons Passed Garriton

Zalghar was in a good mood because he knew that soon there would be no opposition left anywhere in all of Adjemir after he had killed Ram of Darmonarrow. With his Haddron warriors and his strong magic they would then easily conquer all of Adjemir at their leisure. The Kilpacx were making really good time and Zalghar was also happy because he had removed one of the biggest problem which opposed him and this had been the troublesome mage called Salbuk. Zalghar smiled even more deeply with an evil look which crossed his face he remembered all of the events leading up to the death of Salbuk. He was deeply happy inside. This was only a little after as they had passed by the walls of Garriton Zalghar and his troops had not turned in. They had just continued traveling past Garriton at a steady pace towards Darmonarrow.

As they had passed the city Zalghar had seen the sentries running around on the walls of Garriton and pointing in the direction of him and his troops. He had just nodded and smiled towards the walls of Garriton. Turning to his men Zalghar said calmly. We'll come back here I promise. And next time we will flatten this place." As he waved his arm towards the walls of Garriton he was unaware of the fierceness of his voice, or the fact he was almost growling in a satisfied yet evil manner.

In his mind Zalghar knew his warriors were looking for a good fight because the fight they had the night before when they did away with the mage called Salbuk was too short and therefore not much fun. This same feelings seemed to apply to the Kilpacx. The Kilpacx have not had a good feeding since they smashed the Krug village of Theoris, nor had they been used in a real battle since they first attacked Darmonarrow. The Kilpacx would need the exercise and they would feel good completely destroying Darmonarrow this time. Zalghar smiled his evil smile again as he knew in two days at the most he and his men would have complete control over all of Adjemir. The only real problem which remained was this Bobbiur, Hagjel and the old Human sorcerer from Darmomarrow. Zalghar had smiled as they had passed by Garriton because he knew deep inside Darmonarrow had put their best men into battle against him and now their main power Salbuk was dead. He started to laugh because he knew exactly how much magic power he had and he knew there was no magic in all of Adjemir which was even close to being as strong as his magic powers were. Zalghar's magic was Haddron magic.

Some thoughts kept going through Zalghar's mind. "These people of Adjemir have not ever seen the full force of Haddron magic. They did not have any idea as to what they were up against. Not even this Ram would be prepared to fight the full power of Haddron magic."

Then Zalghar had began to laugh out loud. His men including the Haddrons who were riding point turned to look. The Haddrons riding point when they had heard Zalghar laughing also had a big smiles on their faces. The Haddron warriors whom had been closest to where Zalghar was riding had showed their enthusiasm because they also felt what Zalghar was feeling. These stupid Adjemirians had not yet been in close combat with fully prepared troop of Haddron warriors. Each Haddron warrior had powerful magic tremendous fighting skills and they would take no prisoners.

Each and every Haddron warrior who came to Adjemir with Zalghar, on their own were complete and efficient killing machines. All of Zalghar's warriors had been well trained to fight viciously to any end, by Zalghar himself.

From what the Haddrons had seen in the Red Valley battle between the Humans and the Elves was that neither the Humans nor the Elves had any special skills. At this Zalghar thought to himself when they would fight with Bobbiur and Ram from Darmonarrow his enemies would feel the complete ruthlessness wrath of Haddron power. Zalghar had looked down at his hands and while flexing his fingers he could tell that his powers were at their best. Zalghar had a really good nights sleep and he knew deep inside he would be ready for anything or anybody that Darmonarrow could send against him. The evil dark look returned to his face as he knew when he attacked Darmonarrow today there would be no surprises. This time he would kill everybody from Darmonarrow and if he was lucky enough to capture Bobbiur and Hagjel he would make their deaths very painful and very slow.

As he turned and surveyed his warriors. He could tell that they were looking forward to this battle. It was just too bad that Bobbiur and Hagjel had gotten away the night before because it would have been a lot of fun killing them both back at the tunnel's entrance.

Today would be a different story. They would both be very dead very shortly. Zalghar then remembered how he had sent the Rune axe into Darmonarrow the day before the first attack on the town of Darmonarrow. This made him turn around and look at Obmar with a smile. The Rune axe which Obmar carried was very powerful and once it had been dispatched it did not require any energy to function. Therefore Zalghar could use all of his energy to kill anybody from Darmonarrow, at his will.

Thinking to himself Zalghar mused. Obmar had fit in really well and was proving his worth more and more all the time with interesting information about Adjemir and more importantly Darmonarrow. The information given to him by Obmar is what enabled Zalghar to know that the only problem with the conquering of Adjemir now was the power of the sorcerer Ram from Darmonarrow.

Looking down Zalghar could also tell that the huge Kilpacx knew there was going to be a battle because of the quickness in their step. Zalghar knew the Kilpacx were not all that intelligent but some instinct from within them always seemed to let them know when they were going into battle. Zalghar knew how the Kilpacx felt because they were not looking around. These huge lumbering Kilpacx continued looking straight ahead as they marched up the road. It was as if there was something right around the corner. There was a determination in their step and this made Zalghar feel warm inside. It was a good feeling. It was always interesting to watch these magnificent beasts doing their work while destroying the enemy.

Just then the warrior who had been riding the first Kilpacx on point from the front of the column, turned and rode back towards Zalghar. The warrior stopped beside Zalghar and said. "Zalghar there are riders just in front of us." Quickly he added. "It looks like about twelve or more and it looks like they have just left from Garriton." Zalghar was listening intently as the rider continued. "There may be an ambush in front of us. So what do you want to do?"

The rider waited as Zalghar slowed his Kilpacx down and was in deep thought. The question for Zalghar was. Should I stop the march and send out the 'Spirit Eye' or not? Zalghar decided not to send out the 'Eye' because of the amount of energy which it would need because he wanted to keep full power for the up and coming battle with Darmonarrow. Turning to the rider he gave the order. "I will not send out the 'Spirit Eye' because there are no powers strong enough from Garriton which we have to worry about." Then he said further. "It is just as well because it appears these warriors in front of us are going to help Darmonarrow and therefore we can kill them all at the same time." Then Zalghar added. "But I want the march to slow down slightly and we will require the point rider to be farther out in out in front of us at all times. Just in case there is an ambush."

He went on to say. "These riders from Garriton who are just in front of us are not that important and I don't want to waste any of our power on them. Also I don't want the Kilpacx using up a lot of energy chasing those riders from Garriton. So just let them go. As I said earlier will kill them all at one time when we get to Darmonarrow."

Then Zalghar said after a short pause. "I will want the rider who is presently in front of us to set up his protection shield just in case there is an ambush. When the battle starts with Darmonarrow. Which ever warrior is leading us with the protection shield may have to stay the back when the battle commences ." Then he went on slowly to say. "His powers will be weakened from keeping his protection shield up for such a long time."

The orders from Zalghar were initiated. The march in the direction of Darmonarrow continued but at a much slower pace.

Ram's Strategy for the Battle

Knowing the directions of were Haddrons were coming from was of a great assistance for Ram. He had brought his troops away from Darmonarrow so the battle with the Haddrons would not be so close to Darmonarrow. This was in order to make it safe for the women and children. But he also had a secret reason for bringing the fight with the Haddrons to this place. A secret which nobody not even Bobbiur knew anything about.

When they arrived at the place where Ram had chosen to confront the Haddron warriors it was very close to the Temple of The Ancients but it was even closer to the Cemetery of The Ancients.

Bobbiur had ridden up closer to Ram and asked in a questioning tone. "Why do we stop here this does not seem like a very good place to fight the Haddron warriors?" In a questioning tone he then asked. "Is it?"

The place where Ram had stopped the march was in a small clearing just off the road about half way between Darmonarrow and Garriton in the Valley of The Ancients.

Ram looked at Bobbiur with a kind gentle smile and said. "I cannot tell you why but this is the best place to beat the Haddrons." Ram quickly and before Bobbiur could ask any more questions said. "We do not have too much time so call all the troops in close and I will tell you how I would like the battle to proceed." Bobbiur could see a quiet determination yet sadness in the eyes of Ram, which he had never seen before. This puzzled him. Without saying anything Bobbiur obediently turned and rode out to the troops and brought them all closer to where Ram was waiting.

Once all the troops were in close enough for Ram to speak to them all Ram looked them over very slowly. Other than the Spaggidons who were making a small fuss, all was quiet. Then Ram started to give out his strategy. "Bobbiur you will take up a position on the far side of the valley just past where Fondrall will have some of the archers." Ram pointed as he continued. "You will be with the spear throwers who will place themselves over there beside that small hill." Ram paused after he had pointed in the direction where he wanted the archers to place themselves. Then he turned to Hagjel. "Hagjel you will be in charge of half of the Archers."

Then turning to Fondrall Ram said. "Fondrall you will in charge of the other half of the archers and you will position your troops over there." Again Ram pointed in the general position where he wanted Fondrall to place his troops. "Fondrall if something should happen to Hagjel then you will be in command of all of the Archers." Ram paused for a short time as he asked. "Is this understood and do any of you have any questions?" Ram waited and as there were no questions from the archers he continued in a matter of fact tone. "I will explain further what I would like you to do when the Haddrons get here but for now I will explain to you where I will be placing myself."

Turning in another direction Ram said quietly and sadly. "I will be over there." He had just pointed to another small hill which was not very far from the Cemetery of The Ancients. Everybody wondered why Ram would want to separate himself from the main force and why he had chosen the small hill to do his fighting from. But nobody who was present raised any questions.

Speaking to Bobbiur Ram went on slowly but made his point clear. "Zorp has given me thoughts of how the Haddrons will fight." Then he added. "They will start off by throwing their fire balls and they will do this from a distance."

Looking calmly towards Bobbiur Ram said. "Bobbiur you should not fight early in the battle but you should help out where you can. If my strategy works the way I think it should you will be better off getting the Haddrons to throw as many fire balls as you are able to early in the battle." Ram paused before he said. "When the fire balls start to grow weak you should be able to get close enough for hand to hand combat."

Then speaking to the spear throwers Ram laid out the rest of his plan. "You spear throwers should come in last." Then nodded in Bobbiur's direction, Ram continued. "Bobbiur will decide when it is best to start to your attack." In a strong tone Ram said. "The main purpose of the spears throwers should be to concentrate on the Kilpacx." Pausing for a short time while he gathered his thoughts Ram continued. "After the magic energy of the Haddron warriors becomes weak the Haddrons will start to depend on the fighting and killing skills of the Kilpacx to finish you off." Then he added. "Everybody here should know by now just how dangerous those giant Kilpacx can be."

Ram pointed towards some bushes just beside where the archers were to be placed in position. There were also some large rocks where the spear throwers could hide and be in waiting for the Haddrons in an ambush. "When the Haddrons try to pass your position you should try to hit them in their flanks." Then the old sorcerer said. "You should be able to charge into them with a surprise attack." Ram continued. " But you will have to get very close to the Kilpacx. The skin of the Kilpacx, is very strong so you will need to hit them with your spears with great force."

Turning his attention back to the archers Ram mentioned how the arrows should be used. "Use your arrows sparingly." Then turning his attention towards Hagjel Ram continued slowly but confidently. "Do not shoot more than one or two arrows at a time." Nodding at Hagjel Ram added. "Hagjel get your people to take turns in shooting at the Haddron's fire balls. What we do not want is to be firing a large number of arrows at the same fire ball. If this happens you will run out of enhanced arrows before the Haddrons run out of their fire balls." With a thoughtful tone Ram stated. "This would be disastrous."

As Ram continue to speak to Hagjel he said. "Hagjel you should spend some time getting your archers into a firing sequence." Then without pausing Ram asked. "Do you understand?" Hagjel nodded and said nothing.

Then Ram turned to Fondrall and he said. "Fondrall the same applies to your archers also. You must set up a firing sequence with your arrows just like I have instructed Hagjel and his archers to do.

Just then one of the archers who was standing towards the outside of the group yelled. "Somebody is coming." Fondrall glanced in the direction that the archer was pointing and said almost instantly. "It is alright he is from Garriton." Then he added. "He is with us." As it turned out it was the messenger from Garriton which General Yauddi had sent to advise Bobbiur and Ram that Kirwynn was being followed by the Haddrons. The rider from Garriton did not come down the main road but had come from out of the bushes, which meant he had come on the shorter route.

The messenger came directly towards Ram. The messenger dismounted and bowed to Ram. Without any introductions the messenger quickly told Ram that Kirwynn was coming with about twelve well trained soldiers from Garriton and that the Haddrons invaders were very close behind them. Without saying anything to the messenger Ram instantly turned directly towards Hagjel. "Hagjel take a fresh mount and ride towards the Garriton troops at the fastest speed you can." Then Ram quickly added. "When you meet up with the soldiers from Garriton tell Captain Kirwynn to come here as quickly as their mounts can carry them." Without any hesitation Ram continued. "Tell them not to stop for anything and make sure Captain Kirwynn fully understands just how close the Haddrons are following behind her and the Garriton troops."

Shaking his head Ram said. "They will not be able to defend themselves against the Haddrons without power magic." Before finishing he added. "That is if the Haddrons should catch up to the Garriton troops."

Immediately after Hagjel had left the troops were told to take up their positions and Ram said to Bobbiur. "Bobbiur come with me. I need to tell you some more about what should happen here today."

The day was starting to warm up as Ram took Bobbiur off a little ways. Ram gave some of his ideas to Bobbiur on how he wanted to fight Zalghar separately. "Bobbiur I am not sure just how powerful Zalghar is but he must be quite powerful or he would still not be roaming around Adjemir this freely. I want to keep Zalghar away from our soldiers. I will also want to keep you and the soldiers, away from Zalghar and in a position of safety and a good distance from his magic."

Then placing his hand on Bobbiur's shoulder and speaking in a very quiet tone Ram said. "I must fight Zalghar by myself."

Bobbiur who had been standing quietly was frowning when he spoke. "There is some reason why you brought us to this place to fight the Haddrons." Then gritting his teeth Bobbiur asked. "I must know why we are fighting here." Standing tall with a fierce look in his eyes Bobbiur was looking questioningly at Ram as he said. "Ram. There is something you are not telling me." Bobbiur did not realize that his voice was getting louder and there was also a quiver in his voice when he was speaking. Bobbiur continued showing his concern by saying. "It makes no sense for us to fight the Haddrons this close to the Temple of the Ancients."

Bobbiur kept talking without any pause. "If we are beaten by these Haddrons they will surely attack and demolish the Temple." Again Bobbiur paused briefly. "So I have to ask you. Why we are here?" After thinking for a short period of time Ram said in a very quiet tone. "Bobbiur you have to trust me. Do you understand? Without waiting for Bobbiur to reply Ram said. "I understand things which I cannot tell you about at this time." Ram paused and then said to Bobbiur in a very quiet tone. "I promise to tell you why we are here sometime in the future. But for now you must understand that we have very little time to plan for our battle against these Haddrons."

Before Bobbiur could ask any more questions Ram continued. Ram quickly pointed at the little hill where he would be situated when the Haddrons got close. "I will be there as I have told you before. I will stay there until Zalghar comes after me." Then Ram said. "It's me who Zalghar wants and I will make him chase me. This will also keep Zalghar away from the others." Ram then said. "Its safer for all of our people if we do it this way. The Darmonarrow and the Garriton troops will have to keep the Haddron soldiers busy and away from where me and Zalghar when have our battle."

Then Ram changed the conversation slightly. "You must keep Kirwynn away from the main fighting. And you should stay with her until the Haddrons fire balls start to show that they are becoming weak. This is when you and the spear throwers should attack them on their flank with all your forces. If we are able to keep Zalghar away from the main fighting then you will have a chance of winning against the Haddron warriors and their Kilpacx."

At this time Ram lowered his voice as he looked Bobbiur straight in the eyes. "Bobbiur. No matter what happens in the battle which I will have with Zalghar. You and Kirwynn must stay in the clear. You must under no circumstances come to close to this place while I am battling Zalghar." In a solemn tone Ram continued. "You should also tell your men and the men from Garriton that while I will be battling with Zalghar they must, under all circumstances stay well back."

Bobbiur then asked why he could not help Ram fight Zalghar by saying. "You at least should let me stay close in case something goes wrong then I could help."

Bobbiur quickly went on in the same pleading tone. "You may need me to cover your back just in case something goes wrong."

Raising his voice Ram only shook his head. "You do not understand. The magic powers which will be used in this battle will be strong enough to kill anybody who is too close." Then Ram quickly added in a pleading way. "You must promise me that you will stay well back regardless of how the battle is going."

Before Bobbiur could ask or say anything more Ram changed the subject. "I want you to be ready to travel out and to show your self to Zalghar when he gets close." Ram spoke softly as he continued. "When Hagjel gets back here with the troops from Garriton you should advise Kirwynn of the battle strategy which we have planned. You should also tell Fondrall to share the enhanced arrows and spears with the troops from Garriton and to instruct them on the use of these weapons."

As Bobbiur was listening to Ram speaking he saw the same sadness in Ram's eyes which he had seen earlier. Bobbiur was also aware that Ram seemed to look older and more tired than he had ever looked in the past. Bobbiur swore to himself that after they had beaten the Haddrons he would do more work and he would take on more responsibility around Darmonarrow. This way he could take some of the stress off of Ram because he was getting older.

Bobbiur started to think of Kirwynn just as Ram started to speak further about the defenses of their position here near to the Temple of The Ancients. Without looking in the direction where the Haddrons would be coming from. Ram raised his arm in a sweeping motion of the general direction of the road between Garriton and Darmonarrow when he said. "If the rider from Garriton is correct then you will have only a short time after Kirwynn and the Garriton troops get here to speak with Kirwynn."

Changing the subject Ram then said. "When you have seen Kirwynn and you have spent some time with her then I will want you and Hagjel to travel out to the main road and travel directly towards the Haddrons."

Before Bobbiur, who still had a puzzled look on his face could say anything, Ram continued. "Where this road meets the main road between Garriton and Darmonarrow there is a small open valley. You must let the Haddrons see you at that location." At this time Ram in a solemn tone gave his plan to Bobbiur. "You will have Hagjel with you. If you can get close enough without any danger to yourself and Hagjel then Hagjel should fire some ordinary arrows at the Haddrons. You must be seen clearly by these Haddrons." Glancing towards Bobbiur Ram then said. "I will want the Haddrons to chase you." Further emphasizing with a wave of his hand Ram then said. "I want the

Haddrons to come here. And remember to keep your distance. If you get to close then the magic of Zalghar could kill you both."

Without any hesitation, just like a good soldier who always follows orders Bobbiur said. "I understand how powerful Zalghar is and I understand what you want me and Hagjel to do."

Bobbiur was looking at Ram with a curious look on his face just as Ram walked up to him and put his arms around him as he gave Bobbiur a hug. Bobbiur had never seen Ram act like this before. Ram had never shown any affection for anybody in Darmonarrow and this caught Bobbiur by surprise. Bobbiur was also surprised as to how much strength Ram had in his upper body as he put his arms around Bobbiur.

Ram then said. "You must be very careful and please do not become over confident with the Haddrons because they are more powerful and dangerous than even you can imagine. Especially Zalghar." Then Ram said as he turned away. "Bobbiur I must rest as much as I can before the Haddrons come. I will need all of my powers to be at their very strongest. Good luck my son."

Bobbiur nodded and only said. "Thanks Ram." At this time Bobbiur had wanted to tell Ram when he was growing up he had thought of him more as a father than as the leader of Darmonarrow, but he didn't. He didn't know why but Bobbiur did not turn away immediately instead he just stood there and watched as Ram walked slowly up the small hill. Ram had his back towards Bobbiur and he never looked back. At this time Bobbiur could see the strength in Ram's movements but he could also tell that Ram looked tired. Bobbiur hoped that Ram would do alright in the battle today. That is if he and Hagjel were able to bring the Haddrons in this direction.

Bobbiur turned and walked in the direction of Fondrall and the other soldiers who were still practicing with their new weapons. As he was moving back towards the main group of soldiers Bobbiur thought to himself. "I may never see Ram again. This fight with the Haddrons could be a disaster." Bobbiur turned and looked back towards Ram who was now sitting cross legged on the ground, on the small rise with his back towards the valley. Reaching up Bobbiur noticed that he had a tear in his eye which he abruptly wiped away as he turned and continued walking towards Fondrall.

Bobbiur started to give orders even before he had gotten up to where Fondrall was with his men. "Fondrall. The Garriton troops should be here shortly. Ram has asked that you share your enhanced weapons with them." Then Bobbiur added. "You should also instruct the men from Garriton on the proper use of these weapons and how they should concentrate mostly on the fire balls which will be used by the Haddrons." Continuing on Bobbiur then said. "I would also think that you should spread your troops out as much as you can so that a single lucky shot from the Haddrons doesn't injure or kill all of you at the same time." Nodding for a short moment Bobbiur repeated what he had said earlier. "You will be in the open so don't forget to spread the troops out as much as you are able too."

"I understand Bobbiur." Fondrall had said this while smiling and nodding with enthusiasm.

Just as Bobbiur was finishing speaking to Fondrall Hagjel rode into sight with Kirwynn and the troops from Garriton. They had been moving quite fast because he noticed all of the horses were breathing heavy and all of the mounts were completely covered with sweat and lather from the extreme run.

Bobbiur smiled and went directly to meet them.

Fondrall yelled as Bobbiur was walking away. "The men are all ready and we will distribute the new weapons amongst the Garriton soldiers." It was as if Bobbiur had never even heard Fondrall. He just kept walking towards the Garriton troops and never even looked back.

Fondrall smiled to himself because he knew that Bobbiur was very interested in Captain Kirwynn. "The rumors must be correct." His smile deepened because Fondrall had seen just how fast Bobbiur had left him. The movements of Bobbiur were swift, deliberate and immediate, in order for him to go and see the Captain. Again with the same smile Fondrall just shook his head as he turned back to his task.

As Bobbiur got close to where Kirwynn was he could not help but notice that his heart started to beat faster. He looked down at his chest, just to make sure that the way his heart was pounding away, that it would not be visible to the others. He did not want anybody to know how he felt about Kirwynn. His feeling must be kept secret. He got a serious, business like look, on his youthful face.

But all of this was about to change.

As he got closer to Kirwynn and Hagjel, Bobbiur was completely unaware that all of the men who were around him were actually watching. Most of the soldiers were turned in his direction and all of them had a big smile on their faces.

The Nine Moons of Adjemir

Apparently Bobbiur only had eyes for Kirwynn.

Even Hagjel who had just dismounted was going to say something to Bobbiur when he saw the look in Bobbiur's eyes. As Hagjel saw the direction Bobbiur was headed in he stepped back smiled and spoke to himself. "Bobbiur your in love."

Then still smiling Hagjel while shaking his head whispered to himself. "And you are in for a big surprise because you think you are in control." Then Hagjel whispered. "But your not."

Hagjel just kept mumbling to himself as he continued to watch Bobbiur. "The men are really going to tease you and I am going to be the first." Hagjel had such a big smile on his face and he was completely unaware that he was so close to laughing that it was having an effect on Jakka. Jakka had poked his head up out of the tote bag and looked upwards at Hagjel. Following Hagjel's eye direction, Jakka then looked towards Bobbiur and Kirwynn. Even Jakka found it amusing because he began to chatter and started to giggle as best a JymmKat can do.

At this, Hagjel looked down at his friend Jakka and he also began to giggle.

As Bobbiur neared Kirwynn she was just taking off her helmet and was shaking out her hair. Bobbiur walking straight towards her went to shake Kirwynn's hand as he was about to say, how glad he was to see her when their eyes had locked on each other. To Bobbiur complete surprise and complete embarrassment as he was reaching out his hand towards Kirwynn, it happened. In front of everybody Kirwynn stretched up put her left hand at the back of his head pulled him down towards her. Then she kissed him.

Bobbiur red faced drew back and whispered between clenched teeth. "Kirwynn not in front of the men." Kirwynn was having no part of this and with a short shake of her head and a impish smile on her face, she only said. "Bobbiur don't be such a coward." Then she quickly added. "You will find that the men will feel good about how we feel for each other."

Bobbiur red faced looked around at the men who had gathered close to him and Kirwynn. He became even more red faced and bent his head towards the ground as the men who were closest, started to slap him on the shoulder. Kirwynn continued to smile ear to ear as the Garriton troops started to chant. "Kirwynn. Kirwynn."

Ram who was resting on the other small hill heard the commotion. He just continued looked straight ahead, at nothing in particular. With a big smile on his face he whispered slowly and quietly to himself. "Bobbiur you fool. Give it up." With his eyes wide open and glancing off into the distance with a slight chuckle Ram whispered. "Surrender you fool because you have lost." Still smiling and very relaxed while shaking his head slowly from side to side Ram then said. "And it's about time."

Ram felt good about the relationship between Kirwynn and Bobbiur because he knew a relationship like this would change things in all of Adjemir. Ram then thought. "That is if we are able to beat these Haddrons today."

Back with Bobbiur and Kirwynn to everybody's surprise, Bobbiur slowly leaned over and returned the kiss to Kirwynn. Turning quickly towards Hagjel before any of the soldiers had a chance to tease or make fun of him, Bobbiur said with a growl in his voice and a scowl on his face because Hagjel could not wipe the grin off of his face. "Hagjel we have fresh mounts here so lets go. I will tell you what we are going to do as we ride out."

Just before Bobbiur mounted his Spaggidon he gave instructions to Fondrall and also to Kirwynn that the soldiers should dig some trenches. He wanted the soldiers to have some place where they could shield themselves if a fire ball was missed by any one of the archers. After they had mounted the two fresh Spaggidons and had started out towards the direction of the main road Bobbiur said to Hagjel. "Ram wants us to go to the main road and intercept the Haddrons."

Hagjel looking at Bobbiur had a surprised look on his face as he spoke in a questioning manner. "Does he want us to stop and fight the Haddrons by ourselves?"

Bobbiur after having gotten over the incident between Kirwynn and himself had a grin on his face as he said. "No were are not to fight the Haddrons but we have to get their attention and make sure they chase us here. Ram wants to fight them at the location where he is and for whatever reason, he made it very clear that we are to bring the Haddrons here."

They rode silently for a little while when Bobbiur gave Hagjel his idea on how they could get the Haddrons to chase them. "We should stay just out of reach of Zalghar's magic and shoot some arrows in their direction. We must make ourselves clearly visible and see if we can make the Haddrons angry." Hagjel thought for a second and then he said. "I can shoot fire arrows at them from a considerable distance. I will hit one of the Kilpacx."

Then Hagjel added with a questioning nod to his head. "That should get their attention."

Bobbiur only nodded as he was keeping all of his attention to the front of them as they were nearing the main rode.

The Haddrons Are Coming

Bobbiur and Hagjel waited just off of the main road in a small clearing where they had a clear view for a considerable distance up the Garriton road which was off towards their right. Neither of them spoke as Hagjel with his Elf hearing wanted as much warning of the coming of the Haddrons as possible. After only a few moments Bobbiur turned to Hagjel and broke the silence by speaking softly. "Hagjel I know that you have not said much about Salbuk and I know you miss him." Speaking very softly. "I miss him too."

Bobbiur lowered his voice as he said. "I just wanted you to know this. He was a good Human and he was a good friend of yours."

Hagjel with a slight showing of tears gathering in the corner of his eyes while continuing to concentrate on the road ahead only nodded. After a few moments Hagjel swallowed and changed the subject as he said to Bobbiur. "Bobbiur you're a good Human and I hope you are safe after the battle with the Haddrons. I am happy for you and Kirwynn although I find your behavior towards Kirwynn kind of puzzling. Elves do not behave in this fashion and if we like someone we show it without any concerns." Looking towards Bobbiur he then said. "You should do the same because I know that Kirwynn really likes you and she is not afraid to show it."

Hagjel continued to look straight ahead as he whispered while concentrating on the road. "The Haddrons must be getting very close so we will need to be even more quiet."

Jakka had popped up was looking around wide eyed at Bobbiur and Hagjel but was unable to figure out why they were talking in whispers. Then both Jakka and Hagjel looked instantly down the road because Jakka had heard something.

Bobbiur knew that something was up because without saying anything with his full attention on the road Hagjel drew three arrows from his quiver. Hagjel rested two arrows on his saddle and placed the other one into his bow.

These were not flaming arrows and Hagjel remembering the conversation earlier with Bobbiur spoke softly as he said. "It will be faster if we don't stop to set flame to the arrows. They are very close because we, Hagjel nodded down at Jakka, just heard one of the Kilpacx sneeze."

At this Bobbiur said. "Hagjel just in case I will cover your back so you can have your full concentration on the Haddrons when they appear."

Hagjel nodded and then started to raise his bow. They had some cover just behind some bushes which were large enough to hide them from anybody riding on the road.

The Haddrons Give Chase

When the first Haddron, the Haddron riding point and his Kilpacx appeared, he was just riding around the curve in the road as he came into clear view. Once Hagjel was certain he could reach the Haddron with a shot. He let loose.

Bobbiur saw the arrow leaving the bow with a high rising arc. The arrow flew straight at the target and it hit the Kilpacx in the neck. Bobbiur shook his head as he said to Hagjel because the distance was so great. "Nice shot Hagjel." But Hagjel did not answer as he had already sent his second arrow which hit the Kilpacx in almost the same place. The third arrow which Hagjel fired at the target was aimed at the Haddron rider. The two arrows which were shot at the Kilpacx did not do any damage at all because of the heavy skin of the Kilpacz. The arrow which was aimed at the rider was stopped by a protection shield.

The third arrow when shot by Hagjel was sent immediately after Hagjel had placed himself in full view. Bobbiur could not help but admire the speed with which Hagjel could loose his arrows. All three arrows were in the air in a huge arc, even before the first arrow had hit the Kilpacx. Bobbiur had also ridden into view just as the third arrow was striking the protection shield of the Haddron rider.

The Haddron had not been hit because the arrow glanced off of his protection shield with a loud, 'thunk' and went harmlessly into the ground just behind the Haddron. The arrows which were shot at the Kilpacx had stuck into the thick skin of the animals neck. But because of the distance of the shot, these arrows did not penetrate deeply. At this distance most of the force was lost and the Kilpacx was not harmed. After this quick succession of arrows the Haddron warrior saw Bobbiur and Hagjel. He then turned and quickly disappeared back behind the trees which were near the curve in the main road.

The Haddron went quickly to see Zalghar at which time he told Zalghar that Hagjel and Bobbiur had set an ambush for them. Zalghar began to laugh as did the other warriors but Obmar remained quiet.

Zalghar asked. "How many men does Bobbiur have with him?"

When Zalghar heard that there were only the two of them just like the night before he said. "Lets go after them and they will lead us to Ram."

Obmar chose this time to speak. "What if Ram and Bobbiur have set a trap for us?"

Zalghar just shook his head as he spoke through clenched teeth. "If they have set a trap for us that will be their undoing. As I will destroy anything or anybody they place in front of us. Mostly I want to kill Ram and this young upstart Bobbiur." Zalghar kept on talking as he was going into a bit of a rage. Zalghar then said in a vicious tone. "Adjemirian magic is no match for Haddron magic and anybody who tries to use their power against me will be smashed into little pieces and fed to the Kilpacx. We do not have to be worried about any ambush which these Adjemirians might have planned."

Then Zalghar said in a determined tone of voice."I only want Ram." Nodding with satisfaction. "These two fools should lead us directly to him." Zalghar waved his hand as he said. "So lets proceed." Zalghar looked over his men. He then pointed to three of them and he ordered. "You three ride the point but go a little slower. If something does not look right to you then you should come back immediately to where I am."

Rubbing his chin Zalghar gave further advice to the warriors he was sending to the point. "If Bobbiur is traveling fast then he will be leaving a good trail. But I would think he will stay on the road so following any trail which they may leave is probably not important."

Before these warriors turned and went to the front Zalghar finished by saying. "Be careful." Zalghar then turned to a different two warriors and said. "You two bring up the rear." Glancing sideways Zalghar told Obmar. "You ride close to me and if I need information or if I want to ask you some questions about anything you will be close."

The Nine Moons of Adjemir

Obmar was still concerned about a possible ambush from Bobbiur and Hagjel but Zalghar just laughed and repeated what he had said before but this time it was a bit different. "If they have set an ambush for us I hope they have Ram with them because it will save us time searching for him." At this last statement Zalghar laughed.

The Haddrons traveled in this formation for about forty minutes when the three leading Haddrons came back to where Zalghar was riding. They looked excited. One of the point Haddrons spoke directly to Zalghar. "Zalghar it's just like Obmar had said earlier." The Haddron quickly added. "This Bobbiur has set a trap for us." Then with a questioning look on his face the Haddron added. "But they are not hiding. They are out in the open." Continuing to give information to Zalghar the Haddron warrior then said. There is an old man on a different hill on the other side of this small valley. He was to our right."

The Haddron warrior added. "It might be Ram!"

"They did not attack us and they just stayed where they were." Again with a questioning look the Haddron spoke further. "They were just watching us and it was strange." With some excitement to his voice, with a slight shake of his head, the Haddron gave some more information to Zalghar. "It is kind of strange because the old man is sitting near an old cemetery and he just continued sitting with his back to us."

With a squint to his eyes Zalghar looked at the warrior before he asked. "Is this old man wearing any armor?"

"No." Came the answer and just then the Haddron jumped to the ground and drew a picture in the dirt to show how the Adjemirians had placed their fighters.

The next question from Zalghar was to the same warrior. "Do you think there were any large groups of soldiers around other than what you have told me about." To this question the warrior just shook his head as he said. "No! There were no signs of any other larger groups of warriors." The Haddron warrior was starting to smile as he gave all this information to Zalghar.

Zalghar thought for a moment to himself as he whispered to himself. "This is going to be easy." He was very interested in the old man who was by himself on the opposite hill. He also thought to himself. "This must be Ram?"

Slowly Zalghar spoke out loud after again viewing the map which the warrior had made on the ground. Then he spoke about how they would attack. "You must divide yourselves into two groups and then you should attack both of their stations at exactly the same time." In a confident tone Zalghar said. "You should send in a large barrage of fire balls before you let the Kilpacx into the battle." In a vicious tone Zalghar said through clenched teeth. "Kill as many of them as you can with fire balls before you get to close." As an after thought he added. "You should also put a protection shield around the Kilpacx eyes."

The warriors nodded as Zalghar commented further. "We do not want to have the same thing happen which happened at the city of Garriton when we attacked them the other night." With a fiendish vicious grin on his contorted face and a look of pure evil in his eyes Zalghar sneered. "Concentrate your heaviest fire power towards that archer Hagjel and when you see Bobbiur I want you to smash him. But don't kill him." Then Zalghar growled. "After the battle is over he is mine."

That same mean and vicious look was back in his eyes as he repeated. "Capture him for me."

Then Zalghar added. "The old man on the hill must be Ram." Zalghar with a vicious look in his eyes was smiling off into the distance in the direction of where the Adjemirians had chosen to try to defeat him and his Haddron warriors. "I will personally go after Ram myself."

After this conversation Zalghar got back on his Kilpacx at which time he motioned for his men to proceed. The Haddrons then got into battle formation and began to travel further up the road towards the battle site.

The Kilpacx, knowing that a battle was about to start quickened their pace. The older and bigger Kilpacx were starting to lick their chops in anticipation of a feeding frenzy.

Bobbiur and Hagjel Prepare for Battle

Soon after the arrows were fired at the Haddron warrior both Hagjel and Bobbiur had hurried back to the spot which had been chosen to fight the Haddrons. When they had arrived back at the Valley of the Ancients the first thing that Bobbiur did was go directly to where Kirwynn was waiting. Bobbiur jumped off of his mount and asked Kirwynn. "Have your men been properly instructed on how to use the enhanced weapons which we were given by Zorp?"

To this question Kirwynn responded. "Yes." And she went on to say. "Fondrall has shown the Garriton troops everything that they should know about the use of these weapons." Bobbiur had nodded and then he said to Kirwynn. "Kirwynn I need to spend some time with my soldiers before the Haddrons arrive. Ram also said that we should stay away from the main fighting because the heavy fire will be directed towards the archers when the battle starts."

To this statement Kirwynn's eyes showed a little disappointment but she had only asked. "Will you be with me Bobbiur?" Bobbiur had nodded as he replied. "Yes. But we should not be with or near the archers." "I think we will be better off and of more help if we stay with the spear throwers. The spear throwers will be used in a surprise attack but this will not be until the magic of the Haddrons starts to show signs of weakness." Continuing Bobbiur stated. "Both Zorp and Ram said this will be the best way to fight the Haddrons and that will be from a distance."

Kirwynn had become silent for a moment and then she had spoken. "Bobbiur this makes sense. We should fight them at a distance if it is possible otherwise the enemy Kilpacx will do most of the fighting." Then she continued. "I agree. The Kilpacx are a little too powerful for the arrows, unless we are able to get close enough until the magic of the Haddrons becomes weak. Then we can attack them with our spears."

With a short nod of his head Bobbiur had said. "I will be right back." With this last statement, Bobbiur went to speak to the men from Darmonarrow. When Bobbiur neared the troops Hagjel and Fondrall came over to speak to him. As they were getting close Bobbiur noticed that Hagjel was smiling and Bobbiur thought. "This is a good sign." Bobbiur knew that the death of Salbuk was still bothering Hagjel. Bobbiur had mused momentarily and then said to himself with a slight smile catching the corners of his mouth. "Nothing like a new battle to take your mind off the past." He continued thinking to himself. "Hagjel will have plenty of time to grieve the loss of Salbuk after this battle is over. That is if we are still alive." At this thought the smile had left Bobbiur's face.

"Good to see you before the battle." Fondrall had said just as Hagjel was nodding towards Bobbiur. Bobbiur glanced at the troops and then back to Hagjel just as Fondrall began to speak. "The men will be shooting their magic arrows in a sequence and as they shoot an arrow they will call a number." Fondrall continued on. "There will be eight sets of two archers and the groups are numbered one through eight."

As Fondrall glanced towards his archers he continued. "Each archer after they are paired will call a number as they shoot." Then Fondrall said. "We are using sixteen archers in total between the Darmonarrow archers and the Garriton archers and our main concentration will be on the Haddrons fire balls." Just then Hagjel had broke in to say. "In each pair of archers we will have two arrows loaded at the same time. But only one arrow at a time will be shot at the Haddrons fire ball." Hagjel added in a surprisingly relaxed fashion. "Should the first arrow miss it's target the second arrow will be ready to be let loose immediately."

Then it had been Fondrall's turn to speak. "If everything goes as we have planned it, there should be no waste of the enhanced arrows." After hearing everything that Hagjel and Fondrall had to say about the archers Bobbiur gave them some praise by saying. "Fondrall you have the archers very well prepared and we can be thankful for that."

Then Bobbiur turned to his friend Hagjel. "Hagjel I know just how good an archer you are so there should be no fear of wasting or running out of enhanced arrows. I just came over here to see how everything was going and it looks like all of you are very ready." As he was saying this Bobbiur had glanced back in the direction of where Kirwynn and the spear throwers were stationed before he said. "I have to get back with the spear throwers and Kirwynn."

This brought a smile to Fondrall's face as he changed the subject. "You have both Shantok and Alandaugh with you." At this time Fondrall asked. "Do you know of them?" Bobbiur said with a questioning look on his face said. "I don't." Fondrall with admiration spoke with respect. "They are probably without a doubt the best soldiers that Garriton has ever turned out. Alandaugh is a little crazy when he fights but he is really fast, very strong and very brave. Shantok is very smart, strong and he fights fiercely."

As Fondrall turned to walk back to the men with a smile on his young face he had yelled over his shoulder. "You will like them both."

Bobbiur turned to Hagjel and then he put his arm around Hagjel's shoulder and said. "Good luck." Bobbiur then put his hand inside the tote bag and patted Jakka on his fuzzy little head as he said. "See you later Jakka."

The Defenders Dig In

Earlier when Bobbiur had told Kirwynn and Fondrall to have the men dig small trenches in the ground in which to throw themselves into, if any Haddron fireballs were missed by any of the Archers. The soldiers had undertaken this task in an organized fashion. Bobbiur had noticed that all of his orders had been followed. The defenders had gone about this task very quickly and efficiently because nobody wanted to be cooked like a ham, by a powerful Haddron fireball. Being sizzled was not in the best interest of the defenders.

As Bobbiur had walked back to the location of the spear throwers and Kirwynn he had gone over in his mind some of the discussions had with Fondrall and Hagjel. In a soft tone of voice Bobbiur had told the defenders. "You must fight with the greatest skill which you are able too. If we lose here today then we will all be killed before the end of the battle by Zalghar because as you know his magic is very strong."

When he had to spoken earlier to Hagjel Bobbiur had said. "I will keep Kirwynn myself and the spear throwers completely hidden until the magic of the Haddron warriors starts to grow weak. That is when we will attack the Haddrons and the Kilpacx from their flank." Then with a sad tone Bobbiur had said to Hagjel. "Hagjel the spear throwers Kirwynn and myself will be on the other side of the Valley of the Ancients which is going to be closer to Fondrall and his men and farther from you and your archers." Looking directly into Hagjel's eyes and then glancing down towards Jakka, Bobbiur with a very quiet and soft voice had said. "You will have to fight the Haddrons by yourselves when the battle starts because the spear throwers will be hitting the Haddron's flank from the other side of the valley and we won't be able to help you right away."

To the surprise of Bobbiur Hagjel had the same old smile on his face when somebody was worried about his safety. Hagjel had only said. "Bobbiur you take care of yourselves and I'm sure we can look after what will be happening on this side of the valley. When you are successful with your flank attack on the Haddrons and when you have finished helping Fondrall and his archers you can bring all your forces together at one time. You will be able to hit the flanks of the group of Haddrons which my men and I will be fighting with an even stronger force. You must not worry about us too much because you will not be able to concentrate on the Haddrons completely and this will weaken your fighting skills."

With the same smile of confidence and with his head tilted to the side, Hagjel had commented further. "I think these Haddrons might be in for a little surprise here today." Bobbiur had been surprised at the strong sound of confidence which Hagjel was using and it had reminded Bobbiur about just how good Hagjel was with his bow.

Jakka had been sitting up and looking out of the tote bag directly at Bobbiur and without even thinking Bobbiur remembered reaching out and stroke Jakka's head. Jakka had started his friendly chatter and at the time Bobbiur couldn't help but think to himself. "I am amazed at just how comfortable I am with Jakka now. Hagjel and Salbuk had been right when they said that I would start to like Jakka once I had time to spend with him."

Jakka seemed to understand when Bobbiur said. "Jakka you have been very helpful and I am starting to understand you better. It's good to have you on our side." At this time it had surprised Hagjel that Bobbiur would be talking to Jakka like this but after what he had seen in the last few days and the fact that they were getting ready fight these foreign Haddrons, Hagjel had thought to himself. "Nothing should surprise me any more."

Bobbiur knowing that this battle may be the last time he would see Hagjel alive without saying anything he reached over and shook Hagjel's hand. Then with a sad look on his face Bobbiur had again wished Hagjel lots of luck.

Bobbiur had then turned mounted up and rode over to the position which was being held by Fondrall and his men. Once he arrived at the location where Fondrall had dug in he had asked one of the archers to take his Spaggidon over to the trees and tie it up with the rest of the animals. The trenches which had been dug by

Fondrall and his men were a bit farther apart and a little wider than those which had been dug by Hagjel and his archers. Although these trenches were wide Bobbiur was rather concerned that they might not be deep enough.

Bobbiur asked Fondrall. "I think you should have dug your trenches deeper." Fondrall with a slight smile on his face had simply said. "Our trenches are not as deep but we made them wider because our shields are bigger than the shields carried by Hagjel's archers."

Fondrall had went on to say. "I have spoke with my men and they understand what the Haddrons will be doing when they first attack. Should our archers miss a fire ball they will jump into the trench and place their shield over themselves covering their upper body. "Fondrall pointed down as he said. "These wet blanket will cover their legs."

Fondrall had continued to speak in a matter of fact tone as he said. "I have also instructed these archers to go to the stream and get soaking wet." At this Fondrall had pointed at some of his men returning from the stream which was close by and Bobbiur also noticed some of Hagjel's archers were doing the same. "Good idea." Bobbiur had said as he thought to himself. "These men are actually quite smart and really don't seem to need much training at all." Bobbiur said to Fondrall. "I think your all doing a good job." Bobbiur had said this with a assuring smile on his face as he then stepped closer to Fondrall.

Bobbiur had reached out and shook Fondrall's hand as he was nodding his head. "Fondrall I wish you and your men lots of luck. And thanks for helping out."

When Bobbiur returned to where Kirwynn was waiting with the spear throwers he was happy to see that these men had also dug holes in the ground but these were not trenches like Hagjel and Fondrall's men had dug. These were actually holes in the ground right out in the open and just slightly onto the Temple side of the valley. These holes were on level ground and Bobbiur also noticed that these soldiers had several earth colored blankets with them.

Smiling Kirwynn approached Bobbiur and to save him further embarrassment because all of the spear throwers were watching she reached out and shook his hand in the Adjemirian fashion. To everybody's surprise Bobbiur leaned in towards Kirwynn put his arms around her and kissed her. The men who were watching instantly cheered gleefully. As the two parted Kirwynn had a slight flush on her cheeks but then she quickly got right down to what was important.

Kirwynn pointed towards the freshly dug holes in the ground and spoke in a quiet tone. "I had the men dig these holes in the ground because it would have been to too obvious if we had decided to hide behind those rocks."

Kirwynn was pointing in the direction of a rocky place off to the side of the valley. As Bobbiur listened Kirwynn went on as she again pointed in the direction of the rocks. "I did not want the fighters placing amongst those rocks because they would be too far from where the main fighting should commence and if Zalghar was too send in his 'Spirit Eye' then we would not be able to make a surprise attack." Smiling at Bobbiur's look of concern Kirwynn added. "I wanted them closer because when we attack we cannot be spending too much time charging towards the Kilpacx. We would be out in the open for such a long time."

Without waiting for Bobbiur to reply Kirwynn continued on. "This way being this close we can surprise these Haddrons."

Bobbiur looked directly at Kirwynn with a new respect then he asked questioningly as he rubbed his chin. "I have to ask you what the blankets are for?"

Kirwynn had an impish smile on her face as she looked towards the spear throwers, she answered Bobbiur's question. "These blankets are the same color as the ground and what we will be doing is going under them shortly so we cannot be seen by the Haddrons as they approach. Nor will we be seen by any 'Spirit Eye' which Zalghar may be sending out shortly."

Kirwynn pointed at the archers who were with Hagjel and Fondrall and then said. "When we are hidden the Haddrons will only see the archers and their attention will be on the archers only. They will not even know that we are hidden here."

As they were talking Shantok and Alandaugh came up to them and without any introductions they spoke directly to Kirwynn. Shantok spoke first after nodding towards Bobbiur. "Kirwynn we are all ready with the holes which we have had the men dig." Alandaugh spoke next. "We must get out of sight as fast as we can because if the Haddrons know where we are hidden we will be at their mercy."

Without waiting for Kirwynn to answer Alandaugh being the most outspoken of the two turned and walked up to Bobbiur and put out his hand while saying. "My name is Alandaugh. I am very pleased to meet you and I want to fight beside you. My parents have told me that you Hagjel and Salbuk saved Garriton from these Haddrons."

The Nine Moons of Adjemir

Then Alandaugh quickly yet solemnly added. "I will watch both your and Captain Kirwynn's backs."

He had meant what he said and Bobbiur was always thankful for any help he could rely on in any battle. Alandaugh had a simple and direct way of speaking his thoughts and Bobbiur instantly had been put at ease as he found this young warrior very likeable.

Shantok who was somewhat more reserved had been standing back a little ways. Then Shantok slowly reached out his hand and he also said he would watch their backs in the battle.

In the battles of Adjemir for any soldier to say they would watch your back it was a way of showing extreme respect and this feeling of respect from both these soldiers made Bobbiur feel very comfortable with both Shantok and Alandaugh.

Because Bobbiur had found both Shantok and Alandaugh very likeable he thought to himself. "We will watch your backs also." Before Bobbiur could speak further, quietly Shantok added. "We are calvary soldiers but our horses would be of no use in this type of battle so we have joined our brothers and we will help in the spear attack." Then Shantok with some urgency in his voice said. "But we must get under the blankets and into the holes as soon as possible otherwise if we are not properly hidden then we will not be able to surprise the Haddrons."

"Our horses are tied to some trees over there." Shantok was pointing in the direction of a small group of trees a short distance from where they were standing.

Understanding the urgency and with a questioning look on his face Bobbiur asked Kirwynn. "Is there a hole for me?"

Smiling with the smile that only Kirwynn could muster she mentioned. "We have a bigger hole dug than the rest. And Bobbiur." She paused and spoke huskily with an impish smile on her face. "You have to stay with me." Bobbiur blushed slightly and he turned to Shantok and Alandaugh while changing the subject. He spoke in a relaxing tone. "You men have done really good at getting ready for the Haddrons. And I want to thank you for saying you will watch our backs. We will watch your backs also."

Then nodding towards both Shantok and Alandaugh Bobbiur said. "Good luck."

Just then an outer guard who had been sent out by Shantok and Hagjel came riding up and yelled. "The Haddrons are coming."

Shantok quickly called to the spear throwers. "Into the holes we don't have very much time before the Haddrons are here." When the order was given the men and their equipment quickly disappeared into the holes and the blankest were pulled over them for cover from above.

It was as Kirwynn had said earlier that they would not be seen, and this was true. The camouflage was so good that nobody was going to know that the spear throwers were in this location and very well hidden. Once they were all in the holes it was as if there had never been anybody here. Unbeknownst to the men in the holes only a few minutes had gone by before the 'Spirit Eye from Zalghar was to fly in the sky's over the valley. But the men were already invisible from above. Therefore the Haddrons had no knowledge of the hidden spear throwers.

Once they were in the hole and under the blankets Bobbiur became very aware of the closeness of Kirwynn. He became somewhat nervous and felt compelled to say something. Bobbiur then asked Kirwynn. "How is your father?

At which time Kirwynn knowing that Bobbiur was nervous answered with the same old impish smile on her face. "Dad is doing just fine." And before Bobbiur could say anything more Kirwynn kissed him. This kiss was not like any of the other kisses which Kirwynn had given Bobbiur before. This kiss was much longer and more intimate. And although he liked it and he responded, Bobbiur when he was given a chance said very quietly. "Kirwynn I like you very much but I cannot be distracted when the Haddrons come."

They were in the small ditch lying side by side when Kirwynn said.

"Bobbiur. I love you." And to Bobbiur's surprise and without any hesitation he said to her. "Kirwynn. I love you."

Kirwynn giggled in delight and Bobbiur was quite surprised at how easy it had been to say this to Kirwynn. Bobbiur was also surprised at how comfortable he felt lying side by side with Kirwynn and then he wondered why he had never felt this way before. He was very relaxed which he found quite strange. He had just told Kirwynn he loved her and he was just about to enter into a battle where they all might die and yet he was the most relaxed he had been in years.

The Haddrons Attack

When the Haddrons had started to follow Bobbiur and Hagjel all of the Haddrons were smiling. They feared nothing and they had not been in a good battle for so long that they needed this fight just to keep up their interest in conquering Adjemir. The group of Haddron warriors and the Kilpacx which he had brought with him to Adjemir were a very powerful force of individuals. Zalghar was very aware of this and his smile became even more evil than it had been before. He chuckled to himself and the sound coming from him was so evil that even Obmar who was riding beside him had a cold shiver run up his spine. Zalghar was also thinking about these people from Adjemir being smashed completely today unless they had a whole army with them.

Even if there was a whole army present his men could smash any army which the Adjemirians could bring against them from anywhere in Adjemir. The only question in his mind would be. "How long it would take for his men to kill all of the Adjemirian army?"

When Obmar who had been riding beside Zalghar heard the evil sounds coming from Zalghar's direction again he became instantly nervous because the sounds were so very evil. But because he was now filled with an ugly form of evil himself, he smiled as he thought. "It's good to be with a band of warriors like these Haddrons who are so powerful. Buying this war axe the day before the attack on Darmonarrow was the best investment I have ever made."

Even though it made Obmar nervous when he was too close to Zalghar the power of his axe and the knowledge that he would be given his own city after these Haddrons conquered all of Adjemir, he found himself grinning an evil grin, just like Zalghar.

"It is almost like Zalghar knows what I am thinking." Obmar had thought.

The Haddrons had been traveling like this for almost an hour when the warriors riding point, called a halt.

While they had been following Bobbiur and Hagjel they still had to be careful so traveling had been somewhat slowed up. Although this lush valley which they had been riding in was very beautiful it was somewhat narrow. Even though the valley was very narrow there had been no place for the Adjemirians to form any ambush. But it did not hurt to be safe therefore the travel was slowed for this purpose.

The Haddrons were now coming to a wider place in the valley when the Haddrons riding point, motioned all of the warriors including Zalghar to come forward. From this position at the point they were able to observe the widening valley ahead. When Zalghar got up to where the point men had called the halt he saw something which surprised him and this brought the evil smile back to his face.

Off to his left farther down the valley he saw about eight archers in a group. This group of archers were not running and there were no Spaggidons or horses in sight. Farther and off to his right he saw another group of warriors about the same size. Again they just stood there. This group did not have any Spaggidons with them either and Zalghar could see that they only had what appeared to be bows, as weapons with them.

Then Zalghar saw what interested him the most. There was what appeared to be an old man without any armor who was sitting alone on a small hill slightly off to the far right side of the valley. This old man was just a short distance from the center group of archers. Zalghar spoke loud enough while pointing towards Ram, for all of the Haddrons to hear. "This must be Ram." Zalghar with a smug smile on his evil face had spoken to nobody in particular but Obmar had heard Zalghar say this. At this time Obmar quickly rode up to Zalghar and spoke in a quiet tone. "That old man is Ram." Before Zalghar could say anything Obmar added. "You must also know that Ram has some very strong magic and you should not under any circumstances ever underestimate him."

This statement by Obmar angered Zalghar who turned to Obmar and through clenched teeth growled. "Ram only has Adjemirian magic and he is no match for me."

Then Zalghar still speaking in a vicious tone said. "I will smash him. Just you watch."

At this, Obmar backed away with a puzzled and nervous look on his face as he became silent. Zalghar turned his attention back towards the enemy at the far end of the valley and he saw on his left beside the first set of archers through some trees, what looked like an old Temple. As he again observed the positioning of his enemy just to the right of where Ram was sitting with his back to them, Zalghar observed what appeared to be an old grave yard. Then Zalghar thought to himself. "Old man you will not need a grave yard because when I finish with you all that will be left will be food for the Kilpacx."

At this thought Zalghar laughed out loud as he said to his warriors. "Come gather around a little closer." At this time he quickly said. "I am going to send out the 'Eye' just to make sure that this pathetic group of Adjemirians does not have any army hidden close by." Then speaking in a tone of extreme confidence Zalghar added. "I will only be a few moments and I will also see if there are any other surprises anywhere else around here." At this time Zalghar commented in a softer tone as he glanced at Obmar and in order to reassure his soldiers. "We have come this far and there is no reason why we should take any chances just in case these people have any hidden surprises."

Obmar with a slight yet nervous smile on his face, nodded quickly in agreement. The Haddrons quickly gathered around Zalghar who had jumped down to the ground. Zalghar got into his trance position very quickly and was in the process of resting his head on his knees just as the circle of Haddron warriors on their Kilpacx finished closing in around him.

Obmar who was not yet considered a part of this practice sat on his Kilpacx at the side of the grouped circle. Obmar looked across the valley at the two groups of Archers and then at location where Ram was sitting. Then thinking to himself with a questioning look on his face, at which time he was almost growling, he muttered under his breath. "There is something about this picture which I don't understand and I don't like." Obmar had kept this to himself as he just sat there away from the main group of Haddrons. Obmar did not know that he was bighting his lip in anxiety, to the point that his lip was now bleeding. He just kept shaking his head slightly. He remained somewhat confused. Obmar knew how strong Ram actually was and Zalghar should never underestimate Ram for even a moment.

Zalghar had been true to his word. He had only been in the trance for a short time when he broke out of his spell. As Zalghar stood up he began to speak in a determined fashion. "These people of

Adjemir have not seen our total strength." Zalghar then spoke while waving his arm over the valley. "There are no hidden armies and no real surprises."

He then pointed his arm towards six of the Haddrons while saying. "You six will attack the group of Archers on our left." Then waving his other arm at the remaining Haddrons Zalghar said in a deeper voice. "You men will go after the group in the middle."

Without pausing Zalghar added. "I will kill Ram on the hill to the right. There are no armies close by and there are no extra men hidden in the old Temple on the left. I have searched the grave yard and I did not see any hidden soldiers there either." With a smile of confidence Zalghar said. "All we have to kill is those soldiers which we see in front of us. We should have this job done in only a few minutes." Then in a scowling tone Zalghar said. "There is barely enough enemy in the ranks of those archers to properly feed the Kilpacx."

At this Zalghar spat at the ground as he scowled. "How pathetic."

Then as an afterthought and speaking somewhat softly Zalghar turned his attention to Obmar. "Obmar you are to stay here and make sure that no fast moving armies come at us from behind. Is that clear?" Obmar commented that he understood and then Zalghar added. "If something should go wrong then you are to get that information to us as soon as possible."

Looking directly at Obmar while nodding his head Zalghar asked. "Okay?" Obmar again nodded but he then stated with a worried look on his face as he raised his concerns again. "Zalghar. I understand that you have some tremendous powers but you should never underestimate Ram. I am having some trouble understanding why Ram and Bobbiur have brought so few soldiers to this place to try and stop us." Still with the worried look on his face and glancing sideways at the Kilpacx who were starting to chomp at their bits while scratching the ground with their huge claws, in the excitement about the up and coming battle. Obmar raised his concerns again as he said. "I am very concerned and confused that Ram has met us here." Speaking softly Obmar added. "There must be a reason for it? Ram's best defense would have been to remain in Darmonarrow and then he could use the walls of Darmonarrow for protection." Then shaking his head in a bewildered fashion Obmar said again. "I just don't understand."

Zalghar only said in a friendly and softer tone. "These people cannot stop us Obmar. Remember they are only Adjemirians." Then as Zalghar felt he had not put Obmar's concerns to rest he went on. "You can be sure of that."Then with a friendly smile on his face as he looked down at Obmar, Zalghar said. "Just to show you how powerful we are you will be our audience."

Then with the friendly grin still on his face Zalghar added. "Sit back and enjoy the festivities." At this Zalghar nodded to the Haddrons who were all smiling to themselves about Obmar's concerns but they never said anything. Haddron warriors never did speak very much and this time was no different.

Turning to his men Zalghar then said in a commanding tone. "I want you to take your time. I also want you to take as many prisoners as you can but let at least two of them escape."

Thinking further Zalghar said. "I want some of them to escape so that they can spread the word on just how powerful we Haddrons are." With confidence Zalghar added. "I want all of Adjemir to know fear just at the mention of us."

As Zalghar made this statement it caused the Haddrons to smile amongst themselves. "The prisoners will be used for some fun after the battle." Zalghar spoke further. "This will be the best of all. But I want you to definitely keep, Bobbiur and Hagjel alive because I want to make their deaths as slow and entertaining as I can."

Zalghar had a fiendishly, evil, mean, and vicious, grin on his determined face. At this last statement the Haddron warriors broke out laughing. The look on Zalghar's face made the Haddron warriors smile knowingly to themselves.

Without saying anything further Zalghar abruptly turned and walked over to his Kilpacx and jumped on it's back. Then with extreme confidence he gave a short order. "Everybody knows what to do so lets get this thing done."

The Haddrons broke into two groups and they both slowly started to travel in a spear head formation towards the waiting Adjemirians. At the same time Zalghar very slowly began his stalking of the old man on the small hill directly ahead. Zalghar was in no hurry because even if the old man tried to get away he would be unable to. The Kilpacx Zalghar was riding knew that the old man towards where Zalghar was traveling was to be it's next meal. Zalghar and his Kilpacx moved slowly but deliberately in the direction of Ram.

The huge Kilpacx never took it's eyes off of Ram's back and then as they got closer the Kilpacx began rapidly licking it's lips. While they were traveling towards Ram. The eyes of the Kilpacx became even more fierce and a low throaty growl was coming from this huge beast.

This growl seemed to become even louder with each step. Actually it was now a low throated roar.

Ram remained sitting on the hill with his back to Zalghar and his head was bent down as if he was asleep. He had not moved, even in the slightest and he had been in this position since he had first arrived at this location.

Zalghar started to wonder if this old man on the ground would have any fight in him at all. "Maybe this is going to be so easy. I might get bored."

Then Zalghar thought to himself. "Maybe the old man has fallen asleep

The Battle Begins

Looking over his shoulder to his left Zalghar noticed that his men are just nearing the warriors from Darmonarrow. Zalghar ordered his Kilpacx to a halt as he watched his warriors line up un their battle formation which was simply to bring themselves in a straight line at a distance where they could fire their magic fire balls at the enemy. Yet they would be out of reach of any weapons which the Adjemirians had. It amazed Zalghar that the enemy was not running away and the Adjemirian Archers just remained motionless. But he thought to himself. "These people from Adjemir were not that smart anyways."

With this in mind Zalghar then turned his attention towards Ram and again Zalghar moved even closer. Zalghar had never known any fear but just in case he had in place a very powerful protection shield because he always felt there was no need to take any unnecessary chances. Still in the back of Zalghar's mind there was now a strange feeling because Ram, had still not gotten up nor had he tried to run away. Ram just sat there with his back still turned towards him and his Kilpacx. Ram with his head rested on his knees never even moved, not in the slightest.

Staring at Rams back intently as he got nearer, Zalghar again thought to himself as he neared the place where he would be close enough to send a magic spell at Ram. Somewhat puzzled Zalghar thought the same thought he had before. "Maybe the old man has fallen asleep!" The only sound which could be heard was coming from the Kilpacx which Zalghar was riding. The huge animal who thought there was going to be a meal was licking it's lips so rapidly that a loud smacking noise was getting louder as they drew closer to the old man sitting on the ground. The piercing eyes of the Kilpacx stared intently at the back of it's next meal sitting motionless on the ground.

Ram who remained motionless just sitting with his back towards Zalghar. With steel cold eyes just stared off into the distance at nothing. The steely stare by Ram was focused and unblinking.

Even though Zalghar had never known any fear in his entire life he had a cold chill run through him and up his spine. The hair on the back of his neck stood up. This was all brought forth as a very powerful mind message came forcefully into his head. Zalghar involuntarily and with considerable force again drew his Kilpacx to a complete halt.

The message coming into his head was in the Haddron language and it said this. "Zalghar you can take your warriors and return to Haddron right now or face the consequences."

Zalghar stared fiercely at the back of Ram as he thought questioningly to himself. "This is not Ram this person on the ground must be Haddron. No one in Adjemir has the power to send a mind message into the mind of a Haddron." Then a new mind message came to Zalghar from the person or thing, on the ground. "This is your last chance Zalghar you must leave Adjemir right now or as I said earlier, you and your warriors will face the consequences. I am Ram of Darmonarrow. I have Haddron blood and I have Haddron magic."

With this last message from Ram Zalghar turned and glanced at his men who were just getting into position and were just getting ready for battle. Zalghar quickly thought to himself. "We cannot go back to Haddron and these Adjemirians on the battle field will be no match for us."Turning his attention towards Ram who had still not stood up, nor had he even looked towards Zalghar as words came to the curled lips of Zalghar. He yelled. "Old man you are no match for me." Then in a defiant tone Zalghar almost spat the next words, as he became completely defiant. "I will smash you old man and I will feed you to my Kilpacx." Then in a quickly gathering rage through clenched teeth Zalghar growled. "You are not only old but you are also very stupid."

Zalghar sent a mind message to his warriors to commence killing the enemy. At this time Haddron fire balls began flying across the battle field towards the waiting defending Archers from Adjemir.

Obmar Views The Battle

Obmar quietly sat on his Kilpacx watching the movement of troops in the valley in front of him. He was calmly paying most of his attention to Zalghar's advance on Ram but then he noticed Zalghar stop short of where Ram was sitting. Then after only a few moments Obmar had seen Zalghar turn and glance at the Haddron warriors who were nearing a position to commence fighting against the warriors from both Darmonarrow and from Garriton. For a very short time Obmar felt feelings for his old friends from Darmonarrow.

Obmar was sitting in a relaxed position with an almost friendly smile on his Dwarfen face as he remembered all of the good times he had while he was still a citizen of Darmonarrow. Obmar's conscience was starting to turn him back into the being he was before the spell from Zalghar's Rune axe had gained it's control over him. Obmar started to hope that his old friends would not die and that all would be safe. Instantly because Obmar's thoughts were starting to turn to goodness, the axe which Obmar had strapped over his shoulder started to glow. Then shortly after it had begun to glow it started to pulsate. Suddenly the smile left Obmars's face changed and his face began to twitch violently.

First Obmar's lips had begun to twitch. Then the twitching moved slowly and soon the twitching covered his entire face. This twitching was beginning to take greater control and then these magic powers started to move slowly down his arms and also into his legs. Soon the twitching was completely throughout his entire body. The twitching was becoming so violent that Obmar nearly fell off of his Kilpacx. What had been happening was the evil from the axe was now taking complete control of Obmar. Any good feelings which Obmar had for any of his old friends from Darmonarrow was being completely removed and now was being replaced by an extreme and very powerful evil which was moving throughout Obmar's body.

The level of evil which was moving through Obmar is one of the strongest evils ever. The evil which now controlled Obmar was equal to the evil feelings which Zalghar possessed. The evil which was now in complete control of Obmar could never be removed. The evil which now controlled Obmar would never change, until his death. Obmar was now a complete slave to this evil.

Obmar had now been turned completely into an evil being and he was being controlled totally by the axe. Obmar suddenly snapped out of the trance with an intense mean, uncontrolled, vicious look on his face. As he observed the valley in front of him he was more and more, desiring to get into the fight. There was an intense killing blood flowing through his veins which was so strong that he could barley sit still on the back of the Kilpacx. Nor could he wait any longer until he could kill somebody or something. He was so out of control that there was saliva drooling from his mouth. His eyes were now enlarged, twitching and bloodshot. Obmar began to growl an evil sound as he saw the battle beginning to start.

The fiendishly evil grin which was on Obmar's face faded slightly. The Adjemirians were not going to run away and Obmar knew how tough the Adjemirians could fight. He had warned Zalghar of some of the dangers. Now he would have to enter the battle soon just to make sure that there were no mistakes made by the Haddrons in this fight. At this time Obmar disregarded what Zalghar had told him about staying in this place and watching the rear for any advancing armies. Obmar started slowly at first to moved forward but then as the evil fighting blood started to pump faster through his veins he picked up more speed. He was traveling directly towards the group of Haddrons who were just starting to fight with Hagjel's men in the center of the valley.

Fondrall's Men Begin to Fight

When the Haddron warriors had started across the grassy fields of the valley, as planned, they divided into two groups. Half of the Haddrons were coming directly at Fondrall and his archers. The other half of the Haddron force were moving straight towards Hagjel's position. Hagjel and his archers were the farthest from where the spear throwers were situated. Hagjel was actually quite close to the location where Ram remained in his position, who was still sitting on the ground a short distance from the Graveyard of the Ancients.

The defenders who were with Frondrall's group stood their ground right where they were and not one of them moved. Each archer had an enhanced arrow in his bow and all were ready to start to fire in sequence, as had instructed when the Haddron fire balls were being shot towards them. Everything had become very quiet and the entire valley became very still. There was a pause.

Nothing at all was even moving, not even the tall grass. The Haddron warriors looked laughingly at the small and puny force of archers across the field from them who were now very close. The Haddron warriors all had smiles on their faces as they looked at the Humans and Elves who where just inside the striking distance of their fire balls. This was going to be a lot of fun. At this point the giant Kilpacx were now all drooling and all were licking their lips. Just like a puppy at meal time. The only difference was that these were not puppies but instead they were mean vicious killing machines. Then without any visible signal and without anything being said the Haddrons warriors who were directly in front of Fondrall and his warriors with an extreme confidence, sent their most powerful fire balls. The Haddrons had raised their right arms towards the sky and as they brought their arms down the magic fire balls were released from the end of their pointing finger tips.

The first salvo from the Haddrons had an arranged firing order which Fondrall saw was from left to right. These fire balls had barely left the hands of the Haddrons when the enhanced arrows in the ordered sequence, left the bows of Frondrall's Archers. When this volley of fire balls had been launched from the Haddrons side of the battle field Bobbiur from his hiding position with Kirwynn could not help but notice how magnificent the fire ball volley was. If this was not a show of force by a hated and dangerous enemy and was not so deadly towards him and the Adjemirians, he thought to himself this show could all be very beautiful. But this was going to be a battle to the death so there was no time to enjoy any of the strange looking fire show. What had been somewhat interesting to watch when the fire balls had been launched, became even more interesting when the enhanced arrows had been released in the ordered sequence from Fondrall's archers.

'Poof.' Poof.' 'Poof.' 'Poof.' The fire balls, Bobbiur noticed, were exploding in sequence just like the magic show put on each year by the Elves and Humans during the Eight Moons of Adjemir festival. Bobbiur found it strange that he was wondering to himself about the Eight Moons of Adjemir festival which was supposed to be happening any day now. He had been so occupied in chasing the Haddrons invaders over the last few days he had completely lost track of time and had forgotten about the annual Adjemirian celebration.

He turned to Kirwynn and with a slight wrinkle on his forehead asked. "Is today the festival day of the Eight Moons of Adjemir?" Kirwynn with a curious look on her face because she was thinking what a strange question to be asking in the middle of a battle said quietly. "Yes it is." Nothing more was said and Bobbiur turned his complete attention back to the commencement of the battle. Bobbiur noticed the enhanced arrows had all been dispatched as was the plan and the archers, who were with Frondrall, had then immediately dove into their trenches. Bobbiur and Kirwynn smiled and cheered quietly when all of the enhanced arrows had smashed their targets. The plan was at this point working perfectly for Fondrall and his archers.

Bobbiur and Kirwynn could also see the battle between the forces with Hagjel's men and the Haddrons where a very similar thing was happening. All of the fire balls had been hit by the enhanced arrows, except for one. He was not sure but to Bobbiur it appeared one of the arrows from Hagjel's group had been released somewhat late. The explosion from the fire ball when it was hit by the enhanced arrow was too close to the archers. One of the archers with Hagjel's group had been hit by the fallout from the explosion from the fire ball just before he was able to get to the safety of his trench.

From Bobbiur's vantage point he could see the defender running and screaming at first. Then the archer started to roll on the ground in order to stop the burning. It did not seem to matter. When the Haddron fire balls were exploded the grass in the valley had also caught on fire. The injured defender didn't have a chance. Smoke from the exploding fire balls and the burning grass quickly started to cover the valley. As the burning defender rolled around on the ground it only made the burning go faster and for a short time the screaming got louder. But this only lasted for a few moments and then all became ghostly silent again.

After the immediate surprise about the enhanced arrows being capable of exploding the Haddron fire balls by the defenders, the Haddrons hesitated but only for a moment. Then the Haddrons without any clear signal from anybody started to move slowly forward. The renegade intruders kept sending their fire balls at the defenders location as they advanced but now there was no sequencing in the firing order. Fire balls began to come at the defenders at random.

Just prior to the smoke starting to fill the valley Bobbiur had seen Zalghar and his Kilpacx traveling directly towards the location of Ram. This was to be the last Bobbiur saw of Ram before the smoke from the fires quickly filled the valley. The smoke soon made it impossible for Bobbiur to see the Grave Yard of the Ancients, nor the place where Ram was located any more. At this time Bobbiur turned his attention back to the battle which was starting to become fierce between the Haddron's and Fondrall's men. The smoke from the fires was also starting to make it almost impossible for Bobbiur to see the other part of the battle location between the Haddrons and Hagjel's men were just now starting to do battle.

Ram's Back Remains Turned

Ram had continued sitting with his back towards Zalghar right up until the time that Zalghar got within striking distance. Zalghar was more than a little curious about the positioning of Ram and why this old man would not turn and face him. When the second message had come into his mind. The message from Ram surprising enough had again been in the Haddron language. At that time Zalghar had stopped all movement and he continued to glare at the back of Ram. Again the message from Ram was clear and there was no confusion. "Take your men and return to Haddron or you will all be killed."

Speaking in Haddron mind language, at this time Zalghar now responded in an even more vicious tone. "I will kill you all and I will personally make your death last for an eternity. Old Man. You are nothing." To this statement from Zalghar Ram never said or did anything but he just remained sitting with his back to Zalghar. Ram seemed to actually be ignoring Zalghar. Ram showed no fear.

Zalghar waited and then out of curiosity with an angry look on his face Zalghar yelled a question to Ram. "How are you able to speak in the Haddron tongue?" This question, had already been answered but it caused Ram to send one last message to Zalghar. This message from Ram was sent in a business like fashion and there was no idle threat nor was there any evident emotion. Ram had actually seemed a little tired but kept a controlled strength to his message. "Let me advise you Zalghar you should all leave Adjemir this instant or as I told you before you and your men will face complete destruction."

Zalghar never responded immediately and he seemed to be thinking to himself. But the quietness was short lived as without any prior warning Zalghar sent his most powerful fire ball directly at the defenseless back of Ram who still had not risen. At least it seemed that the back of Ram was defenseless. But before the fire ball was half way to smashing Ram an extremely strong protective shield instantly appeared. The force of Zalghar's powerful fire ball was deflected away, in a loud crackling explosion without any apparent harm to Ram. After this attack from Zalghar Ram slowly stood up and turned to face the Haddron invader. A chilling and unknown fear ran up the back of Zalghar. The fear felt by Zalghar was because of the look coming from the eyes of Ram. These eyes were not the eyes of an ordinary individual from Adjemir. These were not the eyes of a Human, Elf, Dwarf, or Krug. What Zalghar actually saw was the eyes of a very powerful Haddron sorcerer. The eyes of this old man showed rage and some unknown strength. These eyes seemed bottomless and they also resembled two hot coals from the bottom of a raging fire pit. The look showed it all. The old man had come to fight and instantly from the look in the eyes of Ram Zalghar knew that he was up against a formidable and very capable foe. In this fight age would not matter.

Zalghar was puzzled but there was no time for him to think about where Ram had gotten the ability to speak in the Haddron tongue nor where Ram had gotten the appearance of Haddron eyes. Ram had said earlier he had Haddron blood but the appearance of the Haddron eyes and the viciousness coming from Ram through those eyes, had caught Zalghar by surprise. Now nothing else mattered. There was no time, because now Zalghar had to immediately defend himself. Ram after turning was now facing Zalghar and Ram immediately went onto the offensive. A burning ray of light, which made a hissing sound, had instantly flashed from the deep set eyes of the old man.

In an instant Zalghar strengthened his own protection shield and the killer ray from Ram's eyes bounced harmlessly off him. The killer ray from Ram's Haddron eyes had harmlessly flown off in a different direction. Zalghar had been fast enough in strengthening his protection shield that the full force of the killer ray actually appeared weak. To his complete surprise Zalghar now found himself in a battle that he did not totally understand. The fight with these Adjemirians was supposed to be easy and all of a sudden Zalghar found himself fighting something or someone who had equal powers to his.

A question was in his mind and that question was. "Who is this old man?"

The Haddrons Close In

Back on the battle field where Fondrall and his men had dug in the Haddrons were now closing in on Fondrall's defenses. The men with Fondrall were still able to smash the fireballs as the Haddrons released them. But now the nearness of the Haddron warriors meant that regardless of whether or not the fire balls were hit by enhanced arrows, the momentum from the exploding fireballs would soon be hitting Fondrall and his archers. Fondrall noticed that no clear shot had hit his men or even got close to his line of defense, but some of his archers were down and injured. These injuries had been a result of the force of the fire balls explosion which showered his men. Fondrall also noticed as the Haddrons got closer the giant Kilpacx began to pick up their pace. Luckily for him and his men the smoke from the explosions and the burning grass fires would give them some additional coverage. The heat from the grass fires might also slow the Kilpacx down.

From his location and observation Fondrall was not sure but it appeared to him that the strength of the Haddron fire balls seemed to be changing color. The bright yellow of the fire balls were now turning to bright orange. This was a clear indication that the magic of the Haddrons was starting to get a little weaker. But he was not sure that he and his men would be able to hold out long enough for the Haddron to completely lose their magic energies.

Fondrall could not see the battle between Hagjel and the Haddrons but it seemed that the battle over at Hagjel's sight was even more fierce than it was with him and his men. He would like to go and help Hagjel but his men had their hands full with the Haddrons who were now starting to close in. The ability of his men to remain firing their enhanced arrows in sequence was becoming more difficult as time went by and this was due to a number of reasons. The closeness of the Haddrons and the increased noise of battle meant that the communications between him and his men were almost impossible. He saw that on occasion some of the fire balls were being destroyed by more than one arrow. He hoped that his men would not run out of enhanced arrows before the Haddron magic grew weak enough to enable hand to hand fighting.

Off to Fondrall's right he saw one of the enhanced arrows had been released somewhat late. This second arrow was slightly behind the enhanced arrow which had just destroyed the Haddron fire ball. The second arrow launched by the archer had been aimed at the same fire ball continued to fly. The second enhanced arrow caught on fire as it went through the explosion and this flaming enhanced arrow was now headed directly at an onrushing Kilpacx. What happed next surprised Fondrall and raised his hopes that these giant Kilpacx could be killed.

The second enhanced arrow exploded just in front of the huge face of this giant Kilpacx. The head of the Kilpacx had caught on fire and at the same time the huge head of this beast was forced backwards by the blast. The recoil of this large animal's head had hit the enemy Haddron. The Haddron rider had been instantly smashed to the ground and was somewhat stunned.

The pain to this huge animal must have been considerable to say the least. The giant beast reared up completely on hit's back legs and began immediately paw at it's face with it's shorter front paws. But the damage to this large animal had been great enough to put this huge beast completely out of the action. The injured animal was making loud screeching noises. This screeching noise was so loud that it was heard by everybody on both sides of the battle field. It was very shortly after this that the large animal, which was clearly in a tremendous amount of pain while it had reared up, tipped right over onto it's back. The momentum of this huge beast instantly crushed the enemy Haddron who was still lying stunned on the ground.

Fondrall could not stop himself from cheering. For Fondrall this was a good feeling.

When all this was happening and the screeching of the injured Kilpacx could be heard across the battle field, the Haddron attack began to slow. The Haddron warriors who had witnessed this lucky shot by the archer with Fondrall's group were somewhat in shock. They had never seen one of these large animals ever go down this fast.

The other Kilpacx who were by nature cold blooded killers, seemed to sense the loss and now were not so quick to continue the attack.

This lucky shot Fondrall thought to himself. "Could be a turning point in the battle."

Fondrall was the next person to shoot in the sequence. He saw that the fire ball he was aiming at was not that strong and so he fired past the fire ball. This time Fondrall's arrow was sent directly at the Haddron. It was very smoky at the time and Fondrall could not see whether or not the arrow was going to hit it's target, mostly because he had to instantly jump back into his hole. He did so just before the Haddron's fire ball had passed directly over him and exploded just passed where he was hidden. But the arrow shot by Fondrall had hit it's target. The arrow did not hit the Haddron's Kilpacx, but just like the shot before, it was a lucky shot. It killed the rider instantly. The timing had to be perfect because the Haddron's protection shield had to be lowered for a very short time, in order for the Haddron to send out his magic fire ball. Before the Haddron could replace his shield completely the enhanced arrow from Fondrall's bow had found it's target. The enhanced arrow hit the enemy Haddron square in the chest. There was an explosion.

"Poof." There was no more Haddron. Only dust, smoke and ashes remained. Fondrall after diving into his hole glanced up just in time to catch a glimpse of the Haddron's death. Even though they were in a deadly battle where all of them might die should they lose to the Haddrons, Fondrall could not help but smile, look to the sky and cheer while saying. "That shot was for you Mom and for you too Dad."

Quickly and with no other thought in his mind Fondrall reloaded his bow.

Hagjel Under Siege

While all the fighting had commenced between the two groups of defenders and the Haddrons the fighting between Fondrall's men and the Haddrons had begun just slightly ahead of the fighting with Hagjel's group of archers.

Hagjel had been the last in his group of archers in sequence, to release his enhanced arrow. He had also been the last of his archers to get into his trench. Because Hagjel was going to be the last person to reach his hiding place he was able to observe the battle group in front of where he was located and also able to see how effective Frondall's men were doing against the Haddrons. At this time there was still not a great deal of smoke in the valley and things were still somewhat visible. The observant eyes of Hagjel had enabled him to see the lucky shot which had been made out of sequence by one of Fondrall's men. This had been the second shot made at the same fire ball. Hagjel saw the second arrow catch fire and explode in the face of the Kilpacx.

Hagjel had made a mental note of the timing of that second lucky shot. Jakka had been watching at the same time and when the enhanced arrow hit the face of the Kilpacx. Jakka had began to chatter. It seemed that Hagjel had only been in his trench for a second when the second sequence of arrows was being released by his archers. With intensity Hagjel watched the archer just to his right and because Hagjel's mind was so observant he had been able to tell who his fellow archer was aiming at. Hagjel was ready.

Out of the corner of his eye he could see the release of the arrow by the defender on his right. Within the blink of the eye Hagjel sent his enhanced arrow directly in behind it. The results were very satisfying because the same thing happened. The fire ball from the

Haddron warrior which they were aiming at exploded and Hagjel's arrow had caught fire as it flew right through the explosion. Because Hagjel had fired his arrow from a kneeling position the arrow which traveled in a slightly upwards direction was headed directly at it's intended target. The target which Hagjel had been aiming for was the throat of the Haddron rider who had been the same Haddron who had sent this last fire ball at Hagjel and his archers. Jakka who had been watching and had seen Hagjel's arrow catch fire as it went through the exploding fire ball started to chatter even louder when the arrow from Hagjel's bow hit it's intended target.

When the arrow from Hagjel's bow hit the Haddron it was at it's full force. The Haddron warrior did not have sufficient time to return his protection shield to it's full power.

The head of the Haddron warrior exploded. The force of this explosion was so great it had also knocked this warriors huge Kilpacx, with considerable force, to the ground. Jakka's chatter almost became a screeching noise because he was becoming so excited. Actually Jakka wanted to get into the fight but the enemy was still to far away for him to effectively use his stinger.

Hagjel said in a very calm tone. "You will probably get your turn shortly Little Guy." Still speaking to Jakka Hagjel said calmly. "When these Haddrons and the Kilpacx are up close they will be even more dangerous."

Hagjel knew that at present he and his men had the element of surprise mostly because of the enhanced arrows, but when the Haddrons closed in this advantage would be lost. Although Hagjel could not see the place where Bobbiur, Kirwynn and the spear throwers were waiting in ambush because of the now dense smoke on the battle field Hagjel thought that they should be getting ready to attack the flank of the Haddrons with the enhanced spears very shortly. This new surprise from Bobbiur's soldiers could and should keep the Haddrons and the Kilpacx confused. Hagjel also knew that while Bobbiur was helping Fondrall and his archers the archers who were with him at this location would still have to defend against the Haddrons by themselves. It was going to be tough.

Just then a fire ball from another Haddron warrior caught the archer who was in the trench next to him. It was a direct hit and the archer died instantly. The archer had just be in the process of releasing his arrow at a different target and did not see the incoming fire ball in time. The killing of the archer in the next trench caused Jakka to become instantly silent. After the death of the archer in the next trench,

Jakka continued to whimper softly while looking upwards at Hagjel. Jakka was now becoming worried for the safety of Hagjel as the Haddrons were getting even closer. The viciousness and the intensity of the battle was increasing. Instinctively Jakka knew that pretty soon there was going to be some fierce fighting with the Haddrons. The Kilpacx looked huge to Jakka. Jakka continued to whimper and while looking around he had a very worried look on his face.

The Spear Throwers Enter the Battle.

Over in the trenches where Bobbiur, Kirwynn and the spear throwers were hidden the time was nearing for the start of the attack on the Haddron's flank.

Bobbiur turned to Kirwynn and said. "I want you to stay behind me." Then he went on in a very serious tone. "I will be getting in very close and when I attack the Kilpacx. I will knock them down and you should come in quickly from behind me and finish the beast off with your spears. Kirwynn only nodded and said nothing. This was when Bobbiur put his hand up out of the trench and waved in a circular movement which was a signal they had discussed prior to start the Haddrons attack. The Haddrons were now slightly ahead of the spear thrower's location so an element of surprise was in the favor of the defenders because they would be attacking the Haddrons from slightly behind.

Although all of the spear throwers rose up at the same time Bobbiur, Shantok, and Alandaugh, were going to be the first to enter into the battle. Kirwynn who had good leg speed, surprised Bobbiur because she was able to move so fast. Kirwynn had three enhanced spears with her. She ran with confidence but there was a worried look on her pretty face. Bobbiur looked behind and saw that Kirwynn was able to stay right up with him, even with the additional weight of the spears. This made him smile. Then he turned his attention back to the battle in front of him. Kirwynn smiled back and the worried look slowly left her face.

Although he had never fought beside Shantok or Alandaugh he was impressed at their courage. Both were attacking at full speed and neither seemed to fear anything. Bobbiur was also impressed by the fact that they, without any earlier discussion, had launched attacks on two separate Haddrons. Both of them remained silent. This should allow them to get as close to the Haddrons as they were able to and surprise them as best they could. All this was designed to happen before the Haddron warriors could turn to protect their flank.

Bobbiur knew in his mind that it would be easier for both Shantok and Alandaugh if they both to attacked one Kilpacx or Haddron at a time. But Bobbiur could see out of the corner of his eyes these two courageous warriors were going to attack a Kilpacx each. Bobbiur was impressed.

Bobbiur never carried any enhanced spears with him but as he was running towards the Haddrons and the Kilpacx as fast as he could, he spoke softly to the Runes on his swords. "Rimejda." "Rimejda." "Rimejda." Quickly both swords began to glow brightly in a yellow, greenish, bluish prism, of pulsating colors.

From close behind him Kirwynn saw Bobbiur's swords start to turn color and the closeness of the Haddron flank surprisingly made her move even faster. All four of them were now very close to the Haddrons flank. The spear throwers where just behind them and were also closing in at a very fast pace. Fast enough that the surprised Haddrons would be slow to react.

Up until this time the battle was in the favor of the defenders as one Haddron was dead and two Kilpacx were out of action. Bobbiur thought that only a small number of soldiers from the Adjemirian side of the fighting were injured or dead. But he thought to himself. "Now we are fighting at closer quarters things could change very quickly."

After charging quietly across the battle field Bobbiur was the first to reach the Haddrons. Without slowing his speed he ran swiftly up behind one of the Kilpacx. Bobbiur swung with his right hand. The sword, with Bobbiur's fierce swing, dug deep into the tendons in the back left leg of the giant animal. The reaction of this large animal was instant. All movement of the killer Kilpacx stopped. The huge Kilpacx stumbled. The Haddrons attackers had been so intense at concentrating on Fondrall and his archers that they still did not know there was an attack on them coming in from their flank. The surprise attack by Bobbiur and the spear throwers had worked out quite well. Clearly the attacking Haddrons had been caught completely by surprise by the spear throwers forward thrust.

After Bobbiur's swing the Kilpacx had gone down into a sitting position, screaming as the Kilpacx do, from the damage done by Bobbiur's sword. Immediately behind Bobbiur's sword attack Kirwynn had almost instantly ran a spear deep into the side of the damaged and sitting beast.

Both Kirwynn and Bobbiur then ran back a short distance because the spear was going to finish the Kilpacx off. Neither Bobbiur nor Kirwynn knew whether or not there was going to be an explosion from the enhanced spears, like the explosions from the enhanced arrows.

But what happened next came as a surprise to all. This huge beast had been screeching in pain after the sword had dug deep into the ligaments of the beast's hind leg. Now after the spear from Kirwynn, which was rammed deep into beast's side, both Bobbiur and Kirwynn were in for an even bigger surprise. The damage from the enhanced spear instantly brought a pained and stunned look to the beast's face.

The large beast instantly grew silent.

The Haddron warrior seemed to know what was happening and he had quickly jumped off of the other side of the injured Kilpacx as he quickly ran into the smoke in the direction his Haddron friends.

The Kilpacx with a stunned, sad and bewildered look on it's huge face, right in front of Bobbiur and Kirwynn, began to slowly melt away, just like soft spring snow on a hot day.

It did not seem that the beast was in a lot of pain at this time as the screeching had suddenly stopped. It also appeared to Bobbiur that the beast was already dead even before the huge beast had completely melted to the ground. The death of this huge and now harmless beast only took a few moments.

Off to Bobbiur's and Kirwynn's right, Alandaugh was next with his attack. In the smoke from the grass fires the other Haddrons were still not fully aware that they were being attack from a new direction. Just within sight of where Bobbiur was, Bobbiur also saw Shantok ram his spear deep into the side of the next Kilpacx. All this took place at almost at the same time as Alandaugh had hit his target.

Both of the Haddron riders had jumped off of their mounts, from the opposite side of the Kilpacx, out of sight of both Shantok and Alandaugh. This time they did something a little different than the rider who was on the Kilpacx which Bobbiur and Kirwynn had just destroyed. These two Haddrons after jumping to the ground, turned to fight. These two Haddrons were out of sight of Shantok and Alandaugh because they had gotten off of their mounts on the opposite side of the dying beast. Both of the Haddrons aimed and fired. Because Shantok and Alandaugh remained out of sight of these two enemies the Haddron fire balls were sent into a group of charging spear throwers. These spear throwers had been charging just slightly behind Shantok and Alandaugh and they had still not gotten into the fight. As it turned out, they were easy targets.

Both of the Haddrons at the same time had let go of their fire balls. The result was devastating. Both fire balls were direct hits on two of the oncoming spear throwers. These two spear throwers were burnt instantly and were probably dead before they hit the ground screaming. This brought a sickening feeling to Bobbiur's stomach, but there was no time to help the injured. Nor would there be any hope because of the extreme explosion from these successful Haddron fireballs.

At this time Bobbiur noticed the enemy fire balls clearly were starting to get weaker. He knew this because the color of the fire balls were starting to change again. The enemy fireballs were now becoming a dark orange, almost a red and Bobbiur knew that there was not much magic left for the Haddrons to use. But Bobbiur also knew that these Haddrons were still to be feared. The Haddrons were probably vicious warriors and they still had the huge and fearsome killer Kilpacx to send against the defenders.

Without thinking or even hesitating Bobbiur ran directly at the closest Haddron who was in the process of putting his protective shield back into place. The Haddron saw Bobbiur running at him and he just smiled because his protection shield was nearly completed. The enemy Haddron never even drew his sword and he never had time to send another fire ball. Bobbiur thought to himself that this Haddron was not yet aware of Bobbiur's enhanced swords. At least the Haddron didn't know this until it was too late. Just before the swords of Bobbiur cut through the Haddron's protection shield a look of complete astonishment came over the Haddrons face. The smile was wiped off this Haddron's face forever. Clearly it was to late for the Haddron to attack Bobbiur and the Haddron knew that he as about die. Complete fear was all which was present on the enemy warriors face.

Swinging both swords with as much force as Bobbiur could muster the enhanced swords found their target. Bobbiur was not aware that he was now screaming a vicious war cry, through clenched teeth. The scream was only. "This is for Salbuk."

The Nine Moons of Adjemir

There was a look of complete rage on Bobbiur's face with such a fierce sound in his voice as he cut this Haddron to pieces that even Kirwynn, who was still very close behind Bobbiur, had an involuntary shudder run up her spine. The Haddron had been cut down so swiftly and fiercely by Bobbiur that he did not even have time to finish his scream. One more powerful swing from Bobbiur's swords had cut his head clean from this Haddron's shoulder's. The Haddron's head tumbled onto the ground. Before the dead Haddron's head had touched the ground Bobbiur was already turning to attack the other Haddron. The second Haddron was also standing on the ground a short distance away but was almost impossible for Bobbiur to see because of the fire and smoke.

Bobbiur knew the general location of the other Haddron so he rapidly moved in the direction where he had last seen this enemy warrior. But Bobbiur in his rage had miscalculated the place where he thought the Haddron warrior would be. He had unknowingly ran right passed the Haddron.

This Haddron saw Bobbiur before Bobbiur saw the enemy. As soon as Bobbiur saw the Haddron he turned in the Haddrons direction. But Bobbiur was too late. Before Bobbiur could get into striking range with his swords the Haddron was raising his arm to send a deadly fire ball, which at this distance could not help but destroy Bobbiur. At this range the Haddron could not miss and Bobbiur knew this. Kirwynn who was directly behind Bobbiur had seen the Haddron through the smoke before Bobbiur had. She was raising her hand to her mouth to scream a warning to Bobbuir. But Kirwynn knew her warning to Bobbiur was going to be to late. To Kirwynn it looked like Bobbiur was finished. At this time Bobbiur looked defenseless.

Stopped dead in his tracks Bobbiur could only stare at the attacking Haddron. There was no place to hide and Bobbiur was not in a position to strike at the enemy. Bobbiur quickly turned and looked at Kirwynn and it was almost like he wanted to apologize for being so foolish to let this Haddron get the better of him. Kirwynn thought that Bobbiur looked a little bit like a child and she also thought that he looked a little embarrassed. Kirwynn knew in this instant Bobbiur was soon going to be dead. They both had just stood there motionless with their eyes locked with each other. The Haddron's hand was being brought down into a firing position.

Just as Bobbiur was about to die by the blast from the Haddron, Bobbiur heard a sound that he would never forget. It was a swishing sound. This strange sound was the sound of a spear thrown, with extreme force.

Alandaugh had just saved Bobbiur from a horrible death. The spear was an enhanced spear and upon impact with the Haddron's chest the Haddron warrior instantly flew apart into a thousand pieces. The enemy had instantly disintegrated. The rage seemed to have completely left Bobbiur as he had been standing there completely defenseless against the Haddron. If the Haddron had more time, some damage could have been done to Bobbiur. In all likelihood Bobbiur would be dead. After Alandaugh had thrown the spear Bobbiur just hung his head. This lesson about losing his temper and going into a rage had almost cost him his life. At the time Bobbiur did not know that this lesson would stay with him for the rest of his life.

Bobbiur saw Alandaugh coming through the smoke and Bobbiur quietly and solemnly nodded his thanks to Alandaugh. Alandaugh without any expression on his face, shrugged his shoulders nodded towards Bobbiur, as if to say. "No big deal."

As Alandaugh, in somewhat of a hurry, turned quickly to get back into the battle. Bobbiur just shook his head in wonder as he saw a slight smile come onto Alandaugh's boyish face. Bobbiur thought to himself. "We are all fighting for our lives and the freedom of all of Adjemir and this young Alandaugh is having fun. He seems fearless."

Shantok had just come into view and he had the same smile on his face. Bobbiur thought to himself. "These two warriors just love to fight."

Turning towards Kirwynn Bobbiur saw that she had an extremely pale look to her face and he knew she had been very worried. Deep inside Bobbiur also knew that he had scared her a great deal, probably more than she had ever been frightened before in her life. Bobbiur still embarrassed, without saying anything took a deep breath, turned and headed directly back into the battle.

Ram Fights Zalghar

Knowing that there had been no possible way for getting the Haddrons to leave Adjemir peacefully, slowly and with a good deal of determination, Ram with his fierce eyes had sent his killer ray at Zalghar. With tremendously swift reflexes Zalghar had actually used a small magic reflector shield and the killer ray from Ram had bounced harmlessly into the sky above.

Ram already had a very powerful protection shield in place and Zalghar from his years of fighting ignored this knowledge. Zalghar almost instantly with a determined fiendish look on his face, while gritting his teeth had sent an extremely strong and tremendously powerful fire ball directly at the waiting Ram. This fire ball although much more powerful than any magic spell ever used against Ram, had just glanced off Ram's protection shield. Ram staggered, but remained on his feet. Just like the killer ray which Ram had used on Zalghar earlier, this magic spell from Zalghar, just disappeared harmlessly into the bright blue Adjemirian sky above.

Ram did not say anything but the behavior of Zalghar was what Ram had expected and wanted. The powers of Zalghar were being wasted. The expression on Ram's face never changed, not in the slightest and as he moved slightly to his right. Then Ram quickly put both hands over his head. As he brought both his hands together in a slapping motion, a huge and a very long handled magic war axe which was made from a pure magic energy, quickly appeared in his hands.

Ram swiftly with a sudden urgency quickly raised this enormous, pulsating colored war axe, farther above his head. Then with a tremendous amount of energy and force, while stepping closer to Zalghar, Ram brought the war axe down onto his enemy. Energy sparks flew everywhere. Even though Zalghar now had in place a very powerful protection shield, the force of the war axe coming down on his protection shield, was so great, Zalghar was knocked staggering to the ground. Luckily for Zalghar his protection shield remained intact.

Miraculously and without even seeming to move, Zalghar was instantly back on his feet, as he said in a loud, confident yet vicious voice. "So it's war axes that you want to fight with old man."

With lightning speed a huge war axe instantly appeared in Zalghar's hands. Zalghar's war axe was very similar to the weapon which Ram had just used. Quickly and with power the war axe swung by Zalghar was smashed down with an extreme force, at Ram's protection shield. Similar to the force which Ram used on Zalghar this war axe, although it had extreme magic powers could not break through the barrier of Ram's protection shield. Although Ram was staggered, he had not been knocked to the ground.

The battle was to continue like this for some time and Zalghar would now have admit that Obmar may have been right. Ram was more powerful than he had first thought. But Ram is old and in the end Ram would be dead. Zalghar knew that he was going to win.

Ram then changed his strategy. He went directly to the use of two enhanced swords. Putting both hands out in front of himself and clapped his hands two times. Without showing any expression and without saying anything, two magic swords instantly appeared in his waiting hands. These two swords were just like the magic war axe. They were constructed of pure energy. Although these swords were very strong they were not made of metal but each appeared to be more like a lightning bolt. The energy which constructed these weapons was a bright blue. Both swords were pulsating and there were large number of sparks escaping from the tip of each weapon. Without saying anything, with a simple nod of his head and the partial closing of his eyes, two swords which were very similar to the swords held by Ram instantly appeared in the hands of Zalghar. Still without any expression showing on his face, Ram advanced closer to Zalghar.

What Zalghar did not know was that while Ram had been sitting and resting he had been conserving all of his magic energies. Ram knew that he had in his possession some very powerful magic but he also knew he would also require a considerable amount of intelligence. He would have to think clearly while battling with Zalghar. He would never overestimate the power of any enemy. Nor would Ram ever overestimate the power and magic of Zalghar. Ram would never make this type of mistake. Ram would also be patient in this battle and he was not about to rush anything. Although Ram was very concerned about the battle between the Haddrons and the warriors from Adjemir, he was not able to follow that part of the battle because of the smoke and fire in the valley. Still he remained concerned about the welfare of his people and also the warriors from Garriton.

As he continued to advance towards Zalghar with his weapons at the ready, he could not help but take a look over his shoulder for a quick glance at the battle ground but the smoke still remained thick. It remained impossible for him to see the fighting which was now well underway in the main part of the Valley.

Unknown to Ram or Zalghar the battle between the warriors on the battle field, up until now was favoring the Adjemirians, but this was about to change.

In the skirmish where Hagjel was fighting the battle it was now getting into closer quarters where the giant Kilpacx could do severe damage. Hagjel felt safe because if any of the Kilpacx got to close to him, he knew Jakka could and would stop any of these large animals in it's tracks. But he knew there were problems with the battle, as he could hear through the heavy smoke, screams from some of the men who were fighting close to him. The surprise from the enhanced arrows and the damage which was created by their earlier use was now being overcome by these fierce Haddron warriors. The screams which the worried Hagjel was hearing through the heavy smoke covering the battle field were now all Adjemirian screams.

Hagjel had assumed that the ability to see through this intense smoke was as difficult for the Haddrons as it was for the defending Humans and Elves, but he was about to learn the killer Kilpacx, were not bothered very much by this dense smoke. Because the heavy smoke did not bother the Kilpacx very much the Haddrons now had an enormous advantage over the defending Adjemirians.

Suddenly bursting through the haze came one of the Haddrons riding his Kilpacx and although Hagjel already had an arrow notched in his bow there was no time to fire. As it worked out Jakka who was able to see into the smoke a little better than Hagjel, never even hesitated.

"Ka, Ka, Ka, Hawusssss." Jakka's stinger had been sent immediately. What really surprised Hagjel and what he found most interesting was the stinger sent by Jakka, was visible to the naked eye, because the sting had to force it's way through the smoke.

Hagjel had been temporarily caught by surprise, mostly because the Kilpacx was onto him so suddenly but also because the, stinger sent by Jakka could knock this enormous beast to the ground so fast. The Kilpacx had just been in the motion of biting down on Hagjel when Jakka had sent his stinger. The Haddon warrior, who was just as surprised as Hagjel was in regards to this big beast going down so fast was just able to get moving fast enough to disappear into the smoke before Hagjel could release his arrow. Hagjel followed the Haddron but he had to move very slowly. Without looking down he whispered. "Thanks Jakka."

This was all Hagjel had time to say and Jakka who seemed to understand just smile up at Hagjel as he began to chuckle to himself in his GymmKat fashion. Although he was in the middle of a fight to the finish Hagjel was moving very slowly. He was concentrating with extreme attention while he was fallowing the Haddron, but he now had time to reach into the tote bag. As he patted Jakka on the head he said with a warm feeling. "Good work Jakka."

Hagjel was not familiar about fighting in smoke like this, so he continued to move stealthily and very slowly in the direction of which he had last seen the escaping enemy.

Over in the other battle where Bobbiur and Kirwynn were fighting side by side with Shantok and Alandaugh the battle was going a little better. The spear throwers combined with the archers ability with enhanced arrows were at least able to hold their own. But the battle was clearly turning in favor of the Haddrons, mostly because of the ability of the Kilpacx to see through the smoke.

Bobbiur and Kirwynn could hear very clearly the screams from some of the Adjemirians as they were being viciously attacked, probably and mostly by the killer Kilpacx. Through the smoke and haze a Kilpacx was suddenly charging down upon Bobbiur and Kirwynn. Without any notice or clear sign between the two of them, they parted instantly, just in time enough so the Kilpacx, with it's tremendous momentum ran right between them. Although Bobbiur had to almost dive out of the way of the charging Kilpacx as did Kirwynn, Bobbiur was back on his feet so fast that he was able to slash the large beast in it's back legs, as it charged by.

The enhanced swords of Bobbiur's were still nearly at their maximum power and as Bobbiur's swing cut deep into the Kilpacx rear right ankle tendons, the beast began to roar in agony. Within a millisecond and without saying anything, Kirwynn ran an enhanced spear deep into the side of the injured animal. As before there was no explosion but within a matter of seconds the giant Kilpacx with a sad look in its vicious face, started to melt to the ground right before their eyes. The rider Haddron who had jumped of the injured animal escaped quickly into the ever thickening smoke.

At this time Kirwynn through the smoke, could tell that Hagjel and his warriors were having a very tough time in the hand to hand combat with the Haddrons. She quickly said to Bobbiur. "I think we should go and help Hagjel and his archers."

Bobbiur shook his head as quickly he answered back in a negative way. "We must concentrate on this battle here." Then he added. "If we break from the earlier strategy then the battle may turn completely against us. We have been very lucky up till now but the Kilpacx in these close quarters are very dangerous. We have lost the element of surprise and we will be lucky to survive the next few minutes." Then Bobbiur repeated himself as he continued to speak to Kirwynn. "These Kilpacx in close will be doing us some severe damage to our soldiers but we must not now go running all over the battle field."

While trying to see through the thickening smoke Bobbiur said. "We have to stay here and concentrate on these Haddrons. If we are able too beat these Haddrons and if we still have some spears and enhanced arrows left then we will be able to go and help Hagjel. I understand we should be helping Hagjel but we must concentrate on these warriors first before we can effectively help Hagjel."

Then Bobbiur added with a worried look on his battle stained face. "My biggest concern is how well Ram is doing?" Bobbiur quickly finished. "If Ram loses to Zalghar today then nothing else will matter and we will all be killed by Zalghar before the day is finished."

Kirwynn also trying to see through the heavy smoke was biting her lower lip. She had a very worried look on her face. Bobbiur noticed that she was down to her last spear and nobody was sure how many Haddrons or Kilpacx were still mobile on the battle ground. Neither could anybody on the Adjemirian side know just exactly how much magic power these Haddrons still possessed.

Just out of sight from where Bobbiur and Kirwynn were positioned Alandaugh and Shantok were being chased by two Haddron Kilpacx. They were down to one spear each but these were two courageous warriors were able to stay out of the reach of the Kilpacx and just out of sight by the Haddrons, who were unable to use their fire balls in this ever thickening smoke.

Bobbiur got really close to Kirwynn at which time he took up a defensive stance as he looked around. He wished he could see how the battle was going. But deep in his mind he knew that they were about to lose this fight. At these close quarters the Kilpacx clearly had the upper hand. This matter became even more evident as the Adjemirian warriors were running out of enhanced spears and arrows. Nobody from Adjemir had ever seen the ability of the Haddron warriors in hand to hand combat but Bobbiur knew, deep down inside himself that these warriors were probably very capable and very deadly in close combat. In fact he was sure about this.

The battle was now completely in the favor the Haddrons and he knew this also. The question which was in his mind now was whether or not, he should get Kirwynn back to a safer spot. But as this thought came into his mind, he thought of Salbuk and the warrior instincts deep inside him quickly rose to the surface. With determination Bobbiur turned back into the battle and bravely got ready for what ever was to happen next.

Obmar Enters The Battle

When he was crossing the battle field Obmar knew that the defenders had surprised the Haddrons but he also knew by the screaming from the Adjemirian soldiers in the battle field in front of him, the battle was now turning in favor of the Haddrons. The Kilpacx were now at close quarters and the ability of these giant beasts to finish off the Adjemirians was to be assured. Obmar had changed his mind and instead of going into the battle against Hagjel and his fighters Obmar change directions. He was moving slowly in the direction of where he had last saw Zalghar which was close to the spot where Ram had been waiting to do battle.

Just then a gently but steady wind started to blow. It was coming from the direction of Darmonarrow and this wind slowly began blowing some of the denser smoke out of the valley. The smoke was being pushed towards the other end of the valley from where the Haddrons had entered the battle.

Right in front of Obmar as the smoke was being thinned away by this slight breeze, he saw two figures start to come into view. It was Ram and Zalghar. They were close together and at this time Obmar saw that they were using very powerful magic swords. Bright sparks were flying in all directions. Even over the sound of the general fighting on the battle field Obmar could hear the forceful clashing, of a magic sword smashing against the other magic sword.

Obmar also thought, even from this distance that Ram appeared to be trying to force Zalghar into the Graveyard of the Ancients. Obmar wondered why. Obmar could see quite easily that these two warriors were in an incredibly vicious fighting mood. At this time Ram had his back towards Obmar and Ram clearly did not know that Obmar was watching him from behind. Just then the smoke closed back in temporarily. Ram and Zalghar were fighting fiercely with sparks flying from the swords so intensely that Obmar could tell exactly where the fight was just by the flashing of sparks and the loud crashing sounds, coming forcefully through the smoke. Obmar thought to himself. "I tried to tell Zalghar just how powerful Ram was now he is in trouble."

Obmar began to move closer but very slowly and very cautiously.

Ram, even though he was quite old confidently and efficiently stepped steadily towards Zalghar with both swords flashing and striking so rapidly they looked just like a blurring whirlwind. To Zalghar's intense surprise he was being greatly overpowered by this somehow very strong old man. Unknowingly Zalghar had been steadily backed up. His direction without knowing it was in the general direction, as seen earlier by Obmar, was directed towards the Graveyard of the Ancients. Ram with intensity without Zalghar knowing it, was purposely steering Zalghar into the grave yard with his ever increasing forward momentum. But Ram did not want to bury Zalghar. He just wanted to kill him.

Ram was now winning without question as Zalghar was starting to tire. With this knowledge at this time Ram pressed on with a greater and complete abandon. Ram's forward motion could not be stopped or even slowed by Zalghar's now, almost feeble attempts. In his entire life before coming to Adjemir Zalghar had never witnessed such power and speed with which he was now seeing coming from this old man Ram. Some of the movements by Ram Zalghar noticed, were almost a blur. Ram seemed to be in one place and almost instantly, he would appear in a completely different location. Some questions now came into Zalghar's mind. "How can this old man move this fast? This old warrior is very powerful and strong." Zalghar now had to admit this out loud through gritted teeth. After a few more swings Zalghar finally had to admit to himself through his gritted teeth as he had been swinging his sword swiftly, but only in defensive moves. "Obmar had been right. This old man is very powerful."

Even through his protection shield Zalghar now had injuries to his right arm, his left leg and his left side. Even through the protection shield the ever increasing power in Ram's swings damage was being done. As the battle between these two tough warriors continued, Ram still seemed to be getting even stronger and more powerful as the battle progressed. This was hard to understand. Now as Ram successfully continued to back the now nearly exhausted Zalghar into the Graveyard of the Ancients the fierce battle seemed to be all but over. Ram with a tremendous amount of force from a single blow knocked Zalghar to the ground. Zalghar was in disbelief because firstly he had been completely surprised by this old man but now more so because he was actually being smashed to the ground by this old warrior.

All Zalghar was able to do was to increase the magic power to his protection shield. Zalghar knew he was about die as he thought to himself. "How can this be happening?"

Ram knew quite well that he had beaten Zalghar. Now all had to do was wait until Zalghar's protection shield grew weaker. Ram knew that after only a short time he would be able to kill Zalghar and then he could go and help his fellow Adjemirian warriors in the main battle field. In order to be able to get to the Adjemirian warriors and help them as fast as he could, Ram with considerable force began using both of his swords in order to increase the bombardment of the weakened protection shield of Zalghar. The smashing of Zalghar's protection shield, now began in earnest. The smashing sounds increased.

Ram knew in his mind that once he smashed through the shield he could kill Zalghar easily and all of Adjemir would be saved. So he pressed on in earnest. Sparks continued flying from the weakening shield and now Zalghar lying on the ground looking finished, had deep furrows on his brow. Ram knew by the sparks which were flying from the shield that he was almost through the magic barrier of the forces of the shield. Ram with a determined look on his now sweating face unbelievably was actually able, even at this time to further increase the onslaught. Lying on the ground with a worried and confused look on his face all Zalghar could think was. "Where did Ram get these powers from?"

Zalghar knew he was about to die and there was absolutely nothing he could do about it. Zalghar was now afraid and this was the first time in his life that he actually knew real fear of any kind. This was not something he liked. He found this feeling very strange. He had some small fears before in his life but nothing like he was feeling now.

Yet even at this time the evil look had never left his eyes.

Ram knew as he was about to kill Zalghar right where he lay. Yet for some unknown reason the evil in Zalghar, brought a fiendish smile to his enemy's face. A big smile. A very, very big smile now spread across Zalghar's evil face. Ram could not figure out why Zalghar was smiling so fiendishly but he was about to find out shortly.

The smoke from all the burning grass had cleared slightly and just behind Ram Zalghar had seen Obmar approaching. The evil smile on Zalghar's face had nothing to do with his possibly dying. It was because he had seen the war axe was being swung by Obmar. A sense of foreboding had suddenly come over Ram and he started to turn quickly. But it was too late.

Up until this time Ram was completely unaware that Obmar had snuck up behind him. Obmar had swung the Rune axe and at the same instance Ram had caught Obmar's mind message, which simply was. "Ram you are going to die." The pure evil Rune axe which was swung so fiercely by Obmar cut horizontally and slightly downwards, as it slammed deeply into Ram's right side. Ram was knocked viciously to the ground and was in tremendous pain. Ram although in this tremendous pain could only think. "This battle was now going to turn completely into the favor of Zalghar and his Haddron warriors. All of Adjemir is lost."

But when the evil Rune axe had struck Ram in the side, it resulted in a good force being hit by an evil force. From this energy explosion Obmar had been knocked stunned and dazed to the ground. Ram also lay defenseless and stunned where he had landed on the cold rough ground.

Ram had been so intent and so close to killing Zalghar that all of his attention was directed only towards the task at hand. He had not seen nor felt the presence of Obmar sneaking up behind him. Ram had a puzzled look on his tired old face and as he lay on the cold ground he turned to see Obmar laying on the ground behind him. Ram had been severely hurt and he was bleeding quite heavy from the deep wound in his side. At this moment he then turned slowly and he could see Zalghar slowly and weakly starting to regain some strength. Ram could see the power of Zalghar was starting to return and he also fully understood clearly at his time that he would be unable to fight Zalghar any further.

Ram had a question in his mind and the question was. "Why did Obmar attack him from behind?" Then he saw through squinted eyes, the Rune on the handle of the war axe and instantly everything became very clear.

With a sad look on his face Ram turned and watched Zalghar. Zalghar was quickly getting his old form back and his strength. Then slowly Zalghar rolled completely onto his side where he could face

Ram. The look of pure evil was returning to his face as Zalghar started to smile. As Zalghar glanced sideways he had said to Obmar. "You have done really good here Obmar and I will repay you fully for your help." Obmar only smiled weakly and nodded in Zalghar's direction as he was still somewhat dazed and stunned from the energies which were released from the war axe when it had sliced through Ram's protection shield and had cut deep into the side of Ram. Still lying prone on the ground Obmar smiled as he heard new screams coming from the center of the battle field which meant the Haddron Kilpacx were in very close to finishing off the Adjemirian defenses. Obmar had a cruel, evil and fiendish smile on his wrinkled face because the sounds of screaming coming from the battle field, meant the Haddrons were having great success.

The Haddron Warriors Are Winning

The surprises which the Adjemirians defenders had when the battle first began were now non existent. In close quarters and with the ability of the Kilpacx to see through the smoke or maybe their ability to smell the enemy, through the still lingering smoke had given a distinct advantage to the Haddrons attack. A number of Kilpacx had been killed and the number of the Haddrons had been reduced, but they were still an extremely strong and dangerous force.

Fondrall's group had been hit hard at first and were being smashed but Fondrall knew he could depend on the spear throwers once they had entered the battle. Fondrall and his soldiers could hear the increase in the sounds of the battle and Fondrall knew when the spear throwers had finally hit the Haddrons in the flank.

The noises coming through the dense smoke was noise which had made Fondrall think that their side, at that time were winning. Fondrall had heard screams from some of his men but he had also heard sounds which he knew were injuries to the Kilpacx. Fondrall had also known the spear throwers had entered the battle at exactly the right time and none to soon.

These huge beasts up close would have made short work of him and his men but the surprise attack on the Haddrons flank by Bobbiur and his men had giving sufficient time to Fondrall's men to regroup. Hagjel's men had not been quite this lucky and the screams coming from Hagjel's archers, which Fondrall heard had meant that the battle over there was even very much more in favor of the Haddrons.

Fighting on the flank of the Haddrons and trying his best to help Fondrall and his men, Bobbiur knew the battle where he was fighting the Haddrons, was actually taking too long. Bobbiur was worried for Hagjel and Bobbiur also knew he would have to hurry things up or Hagjel and his men who were fighting the other group of Haddrons would all be dead very soon. That is unless Bobbiur and his men could finish off these Haddrons and get over to the location where Hagjel was fighting. Because Hagjel had been greatly outnumbered Bobbiur continued to be very worried for him. Because the element of surprise by the Adjemirians had been used to attack the side of the Haddrons there was now no reason why the spear throwers had to be quiet any longer.

Bobbiur began his blood curdling war scream. A scream, which through the somewhat dense smoke was not lost on the Haddrons. The war scream which Bobbiur used was almost unreal and it sent chills up the backs of some of the Haddrons who Bobbiur had been fighting. Then through the smoke Bobbiur heard the war cries of Shantok and Alandaugh. Bobbiur instantly renewed his charge as did Shantok and Alandaugh. The renewed charge of these three fearless soldiers caught some of the Haddrons by surprise and for a few moments even the Kilpacx were caught off guard. The momentum now seemed to be starting to swing in favor of Bobbiur and his men.

Kirwynn did not realize until after she had also begun her charge the scream which she was hearing the loudest, was actually coming from her own mouth. Even Bobbiur was surprised by the sound coming from Kirwynn and he glanced back with a short quick grin on his smoke stained face. He then turned his head back into the battle just as an attacking Kilpacx was coming into view through the smoke.

The enhanced swords were being swung so hard and furious that Bobbiur looked just like an uncontrolled whirlwind. Coming through the dense smoke Bobbiur's charge continued right into the huge animal's face. The mouth of the Kilpacx had been opened in a motion of attempting to bite down on Bobbiur. But this was just as the vicious swords of Bobbiur sliced deep into the animals mouth. This Kilpacx had been injured severely on his outer mouth which also included his large tongue. Some teeth although very strong, had been knocked clear out of the animals mouth by the extreme force of Bobbiur's swings. Some large and very sharp teeth from this wounded Kilpacx, were scattered on the ground.

As the giant beast drew to a quick halt, Bobbiur never even slowed down in the slightest. Bobbiur also knew that the magic fire balls of the Haddron warrior could not be used against him this close.

He knew he had some time before the Haddron could dismount and attack him. Therefore Bobbiur was able to quickly run along the right side of the Kilpacx. Swinging with a tremendous amount of force Bobbiur cut completely through the large animals tendons in it's left hind calf. The animal went down. Bobbiur had swung downwards with tremendous force slicing deeply into the lower portion of the animal's leg and partly through the animal's left rear paw. The Kilpacx was now completely immobile. The last spear that Kirwynn had was quickly and deeply slammed into side of the wounded Kilpacx.

Before the Haddron could get off the wounded animal and start to fight him or Kirwynn, Bobbiur had turned and was thrashing his swords in a circular fashion as he jumped up the side of the beast. This Haddron never had a chance.

Although it seemed like Bobbiur and his men were winning the screams coming from some of the Adjemirian soldiers from other locations on the battle field, meant that the Kilpacx and the Haddrons were winning against them. Fortunately for Bobbiur the Haddrons could not make use of their fire balls. If the Haddron had used his fire balls this close then they would be killed because the heat from the explosion would kill them also.

The Kilpacx which Kirwynn had speared in the side had died quickly and quietly. On the other hand the Haddron warrior when Bobbiur had slashed through him with his two magic swords, screamed louder than even the Kilpacx were capable of screaming. This brought a instant smile to Bobbiur smoke stained, sweaty face, as he again without hesitation turned quickly back into the battle.

Off to Kirwynn's and Bobbiur's left, Shantok and Alandaugh had came at a Kilpacx and the Haddron warrior from both sides. The Haddron was the first to die with a spear thrown by Alandaugh, which caught the Haddron warrior clean in the side. The spear had been thrown with such force that at the point of impact the spear had lifted the Haddron completely off of the Kilpacx back and slammed him dead onto the ground. Shantok who was in really good condition also had incredible strength. Shantok ran the enhanced spear so deeply into the side of the Kilpacx that this spear was buried at least, half way into the animal's side. This beast was dead before it hit the ground.

Both Alandaugh and Shantok had heard the Haddron screaming and they both had understood immediately, Bobbiur and Kirwynn were also doing really well in this battle. Without even so much as a word being said between the two of them they both turned and went directly over to where Kirwynn had just finished off the

Kilpacx. Between Alandaugh and Shantok they had three spears left because they had been able to get some fallen spears from dead or injured Adjemirians. Alandaugh immediately gave one of his two remaining spears to Kirwynn. While they were discussing what they had just accomplished two things were happening. What they did not know was the remaining Kilpacx at close quarters were smashing their way through the Adjemirian defenses and a number of the defenders were down. Four archers had been killed. Three spear throwers were dead two spear throwers were wounded severely and were eventually going to die.

The Battle Starts to Change

Of importance and something which none of the Adjemirian defenders on the battle field had any knowledge of, was the entrance into the battle of a very large group of Elf Archers. Zorp had been to the Village of WynnFred and had spoken with Pendahl very earlier in the morning. The visit to the Elf's village of WynnFred had been made shortly after Zorp had visited Garriton. The visit to WynnFred was after Zorp had been to Garriton when General Yauddi had sent Kirwynn with the Garriton soldiers to help Ram and Bobbiur fight the Haddrons. Reinforcements were on the way and of great importance to this battle was when Obmar had left his post. The entrance of Pendahl and his troops into the fight was going to of a great surprise to the Haddrons.

What had happened earlier in the morning at WynnFred was when Zorp had finished speaking to Pendahl there was immediate action. Pendahl was quickly able to gather nearly thirty soldiers, mostly archers, from WynnFred. The Elves had then started to travel quickly towards the valley where Temple of the Ancients was situated. At the same time Pendahl had dispatched a messenger to travel to the two nearest Elf cities with instructions to gather as large a force as they could and to meet him and his troops on the road to the Temple of the Ancients. Pendahl wanted to combine forces before they met up with the Haddrons. The additional forces caught up to Pendahl and the WynnFred archers only moments before they came to the valley were the battle was being fought. Pendhal, through the use of messengers was able to have an agreed truce between the Elves and Humans in order to battle the Haddrons. Of course this was easy because Kirwynn was in charge of the Garriton troops.

The smoke from the battle by the time of the arrival of the Elf reinforcements was starting to get thinner because of a gentle wind which was now getting stronger was blowing steadily through the valley. What the advancing Elfen troops saw as they entered the valley was a fairly large battle.

When Pendahl and his archers first came to the valley he was unable see the battle between Ram and Zalghar, because by now the battle between Ram and Zalghar had already moved deep into the Grave Yard of the Ancients, which was well out of Pendahls sight. Because there was a slight rise where Pendahl was stopped he was able to see over most of the remaining smoke. He could see that the center of the valley where Hagjel was fighting. Pendahl knew instantly the Hagjel needed immediate assistance. Quickly he ordered nearly two thirds of the soldiers to go and help Hagjel. Pendahl took the remaining soldiers and was traveling very quickly across field towards the backs of the Haddrons who where in close combat with Bobbiur, Kirwynn, Shantok, Alandaugh and the remaining archers and spear throwers who were still alive.

Bobbiur saw Pendahl and his soldiers coming through the remaining smoke before the Haddrons did and there was an instant smile on his face. With a new feeling of confidence Bobbiur thought to himself. "We may win this battle yet." Then just for an instant Bobbiur wondered how Ram was doing in his fight with Zalghar. He hoped all was well with Ram.

At the location where Hagjel was still able to hold the Haddrons off, through the smoke and with the incredible eye sight which JymmKats have Jakka saw something and he began to whimper. Hagjel who at this time was being stalked by one of the killer Kilpacx quickly looked down and asked. "What is wrong Jakka?" But Hagjel was unable to see what was bothering Jakka. Hagjel had then turned his attention back to trying to find the location of the Kilpacx and to fighting the Haddrons.

What Jakka had been watching was the attack on Ram by Obmar with the Rune emblazoned war axe.

Jakka had whimpered a little more and a short time later when he seen Zalghar starting to try to rise up from the ground. In a flash and without Hagjel being able to stop him Jakka sprung up and bolted out of the tote bag. Hagjel was slow to respond and before he could do anything Jakka had disappeared into the smoke, which still remained fairly heavy in this part of the valley. Jakka instantly headed at an incredible speed, that is for a JymmKat, directly towards the location of Ram and Zalghar.

Back in the part of the battle field where Bobbiur was fighting the Haddrons the battle was about to change. The incoming Elves as it turned out, would be enough to completely overwhelm the remaining Haddrons who had been fighting Fondrall and his archers. Even though Zalghar was still alive and Bobbiur knew this he could not help but smile to himself, because it appeared that the presence of the incoming Elfen soldiers were a compete surprise to these Haddron enemies.

On the other hand if Zalghar was able to defeat Ram then all of the remaining Adjemirian soldiers on the battle field would be killed by Zalghar. Bobbiur knew just how powerful Zalghar was but he continued to smiled knowing that Pendahl and his Elves had joined the battle. This was good news.

Actually if the Haddrons still had their full magic powers then Pendahl and his men would have been smashed to bits. But the long fight with Bobbiur and his soldiers had left all of the Haddrons on the field, with their full powers being considerably reduced. The battle on this part of the field, was all but over. Bobbiur knew this and he also knew that Hagjel could be in trouble. Unlike Bobbiur and Fondrall's forces, Hagjel and his archers had to take on the same size of Haddron force and there was no spear throwers hidden nearby to surprise the the foes of Hagjel.

Hagjel could not rely on any ally to come to his aid and attack the Haddrons from the flank similar to what had happened in the battle between the Haddrons and Fondrall's men. Hagjel and his men had to defend against these Haddrons by themselves. Now the Haddrons and the vicious Kilpacx were closing in and in Hagjel's mind, things appeared hopeless. Hagjel was not aware of just how the battle was going elsewhere in the valley all he knew for sure was that he and his men were being severely beaten.

Feeling that things might not going so well for Hagjel and his troops Bobbiur left his part of the battle and with good speed moved directly to the location where Hagjel had been fighting. There was still enough smoke in this part of the valley, which enabled him to reach Hagjel's location without any of the Haddrons trying to stop him. Bobbiur was unaware that Kirwynn was right behind him and right behind her came Shantok and Alandaugh. There were three spears remaining amongst these three fighters. Bobbiur was right, the reinforcements from the Elves had not yet arrived to help Hagjel and the Haddrons were starting to circle the remainder of Hagjel and his men.

When Bobbiur arrived at the location where the Haddrons were closing in on Hagjel and his men there was not much time left. Bobbiur did not hesitate and he was able to catch one of the Kilpacx and the Haddron rider by complete surprise. The Haddron rider closest to Hagjel was in the motion of raising his right arm, to send a fireball at Hagjel. The Haddron was so focused on killing Hagjel that neither he nor the Kilpacx were aware that Bobbiur was coming.

Just as the Haddron's arm started downwards to send the fireball to smash Hagjel who was completely helpless at this time, Hagjel started to smile. He had seen Bobbiur entering the battle.

As Bobbiur had done before with his enhanced swords, with his speed and his surprise, the attack was swift. With his first swing he sliced the tendons of the Kilpacx. As the injured Kilpacx was going down and knowing the Haddron had dropped his protection shield to fire his fireball at Hagjel Bobbiur knew he must strike immediately. The Haddron was just in the process of turning in order to see who was attacking, so Bobbiur still had the element of surprise against this warrior. With an opening for Bobbiur's attack and with his momentum, he was onto the Haddron, in the blink of an eye. The surprised Haddron never had a chance.

With extreme force and showing no mercy Bobbiur swung his sword. The head of the Haddron flew into the air and the Haddron's head smashed rolling onto the ground right in front of the injured Kilpacx. This battle was over so fast that Bobbiur never even slowed down. He ran right up to where Hagjel was and then he turned quickly as he raised both swords in order to protect Hagjel from any further attack.

Hagjel seemingly quite relaxed but with a worried look on his battle wary face, he turned to Bobbiur as he said. "I had things under control Bobbiur. I had the Haddron in my sights." Bobbiur laughed with a friendly grin on his face as he said. "No you didn't and now you owe me one."

But knowing something was not right Bobbiur looked closer at Hagjel and he instantly knew that something else was wrong. Then it became evident as Bobbiur noticed the tote bag was empty, meaning Jakka, was not with Hagjel. Bobbiur's first thought was that Jakka had gotten scared by all the fighting, or the appearance of the large Kilpacx and had run away. To his surprise Bobbiur also noted that Hagjel looked kind of lost without Jakka's presence.

Immediately and without thinking further Bobbiur launched himself. He was fully in the air when he swung with all the force his body could muster. Bobbiur's timing was perfect. The strike came just as another enemy Haddron's arm was coming down into a firing position. Hagjel, who was in the process of loading an arrow to defend himself, stopped. Hagjel smiled as he saw the arm of the Haddron fall to the ground.

This Haddron had taken Bobbiur and Hagjel completely by surprise as he had apparently snuck through the remaining smoke. What was more surprising for the Haddron was that his protection shield did not stop the enhanced swords swung by Bobbiur.

The next surprise for this Haddron was instant and it was to be the last surprise for this Haddron. Right behind his arm being cut off, was when his head came off from a powerful left handed swing, from the second sword wielded by Bobbiur.

The Haddron's death had been swift. Even Hagjel could not believe how fast Bobbiur could attack and kill a Haddron. Hagjel thought to himself. "Bobbiur is turning into a pure killing machine. The longer the battle goes on the stronger and faster he seems to be getting."

Then Hagjel was even more impressed when he saw, just as Bobbiur landed on the ground and without even stopping for an instant, he was on the attack again. Headed directly into the dense smoke and again slashing with his right arm, then his left, he severed the tendons of the Kilpacx rear legs from which this last Haddron had dismounted from before sneaking through the remaining smoke. The Haddron had left his mount hidden in the smoke from the grass fires before he had successfully snuck up on Bobbiur and Hagjel.

The animal was instantly made immobile and without even stopping to say anything to Hagjel, Bobbiur disappeared back into the smoke. Bobbiur was now looking for another fight. All Hagjel knew was that it appeared that Bobbiur had just saved his life and Hagjel also knew he had just witnessed a new and fully mature, Bobbiur.

Hagjel said to himself. "These last few days seemed to have really toughened Bobbiur up. He was just like a kid when we originally went after the Dark Storm Clan."

Then turning to also went back into the battle, Hagjel with a deeply worried look on his face, spoke out loud to himself. "I wonder where Jakka is."

Then Hagjel heard the war cry from Bobbiur and Hagjel smiled broadly. What Hagjel didn't know was that Bobbiur had given his war cry because he just encountered the Elfen reinforcements. Hagjel was just about to release his arrow at the Kilpacx to finish it off when a swishing sound passed his ear. Hagjel saw an enhanced spear being slammed into the side of the Kilpacx. Right behind the spear came Kirwynn, Shantok, and Alandaugh. Hagjel laughing said. "Its good to see you." Then pointing. "He went that way." Hagjel had been referring to Bobbiur as he went on to say. "Bobbiur's speed and his ability to fight these Haddrons, is incredible."

Turning to Kirwynn Alandaugh said. "Good throw Kirwynn but now you are without any spears so you must stay behind us." Shantok agreed by saying. "Yes you must stay behind us and we had better get over there and cover Bobbiur's back." Then he quickly added. "He may not be wanting to stay out of trouble and we don't want to lose him this late in the day." Hagjel agreed and laughingly he stated. "We had better get moving because Bobbiur seems to be acting a little strange."

Then with a smile on his face Hagjel said. "He is taking all the fighting away from us." With a laugh they all moved of in the direction where they had last seen Bobbiur.

Ram Has One Last Surprise

Back near to Grave Yard of The Ancients as Ram lay on the ground still stunned and slowly going into shock from the pain and the loss of blood. He could tell that the magic powers were starting to return to Zalghar. Ram also knew that if Zalghar was able to gain, even a small amount of his magic powers, there would be no Adjemirians on the battle field who would be safe. He would kill everyone.

During the battle between Ram and Zalghar which actually lasted for quite a while, unknown to Zalghar, Ram had been slowly edging Zalghar further into the Graveyard of the Ancients. Just about the time when Obmar had slammed the Rune axe into his side, Ram had been able to move Zalghar, very close to a large Pedestal. This large Pedestal was situated in the exact center of the Eight Graves of the Ancients.

Ram in his injured state now heard a slight noise from behind his back. Wondering what was making these noises. He turned his head slowly and saw Obmar had regained enough of his strength to be able to stand up and he had again picked up the Rune axe. At this time Ram saw that Obmar was in the process of raising the axe over his head and Ram without showing any expression, also knew he was powerless to do anything. Ram was quite surprised because he thought earlier Zalghar would have recovered faster and would be the enemy who would be back into action first. Ram also thought it was going to be Zalghar who was going to finish him off in the end and not Obmar. But apparently he had been wrong.

Instinctively Ram knew he did not have enough time or strength to defend himself and all was about to be lost. Ram was now becoming very worried about all of his friends on the battle field but he was even more worried about Bobbiur. Then Ram, wincing in pain, thought out loud about Bobbiur. "Maybe Bobbiur could still escape?"

Just as Ram was preparing to give up all hope he was suddenly aware of a strange new noise coming from close by. It was a loud clucking sound and he wondered what was making this strange noise. But Obmar recognized this sound immediately. Obmar, through fear, had stopped his upward swing. The war axe was just reaching the exact height which was needed to start it's downward killing blow at Ram.

Obmar was right, the sound he was hearing was the sound of a full grown GymmKat. Obmar's eyes were open wide as he heard the sound reaching it's conclusion. The evil look on Obmar's face now turned to a look of complete and uncontrolled fear.

Cautiously Obmar slowly turned part way around with a slight smile on his face, so that Jakka could see it was him. Obmar seemed to think that maybe Jakka would think he was still on the side of the Adjemirians and Jakka might not send his stinger. For a GymmKat, Jakka was actually very intelligent and he wasn't easily fooled. Not even in the slightest. Fates were sealed. "Ka,Ka,Ka, Hawusssss." Jakka sent the stinger and at this close range the impact of Jakka's stinger was dead center in the back of Obmar, right between the shoulder blades.

The Rune axe fell from the helpless hands of Obmar.

Then Obmar involuntarily staggered off in extreme pain where he crumpled to the ground in a big heap, almost at the side of Zalghar. Obmar was now screaming in extreme pain as the entire stinger had finally entered his body.

From where Ram still lay on the ground he was quite satisfied with how Jakka had stopped Obmar. A small grin came to Ram's tired looking face. Hearing another noise Ram now glanced towards Zalghar. Ram could now see the pinkish color returning to the hands of Zalghar and he knew, deep inside, that Zalghar would have enough power in only a very short time to return to his evil self. Ram, knowing the magic power was quickly returning to Zalghar and also knowing that a stinger from Jakka would be useless against Zalghar at this time, turned towards Jakka as he said. "Thanks Jakka but I cannot be saved. Go back to Hagjel now. You cannot stop Zalghar."

Then in a very sad and weak voice Ram spoke further. "Your sting cannot stop the magic of Zalghar." Jakka stood there looking at Ram and then he started to whimper. Looking over towards Zalghar,

Jakka saw Zalghar starting to rise and Jakka was starting to look from Zalghar to Ram. Jakka quickly repeating this behavior.

Calmly and sadly Ram said again. "Jakka you should go to Hagjel right now." Jakka finally understood and he turned and ran quickly back towards the location of Hagjel. Then the JymmKat paused and turned for a short time. Ram in a very weak but friendly voice, with a slight smile on his face and a weak wave of his hand yelled as forcefully as he could. "Go."

Jakka now turned and swiftly disappeared back into the smoke filled battlefield.

At this time Ram turned his attention back to Zalghar who was now moving towards Ram. For a short time Zalghar stopped and looked at Obmar withering on the ground in severe pain as he said. "I will stop your pain in a few moments."

Zalghar took a few more feeble steps before stopping again and picked up the Rune axe. The evil and vicious look returned to Zalghar's face as he felt the familiarity of the evil contained in the axe. Zalghar took about five steps closer to Ram and then he started to raise the axe.

All was lost, and Ram knowing he was about to die, looked Zalghar straight in the eyes. Zalghar stopped all movement for a second. Unknowingly Zalghar felt a new fear. Strange thoughts were running through his mind and he didn't know why. There was a fuzzy unknown feeling in the back of his head. He turned to see if anybody had snuck up behind him but there was nobody. Things became eerily silent. Even Obmar had become silent. All movement in the entire area seemed to become slowed. Zalghar did not understand.

Then shaking his head in disbelief, Zalghar sneered, as he attempted to put these thoughts out of his mind. He then stepped closer to Ram and while starting to raise the axe over his head and in a vicious sounding voice he screamed loudly. "Old man I'm going to slice you into little bits and feed you to my Kilpacx." With his hateful Haddron eyes bulging from his head, in an even more vicious tone, Zalghar growled between clenched teeth. "Old man I'm also going to kill you slowly."

Ram laying there, in an apparent helpless position had never, in his entire life seen such an evil look as he saw on Zalghar's now distorted and ugly face. Just before Zalghar was finished raising the axe over his head, Ram slowly pointed the open palm, of his right hand, directly at Zalghar's chest.

Smiling, Zalghar stopped and began to laugh out loud and then he growled, with an evil laugh of extreme confidence. Clearly Zalghar was savoring the moment. There was saliva and some form of froth at the sides of his evil grinning mouth. The veins in the side of his throat were protruding. His eyes seemed to bulge even more as he screamed.

"Old man. I know you have no magic power and you cannot stop me." Then with a disgusted spitting sound Zalghar shouted through clenched teeth. "So do not try to scare me."

Zalghar lowered the axe just slightly to step even closer while he savored the moment . Zalghar seemed to be enjoying himself immensely, because he was about to kill the now helpless old man laying bleeding and already dying, on the ground.

Zalghar shaking his head spoke one more time in a calmer voice. "You know you cannot stop me."

Without so much as even blinking, while continuing to stare deeply into the somewhat insane eyes of Zalghar, Ram said in a stern and a very crisp voice, three words. "Jedarim." "Jedarim." "Jedarim." Zalghar stopped. He was unable to take another step forward.

Instantly after Ram had finished repeating the words. "Jedarim." A sequence of events immediately went into motion. First the ground close to the base of the Pedestal began to tremble and rumble. Then flashes of energy, which looked like small lightning bolts, instantly left each of the eight graves of the Ancients and traveled at an incredible speed about a foot off of the ground, directly towards the pointed base of the huge Pedestal. As these energy bolts neared the ground at the base of the Pedestal, they at the exact same time, directed their energies downward into the ground. With a loud crackling sound these energy bolts, entered through the ground into the base of the Pedestal.

In a flash the Pedestal from the ground all the way up to it's uppermost point high above the ground, became fully and instantly energized. The once quiet and lifeless Pedestal now seemed fully alive as it was instantly lit up in a bright blue, pulsating color. Through all this and although it had only taken less than a second, Ram continued pointing the palm of his open right hand, directly at the chest of Zalghar.

Zalghar again started bring the axe upwards into a striking position but he paused for a 'milii' second and glanced at the Pedestal. The huge Pedestal was now completely lit up even brighter than it was only a second before and the entire immediate area surrounding the Pedestal was now energized.

The Pedestal was making a very loud crackling noise. Sparks were starting to fly off of the Pedestal in all directions. The entire area around the Pedestal was now lit up by the ever increasing sparks.

The eyes of Ram never blinked, nor did the piercing eyes of Ram ever leave the evil eyes of Zalghar. Not for a second. Even though the cracking noises coming from the Pedestal was becoming even louder it never took Ram's attention away from the eyes of Zalghar.

As his eyes remained glaring into the eyes of Zalghar Ram continued pointing, the palm of his right hand at the exact center of the chest of Zalghar. Ram could also tell that the power of Zalghar was returning even faster than he had thought it could. But even this didn't matter not even in the slightest. "Not any more." Ram had quietly whispered to himself.

Zalghar tried to take one last step closer to Ram but he couldn't. Although he raised the evil killer axe even further above his head, it took considerable energy. It was as if something was controlling his movements.

The evil look in Zalghar's eyes grew more intense as he said. "Old man I am not sure what you have done to this stupid Pedestal but it is all to late."

The evil in Zalghar's eyes seemed to even increase if that was possible, as the Rune axe started it's powerful, downward killing swing.

Then it happened.

Ram whispered. "Jedarim." One more time.

Magic powers from the now fully energized Pedestal instantly exploded out from the uppermost point of the Pedestal in a loud and powerful crackling noise. This tremendous energy bolt, with incredible speed flashed streaking through the air downwards. With considerable force and speed the energy bolt slammed right into the chest of Ram.

All this took less time than it takes to blink.

The power which had come from the Pedestal now instantly flashed through the upper body of Ram. The huge magic energy bolt with force and an incredible speed jumped out of Ram's opened palm. With an even greater speed it slammed Zalghar, with it's full force squarely in his chest. Zalghar was forced back a few steps, but he did not go down. It was if he could not fall down and he appeared to be anchored in this position.

The power bolt from the Pedestal continued flashing steadily from the Pedestal, through Ram's upper body, whose body was now becoming nothing more than an electrical conduit and this power continued to slam directly into the chest of Zalghar. There was a very loud cracking sound as the energy entered Zalghar's chest and a large cloud of smoke exploded from his now motionless body. As the energy continued to slam into Zalghar's body, Ram could see a continuous line of burning smoke coming from Zalghar's eyes, nose, ears and mouth.

The evil Rune axe remained in Zalghar's hands but Zalghar could not finish his swing. All of Zalghar's movements were now frozen in time. The power from the Pedestal was so strong that the energy now began burning a huge hole into the chest of Zalghar.

Almost immediately after the energy had burnt the hole in Zalghar's chest, the energy force then started to gel together and collected inside the partially lit up body of Zalghar. The eyes of Zalghar had become huge and blood shot. His hair on his head was electrified and was standing straight out from his head. Within only a few more seconds Zalghar's entire body was now fully lit up and looked just like a candle in a darkened room.

When the energy force had built to a vibrating, pulsating, aura of light, the body of Zalghar convulsed and snapped backwards. Instead of the killer axe being brought downwards and killing Ram, the axe was flung backwards about thirty feet and landed in a slight hollow in the ground. There was now a loud and continuos scream coming from Zalghar and although Ram was in a great deal of pain, he smiled. The deed had been done.

Ram, who was now in a tremendous and increasing pain could not help but say, in a husky, whispering voice. "Surprise. Surprise. Now you die Zalghar." Just as Ram finished saying this the energy from the Pedestal ceased. Staring wide eyed at Ram, Zalghar in shock and disbelief, was now able to stagger backwards, in a jerky, swaying, weakened form of movement.

Still stumbling Zalghar continued to back up far enough, that he actually fell down close to Obmar who was still withering on the ground and in severe pain. Rolling around in severe pain Zalghar tried to sit, but slowly sank back towards the ground. But before his body had hit the ground the evil Zalghar was dead.

The pressure of the magic energy which was still contained in Zalghar's lifeless body, exploded. The explosion from the now dead body of Zalghar, had considerable force. The explosion was so great that it was possibly the biggest explosion that had ever been witnessed in all of Adjemir. The force from this explosion, was also strong enough, it resulted a number of other things .

When the force from this explosion hit Ram it rolled him over about six times and left him even more broken than he had been before. Because Zalghar's body had exploded with such great force. Obmar had instantly caught on fire where he had lain, still withering in severe pain, since he received the sting from Jakka. The force from the blast was so strong that the loose materials which was on the ground close by, such as leaves, dirt and other loose materials, buried the evil Rune axe, where it had fallen into a hollow in the ground.

The sound from this explosion, was so strong that the troops on the battle field, including Bobbiur were instantly aware that something incredible, had just happened. Everything on the battle field came to an instant and complete standstill.

Ram who was in a great deal of more pain now rested his head on the ground. He was breathing deeply but he had a satisfied smile on his old and tired face. He then glanced up at the Pedestal as he spoke softly to himself. "The sacrifice was worth it."

Ram was feeling very tired and he closed his eyes.

From across the battle field, Bobbiur after hearing the scream from Zalghar, which was followed by the explosion, went into instant action. Quickly and without saying anything to any body he turned and started running, in somewhat of a urgent and determined fashion as fast as he could, towards the direction of the scream.

Bobbiur knew that the remaining Haddrons were surrounded and the battle was all but over. Because Bobbiur had been so busy fighting the Haddrons he had forgotten that Ram was up against Zalghar all by himself.

With determination Bobbiur moving swiftly towards the Graveyard of the Ancients, was hoping he would not be to late. There was now a very worried look on Bobbiur's young, but battle hardened face.

Transfer of Magic

Bobbiur continued to run through the thinning smoke with complete abandon, and without any fear for his own safety. He was able to run very quickly up and into the Grave Yard of the Ancients. Seeing the large Pedestal above the low hanging smoke and using it as a guide, he traveled directly towards it.

Arriving at the location of the battle between Ram and Zalghar, Bobbiur drew to a sudden halt. Everything he saw showed that there had been a hard fought battle between these two very powerful individuals. Firstly he saw a large hole in the ground with a misty smoke still rising from it. This smoking hole in the ground was where Zalghar had been only moments before. A little farther on Bobbiur saw Obmar, still withering in pain and murmuring something in his death throws.

Just past Obmar, Bobbiur saw what looked like a dusty dirty bunch of old rags laying motionless on the ground. It was actually Ram what Bobbiur was looking at, lying motionless in a large pool of blood. Gasping in surprise Bobbiur moved closer and he noticed, that Ram looked older, smaller and thinner than he had ever looked before. Frantically Bobbiur went straight to Ram and showing great concern bent down to see if Ram was still alive.

As soon as Bobbiur had leaned down Ram became aware of a person being close to him. At first Ram thought that it might be Obmar. Then Ram saw Bobbiur and even though he was in a tremendous amount of pain, the old man smiled.

Sputtering Bobbiur could hardly speak, because he had been so afraid that Ram was dead. Finally after swallowing, Bobbiur spoke. "Ram I was so worried for you." Bobbiur was now smiling because he was so happy that Ram was still alive as he said. "I should have come sooner." In an anxious fashion Bobbiur speaking in a rapid tone continued on. "We have to hurry. We must get you to a Healer as fast as we can."

Ram just weakly held up his hand as he said. "Bobbiur I cannot be saved. I have been damaged beyond repair."Again in a sputtering form of speech Bobbiur said. "It's my fault. I should have fought Zalghar myself." Speaking just above a whisper the old man said."You would have been swiftly killed by Zalghar."

"I am the only one who could fight Zalghar and in the end I was not so sure that I could beat him. That was why when I still had all of my magic powers available, at my finger tips, I was able to force Zalghar into the Graveyard of the Ancients."

Trying to take control, Bobbiur in an insistent sounding manner again said. "Ram you must let me get you to a Healer."

Speaking softly almost in a whisper Ram spoke pleadingly."Listen to me carefully my son because I do not have much longer to live."

Ram took a deep breath, winced in pain as he continued. "The reason I met Zalghar and the Haddrons in this location and the reason I forced Zalghar into the Graveyard of the Ancients, was because it is the location of the Pedestal of Life."Then Ram softly added. "You see. I have never told this to anybody before but I am the offspring of one of the Ancients. I am half Human and half Haddron." Ram continued slowly. "It is the half of me which is Haddron which makes my magic so strong."

Just then Kirwynn, Shantok, Alandaugh and Hagjel came through the smoke, all chattering. Before they saw Ram on the ground, Hagjel in a happy voice had said. "The Haddrons and all the Kilpacx are dead." When they saw Ram on the ground at which time the joyful sounds in their voices stopped.

Kirwynn immediately knelt down beside Bobbiur and without saying anything she held onto his arm. Bobbiur with some urgency in his voice nodded quickly to the new comers. Ram while looking straight into Bobbiur's eyes urgently continued.

"I do not have very long so I must finish what I have to say." "I feel I can speak in front of these people because I can tell that they seem to be very good friends of yours, but you must listen very carefully."

Everybody became silent as Ram who was quickly getting weaker and in a very great pain pressed on. "The reason I angled Zalghar into the Graveyard of the Ancients was just because if he was getting the better of me, I had secret weapon which nobody in all of Adjemir knew about except me."

Pressing onwards Ram spoke softly."The Ancients were actually Haddrons who came to here to Adjemir a very long time ago." With considerable pain on his face Ram kept explaining things to Bobbiur and the others. "They were a very careful people. My father was actually one of the younger Haddrons out of the group of eight and he fell in love with a young Human girl by the name of Jeffla, a long, long, time ago."

Ram paused momentarily and then he weakly continued. "All of the Ancients, my father included, agreed before they died to be buried with their magic powers intact."

"The Pedestal of Light, receives it's power from their magic which remains buried in the Graveyard of the Ancients. As well the power for the Pedestal of Life, comes from the Graveyard of the Ancients." Softly and weakly Ram continued on. "The power to operate the Pedestal of Light, is just a small amount of power. But the power from the Pedestal of Life requires a much greater amount of energy."

In a great amount of pain Ram suffered on by adding.

"When I was a young man it was well after the death of my Haddron father I was summoned to the Temple of the Ancients and it was then that I had been told about my Haddron father." Then with a weak smile Ram said. "Up till that time I was always told that I was a Human." Uninterrupted Ram continued to tell his story. "One of the older monks had all the knowledge and he was told by my father to give this information to me, but not ill after he was dead. The Ancients, must have foreseen the future and that is why the old monk also told me that if required, I could get a tremendous energy from the Pedestal of Life but it was all to be kept a secret. I was also told that if I was to call on the Ancients magic which was buried here, and use the power for a good cause that the energy which would be channeled through my body would in the end also kill me."

With a sad look on Rams face he went on. "I have to be completely honest with you Bobbiur. I am going to die very shortly." Bobbiur could not help himself he began to sob softly. Then he said through his tears. "I will get the best Healer in the country." Then Bobbiur quickly added. "With your magic and the use of a good Healer there may be a chance of saving you."

Ram just shook his head slowly. "Bobbiur I can tell you that I cannot be saved. The force that killed Zalghar had to run through my body." In a pleading fashion Ram said. "I knew this was going to happen and the use of the power was a last resort but I had to do it. Zalghar was going to kill me anyways. Obmar impaired the use of my magic powers temporarily when he hit me with his evil war axe. If I did not kill Zalghar with the energy from the Pedestal of Life then he would have regained all of his powers very shortly and nobody on the battle field would have been safe from him."

Bobbiur noticed that Ram's voice was growing weaker so he leaned in a little closer and put his left hand under Ram's head. There were still tears in the eyes of Bobbiur. Kirwynn was crying softly to herself and all the others were silently shuffling their feet.

Except Shantok. He had signaled to Alandaugh. Nothing had been said between the two of them. Alandaugh had walked off silently after they had heard Ram tell how Obmar had attacked him from behind with the war axe.

Alandaugh spoke softly to himself. "Orders are orders." He moved over to where Obmar was still quivering on the ground. Alandaugh did not know that Jakka had jumped down from Hagjel's tote bag and had followed him. Without any emotion at all and very business like, Alandaugh drew his knife. Alandaugh actually felt uncomfortable with slicing Obmar's throat and this was probably mostly because he would have preferred to let Obmar suffer a little longer. After the deed was done Alandaugh started to move back over to rejoin the group at which time Jakka followed him, chuckling to himself.

Jakka seemed quite happy to see Obmar gone.

Kirwynn who had been kneeling on the ground beside Bobbiur, could tell that there was not much time left for Ram so she got up and moved back over to where the others were standing. She felt that Bobbiur should be left alone with Ram, in Ram's final moments.

Ram with very sad eyes looked deep into the eyes of Bobbiur as he whispered softly so only Bobbiur could hear. "I want you to do some things for me after I am gone."

Bobbiur nodded and said to Ram. "For you Ram. I will do whatever you want."

Then Bobbiur said again. "But Ram why don't you use your magic powers to save yourself?" Ram smiled and repeated himself. "My magic cannot save me now and I knew this when I called on the magic power of the Ancients."

Then Ram with a very weak grimacing smile on his face, said.

"Marry the girl."

Ram had glanced over at Kirwynn and Bobbiur only nodded that he understood.

The tears in Bobbiur's eyes, remained steady.

Quietly Ram added.

"Unite all of Adjemir. The time is right. By marrying Kirwynn you can get the Humans on your side."

Ram quickly went on by saying in an ever weakening voice. "You may not completely understand the Elves but your friendship with Pendahl will be a great assistance."

In a faltering voice Ram whispered.

"Bury me with the Ancients. Just outside of the ring of the Ancients."

In a very weak voice Ram continued. "Place me as close to the grave which is marked as, Mijerda. He was my father. I have very little time left so you must be quick."

Ram's voice was so soft Bobbiur could barely hear him. "Now place my hands together on my chest and hold them tightly while you place your other hand on my forehead." Then Ram said. "Lean forward and listen to me very carefully." Bobbiur did a s Ram instructed. "I will tell you about the powers of the Ancients, which you may need some day but you must always remember, these powers can only be used for good deeds only and the use of this power in the end will kill you. Just as it is now killing me. This power should only be used in extreme circumstances."

At this time Ram told Bobbiur how to call on the powers of the Ancients, by saying the magic words three times and the magic words were then given to Bobbiur. "Jedarim. Jedarim. Jedarim." Ram in a very weak voice also said. "In order to make the magic powers work your heart must be pure." Ram paused. "You must also form in your mind what you want the powers to do." Ram added. "Remember the power when it is being used by you will be the full power of the Eight Ancients and I can tell you that no Human nor Haddron can carry the full magic powers of the Ancients without severe damage being done."

After a slight pause Ram questioned. "Do you understand me?"

Bobbiur nodded that he understood fully and then Ram continued on. "You must be sure when you are ready to use the powers and then you just say "Jedarim. One last time. This is when the magic will transfer from the Pedestal of Life over to you, and through you."

"Remember it will in all instances kill you. These powers can be used anywhere in Adjemir but these powers are the strongest the closer to the Pedestal that you are situated."

Bobbiur now noticed that the voice of Ram was growing steadily weaker and he knew that Ram was in a hurry to explain things to him so he listened intently without interrupting.

"In the Temple of the Ancients there is an old monk by the name of Dhavden and he is my friend and also my counselor. He will explain to you further how to use the Pedestal of Light. Now I am going to leave you."

After another short pause Ram in a very weak voice continued. "Now you must keep your hands where they are and you must look deep into my eyes. Try to see the backs of my eyes. The good magic contained in my soul will be transferred from me to you."

Bobbiur did this somewhat reluctantly but he now knew that Ram would be dead very shortly. All Bobbiur could say was. "Good bye Ram. You were like a father to me."

It was only moments after Bobbiur, following Ram's instructions, looking deeply, while trying to see the backs of Ram eyes. The transfer of magic commenced. At first there was a soft greenish light which began to glow from Ram's prone body. Then the glow appeared to travel into Bobbiur's body, through his arms.

Shortly after this the greenish light started to get brighter and then the light became equally as bright over Bobbiur also. Both Ram and Bobbiur were now encased with this light and both of them were then raised upwards from the ground by the power of the light.

All of Bobbiur's friends stood back in awe and wonder. No words came from any of them. All of this was like a dream. Everything around them became dark except the place where Ram and Bobbiur were. Once both Ram and Bobbiur had been raised by unseen forces and by the light to about three feet off the ground the lifting motion stopped.

A loud buzzing sound now started and then eight small lighted spheres of a bluish color, began to circle them both. Neither Ram nor Bobbiur moved, not even in the slightest. They became like statues floating softly in mid air.

Without any notice the sounds from the forces became louder, the greenish light became brighter and the bluish spheres started to spiral even faster. Within moments the spheres were spinning so fast that the spinning of the spheres made both Ram and Bobbiur disappear. All that could been seen now was a larger sphere, hovering in the same place and still encompassing both Ram and Bobbiur. This scene remained as it was for only a few moments.

The spinning motion then began to slow down and soon both men were becoming visible again. The more they became visible the closer they were lowered to the ground. Then even the lights began to dim and then slowly the lights completely disappeared.

When the light had finally disappearing Ram was dead. The transfer of magic was complete.

Bobbiur hung his head and was crying gently. He removed his cloak, softly laying it gently over the broken frail and lifeless body of Ram. After a short time Bobbiur stood up and turned to his friends. Without showing any emotion he stated in a quiet fashion, with his head bowed. "Ram will never be very far from me and although I will miss him greatly a part of him is inside me. What we have just done here is to transfer his magic powers over to me. He did this just before he died."

Then after a short pause Bobbiur went on. "We will be burying him in the Grave Yard of the Ancients." Bobbiur had just finished saying this when Pendahl and a couple of his soldiers rode up. Pendahl without saying anything to the others and knowing that Ram must be dead, dismounted. He walked straight up to Bobbiur and offered his condolences. "Bobbiur, I am sorry to see you have lost Ram."

Then Pendahl placed his arm around Bobbiur's shoulders as he said. "All of the Haddron's have been killed and the Kilpacx all have been taken care of."

Bobbiur nodded as he spoke to Pendahl. "Pendahl thanks for coming here to help." Then Bobbiur stated further. "Pendahl I will need to talk to you but I must to do something else first. So if you could wait a moment I will be right back." Without waiting for a reply from Pendahl Bobbiur turned and walked confidently over to Kirwynn as he said. "Kirwynn. I don't have very long."

As Bobbiur was saying this he was taking her right hand in both of his hands, and as he leaned forward, Bobbiur kissed her hand. Before Kirwynn could say anything Bobbiur out of hearing distance from the others, spoke softly. "Kirwynn. I am going to speak to your father and I will ask him if I can marry you." Kirwynn only smiled and did not say anything but she stepped forward and hugged Bobbiur fiercely. Bobbiur looking over her shoulder saw that Hagjel, Shantok,

Alandaugh Pendahl and the two Elfen soldiers who had come with Pendahl, all smiling.

Bobbiur could see that they were all starting to grin. Then Bobbiur scowled at them and this look from Bobbiur made them all break out laughing. Alandaugh, who for a moment seemed to read Bobbiur's thoughts, with a wispy smile at the corners of his mouth, raised his sword to his head and saluted Bobbiur and Kirwynn. In a more serious tone, all of the group then raised their swords and saluted with Alandaugh.

Fondrall was just coming up to where everybody was standing around and instantly asked why everybody was so happy and Shantok told him what had just happened. Smiling fondly Fondrall also raised his sword to his forehead and saluted Kirwynn and Bobbiur. Acknowledging with a slight grin on his tired face Bobbiur nodded back. Bobbiur said to them all, out of respect for Ram that his body should be picked up and taken to the Temple of the Ancients. Shantok took charge of the soldiers who were close. Bobbiur abruptly walked over to Pendahl.

Before reaching Pendahl, Bobbiur turned and quietly said to Kirwynn. "Kirwynn. I need to speak to Pendahl for a few moments."

Kirwynn only nodded with a slight smile and a questioning look on her face.

Jakka who knew something was up, was on the ground, rubbing up against Hagjel's legs and making his friendly chuckling sounds. Bobbiur kissed Kirwynn on her cheek as he said. "Kirwynn. I must go and speak to Pendahl now."

Kirwynn who was now more comfortable with Jakka walked over to Hagjel and with a very happy smile on her face, stooped over and picked Jakka up. It was Jakka's turn to be hugged. The chatter from Jakka got considerably louder. Kirwynn was surprised because she was sure that Jakka had a smile on his furry face.

Diplomacy Will Unite Adjemir

Nearing the place where Pendahl stood waiting Bobbiur began speaking in a friendly tone as he put his hand onto Pendahl's shoulder. Both turned as they continued to walk further away from the group. Bobbiur wanted to talk to Pendahl in complete privacy because the matters to be discussed were very important and even though everybody present were close friends of his, these issues must be kept in complete secrecy until some decisions had been made.

After a short distance Bobbiur stopped and without saying anything for a few moments, while he gathered his thoughts, he looked off into the distance.

Then in a serious tone Bobbiur began to speak. "Pendahl. Just before Ram died he asked me to unite all of Adjemir." At this statement Pendahl in a little shock and surprise remained very still and said nothing. So Bobbiur continued. "Ram also said that I should rely heavily on you to bring the Elves on side. He had said this because of the friendship which you and I have." Bobbiur was looking off into the distance as he chose his next words very carefully. "We worked well together at the battle in the Red Valley and it made a lot of sense to stop the fighting."

Bobbiur paused for a short time, while he was thinking on what he wanted to say next. "Nobody is even sure why the Humans and Elves fight the way they do and you have said this yourself."

This time when Bobbiur paused Pendahl started to speak with a calm and thoughtful understanding. "I understand the problems between the two races and I agree with you that this matter should be fixed. But how?"

Bobbiur thought for a few moments and then he responded by saying. "Pendahl. We were successful in beating the Haddrons today. In fact the Haddrons were the biggest enemy that Adjemir has ever had to face and the Elves and the Humans together defeated the Haddrons." Then changing the subject Bobbiur raised the issues of the Krugs and the Dwarves. "If the Humans and the Elves are able to settle their differences then combined our races will be strong enough that the Dwarves and the Krugs will be powerless to attack either of us."

Bobbiur with a slight smile on his face went on. "It makes sense for our two races to form an alliance because then it should bring peace to all of Adjemir."

Pendahl was quiet for a moment while he was spending some time thinking of what Bobbiur had just said. Then nodding his head he spoke softly. "I agree. But as before. How will we do this?" Bobbiur spoke with a newly found confident tone. "We should get General Yauddi and General Karridhen together with General Charranoid and yourself. Then we can talk about how a long lasting truce can be brought into being."

With a even bigger smile on his battle weary face, Bobbiur spoke in a friendly way. "As you know I have just asked Kirwynn to marry me and General Yauddi is on the battle field right now. General Yauddi after I ask him for Kirwynn's hand in marriage should get him on side without many problems. We should also invite some senior Dwarfs and some senior Krugs to a meeting in the very near future."

Without pausing Bobbiur added what he thought was important. "Pendahl. You should also know that before Ram died he transferred his magic powers to me, which was what he was doing just before he died. I have enough magic power now to enforce a long lasting peace but I feel the use of magic power in a forceful way, in this case, would be very wrong."

Nodding his head Pendahl said. "I agree." Bobbiur was looking down at his hands and even Pendahl could see the magic powers traveling through his forearms and into his hands. They had been turning a strong pinkish color which meant that he was now fully powered in magic. He would still need to polish his new skills but this would come with time.

Then looking up Bobbiur went on in his quiet tone. "I feel I can tell you this Pendahl. Ram was the child of one of the younger Ancients, whose name was Mijerda and therefore Ram was part Haddron. The magic which he has placed inside me is very powerful."

"After I marry Kirwynn, there should be without a doubt a fairly strong friendship between Darmonarrow and Garriton."

Pendahl who was considerably more powerful in the Elfen community than most Elves now rubbed his chin and began to speak. He had been thinking before he started to say anything. His friend Bobbiur seemed to be becoming more mature by the minute. "It's nice that you feel you can unite all of Adjemir but what ever we do, we must treat all the four races equal. We will be powerful enough when we combine our forces that organizing the Krugs and the Dwarves should be a doable thing. But we should get together with our elders before we meet any of the Krug or Dwarf leaders and put together some sort of a working agreement or constitution."

Then Pendahl while pausing for a second, as he looked over at the group which had gathered around the dead body of Ram. There were three Human soldiers and three Elfen Soldiers who had placed a large Garriton war shield under Ram's body. Under the instructions of Shantok they had picked him up onto their shoulders and were starting a slow march, carrying Ram, towards the Temple of the Ancients. Pendahl pointing towards these soldiers as he said. "See our races are already starting to work together."

Bobbiur with a sad look on his face because of Ram's death, turned towards Pendahl and said. "Your right Pendahl. Our people have already started working together and this is good." Bobbiur then without saying anything further turned and started back to his other friends.

Zorp and Dymma Return

Just then Bobbiur saw Kirwynn looking into the sky in a direction towards the end of the valley from where the Haddrons had just come before the battle. She was using her hand cover her eyes because it was getting late in the day and she had to look almost directly into the sun. What she had been watching was a large Dragon flying into the valley and coming directly towards them. As it turned out it was Dymma and Zorp.

Dymma landed very softly, not too far from where Kirwynn was standing. Bobbiur thought that Zorp would want to speak to him so he asked Pendahl to come with him. As it turned out Dymma had landed beside Kirwynn because Dymma had wanted to speak to Kirwynn. As they landed Zorp had jumped like a young man off of the back of this incredible beast and then he turned to speak to Bobbiur. Dymma moved closer to speak to Kirwynn.

"Dymma are you going to introduce yourself to Kirwynn as you are, or are you going to be a lady and show her your true side?" Zorp had that same mischievous smile on his face and the same twinkle in his eyes, which he always had when he was about to tease or trick somebody.

Bobbiur with a questioning look in his eyes instantly wondered what Zorp was up to now. As it turned out he was about to find out shortly.

Dymma, scowling at Zorp in a scolding tone only said. "You foolish old man you really don't have any manners do you?" Then with that same surprising Dragon smile, Dymma in a pleasant voice said. "You are supposed to introduce me to Kirwynn first." Dymma the Dragon turned and looked at Kirwynn. Bobbiur was still somewhat amazed and surprised that a Dragon could smile because he had never seen a Dragon smile before. But this huge and friendly Dragon Dymma was smiling.

Then in a gruffy sounding manner Zorp said. "All right. If you say so." Then turning to Kirwynn Zorp went through the formalities of the introduction. "Kirwynn this is Dymma the Dragon and this is also Dymma my wife." At this last statement Zorp pointed the three center fingers on his right hand in the direction of Dymma and waved his hand horizontally two times, then he paused for a short time. On a third wave of the same three fingers Dymma the Dragon was instantly replaced by Dymma the Lady.

Everybody who present were in awe. This huge beast had been instantly replaced by a very beautiful young lady. Dymma the Lady was very slim, graceful and very beautiful. Her smile was infectious and even Bobbiur was caught by surprise. Dymma in her Haddron form, walked immediately over to Kirwynn and gave her a friendly hug as she said. "Congratulations on your proposal from Bobbiur."

Then placing her arm around Kirwynn's shoulder the young lady who had replaced the Dragon said. "Lets go off a little ways and we'll let the men talk." The two young ladies walked off a little ways to talk by themselves but after they had gone only a short distance Dymma stopped abruptly, turned and spoke to Zorp. She had a sly and impish grin on her face as she said. "Old man. I have shown my true identity now its your turn."

Then Dymma turned quickly and caught up with Kirwynn.

"Dymma. You never stop your nagging do you?" It was all in jest because Zorp had the same friendly smile on is face as he always had when he was in Dymma's presence. Turning to Bobbiur Zorp said. "That woman is going to drive me into an early grave. I swear." Zorp was nodding his head with his eyes wide, in an exaggerated, smiling, mock jester, then he said.

"I'll just be a minute."

With this statement, Zorp repeated what he had done earlier when he had changed Dymma back into her Haddron form.

"Step back for a moment Bobbiur. You too Pendahl please." On the third wave of the same three middle fingers which had changed Dymma back into her Haddron form a very handsome and very young Haddron about the same age as Dymma, stood looking very relaxed right in front of Bobbiur and Pendahl.

Pendahl was quite impressed. But Bobbiur could not be surprised by anything Zorp did. Not anymore.

A serious mood came over Zorp, almost immediately after this transformation and he got right down to business. "Sorry about Ram but as I have told you earlier Bobbiur we could not get involved." In a solemn tone Zorp continued. "As I said earlier for me and Dymma to get involved with Zorp it would have been against Haddron law. But Bobbiur you and the people of Adjemir have done really well. All of the renegade Haddrons have been destroyed." Then to explain things further Zorp said. "Both myself and Dymma had to be in disguise just in case you were captured by Zalghar and his men. As we have discussed earlier we are not able to take Haddron laws and apply them here in Adjemir. We would have been breaking some old Haddron laws and as bad as Zalghar and his renegades were Dymma and myself could have been punished if we attacked Zalghar outside the land of Haddron."

Zorp continued on with this explanation. "I'm not sure that you can properly understand this old Haddron law but our law is our law."

It was Bobbiur's turn to surprise Zorp when he asked. "Did you know that Ram was a child of one of the Ancients? He had Haddron blood in his veins."

Zorp became quiet for a minute and then he said. "So you have found the secret that the Ancients were actually Haddrons who came to Adjemir a long time ago. You were not supposed to know this." Zorp then said."But now that you have this knowledge. I best tell you the rest."Zorp began to explain. "Each of the Eight Moons of Adjemir all represent one of the Ancients. Adjemir had no moons until the Ancients died then after each of the Ancients died, Adjemir got another moon. Now there are eight moons in your land."

"The Ancients as you here in Adjemir call them were actually eight of our Haddron elders. Each of these Haddron elders possessed very powerful magic. These elders left the land of Haddron a very very long time ago."

Zorp slowed in his talking for just a second while he was thinking about something and then he continued. "Apparently they had just felt the need to move on."Looking at Bobbiur with a slight quizzical smile on his face Zorp added. "They chose Adjemir and I have been told that they gave some magic powers to some of their more trusted Human and Elfen friends. The rest is all of your history."

Zorp paused for again for just a very short time and then he began to speak again. "I cannot tell you why Adjemir started to make war all the time."

Looking at Bobbiur for just a moment and then Zorp continued. "While the Ancients were alive Adjemir had a long and gentle peace." Pendahl was listening and was very interested in all of the past history but he felt he had to ask. "Zorp do you really feel Bobbiur can bring a lasting peace to Adjemir?"

Zorp turned to Pendahl and answered quickly. "Yes. But he is going to need your loyalty and your help. Pendahl." Turning towards Pendahl in an explaining tone Zorp then said. "You see everything you need for a lasting peace is right here in front of you." "Pendahl. Your new friendship with Bobbiur is very important. The marriage between Bobbiur and Kirwynn is also very valuable in regards to a lasting peace in Adjemir. Clearly these two things are very important and should bring the Elves and the Humans together."

Zorp, again speaking in a matter of fact tone added. "Once you two have formed an alliance then with the Human's and the Elfs placed into a position of power the Dwarves and the Krugs will be forced to abide by your decisions.

Then Zorp asked of Pendahl. "Does this make any sense to you?"

Without waiting for an answer Zorp made a further comment. "This will not be an easy task and it will take lots of hard work but I'm sure you two can do it."

The men turned as they heard Dymma and Kirwynn approaching and then Zorp made one further statement. "My main concern for a peace in Adjemir is to finish some of the work which was started by the Ancients and also to help your people too stop killing each other."

Turning and facing Dymma and without giving any reasons Zorp said. "We have to go."

Zorp was speaking mostly to Dymma who seemed very happy, but the statement by Zorp was actually for all of the group.

Dymma said to Kirwynn. "Well Kirwynn. It has been nice talking to you and if we lived closer to each other we could be friends. But we live a very long ways away so I guess this is goodbye."

Kirwynn had tears in her eyes and she was very surprised to see tears in the eyes of Dymma. Then these young ladies hugged.

Dymma and Zorp Leave Adjemir

Very quickly Zorp shook the hands of Hagjel and Fondrall who had just walked up. Zorp then shook hands with Shantok and Alandaugh before he walked over to Pendahl. Speaking softly Zorp said. "Pendahl. You are a good Elf and you shall be a very good friend to Bobbiur and Kirwynn."

Then turning quickly to Dymma, Zorp brought up the three fingers which he had used earlier to transform Dymma into a lady and with the same wave of his hand, Dymma was turned instantly back into her Dragon form. Dymma instantly started to stretch and flex her huge wings. Then turning back to Bobbiur Zorp shook Bobbiur's hand in the Adjemirian fashion as he said.

"I have to agree with Dymma if we lived closer we would be good friends." Zorp, still in his actual young Haddron form turned and walked over to Dymma. He got on the back of Dymma and as he turned and looked over the group he said. "I don't think we will ever be coming back to Adjemir but there is a slight possibility."

Then with a slight bow Zorp said. "Good luck to you all and good luck to Adjemir." Without saying anything further Dymma and Zorp flew off in the direction of where Haddron must be and they never looked back.

All of the Adjemirians who where with Bobbiur and Kirwynn waved as they watched Dymma and Zorp fly off until they were completely out of sight. Each and every one of them said goodbye in their own way.

Bobbiur turned to Kirwynn and saw tears in her eyes so he held her hand. Kirwynn reached up as she had turned towards Bobbiur and placing her left hand behind his neck. She kissed him. Hagjel who was not far away started to giggle like a little kid and Bobbiur while looking over Kirwynn's head gave Hagjel a menacing look. After she had kissed Bobbiur, Kirwynn spoke out loud. "I wonder if we will ever see them again?" Before Bobbiur could answer she added. "If they had not come to Adjemir we may well have been beaten here today by Zalghar."

Bobbiur agreed by saying. "I'm not sure that we could have beaten the Haddrons today without the enhanced weapons which Zorp gave to us. In fact I'm certain we would have lost this battle."

"Kirwynn." Bobbiur said while breaking away after the kiss. "I have to go to the Temple of the Ancients and tend too Ram's funeral. I'm also going to set up a time so the old monk can give me some proper instructions on how to use the magic which Ram has given me."

Kirwynn nodding spoke softly as she said. "I'll walk to the Temple with you."

Pendahl who had been giving some instructions to some of his soldiers started to move in their direction while saying. "Wait up. I'll walk to the Temple with you."

As they were walking in the direction of the Temple and before Pendahl caught up with they them both looked up into the sky. I was nearly dark and all of the Eight Moons of Adjemir, were together in the sky.

Bobbiur said quizzically as they walked along. "It looks like there are actually nine moons in the sky."

To this statement Kirwynn said with a girlish smile on her face. "Bobbiur don't be foolish. There are only. Eight Moons of Adjemir."

Bobbiur leaned over and kissed the top of Kirwynn's head as they walked along slowly, then he whispered.

"Your right Kirwynn. There are only. Eight Moons of Adjemir."

The Nine Moons of Adjemir

As they walked along Bobbiur counted again to himself. Clearly he saw a ninth moon in the sky. It was a smaller moon right in the exact center of the 'Eight Moons of Adjemir.' At this time Bobbiur happened to glance over to where Hagjel was walking. Bobbiur noticed that Jakka was sitting up in the tote bag, smiling and looking him right in the eyes with what appeared to be an unknown wisdom. Bobbiur could not help thinking that Jakka had also seen a ninth moon.

Bobbiur then smiled to himself because apparently he was the only person, other than Jakka who could see a ninth moon in the sky. He was not quite sure why he was the only person who could see the ninth moon in the sky but for Bobbiur this didn't matter. All this gave Bobbiur some comfort because deep down inside. Bobbiur knew that Ram was still with him and was looking down on all of Adjemir. Bobbiur also knew that Ram as a new and smaller moon, had finally joined with his father, and the other Ancients in the sky over Adjemir. As they continued walking in the direction of the Temple of the Ancients, Bobbiur's arm unknowingly had tightened around the shoulder of Kirwynn. Deep inside he knew that all would be well for all of Adjemir.

As they neared the Temple and before they entered the building Bobbiur with a slight smile while shaking his head from side to side counted again. Then he whispered knowingly and softly to himself.

"Yes. There are. 'Nine Moons of Adjemir'."

The End   Tyler Dhensaw

About the Author: Tyler Dhensaw

Tyler Dhensaw was born, August 8, 1987, in Prince George British Columbia, Canada. The city of Prince George is located only a few miles south of the commencement of the historic Alaska Highway. For purposes of employment, in 1996, his parents moved to a more southern location in the Province of British Columbia, to a place called Squamish. Squamish, for those who do not know of it's location, is only about 35 minutes by highway, from the ski resort of Whistler BC. Tyler is the youngest of three children.

Tyler was only 14 years of age when he finished the unedited version of "The Nine Moons of Adjemir". He had it in his mind to finish his manuscript before his 15th birthday. With this determination in mind and although he had friends visiting from out of town, he left them to play video games. At which time he smuggled himself upstairs to the computer and commenced to finish his book. The book was finished at exactly two minutes before Tyler's 15th birthday. He had promised his father that he would finish his book when he was still 14 years of age and with this singled minded determination and commitment, plus a side bet with his father, the book came to a conclusion.

Tyler at the time of publishing this book was just 16 years of age. He is presently writing a sequel to. "The Nine Moons of Adjemir" but because of some of Tyler's other commitments, things are moving at a much slower pace.

Snow boarding, roller blades, hiking, writing books, reading, and photography, not necessarily in this order are presently some of his primary interests. Subject to the above, it has been secretly rumored through the Dhensaw household, out of all of Tyler's main interests in life, bugging his father, although not listed above, just might be one of his highest priorities. His grades in school are slightly above average and he is presently in Grade 11.

Tyler has stated, once he graduates, regardless of his present plans as a future police officer, he will continue to write books. His family is very supportive in this instance.

With respect. Tyler sincerely hopes all those who read. "The Nine Moons of Adjemir." Enjoy reading it as much as Tyler, subject to the nagging from his father to finish the book, has enjoyed writing it.

Printed in the United States
22414LVS00002B/169-246